FALL OF RUIN
AND WRATH

FALL
OF
RUIN
AND
WRATH

JENNIFER L. ARMENTROUT

BRAMBLE

TOR PUBLISHING GROUP
NEW YORK

FALL OF RUIN AND WRATH

Map illustration by Virginia Allyn

A Bramble Book
Published by Tom Doherty Associates / Tor Publishing Group
120 Broadway
New York, NY 10271

www.brambleromance.com

Bramble™ is a trademark of Macmillan Publishing Group, LLC.

The Library of Congress Cataloging-in-Publication Data is available upon request.

ISBN 978-1-250-75019-8 (hardcover)
ISBN 978-1-250-32320-0 (international, sold outside
the U.S., subject to rights availability)
ISBN 978-1-250-75018-1 (ebook)

Our books may be purchased in bulk for promotional, educational, or business use.
Please contact your local bookseller or the Macmillan Corporate and Premium
Sales Department at 1-800-221-7945, extension 5442, or by email at
MacmillanSpecialMarkets@macmillan.com.

First U.S. Edition: 2023
First International Edition: 2023

Printed in the United States of America

0 9 8 7 6 5 4 3 2 1

For you, the reader

PRONUNCIATION GUIDE

Divinus: Di-vie-nus
Euros: Your-us
Primvera: Prim-vee-rah
Rae: Ray
Vytrus: Vie-trues
caelestia: ca-les-te-uh
divus: di-vus
na'laa: nah-lay
ni'mere: nigh-meer
ny'chora: nay-ko-rah
sōls: souls

FALL OF RUIN
AND WRATH

PROLOGUE

An eerie quiet descended upon the chamber of the foundling home, hushing the soft snores and wheezy breaths from those sleeping on the cots in the chamber. Missing the warm beds found at the Priory of Mercy, I tightened my aching fingers around the scratchy, worn blanket. I never slept well on the floor, where the mice and rats usually scurried all night.

But tonight, there were no glimpses of their thin, slick tails, nor did I hear the rap of their claws upon the stone. That should be a welcome discovery, but something didn't feel right. Not about the floor beneath me or the air I breathed.

I'd woken with tiny goose bumps all over my skin and a bad feeling in the pit of my belly. The Prioress had taught me to always trust my second sight, the pull of my intuition, and the urge of my instinct. They were gifts, she'd told me over and over, given by the gods because I was born from the stars.

I didn't understand what she'd meant by the whole star part, but right now, my intuition was telling me something was very wrong.

I eyed the damp stone walls lit by the gas lanterns, searching for a sign of what made my belly feel like I'd eaten spoiled meat. By the door, a light flickered and went out. The lantern by the window sputtered, then ceased as another did the same. Across the chamber, the last lamp went dead.

No fingers had cut off the light. I would've seen anyone who dared risk inciting the Mister's ire by messing with the lanterns.

My gaze darted back to the fireplace. The flames from the coals still burned, doing a poor job of heating the chamber, but that wasn't what caught my attention. The fire . . . it made no sound. Not a crackle or a hiss.

A shiver of dread stirred the tiny hairs along the nape of my neck and spider-walked its way down my spine.

Beside me, a lump shifted beneath the blanket and rolled. Tufts of curly, messy brown hair appeared as Grady peered over the edge of the blanket. He blinked sleep-heavy eyes. "Whatcha doing, Lis?" he murmured, his voice cracking halfway through. It had been doing that more and more of late, starting around the same time he'd begun to grow like the weeds in the yard behind the home.

"Lis?" Grady rose slightly, holding the blanket to his chin as the flames in the fireplace began to weaken. "Was the Mister bothering you again?"

I gave a quick shake of my head, having not seen the Mister even though my arms were lined with evidence of other nights and his mean, pinching fingers.

Rubbing the sleep from his eyes, he frowned. "Did you have a bad dream or something?"

"No," I whispered. "The air doesn't feel right."

"The air . . . ?"

"Is it ghosts?" I croaked.

He snorted. "Ghosts aren't real."

I squinted. "How do you know?"

"Because I . . ." Grady trailed off, looking over his shoulder as the flames of the fireplace collapsed, leaving the room lit by slivers of moonlight. His head turned slowly as he scanned the chamber, noticing the dead lanterns then. His wide gaze shot to mine. "They're here."

My entire body jerked as an icy wave of terror swept over me. *They're here* could mean only one thing.

The Hyhborn.

The scions of the gods looked like us—well, *most* of them did, but those who ruled the Kingdom of Caelum weren't like us lowborn. They weren't mortal at all.

And they had no reason to be here.

It wasn't the Feasts, when the Hyhborn interacted more openly with us lowborn, and this was the Rook. We weren't in the pretty places with things and people of value. There was no pleasure in anything to be found here for them to feed upon.

"Why are they here?" I whispered.

Grady's hand clamped down on my arm, the chill of his fingers bleeding through my sweater. "I don't know, Lis."

"Are they . . . Will they hurt us?"

"They have no reason to. We haven't done a thing wrong." He pulled us down so that our heads shared the same flat pillow. "Just close your eyes and pretend to be asleep. They'll leave us be."

I did what Grady said, like I'd done ever since he'd stopped shooing me away from him, but I couldn't stay silent. I couldn't stop the fear from building on top of itself, making me think the worst. "What if they . . . what if they are here for me?"

He tucked my head under his. "Why would they be?"

My lips quivered. "Because I . . . I'm not like you."

"You got no good reason to worry about that," he assured me, voice low so the others couldn't hear us. "They aren't going to care about that."

But how could he be sure? Other people cared. Sometimes I made them *nervous*, because I couldn't stop myself from saying something that I saw in my mind—an event yet to happen or a decision that hadn't been made yet. Grady was used to it. The Mister? Others? Not so much. They looked at me like there was something wrong with me, and the Mister often stared like he thought I might be a conjurer and like he . . . he might be a little scared of me. Not scared enough to stop pinching me but scared enough to keep doing so.

"Maybe the Hyhborn will sense something off about me," I rasped. "And maybe they won't like it or think I'm—"

"They won't sense anything. I swear." He pulled the blanket over us as if that could somehow protect us.

But a blanket wouldn't shield us from the Hyhborn. They could do whatever they wanted to whoever, and if they were angered? They could bring entire cities to ruin.

"Shh," Grady urged. "Don't cry. Just close your eyes. It'll be okay."

Chamber doors creaked open. Between us, Grady squeezed my arm until I could feel the bones in his fingers. The air suddenly became thin and strained, and the walls groaned as if the stone couldn't contain what had slipped inside. A tremor rocked me. I felt as sick as I had the last time the Prioress had taken my hand, like she'd often done without any concern for what I might see or *know*, but that day had been different. I'd seen death coming for her.

I didn't take big breaths, but a scent still snaked under the blanket and in between us, crowding out the smell of stale ale and too many bodies crammed into a too-small place. A minty scent that reminded me of the . . . the candies the Prioress used to carry in the pockets of her habit. *Don't move. Don't make a sound*, I chanted over and over. *Don't move. Don't make a sound.*

"How many are here?" a male asked in a low voice.

"The number ch-changes every night, Lord Samriel." The Mister's voice trembled, and I'd never heard him sound scared before. Usually, it was *his* voice scaring us, but there was a Hyhborn lord among us, one of the most powerful of Hyhborn. It would terrify even the meanest of bullies. "Usually th-there's about thirty, but I don't know any that have what you're looking for."

"We'll see for ourselves," Lord Samriel replied. "Check them all."

The footfalls of the Hyhborn riders—the Rae—echoed in tandem with my heart. What felt like a thin layer of ice settled over us as the temperature of the chamber dropped.

The Rae were once great lowborn warriors who had fallen in battle to Hyhborn princes and princesses. Now they were little more than flesh and bone, their souls captured and held by the princes, the princesses, and King Euros. Did that mean one of them was here? I shuddered.

"Open your eyes," Lord Samriel demanded from somewhere in the chamber.

Why were they making us open our eyes?

"Who are they?" Another spoke. A man. He did so quietly, but his voice bled shivery power into each word.

"Orphans. Castoffs, my lord," the Mister croaked. "Some came from the Priory of Mercy," he rambled on. "O-Others just show up. Don't know where they come from or where they end up disappearing to. None of them is a seraph, I swear."

They . . . they thought a *seraph* was here? That's why they were checking the eyes, searching for the mark—a light in the eyes, or so I'd heard, but there was nothing like that here.

I trembled at the sound of startled gasps and quiet whimpers that continued for several moments, my eyes squeezed tight as I wished with everything in me that they would leave us alone. Just disappear—

The air stirred directly above us, carrying that minty scent. Grady went rigid against me.

"Eyes open," Lord Samriel ordered from above us.

I was frozen solid as Grady rose halfway, shielding me with his body and the blanket. The hand around my arm shook, and that made me shake even harder because Grady . . . he stared down the older kids without fear and laughed as the lawmen chased him through the streets. He was never afraid.

But he was now.

"Nothing," Lord Samriel announced with a heavy sigh. "And this is all of them?"

The Mister cleared his throat. "Yes, I'm as s-sure as I can be— Wait." His steps were heavy and uneven against the floor. "He always got this smaller one with him. A girl, and an odd one to boot," he said, nudging my covered legs, and I swallowed a squeak. "There."

"He doesn't know what he's talking about," Grady denied. "There isn't no one but me."

"Boy, ya better watch that mouth," the Mister warned.

I bit down on my lip until I tasted blood.

"How about you watch your mouth?" Grady shot back, and another dose of fear punched me in the gut. The Mister wouldn't take kindly to Grady talking back. If we got through this, the Mister would punish him. Real bad, too, like last time—

Without any warning, the blanket was ripped away, turning my blood to ice. Grady shifted so half his body covered mine, but it was no use. They knew I was here.

"It appears there are two instead of one, sharing a blanket. A girl." The unnamed lord paused. "I think."

"Move away from her," Lord Samriel commanded.

"She ain't nobody," Grady gnashed out, his body trembling against mine.

"Everybody is somebody," the other replied.

Grady didn't move. There was a heavy, impatient sigh, and then Grady was *gone*—

Panic exploded inside me, moving all my limbs at once. I jack-knifed up, reaching blindly for Grady in the sudden, too-bright lamplight flooding the chamber. I cried out as a Rae grabbed him by the waist. Thin, wispy gray shadows spilled out from the Rae's robes and swirled around Grady's legs.

"Let me go!" Grady shrieked, kicking out as he was dragged back. "We haven't done anything wrong. Let me—"

"Quiet," Lord Samriel snapped, stepping between Grady and me. His long hair was so pale it was nearly white. He placed his hand on Grady's shoulder.

Grady went quiet.

His normally warm brown skin took on a chalky gray cast as he just . . . he just stared back at me, his eyes wide and empty. He didn't speak. Didn't move.

"Grady?" I whispered, trembling until my teeth chattered.

There was no answer. He always answered me, but it was like he wasn't even there anymore. Like he was just a shell that looked like him.

Fingers curled around my chin. At the touch it felt like a jolt of electricity shot through my body. I could feel the hairs on my arms stand as my skin prickled with awareness.

"It's okay," the other lord said, his voice almost soft, *almost* gentle as he turned my head toward him. "He will not be harmed."

"We'll see about that," Lord Samriel replied.

I jerked but didn't make it far. The unnamed lord's hold wouldn't allow it.

Through clumps of matted dark hair, I stared up at the Lord. He . . . he looked younger than I thought he would, as if he were only in the third decade of life. His hair was a golden brown, brushing shoulders encased in black, and his cheeks were the color of the sand found along the bank of Curser's Bay. His face was an interesting mix of angles and straight lines, but his eyes . . .

They tilted at the outer corners, but it . . . it was the color of the irises that held my attention. I'd never seen anything like the *colors*. Each eye contained blots of blue, green, and brown.

The longer I stared at him, the more I realized he . . . he reminded me of the faded figures painted on the vaulted ceiling of the Priory. What had the Prioress called them? *Angels.* That's what I had once heard her call the Hyhborn, saying they were guardians of mortals and the very realm itself, but what had entered the foundling home didn't feel like protectors.

They felt like predators.

Except for this one, with the strange eyes. He felt . . .

"What about her?" Lord Samriel's voice cracked the silence.

The young Hyhborn lord holding my chin said nothing as he stared at me. Slowly, I realized I'd stopped trembling. My heart had calmed.

I . . . I wasn't afraid of him.

Just like I hadn't been when I first met Grady, but that was because I *saw* what kind of person Grady was. My intuition had told me that Grady was as good as any of us could be. I saw nothing as I stared into the Lord's eyes, but I *knew* I was safe, even as those pupils expanded. Tiny bursts of white appeared in his eyes. They were like *stars,* and they brightened until they were all I could see. My pulse began to pound like a runaway horse. Then it finally happened. My senses opened to him. I saw *nothing* in his eyes or in my mind.

But I *felt* something.

A warning.

A reckoning.

A promise of what was to come.

And I *knew.*

The Lord drew back, the pupils shrinking to a normal size and the white specks disappearing. "No," he said, his gaze flicking to my arms, exposed by the too-big sweater I wore. "She is clear."

He dropped my chin.

I scooted back across the blanket, twisting to Grady. He was still suspended there, motionless and empty. "P-Please," I whispered.

"Release him," the Lord said.

Lord Samriel did so with a sigh, and life returned to Grady that very second. The pallor faded from his skin as I scrabbled across the twisted blankets, throwing my arms around him. As I held on to his trembling body, my gaze inched back to the Hyhborn lord who had stars in his eyes.

He remained where he was, still crouched and staring at me—staring at my arms as Lord Samriel stalked past him, heading to the entrance. My fingers dug into the thin sweater along Grady's back.

"Your arms," he asked, his voice so low this time I wasn't sure I saw his lips move. "How did that happen?"

I didn't know why he asked or cared, and I knew better than to say who had done it, but I looked at the Mister and nodded.

The Lord eyed me for a moment longer, lifted his fingers to lips that had curved into a faint half smile, and then rose to an impossible height.

The chamber went dark once more, and the heavy silence returned, but I wasn't afraid this time.

A sharp, swift cry tore through the darkness, ending abruptly in a wet, crunching sound. I jerked as something heavy hit the floor.

The quiet came again, and all at once, the heaviness seeped out of the room as the very air itself seemed to breathe a sigh of relief. The lanterns along the wall flickered to life, one after the other. The fire surged in the hearth, spitting and hissing.

By the door, the Mister was lying in a puddle of his own blood, his body broken and twisted. Someone screamed. Cots creaked as the others clambered from them, but I didn't move. I stared at the empty doorway, *knowing* I would see the Hyhborn lord again.

CHAPTER 1

"Do you have a moment, Lis?"

Looking up from the chamomile I'd been grinding into a powder for Baron Huntington's teas, I saw Naomi standing in the doorway of my chamber. The brunette was already dressed for the evening; the gossamer of her gown would've been completely transparent if not for the fabric's strategically placed panels in a deep shade of cerulean.

The Baron of Archwood led, well, an unorthodox life compared to most mortals, but then again, Claude wasn't just a mortal. He was a *caelestia*—a mortal that descended from the rare joining of a lowborn and Hyhborn. *Caelestias* were born and *caelestias* aged, just like us lowborn, and at twenty-six, Claude had no plans to marry. Instead, he preferred to spread his affection upon many. He, much like the Hyhborn, was a collector of anything beautiful and unique. And one would be unwise if one thought to compare oneself to any of the Baron's paramours, but it was doubly foolish to measure oneself against Naomi.

With her glossy hair and delicate features, she was utterly breathtaking.

I, on the other hand, happened to look like someone had taken different traits from other people and pieced them together on my face. My small mouth didn't match the natural pucker of my lips. My too-round, too-big eyes seemed to take up the entirety of my face, giving me the appearance of looking far more innocent than I was. That had come in handy more than once while I was on the streets, but I thought that I vaguely resembled those creepy dolls I'd seen in shopwindows, except with golden-olive skin instead of porcelain.

The Baron once told me I was interesting to look upon— "stunning" in an odd sort of way—but even if that weren't so, I would still be his most favored, the one he kept close to him, and that had nothing to do with my odd attractiveness.

Tension crept into my shoulders as I shifted on the settee and nodded. Dragging my teeth over my lower lip, I watched her close the door and cross the sitting area of my quarters—my *private* quarters.

Gods, at twenty-two years of age, I'd been here for . . . for six years. Long enough for me not to be shocked by the knowledge that I had my own space, my own rooms with electricity and hot water, something that many places in the kingdom didn't have. I had my own bed—an actual bed and not a pile of flat blankets or a mattress made of flea-infested straw—but I still couldn't wrap my head around it.

I focused on Naomi. She was behaving strangely, repeatedly clasping her hands together and releasing them. Naomi was nervous, and I had never known her to be such.

"What do you need?" I asked, even though I had a feeling—no, I *knew* exactly what she wanted. Why she was nervous.

"I . . . I wanted to talk to you about my sister," she began—tentatively, and Naomi was never tentative in anything she did. There were few who were as brave and bold as her. "Laurelin has been unwell."

My chest squeezed as my gaze returned to the bowl in my lap and the yellowish-brown powder within. This was what I'd dreaded.

Her sister had married a wealthy landowner above her so-called station in life. A union heralded as a true love match, something I would've normally scoffed at, but it was true. Laurelin was the rarity in a world where most married for convenience, opportunity, or security.

But what did love really do for anyone? Even her? It hadn't stopped her husband from wanting a son even though Laurelin's last birth had nearly taken her life. So she kept trying, no matter the risk.

He'd gotten his son now, and Laurelin had been struck with the fever that had taken so many after birth.

"I wanted to know if she will . . . ?" Naomi took a deep breath, stiffening her shoulders. "If she will recover?"

"I'm assuming you're not looking for my opinion," I said, grinding the pestle into the mound of chamomile. The slightly fruity tobacco scent increased. "Are you?"

"Not unless you have been moonlighting as a physician or midwife," she replied dryly. "I . . . I want to know what the future holds for her."

I exhaled softly. "You shouldn't be asking this."

"I know." Naomi lowered herself to her knees on the floor beside me, the skirt of her gown pooling around her. "And I know the Baron doesn't like it when someone asks you to do this, but I swear he will never know."

My reluctance had little to do with Claude, even though he didn't like it when I used my foresight—my heightened intuition—for anyone but him. He feared I'd be accused of being a conjurer dabbling in forbidden bone magic, and while I *knew* the Baron did worry about that, I also *knew* that it wasn't the magistrates of Archwood he was concerned about. All of them were in the Baron's pocket, and none of them would go against a Hyhborn, even if he was only a descendant of one. What he truly feared was that another with more coin or power would steal me away.

But his command to keep my abilities hidden and my own fear of being labeled a conjurer hadn't stopped me. I just . . . I just couldn't keep my mouth shut when I *saw* or *felt* something and was foolishly compelled to speak up. It was the same in all the places Grady and I had lived in before the Midlands' city of Archwood, which had caused me to be accused of being a conjurer and led to us fleeing in the middle of the night more times than I cared to remember to avoid the hangman's noose. My terminal inability to mind my own business was how I met Claude.

And it was also how people in the manor and beyond had learned of me—the woman who knew things. Not many, but enough.

The reason I didn't want Naomi to ask this had everything to do with her.

When I first came to Archwood Manor, at sixteen, Naomi had already been here for about thirteen months. The same age as Claude, she was only a few years older than me, and clever, and she was so much more worldly than I could ever hope to be that I assumed she'd want little to do with me.

That hadn't been the case.

Naomi had become, well, my first . . . friend outside of Grady.

I would do anything for her.

But I feared I'd break her heart, and I was as terrified of losing her friendship as I was of losing the life I'd finally carved out for myself in Archwood. Because more times than not, people really didn't want the answers they sought, and the truth of what was to come was often far more destructive than a lie.

"Please," Naomi whispered. "I have never asked you anything like this before, and I . . ." She swallowed thickly. "I hate doing it, but I'm just so worried, Lis. I'm afraid that she will leave this realm."

Her dark eyes began to glimmer with tears, and I couldn't bear it. "Are you sure?"

"Of course—"

"You say that now, but what if it's an answer you fear? Because if it is, I won't lie. Your worry will turn to heartache," I reminded her.

"I know. Trust me, I do," she swore, the rich brown curls spilling over her shoulders as she leaned toward me. "It's why I didn't ask when I first learned of the fever."

I bit down on my lip, my grip on the mortar tightening.

"I won't hold it against you," she said softly. "Whatever the answer is, I will not blame you."

"You promise?"

"Of course," she swore.

"Okay," I said, hoping she spoke the truth. Naomi wasn't a projector, meaning she didn't broadcast her thoughts and intentions like so many did, making them far too easy to read.

But I could get inside her mind if I wanted to and find out if she spoke the truth. All I would need to do was open my senses to her and allow that connection to snap to life.

I didn't do that when I could help it. It was too much of an invasion. A violation. However, knowing that hadn't stopped me from doing it when it benefited me, had it?

Shoving that little truth aside, I drew in a breath that tasted of the chamomile as I set the bowl on a small table. "Give me your hand."

Naomi didn't hesitate then, lifting her hand, but I did, because it was so rare for my hand to touch others' flesh without their intentions, and sometimes even their futures, becoming known to me. The only way I could touch another lowborn was to dull my senses, usually through alcohol or some other substance, and, well, that dulled everything else too and didn't last very long, so there really was no point.

I wrapped my hand around hers, wanting to take just a brief second to simply enjoy the feeling. Most didn't realize there was a world of difference between being touched and touching. But this wasn't about me. I couldn't take that second, because the longer I held Naomi's hand, the more likely it was that I would end up seeing things about her she might not want to know or want me to learn. No amount of humming or keeping my mind active would stop that.

Quieting my mind, I opened my senses and then closed my eyes. A second passed, and another; then a series of tingles erupted between my shoulder blades and spread up, over the back of my skull. In the darkness of my mind, I began to see the hazy form of Naomi's face, but I shut that down.

"Ask the question again," I instructed, because it would help me focus on only what she wanted to know and not everything else that was taking shape and forming words.

"Will Laurelin recover from her fever?" Naomi said in a voice barely above a whisper.

There was silence in my mind, and then I heard what sounded like my own voice whisper, *She will recover.*

A shudder of relief went through me, but my skin quickly chilled. The voice continued to whisper. Releasing Naomi's hand, I opened my eyes.

Naomi had gone still, her hand suspended in air. "What did you see?"

"She'll recover from the fever," I shared.

Her throat worked on a delicate swallow. "Really?"

"Yes." I smiled, but it felt brittle.

"Oh, thank the gods," she whispered, pressing her fingers to her mouth. "Thank you."

Now my smile was a grimace as I looked away. I cleared my throat, picking up the bowl. I barely felt the cool ceramic.

"Has Claude been having trouble sleeping again?" Naomi asked after a handful of moments, her voice lighter than it had been when she walked into the chamber.

Thankful for the change of subject, I nodded. "He wants to be rested for the upcoming Feasts."

Naomi's brows rose. "The Feasts don't start for several more weeks—at least a month or so."

I glanced at her. "He wants to be *well* rested."

Naomi snorted. "He must be quite excited." Leaning back, she toyed with a sapphire hanging from a thin silver necklace she almost always wore. "And what about you? You excited?"

I lifted a shoulder as my stomach tumbled a bit. "Haven't really thought about it."

"But this will be your first Feasts, right?"

"Yep." It was the first year I was eligible to attend, as one must be twenty-two years of age or married, which made little sense to me, but it was the Hyhborn and King Euros who made the rules, not me.

"You are in for . . . quite the show," she said slowly.

I snickered, having heard the stories.

She tipped toward me once more, her voice lowering. "But will you be partaking in the . . . in the *festivities*?"

"Festivities." I laughed. "What a tame description."

She grinned. "What else would I call it?"

"An orgy?"

Tipping her head back, she laughed, and it was such a lovely, infectious sound. Naomi had the best laugh, causing a grin to tug at my own lips. "That's not what happens," she said.

"Really?" I stated dryly.

Naomi feigned a look of innocence, which was rather impressive considering there was little about her that could be called innocent. "The Feasts serve as a way for the Hyhborn to reaffirm their commitment to serving lowborn by sharing their wealth of food and drink." She recited the doctrine as well as any prioress would as she folded her hands demurely in her lap. "Sometimes a lot of drink flows, and with the Hyhborn around, certain *activities* may occur. That is all."

"Ah, yes, reaffirming their commitment to lowborn," I said a bit sarcastically. She was speaking of the uppermost sphere of Hyhborn—the ones known as Deminyens.

When Deminyens emerged from the ground, it was said they came into existence fully formed and were ageless, capable of manipulating the elements and even the minds of others. Some of them were the lords and the ladies of the Hyhborn echelon, but those weren't the most powerful of the Deminyens. The princes and princesses who ruled over the six territories within Caelum, along with the King, were the most frightening in their power. They could take different shapes, whip rivers into a frenzy with a flick of their wrists, and even seize the souls of the lowborn, creating the terrifying creatures known as the Rae.

Not much was known about any of them except for King Euros. Hell, other than Prince Rainer of Primvera, we didn't even know their names. The only other one we ever heard about, and that was usually through the rumor mill, was the Prince of Vytrus, who ruled the Highlands, and that was because he was dreaded by most. After all, he was known as the hand that delivered the King's wrath.

I almost laughed out loud right then. Hyhborn were the Protectors of the Realm, but I wasn't exactly sure how they served us. Even though the Hyhborn were mostly like absentee landlords who came around only when the rent was due, the Hyhborn controlled everything about the lowborn's lives—from who could obtain an education to who could own land or companies. And I was of the mind that the Feasts were more of a way to provide the Hyhborn with what they wanted. Our indulgence in all manner of things, from gorging on food to indulging in the delights of each other during the Feasts, also *fed* the Hyhborn. Strengthened them. Empowered them. Our pleasure was their sustenance. Their life force. It was more for them than it was us.

Because there were so many more ways they could prove that

they cared for us lowborn, starting with providing food throughout the year to those in need. So many either starved or broke their backs in the mines or risked their lives on hunts to keep their families fed while the aristo—Hyhborn and the wealthiest of lowborn— became richer, the poor even more impoverished. It was the way things always had been and always would be, no matter how many lowborn rebellions rose up. Instead, they provided food only once a year, when much of the food went to waste while everyone was engaging in those certain *activities*.

But I didn't say any of that out loud.

I might be reckless, but I wasn't a fool.

"You know, they're not all that bad," Naomi said after a moment. "The Hyhborn, I mean. I've known of a few lords and ladies who have stepped in and aided those in need, and those in Primvera are kind and even caring. I think more are like that than not."

At once, I thought of *my* Hyhborn—the unnamed lord who had touched my chin and asked how my arms had become so bruised. I didn't know why I referred to him as mine. He obviously wasn't. Hyhborn might fuck their way through the entirety of the lowborn race and then some, and a few might even claim a lowborn as theirs, at least for a time, but they were never a lowborn's. It was just that I didn't know his name, and it was an odd habit that had begun since that night.

Honestly, I doubted the Hyhborn lord had ever realized that he'd saved Grady's life that night. The Mister would've punished him for talking back in front of Hyhborn, and far too many didn't survive his punishments.

My stomach took a quick, sharp tumble like it always did when I thought of my Hyhborn, because I *knew* I would see him again.

That had yet to occur, and anytime I thought of it, I was filled with a mixture of dread and anticipation I couldn't even begin to try to understand.

But maybe Naomi was right about many of them being what they claimed to be—Protectors of the Realm. Archwood flourished partly because of the ones in Primvera, the Hyhborn Court that sat just beyond the woods outside of the manor, and my Hyhborn *had* punished the Mister. Though he had done so rather brutally, so I wasn't sure that was a good example of a kind and caring Hyhborn.

"Do you . . . do you think there will be Deminyens at the Feasts?" I asked.

"There are usually a few of them that show." Her brow creased. "I've even seen a lord or two in the past. I do hope they show this year."

Toying with the pestle, I looked over at her.

Her grin turned sly as she twisted the silver chain around her fingers. "There's never a need to use the Long Night with a Hyhborn," she added, referencing a powder made from the seeds of a trumpet flower. The powerful herb, in the right dose, left one drowsy and without much memory of the time after ingesting it. "They are quite delightful."

My brows rose.

"What?" she exclaimed with another robust, throaty laugh. "Did you know that the Hyhborn are known for climaxes that can last for hours—actual *hours*?"

"I've heard." I wasn't sure if that was true or not, but hours-long orgasms sounded . . . intense. Possibly even a little painful.

Her gaze flicked to mine. "Are you able to touch a Hyhborn without . . . *knowing*?"

"I'm not sure." I thought about Claude and then my Hyhborn lord. "I can touch a *caelestia* for a little while before I start to know things, but I've never touched a Hyhborn before, and whenever I'm asked something that deals with them, I sense nothing. So, I'm not sure."

"Well, might be worth finding out." She winked.

I laughed, shaking my head.

She grinned at me. "I need to get going. Allyson has been a mess of late," she said, speaking of one of the newest additions to the manor. "I need to make sure she has her head together."

"Good luck with that."

Naomi laughed as she rose, the gossamer pooling around her feet. She started for the door, then stopped. "Thank you, Lis."

"For what?" I frowned.

"For answering," she said.

I didn't know what to say as I watched her leave, but I didn't want her thanks.

My shoulders slumped as I lifted my gaze to the slowly churning fan above me. I hadn't lied to Naomi. Her sister would survive the fever, but the foresight hadn't stopped there. It had kept whispering, telling me that death still marked Laurelin. How or why, I hadn't allowed myself to find out, but I had a feeling—and my feelings were rarely if ever wrong—she wouldn't live to see the end of the Feasts.

CHAPTER 2

"Would you like a different wine, pet?"

My fingers tensed, then pressed against the skin exposed between two of the many strings of jewels adorning my hip. Normally the nickname didn't bother me, but Claude's cousin Hymel stood within ear range, which was common since he was the Captain of the Guard. Even with his back to me, I knew Hymel smirked. He was an ass, plain and simple.

Thin, delicate chains of diamonds hanging from a crown of fresh chrysanthemums tapped against my cheeks as I turned my head from the throng of those below to the man beside me.

The dark-haired Baron of Archwood sat upon what could be described only as a throne. A rather gaudy one, in my opinion. Large enough to seat two and encrusted with rubies taken from the Hollow Mines, the chair cost more coin than those mining the rubies would likely ever see.

Not that the Baron realized that.

Claude Huntington wasn't necessarily a bad man, and I would know if he was even without my intuition. I'd met too many bad people from all classes to not recognize one. He could be prone to recklessness and indulged in the pleasures of life a bit too much. He was known to be a holy terror if crossed, was obviously spoiled, and, being a *caelestia*, was expectedly self-centered. Rarely had a single wrinkle of worry creased the Baron's alabaster skin.

But that had changed in recent months. His coffers weren't as full. The abhorrent chairs and gold decor Claude insisted on, the near-nightly parties and celebrations he seemed to need to survive, likely had something to do with this. Though that wasn't entirely fair. Yes, Claude wanted to host these parties, but it was also required of him—of all barons. Many types of pleasure were found at these gatherings, be it through drink, food, conversation, or what usually happened later in the night.

"No," I said, smiling. "But it's kind of you to offer."

The bright lights of the chandelier glinted off the skin along his cheekbones and the bridge of his nose. There was a dusting of gold shimmer there. It wasn't some sort of facial paint. It was simply his skin. *Caelestias* glimmered.

Eyes a lovely shade of sea-glass blue searched mine. Everything about Claude was lovely. His perfectly manicured, smooth hands and coiffed, inky hair. He was slim and tall, built perfectly for whatever fashion the aristo were currently obsessed with, and when he smiled, he could be devastating.

And for a little while, I liked being devastated by that smile. It didn't hurt that Claude, being a *caelestia*, had always been extremely difficult for me to sense. My abilities didn't immediately snap into action around him. I could touch him, if only for a little bit.

"But you haven't drunk much of your wine," he observed.

Laughter and conversation droned on around us as I glanced at the chalice. The wine was the color of the lavender that grew in the gardens of Archwood and tasted of sweetened berries. It was tasty, and imbibing wine was welcomed and even expected. After all, there was a pleasure in drinking alcohol, but it also dulled my abilities. More importantly, I knew the truth of why I was the Baron's favorite paramour.

It wasn't my stunning odd attractiveness or my personality. The Baron kept me *and* Grady sheltered, fed, and well taken care of because of my abilities and how useful they could be to him, and I was terrified that the moment I no longer served a purpose was the moment Grady and I would be back on the streets, barely scraping by and living on the edge of death.

Which wasn't living at all.

"It's fine," I assured him, taking a very small sip of the wine as I turned my attention back to those below the dais. The gold-adorned Great Chamber was full of the aristo—the wealthy shippers and shop owners, the bankers and landowners. No one was masked. It wasn't *that* kind of party. Yet. I searched for Naomi among those below, having lost sight of her earlier.

"Pet?" Claude called softly.

I faced him once more. He bent at the waist, extending his hand. Behind us, his personal guards kept their eyes on the crowd. All except Grady. I caught a quick glimpse of the brown skin of his jaw tightening. Grady wasn't exactly a fan of the Baron and this arrangement. My gaze returned to the Baron.

Claude smiled.

Bracing a hand on the velvet pillow I sat on, I leaned closer and placed my chin in his hand. His fingers were cool like always. So were his lips as he lowered his head and kissed me. I felt only a little flutter in my stomach. I used to feel more, back when I thought his attentiveness was born of want of *me*.

Which was why Grady didn't like this arrangement.

If Claude showered me with attention because he wanted me for, well, me, Grady wouldn't care at all. He just thought I deserved more. Better. And it wasn't like I didn't think I did too, but more and better were hard to come by for anyone these days. Having a roof over our heads, food in our bellies, and safety and security always trumped better and more.

His mouth lifted from mine. "You worry me."

"Why?"

He dragged a thumb just below my lower lip, careful to not smear the red paint. "You're quiet."

How could I not be when I sat upon the dais with no one but him and Hymel within speaking distance? Claude had been chatting with everyone under the sun this evening, and I'd rather cut my own tongue out than speak to Hymel. Seriously. I'd cut my tongue out and throw it at him first. "I think I'm just tired."

"What has you so tired?" he asked, tone ringing with just that right amount of concern.

"I didn't sleep well." A nightmare of the past had woken me last night, one that had been a haunting walk down memory lane. I'd dreamt that we'd been back on the streets, and Grady had been sick with that body-rattling cough. The one I could still clearly hear all these years later. I had that nightmare a lot, but last night . . . it had been too real.

Which was why I'd spent most of the day tending to the flower garden I'd made for myself. I'd barely had time to grab something to eat between that and preparing for my presence in the Great Chamber, but in that little garden, I didn't think about the very real past, the nightmares, or the fear that all of this could end at any moment.

One dark brow rose in response. "Is that truly all that it is?"

I nodded.

He slid his hand to my hair, fixing one of the strings of diamonds. "I was beginning to fear that you were jealous."

I stared at him, confused.

"I know I've been paying a lot of attention to the others of late," he said, fixing another string as he glanced out to the crowd, likely at the fair-haired Allyson. "I was worried you were beginning to feel unappreciated."

My brows inched up my forehead. "Seriously?"

He frowned. "Yes."

I continued to stare at him, slow to realize he was being truthful. A laugh bubbled up, but I squelched it. I couldn't even remember the last time Claude had done more than give me a quick kiss or pat on the rear, and I was completely okay with that.

Mostly.

While I felt little real attraction toward him these days, I did enjoy being touched. Desired. Wanted. I enjoyed touching, even if it was for only a few minutes. And even though Claude had no boundaries set upon his paramours, things were a bit more complicated for me. I was more like an advisor . . . or a spy he sometimes showed attention to.

"I've been told you haven't been sleeping in anyone else's quarters," he added.

Irritation flashed through me. I didn't appreciate the idea of him having anyone keep an eye on me, but it was also a rather irrelevant observation.

Claude knew exactly how difficult it was for me to be intimate with others. How uncomfortable it made me if they were unaware of, well, the risks of me touching them without dulling my senses with what felt like my body weight in liquor. And not being able to remember having sex or hoping that it was enjoyable was as disquieting as seeing or hearings things I shouldn't. Maybe even more so.

However, Claude also routinely forgot what didn't directly involve him.

"I don't want you to be lonely," he said, and he meant it.

That's why I smiled at him. "I'm not."

Claude was quick to return my smile and lean away, turning his attention back to whatever. I'd given him what he wanted. Reassurance that I was happy. He sought that because he cared, but also because he was afraid if I wasn't, I'd leave. But what I'd given him was a lie. Because I was—

I stopped myself as if that could somehow change how I felt.

I grabbed the chalice, drinking half of the wine in one gulp as I stared at the gold crevices etched into the marble floors. My mind went quiet, only for a few seconds, but that was all it took for the hum of voices to ratchet up. Closing my eyes, I took a deep breath and held it until I severed all those unseen strings as they began to form in my mind.

After several moments, I exhaled softly and opened my eyes. My gaze flicked out over the crush, the faces a blur and my mind my own.

In front of me, Hymel leaned against the dais. He glanced back at me, the mouth framed by a neat beard twisted into a sneer. "Is there anything you're in need of, *pet?*"

My expression showed nothing as I returned Hymel's stare. I didn't like the man, and the only reason Claude tolerated him was because he was family and because he took care of the more unsavory tasks of running a city. For example, Hymel enjoyed being sent to collect rent, especially if payments couldn't be made. He was unnecessarily hard on the guards and taunted me whenever he got the chance.

He wanted me to respond to him as I did when others stoked my temper. I had what Hymel called "a mouth" on me. However, I'd learned to keep that mouth in check. Well, about ninety percent of the time. But when I was really mad? Or really nervous or scared? It was the only defense I had.

Except, come to think of it, it wasn't really a defense. It was more like a self-destructive tendency, because it always, *always* got me in trouble.

Anyway, Naomi once told me it was because he had problems performing in bed, unable to find release. I didn't know if that was true or not, and I found it ironic that such a being could have such difficulties, but *caelestias* were as close to mortal as any Hyhborn could be. They didn't get as sick as often and were physically stronger. They didn't need to feed as Deminyens did, but they weren't immune to diseases. Either way, I doubted that was the driving force behind Hymel's meanness, or the only one, but I did *know* one thing about him for sure.

Hymel was a particular kind of cruel, and that was what he got off on.

He smirked. "You're like a favored hound, you know that, right?" His voice was low enough that only I could hear him, since Claude had turned his attention to one of his cronies. "The way he has you seated by his feet."

I did know that.

But I'd rather be a favored hound than a starving, dying one.

Hymel wouldn't understand that, though. Those who never had to worry about when their bellies would be full again or if those rats scurrying through their hair at night carried diseases had no idea what one would do to keep fed and sheltered.

Therefore, his opinions and those of others like him meant nothing to me.

So I smiled, lifting the chalice to my lips, and took another, much smaller drink.

Hymel's eyes narrowed, but then he turned from me. He stiffened. I followed his stare. A tall man dressed in finery walked out of the crowd. I recognized him.

Ellis Ramsey approached the dais, heading for the Baron.

The shipping magnate from the neighboring town of Newmarsh stopped to bow deeply before the Baron. "Good evening, Baron Huntington."

Claude nodded in acknowledgment as he extended his arm toward one of the empty chairs to his other side. "Would you care for some wine?"

"Thank you, but that won't be necessary. I don't want to take up too much of your time tonight." Ramsey gave a tight smile that did nothing to ease the harshness of his grizzled features as he took the seat. "I have news."

"Of?" Claude murmured, glancing at me. It was quick, but I saw.

"The Westlands," he said. "There's been a . . . development."

"And what would that be?" Claude asked.

Ramsey leaned toward the Baron. "There are rumors that the Westlands' Court is at odds with the King."

My little old ears perked right up as I lowered my chalice and opened my senses. In a room of so many people, I had to be careful not to be overwhelmed. I focused only on Ramsey, creating this imaginary string in my mind—a cord that connected me directly with him. Thoughts could be hard to make sense of—sometimes I heard more of a collection of words that either matched what one spoke or were something completely different. Either way, it always took me a moment to gain my bearings, to decipher what I was hearing out loud and what wasn't being spoken.

"I have little interest in rumors," Claude replied.

"I think you will in this one." Ramsey's voice lowered as I heard *I doubt you have interest in anything that doesn't spread its legs and isn't wet.* I rolled my eyes. "Two chancellors were sent to Visalia on behalf of the King," Ramsey reported, speaking of the lowborn messengers who acted as go-betweens for the King and the five Courts. "There appeared to be a problem with their visit, as they were sent back to His Majesty . . ." The magnate allowed a dramatic pause. "In pieces."

I was barely able to smother my gasp. I would consider being sent anywhere in pieces to be more than a problem.

"Well, that's concerning." Claude took a deep drink of his wine.

"There's more."

Claude's grip tightened on his glass. "Can't wait to hear."

"The Princess of Visalia has been amassing a substantial presence along the border between the Westlands and Midlands," Ramsey shared, his thoughts reflecting what he spoke. "More rumors, but ones also believed to be true."

"And this substantial presence?" Claude looked out over the crowd below him. "Are we speaking of her battalion?"

"Hers and the Iron Knights is what I'm hearing." Ramsey shifted, dropping a large hand to his knee.

Surprise flickered through me as I set the chalice on the tray. The Iron Knights, a group of rebellious lowborn who were more like raiders than actual knights, had been causing problems throughout the border towns in the Midlands and Lowlands for the last year. From what I knew, they wanted to see the Hyhborn king replaced with a lowborn one, and even though I didn't pay much mind to politics unless I had to, I knew they were gaining support throughout Caelum. It was kind of hard not to when I knew people who believed that Vayne Beylen—the Commander of the Iron Knights—could change the realm for the better, but I didn't see how that would be possible if they were joining forces with the Westlands' Hyhborn.

Claude drew his thumb over his chin. "And have they crossed into the Midlands?"

"Not that I have heard."

"What about Beylen?" Claude asked. "Has he been spotted?"

"That is another thing I cannot answer," Ramsey said, while thinking, *If that bastard is spotted, he'll be a dead one.* Something about that thought was disquieting, because it was almost as if Beylen's death would be upsetting. The Iron Knights were gaining traction among lowborn, but usually the wealthy ones didn't want to see the Iron Knight succeed. Doing so jeopardized the status quo. "But Archwood is quite the distance from the border. There will be at least a warning if the Iron Knights do move into our lands, but if they travel past the border towns? This would no longer be a rebellion."

"No," Claude murmured. "It would be an act of war."

My chest felt far too tight as I severed the connection I'd forged with the magnate. I glanced at Grady, then to the crowd. There had been no wars, not since the Great War that took place four centuries ago and left nearly nothing of the realm behind.

"I do not think it will come to that," Ramsey said.

"Nor do I." Claude nodded slowly. "Thank you for the information." He leaned back in his chair. "I would keep this quiet until we know more for sure, lest we have a panic on our hands."

"Agreed."

The Baron was silent as Ramsey rose and descended the dais. The shipping magnate was no longer visible in the crowd when Claude turned his attention toward me. "What do you know?"

And here was the crux of our arrangement. How I benefited him. Sometimes it was learning of another's future or listening in on the thoughts of another baron, if they were up to something or if they came to Archwood in good faith. There were times when it required a more . . . hands-on approach for me to know.

But not this time.

As soon as he asked his question, a chill moved through me. The coldness settled in the center of my shoulder blades. My stomach hollowed as I reached beneath my heavy length of dark hair and touched the space behind my left ear, where it felt like someone had pressed a cold kiss. The voice among my thoughts spoke a warning.

He's coming.

CHAPTER 3

The dull ache in my head that came from whenever I was around so many people eased only when I returned to my quarters. I was tired, but my mind was far too restless for me to even think of sleep as I entered the bathing chamber.

I quickly scrubbed the paint from my face and braided my hair. After slipping on my nightgown, I donned a lightweight, cap-sleeved robe that belted at the waist as I toed on a pair of thin-soled boots. I slipped out of the terrace doors of my quarters and into the humid night air, then crossed the narrow patio and started across the back lawn. It must've rained a bit ago, but the clouds had cleared. With the glow of the full moon casting silvery light along the grass and stone pathway, I made no attempt to hide my movements from those patrolling the manor walls in the distance. The Baron was well aware of my nighttime travels and had no problem with them.

During the day, city folk often entered the grounds of the manor to wander the gardens, but it was quiet and peaceful at this time of night. The same could not be said about inside the manor, where the party was just beginning in the Great Chamber. All the aristo unaware that something was coming.

Someone was coming.

My stomach wriggled as if it were full of serpents. Could it be warning me of the Iron Knights—their Commander? It was the only thing that made sense, but why would the Iron Knights be working with the Princess of Visalia?

Trying to see into the future where the Deminyens were involved was nearly as unhelpful as trying to see my own. My so-called gifts were no help there when I either heard or saw nothing, or received only vague impressions.

I thought of Claude's response to my premonition. The Baron had gone quiet before deciding that King Euros would surely do something to prevent whatever political unrest was occurring be-tween the Crown and the Westlands from spilling over into the Midlands. His mood improved then, but mine had worsened, be-cause all I could think of was Astoria, the once-great city on the border between the Midlands and the Westlands. It was said to have been not only the birthplace of Vayne Beylen but also where those who sought to join the rebellion had been given refuge.

King Euros had sanctioned the destruction of Astoria, and the Prince of Vytrus had delivered the King's wrath. Thousands had been displaced, and only the gods knew how many had been killed. All that that devastation had accomplished was the creation of more rebels.

So, I wasn't relieved by the idea of the King becoming involved.

Sighing as I passed the darkened buildings where the manor blacksmith and other workers spent their days, I saw the stables come into view. I grinned as I caught sight of Gerold, one of the stable grooms, slumbering propped against the wall, legs spread wide in the straw. Seeing the empty bottle of whiskey between his thighs, I cracked a grin. Gerold wouldn't be waking anytime soon.

I passed several stalls, heading for the back, where a beautiful sable mare nibbled on a late-night snack of alfalfa in the glow of lantern light. I laughed under my breath. "Iris, how are you always eating?"

The mare huffed, ear twitching.

Smiling, I ran my hand over her glossy coat. Iris was one of many gifts from Claude. She was the only horse I'd ever owned, and she was my favorite of all the gifts he'd bestowed upon me even though she didn't . . . she didn't feel like she was truly mine.

Nothing in Archwood did, not even after six years. Everything still felt temporary and on loan. Everything still felt like it could be ripped out from beneath me at any given second.

I picked up a brush and started with her mane, brushing at the bottoms of the strands in downward sections. Besides the gardens and the little section I'd cultivated for myself over the years, the stables were the only place where I felt . . . I didn't know. Peace? Found pleasure in the simpleness of taking care of Iris? I thought it was the sound—the soft whinny of all the horses and the drag of their hooves on the straw-strewn floor. Even the smells—though, when the stables hadn't been mucked, not so much. But I liked it here, and it was where I spent much of my free time. The stables weren't as good at silencing my intuition, though. Only large quantities of alcohol and having my hands in soil accomplished that. Still, it brought me pleasure, and that was important to me and to the Hyhborn.

My nose wrinkled. I had no idea how they . . . they fed on us when there were none around. At least from what I could tell. I supposed it was something we weren't supposed to know, and I also guessed I was probably better off not understanding.

As I brushed Iris's mane, the part of me that was a worrier took over—the part that had learned to expect the bad and fear the worst in all situations. What would happen if the unrest in the west made its way into the Midlands—to Archwood? My stomach knotted with dread.

Before Archwood, all the different towns Grady and I had lived in blurred into one nightmare. Finding coin whatever way we could. Taking any job that would hire people our age and resorting to thievery when we couldn't find work. No real plans for the future. How could there be when every minute of every day was spent on surviving—on all those "not"s? *Not* starving. Not getting caught. Not becoming a victim to any number of predators. Not getting sick. Not giving up—and gods, that was the hardest when there was no real hope of anything more, because inevitably, we ended the same as we had begun.

Running.

Running away.

Grady and I had fled Union City the night the Hyhborn appeared in the orphanage, stowing away on one of the stagecoaches headed out of the Lowlands. I'd been convinced that we'd escaped. And it was kind of funny in a sad, somewhat disturbing way to think back on how scared I'd been that night—so afraid that the Hyhborn would discover that I was different and take me. Hurt me. Or even kill me. To this day, I didn't know why I'd been so afraid of that. Hyhborn had no interest in lice-infested orphans. Not even one whose intuition alerted them to another's intentions or allowed them to see the future.

But after that night, all we'd done was run and run, and if Archwood were to fall, we would return to that life once more, and I . . . My hand trembled. That terrified me more than anything—even more than spiders and other creepy, crawly things. Even thinking of it made me feel as if my lungs were decompressing and I was on the verge of losing the ability to breathe.

I would do anything to make sure that didn't happen. That neither Grady nor I had to go back to surviving all those "not"s.

But as I moved on to Iris's tail, an all-too-familiar itchy, suffocating feeling of loneliness settled over me like a coarse blanket. There were far more important things to be worried about at the moment, but there were few feelings worse than loneliness. Or maybe there actually weren't any, and loneliness was the worst, because it was pervasive, hard to shake, even when you weren't alone, and it worked overtime to convince you that contentment and joy were possible.

But that was a lie.

When you truly spent most of your time alone? When you *had* to? And not because you *wanted* to? There was no joy to be found. That was my future. For however long that might be. But the future wouldn't be any different—whether I was here or elsewhere.

That loneliness would remain.

The darkness of my thoughts haunted me as I used a brush on Iris's coat. I blew out an aggravated breath. I needed to think of something else—

Listen.

My body suddenly froze. Frowning, I turned and scanned the shadowed aisle of the stables, hearing only the sounds of the other horses and Gerold's faint snores. My hand tightened on the brush as an acute sense of awareness washed over me. It wasn't a chill of unease. This was different. The pressure between my shoulders was something else entirely. An intuition that I followed, wherever it led. Or more accurately, it was a *demand*.

Curious, I walked out of the stall, letting my intuition guide me.

I'd learned long ago that I'd get little rest if I actually managed to ignore it, which I was rarely capable of doing.

I walked toward the back of the barn, where the doors were cracked, my steps quiet. Just as I went to push the door open, I heard voices.

"Did you get him?" The muffled words traveled through the wood. The voice sounded familiar. "And you're sure he's not one from Primvera you mistook?"

My breath caught. If the "he" they spoke of could've been mistaken as someone from Primvera, then they spoke of a Hyhborn and likely a Deminyen, as they didn't live in lowborn cities but resided in their Courts.

"Because how do you think I knew what he was in the first place? I saw him and I remembered what he was supposed to look like," another voice answered, and this one I recognized immediately due to his unique, gravelly tone. A guard who went by Mickie, but I knew his actual name was Matthew Laske, and he was . . . well, bad news. He was one of the guards who eagerly aided Hymel when it came to collecting rent. "He's the one Muriel had us waiting for. I'm sure, Finn."

Another of Claude's guards. A young man with dark hair who always smiled whenever I saw him, and it was a nice smile.

I knew I shouldn't eavesdrop; rarely did anything good come from that. But that's what I did, because pressure had settled in the space between my shoulder blades and had begun to tingle. I crossed the foot or two to the shared wall and leaned against it. Unsure of why I was compelled to do so or what my intuition was picking up on, I obeyed the urge and listened.

"And on top of him being a spittin' image of what Muriel said, if he was from Primvera, I doubt he'd be slinkin' around the Twin Barrels," Mickie continued, referencing one of the bawdy taverns in Archwood. I'd been there a time or two with Naomi. It was not a place I'd think a Hyhborn would normally spend time in. "Anyway, I took him to Jac's barn."

"Are you shittin' me?" Finn demanded. "You took that thing to his barn? When Jac is off getting sucked and fucked every way from Sunday?"

My brows lifted. I didn't know of anyone by the name of Muriel, but I did know who Jac was. A blacksmith—the widowed black-smith who was in line to replace the Baron's personal smithy. He sometimes stepped in when the Baron's own fell behind. So did Grady, who had an unbelievable natural knack for forging metal.

"Don't ya look at me like that," Mickie growled. "Porter made sure he ain't waking up anytime soon," he said, naming the owner of the Twin Barrels. "Served him the house special." The guard chuck-led. "His ass is knocked, and what I put in him will keep him down for the count. He ain't goin' anywhere. He'll be there, ready for us to handle him when Jac is finished havin' himself a good night in a few hours."

My stomach hollowed as the tingling between my shoulder blades intensified. Without seeing them, I wouldn't be able to peer into their thoughts, but my intuition was already filling in the gaps in what they were saying, causing my pulse to pick up.

"Got to admit, I'm damned relieved I was right about him and I didn't go and kill one of our own," Mickie said with another raspy laugh. "Porter put enough of the Fool's Parsley in that whiskey he served that if he was a lowborn, it would've dropped his ass dead on the spot, even with one or two sips."

Fool's Parsley, also known as hemlock, could do exactly what Mickie claimed depending on the amount ingested.

My heart sank as I held Iris's brush to my chest, because I knew what was to become of that Hyhborn.

"If ya so worried about him escapin'," Mickie was saying, "I can head back and put another spike in him."

Nausea rose sharply. They put *spikes* in a Hyhborn? Gods, that was . . . that was terrible, but I needed to stop listening and start pretending that I heard nothing. This didn't involve me.

"We need him alive, remember?" Finn's voice snapped with im-patience. "You put too much of that shit in him, he won't be of any use to us."

I didn't walk away.

"We'll wait till Jac's up at dawn," Finn said. "He knows how to get the word out to Muriel. I got a bottle of some good shit out of the Baron's cellars." His voice was fading. "And we'll head over to Davie's . . ."

I strained to hear more, but they had moved too far away. I'd heard enough, though. They had captured a Hyhborn, and I could think of only one reason why someone would do something so insanely foolish—to harvest the Hyhborn's *parts* for use in bone magic. My mouth dried. Good gods, I didn't know that was happening in Archwood, and wasn't that a terribly naive thing to think? Of course, the shadow market was everywhere, in every city in every territory, blossoming wherever desperation could be found.

I closed my eyes as the tingling between my shoulder blades turned to tension that settled in the muscles lining my spine. None of this was my problem.

But my stomach curdled as I turned and started walking. The pressure moved, settling on my chest, and in my mind, I could hear that annoying voice of mine whispering *I am wrong*—that this Hyhborn was my problem. The tension increased, twisting up my stomach even further. And it wasn't just my problem. It was Archwood's. The Hyhborn had destroyed entire neighborhoods to ferret out those believed to be involved in bone magic. Cities had been destroyed.

"But it's not *my* problem," I whispered. "It's *not.*"

But that undeniable urge to intervene—to help this Hyhborn—was as strong as any impression I'd gotten in my life. Maybe even stronger.

"Fuck," I groaned.

Spinning around, I hurried back to Iris's stall, the hem of my cloak snapping around my boots. Going to the manor wasn't an option. The Baron would be utterly useless at this time of night, and I didn't want to involve Grady in this in case things went sideways.

Which was a high likelihood.

Shit. Shit. Shit.

I grabbed the bridle off the wall. "Sorry, girl, I know it's late," I said as she turned her head, nosing my hand. I gave her a scratch behind the ear and then slipped her bridle on, attaching the reins. "We'll make this as quick as possible."

Iris shook her head, and I decided that was an agreement when in reality she was likely showing her annoyance at being interrupted.

I didn't want to waste time with a saddle, but I wasn't a good enough rider to go bareback. So I took the minutes to saddle her, double-checking I had it secured correctly, just as Claude had shown me. A five-minute delay was better than a broken neck.

Gripping the pommel, I hauled myself up and settled into the saddle. I was likely making a huge mistake as I guided Iris out of her stall, quickly picking up speed, but I couldn't turn back as I raced across the lawn. Not when every part of my being was driving me forward. It didn't matter that I had no idea why. Nor did the risks.

I had to save the Hyhborn.

⇛

What are you doing?

What in the world are you doing?

That question cycled over and over, or some variation of it, as I rode through the dark, rain-dampened streets of Archwood, making my way to what I hoped was the blacksmith's, my intuition my only guide. I couldn't answer it. I might be a worrier, but that hadn't stopped me from making extraordinarily bad life choices. This had to be one of the most reckless, foolish things I'd ever done in my life, and I'd done some idiotic things. Like not that long ago, when I tried to usher that little garter snake from the flowers instead of doing the reasonable thing and simply leaving it alone. I ended up with a nice bite on my finger instead of a thank-you. Or when I was younger and jumped out the window of a foundling home to see if I could fly. How I hadn't broken a bone was beyond me. There were many, many other examples.

This went beyond reckless, though. It was insane. Hyhborn were dangerous, and this one could easily turn on me, much like that damn garter snake had. And there was the risk of getting caught by those who had drugged this Hyhborn. No doubt I had been spotted passing through the manor gates by the guards there. The hood on my cloak had been up, but they could recognize Iris. That alone wouldn't arouse suspicion, but I'd been seen and could possibly be identified. And who knew how many other guards were involved in this? Claude was my protector in a way, but the type of people who would capture a Hyhborn weren't the kind to fear a baron's wrath. And if Grady found out? He would surely lose his mind. Or think I'd lost mine—and honestly, I quite possibly could have.

Keeping the hood of my cloak up, I slowed Iris as I passed the darkened storefront of the blacksmith's. I turned the horse toward the mouth of a narrow alley, and she immediately pranced nervously. Something small with claws and a gross tail scampered across the path, causing me to swallow a shriek.

I freaking hated rats more than I hated spiders.

"Let's pretend that was a bunny," I whispered to Iris.

The horse huffed in response as we rode through the alley, splashing water and who knew what. I owed Iris a nice cleaning after this and possibly an apple and a carrot.

Passing stalls full of half-completed metal tools, I spotted the barn Mickie had spoken of. It sat butted up to the woods. There was no sign of life outside, and only the faint glow of either gas- or candlelight leaked between the cracks of the barn doors. I urged Iris past the barn and into the woods, which provided her with some shelter while keeping her hidden. Dismounting, I landed on my feet with a grunt, reins in hand. I tied them to a nearby tree, leaving her enough room to move about.

"Don't eat everything in sight," I warned her as I rubbed her nose. "I won't be gone long."

Iris immediately started grazing.

Sighing, I turned back to the barn and started forward, telling myself I was so going to regret this.

I didn't need any special gifts to realize that, but I dashed across the moonlight-drenched patch of packed earth and reached the side of the barn. Pressing against the weathered wood, I rose onto the tips of my toes and peered into the windows. They were too high for me to really see anything but the faint yellow glow, but the only thing I heard was the pounding of my heart.

Neither Mickie nor Finn had mentioned anyone watching over the Hyhborn, so I didn't think anyone else was inside that barn. I waited a few moments and then prowled around the corner. I made it to the doors, not at all surprised to see that they weren't locked.

Mickie wasn't the brightest of men.

Telling myself yet again that this was a huge mistake, I slid my gloved fingers between the doors. I hesitated and then slowly inched them open, wincing as the hinges creaked more loudly than the floor of my quarters did. I tensed, half expecting someone to come barreling toward me.

No one did.

A fine layer of sweat dotted my forehead as I squeezed between the opening and then forced the door closed behind me. Looking over my shoulder, I ran my hands over the doors as I scanned the shadowy two front stalls of the center aisle. I found the latch and threw it, realizing that the dull light was coming from the back.

I proceeded down the aisle, asking myself another valid question. What in the whole wide realm was I going to do with the Hyhborn? If he was unconscious, I doubted I could move him. Probably should've thought of that before I embarked on the journey.

I didn't think I had ever wanted to punch myself more than I did at that moment.

I neared the end of the aisle. My heart was now like a child's rubber ball, bouncing off my ribs. The lamplight spilled out weakly from a stall to my left. Holding my breath, I reached the edge and looked inside.

My entire body went rigid as I stared into the stall, wanting to deny what I was seeing.

A man was stretched out on a wooden table. Stripped to the waist. Spikes a milky-white color were thrust deep into his forearms and his thighs, and one jutted out of the center of his bare chest, maybe an inch or two from where his heart would be. I knew what they were made of even though I'd only ever heard of them. *Lunea* was the only object able to pierce the skin of a Hyhborn, and it was forbidden for any lowborn to be in possession of it, but I was betting the blades were another thing traded on the shadow market.

Sickened, I lifted my gaze to where his head was turned to the side. Shoulder-length golden-brown hair shielded his face.

A strange sensation went through me—a whoosh as I walked forward, barely able to feel my legs as I looked down at his chest. He breathed, but barely. I didn't see how, with all the blood coursing from the wounds. So much red. Crimson streaked his chest, flowing in rivers that followed the . . . the rather defined lines of his chest and stomach. His pants were made of some sort of soft leather, and they hung low enough on his hips that I could see the slabs of muscles on either side of his hips and—

Okay, what in the world was I doing, staring *that* intensely at a man while he lay unconscious, impaled to a wooden table?

There was something wrong with me.

There were lots of varied things wrong with me.

"H-Hello," I croaked, then winced at the sound of my voice.

There was no response.

I didn't even know why I expected one, with those sorts of wounds. Nor could I really understand how the Hyhborn could still be breathing. Still bleeding. Yes, they were nearly indestructible compared to mortals, but this . . . this was a lot.

The toe of my boot brushed something on the floor. I glanced down, jaw clenching. A bucket. Small buckets, actually. I lifted my gaze to the table. Narrow canals carved into the wood collected the blood running from him, funneling it to the buckets below.

"Gods," I rasped, stomach churning as I stared at the buckets. The blood would be sold to be used in bone magic, as would other parts of the Hyhborn. I honestly couldn't say if any of that stuff actually worked when wielded by a conjurer, but as long as people believed in potions and spells, there would be a demand.

Tearing my gaze from the buckets, I figured I needed to somehow wake him. I stared at the spike in his chest.

Intuition told me what I needed to do. Remove the spikes, starting with the one in his chest. I swallowed again, throat dry as I glanced up. His head was still turned away from me, but now that I was closer, I could see there was a discoloration in his skin along the side of his neck. I peered closer—no, not a discoloration. A . . . a pattern *in* his skin, one that resembled a vine. It was a russet brown instead of the sandy hue of the rest of his flesh, and there was something about the trailing, almost swirling design that struck a chord of familiarity in me, but I didn't think I'd ever seen such a thing.

I looked back to the *lunea* spike in his chest and started to reach for it but halted as my gaze lifted to the damp strands of hair shielding his face. My heart pounded.

That whooshing sensation went through me again.

Hand trembling, I brushed the hair aside, revealing more of that mark in his skin. The russet-brown pattern traveled along the curve of a strong jaw, thinning at the temple, and then following the hairline to the center of his forehead. There was a fingertip-width gap and then the mark began again on the other side, the pattern framing his face. The flesh beneath the eyebrow, slightly darker than his hair, was swollen, as were both of his eyes. Ridiculously long lashes fanned skin that was an angry shade of red. Blood caked the skin beneath his nose, skin had been split open along cheeks that were high and carved, and lips . . .

"Oh, gods." I jerked back a step, pressing my fist to my chest.

The markings framing his face hadn't been there all those years ago, and this Hyhborn's face was terribly bruised, but it was him.

My Hyhborn lord.

CHAPTER 4

What I'd felt the last time I'd seen him surged through me.

A warning.

A reckoning.

A promise of what was to come.

I hadn't understood what that meant then and I still didn't, but it *was* him.

Shock held me immobile. I couldn't believe it even though I'd always known I'd see him again. I'd expected, practically *waited* for his return, but I still wasn't prepared to find myself standing above him.

Suddenly I thought of the premonition. *He's coming.* I'd been wrong. It had nothing to do with the Commander of the Iron Knights.

It had been about *him.*

A high-pitched giggle parted my lips, shocking me. I smacked my hand over my mouth, body tensing.

He didn't move.

Suddenly I wondered if *this* moment was why I'd felt what I had all those years ago in Union City. That maybe it had been a warning that one day our paths would cross, and he would need my help.

Like he had helped Grady and me that night.

I owed him.

But he was a Hyhborn lord—a Deminyen—and all I could think of was that damn garter snake.

Returning to the table, I swallowed. "Please . . . please don't hurt me."

I gripped the top of the *lunea* spike, gasping. The stone was warm. Hot. I closed my eyes, then pulled. The spike didn't budge.

"Oh, come on," I muttered, prying open an eye. I placed my hand on his chest, beside the wound. His skin . . . it was unnaturally hard, but I felt and heard nothing. I didn't know if that was because of what he was or because my thoughts were just too chaotic for my senses to kick in, but there was a far bigger concern than potentially discovering whether I could read a Hyhborn like I could a mortal or if they would be like a *caelestia*.

What if I couldn't get the stakes out?

Taking another breath, I closed my eyes and yanked again. The wet sound of the *lunea* slipping, tearing back through his flesh, turned my stomach. I choked on a gag as it came free. Dropping the stake to the straw-strewn floor below, I opened one eye and then the other. The jagged skin of the hole in his chest . . . *smoked*.

All right, I wasn't going to think about that. My hand shook as I reached for the spike in his left thigh.

A thud from somewhere outside the stall jerked my head around. My stomach dropped. Shit. Making sure the hood of my cloak was still up, I crept back to the edge of the stall and waited for another sound. When I didn't hear anything, I stepped into the aisle. The barn doors remained closed. The sound had likely been an animal running about. Probably a rat. A large one. I'd seen some the size of small dogs.

Shuddering, I started to step back—

A rush of air stirred the edges of my cloak. I went completely still, holding my breath. Shivery awareness broke out across the nape of my neck. Tiny hairs rose there and along my arms. The atmosphere of the barn shifted, thickened. Slowly, I turned.

Four *lunea* spikes remained, glistening with bright red blood, embedded deep in the table—the otherwise *empty* table.

The gas lamp went out, plunging the stall and the barn into utter, absolute darkness.

Instinct, that fickle bitch that had led me here, was telling me something else now. To move. To get the hell out. To *run*.

I made it a step before a body crashed into mine, taking me down. Air punched out of my lungs as I hit the hay-strewn floor hard. What Grady had shown me about how to defend myself over the years— what I'd had to learn the hard way—propelled my body into action. My fingers scraped against the floor as I lifted my hips, attempting to throw the heavy weight off me.

The Hyhborn lord pressed me into the dust and dirt as the sound rumbling out of him, and simultaneously *through* me, turned my blood cold. The growl was something akin to that of an animal—a very angry, very wild animal. Every muscle in my body locked up. In those brief seconds, I realized he might not be able to recognize me—or be able to even see me in the condition that he was in.

"Leaving so soon?" he snarled. "Just . . . as the fun begins? I don't think so."

He moved so fast—everything happened so fast, giving me no time to react. He jerked me off the floor. I stumbled, hitting the edge of the table. Buckets rattled, tipping over. I jumped away from the falling buckets. My booted feet slipped out from underneath me. I went down again, cracking my knees off the floor—the *blood-*covered floor—and it . . . oh no, it was still warm. I could feel it soaking my knees, coating my palms. I gasped, starting to push up.

"You wanted . . . my blood so badly," he seethed, his voice gravelly and nothing like I'd remembered it sounding. "Now you . . . you will drown in it."

My startled cry was ended by the hand that clamped down on my throat, allowing only the thinnest breath to pass. He hauled me to the side like I was nothing more than a rag doll. Panic exploded from deep within as I grabbed his hand and shoved my elbow back into his stomach. Pain exploded along my arm as I met hard, un-yielding flesh. I tried to pry his fingers loose, but they didn't budge as he dragged me across the floor. Straw dug into my hip as my arm banged into one of the still-standing buckets. Horror sank its claws into me. He fully intended to do as he threatened—drown me in his blood.

Tiny bursts of white exploded behind my eyes. There wasn't enough air. My chest hurt as I beat on his arm, getting nowhere. I dug at his grip, legs thrashing as I struggled to free myself, able to force only one word free. *"Please."*

The Hyhborn lord halted, his fingers still pressing into my throat. Then I was suddenly yanked to my feet. Pressure suddenly left my throat. Air poured in, and I gulped it, choking and gagging as my legs gave out.

I didn't hit the ground this time.

The Hyhborn caught me at the waist, his arm tightening. He went completely still against me.

"Please," I repeated, my heart thundering out of control. "I came to help you."

"You're . . . claiming you had . . . nothing to do with this?" he demanded.

"I . . . I didn't."

"Bullshit." That one word brushed up against my cheek.

"I overheard . . . what was done being talked about." I pushed against his chest, needing space—needing more air and light. He didn't budge. Not even an inch. Whatever basic methods of defending myself I knew wouldn't help against a Hyhborn. He held me like I was nothing more than a flailing kitten. "I was . . . I was trying to help." I swallowed, wincing at the rawness as I lifted my hands from his chest. They shook as I held them in the small space between us. "I . . . I swear. They . . . they put Fool's Parsley in something given to you—"

Another growl rumbled out of him.

"I swear. I only came to help," I whispered while my pulse thundered out of control. I no longer felt his breath against my cheek. Another moment passed and then the gas lamp flicked on, causing me to flinch. The dim glow sliced through the unnatural darkness. I blinked until my surroundings came into view.

I was staring at the Hyhborn's chest—at the ragged hole that seeped blood and still smoked. . . .

He grabbed the back of my hood with his other hand, ripping it down. Hunks of damp hair shielded his face as he stared down at me.

Did he recognize me? That seemed improbable given that I looked nothing like I had more than a decade ago.

The Lord suddenly swayed. In the next heartbeat, he went down on his knees, taking me with him, except I landed on my ass before him. The gas lamp sputtered weakly, before staying on.

I started to scoot back, but stopped as he fell forward, onto his fists. Only the curve of his chin and one side of his lips were visible. His shoulders were moving now with rapid breaths.

"Why?" Each breath he took sounded pained. "Why would . . . you . . . help me?"

"I don't know." I pulled my legs away from him. "I just didn't think what they were doing was right, and I needed to help."

He said something too low for me to really hear. My gaze swept over what I could see of his bent body. He was breathing too hard, too fast. Concern rippled through me. "I didn't know what condition you'd be in when I came to help." I glanced at the red, seeping wound along his arm. He had . . . he'd pulled his limbs free from the spikes. "I removed the spike from your chest."

There was no response.

"My lord?" I whispered, the concern growing into full-blown anxiety.

Silence.

"Are you all right?" I cringed the moment the question left my mouth. Of course he wasn't all right. He'd just been drugged, beaten, and impaled to a table.

Biting down on my lip, I leaned forward as I lifted my hands. Carefully, I brushed the hair back from his face—

I gasped, jerking in horror. The striking lines of his face were contorted in pain. His eyes were open—at least that was what I thought, but I couldn't be sure, because what I saw was just pink, raw, and seeping flesh where eyes *should* be.

"They took them," he breathed.

A frayed sort of sound choked me as I stared at him, unable to comprehend how that could be done to anyone. How someone could inflict such damage, such pain. "I'm sorry," I whispered, my own eyes stinging. "I'm so sorry—"

"Stop," he grunted, rocking back, out of my reach. "You have . . . nothing to apologize for if you . . . didn't do this."

A hole opened up in my own chest. "I'm still sorry."

"Don't be. They're already growing back." Another shudder went through him. "Regenerating."

I lowered my hands to my lap. "That's . . . that's reassuring." I swallowed, wincing at the dull ache in my throat. "I think."

He made a sound I thought might be a laugh, but then fell silent, his breathing slowing.

I glanced at the opening to the stall. "We should—"

"Are you hurt?" he barked.

I gave a little jump. "W-What?"

That deep, skin-chilling sound rumbled from him again. "Did *I* hurt you? When I grabbed you?"

"No," I whispered.

His head tilted up, and a few strands of hair fell to the side, revealing just the height of one sharp cheekbone and one eye that no longer looked as raw and mangled. "You lie."

"N-No, I don't."

"You're rubbing your throat. The same throat I was just seconds away from crushing."

My fingers stilled. His reminder was unnecessary, but could he see now? I dropped my hand.

Several more moments passed. Neither of us moved or spoke, and I needed to get moving. So did he. I peeked at the door again.

"I'm sorry."

A jolt ran through me as my gaze flew back to him.

"When I came to, I . . . just reacted," he continued gruffly, his hands falling to his thighs. "I wasn't in my right mind. Thought . . . you had . . . something to do with this."

I stared at him, intuition silent, as it normally was when it came to Hyhborn, but his apology sounded genuine.

The creak of rusty hinges came from the front of the barn, jerking my attention to the opening. My stomach lurched. That was likely not a rat. Dread surged through me. No one could see me here, with him.

"Stay here," I whispered, pushing off the floor as the Lord slowly turned at the waist, to the opening of the stall.

As I hurried past him, I didn't know what I was going to do or say if someone had entered, but as powerful as any Hyhborn lord was, he was gravely wounded. He was likely going to be of little help.

I stepped into the center aisle, my hands trembling. One barn door was half open. I saw nothing as I crept forward, lifting my hood. Wind could've picked up outside, blowing the door open. That was completely possible. I neared the two front stalls, muscles beginning to relax. It had to be—

The shadow darted out of the left stall. I lurched back, but wasn't quick enough. A hand clamped down on my arm, giving it a painful jerk.

"What are you doing in here?"

The gasp of pain turned to one of recognition as I reached back, grabbing his arm. I knew this voice. It was Weber, one of the bakery workers in town, who always flirted with the paramours when he brought fresh pastries that Claude loved—ones he swore no one else could make as well. He was a large man—burly, knuckles bruised, always swollen from the boxing matches held in one of the gambling dens by the wharf.

His hand fisted in my hair, yanking my head back. "Tell me."

"You're hurting me," I rasped.

"Girl, I'm gonna do worse than that if you don't answer me." Weber dragged me farther into the stall, angling me away from the entrance as he folded his other arm around my neck. "You shouldn't be in here."

The smell of sweat and cane sugar swamped me as I blurted out the first thing that came to mind. "I . . . I was out for a walk—"

"Come on now." Spittle sprayed my cheek as Weber bent his head. "You're going to have to—*Wait*. Is that blood on you?"

"I fell," I said in a rush. "That's why—"

"Bullshit. What did you do in here?" he hissed, suddenly going still behind me.

"I—"

"Quiet." His head jerked to the side.

I felt what he heard. The sudden unnatural stillness of the barn—of the air thickening and charging. Then I heard it. The soft, nearly silent footfall. My entire body went rigid. Weber spun us around. The aisle was empty. Of course it was. The Lord could barely stand, had nearly been drained of all his blood, and was possibly still missing at least one eye.

"Is that Hyhborn blood on you?" Weber demanded, taking a step back. "Did you free that thing?"

Before I could answer, he yanked down my hood and cursed. "For fuck's sake, you're one of the Baron's bitches."

"I'm—Oh, fuck it." Giving up on lying, I slammed my arm back. This time I didn't hit hard flesh as I shoved my elbow into Weber's stomach with enough force that his arms loosened with a curse of pain. Spinning around, I thrust my knee up, into his groin.

"Bitch," Weber gasped, doubling over.

I darted around him, but Weber lurched forward. He caught the back of my cloak, throwing me to the floor like I was nothing more than a sack of trash. I landed on my knees for the umpteenth time that evening.

"Stay there," he spat, reaching around to his back. "I'll deal with you in a moment."

In the streak of moonlight, I saw the flash of a milky-white blade—a *lunea* dagger held in his hand. I rose as Weber started for the aisle, snapping forward and grabbing the sleeve of the arm wielding the blade.

The baker cocked his arm, catching me in the face. Pain burst along my nose as I staggered sideways, falling into the wall. Wood groaned under the impact as I lifted my hand to my nose. Wet warmth coated my fingers.

Blood.

My blood.

Tiny hairs rose all over my body as my gaze locked on to his. My thoughts quieted, and it . . . *it* happened. I connected with him, and my intuition came alive, showing me the future—the excruciating crack of bone in my right arm, then my left. The phantom pain traveled to my throat. I felt *it* all.

His *death*.

And I . . . I *smiled*.

"Stupid bitch, you stay there and stay quiet. You've already got a steep price to pay. Don't make it—" His words ended in a choked gasp.

And my breath stalled in my chest.

The Hyhborn lord stood there, moonlight slicing over his bowed head and bloodied chest. He looked like an avenging spirit conjured from the depths of nightmares as he held the baker by the throat with one hand and the wrist with another.

"Attempting to capture . . . me was a bad choice to . . . make." His voice was so soft yet so cold, it sent a chill of dread down my spine. "But striking her?"

My blood-tinged lips parted as the Lord lifted the mortal off the floor, unperturbed as Weber beat at the arm holding him up.

"That was a fatal mistake," the Hyhborn snarled.

Weber sputtered, eyes bulging.

The Hyhborn's head tilted, sending several strands of hair sliding back. The moonlight cut over his profile, glancing over his mouth. His smile was as bloody as mine had been. He twisted Weber's arm sharply.

The crack of the baker's bone was like thunder. The dagger landed with a thud. His wheezy whimper gave way to a smothered, keening wail.

"I . . . remember you." The Lord's head straightened. "You were the one . . . who jumped me outside the tavern." He reached across, grasping Weber's other arm. "You're the one . . . who put a spike . . . in my chest."

I pressed back against the wall at the snap of the second bone, my hand falling from my bloodied nose.

"And you laughed while doing it." The Lord suddenly jerked his hand back—

I turned away but I still heard the sickening crunch—still saw the glossy blue-white of cartilage of Weber's windpipe. I tried not to see even though I already had, seconds ago.

"And that will not be a sound you make again." The Lord tossed the clump of ruined tissue and flesh aside. He dropped the baker.

Bile climbing up my throat, I turned and looked to where Weber lay, a twitching, spasming heap of man. I'd seen my fair share of death. In the streets and in the orphanages as a kid, even long before my Hyhborn lord had come to Union City. I'd seen death so many times, in my mind and before me—those who passed due to ailments that had festered and grown inside them, and those who passed due to the evils that had grown inside of others. I'd seen so much death that I would think I'd have grown used to it by now, and maybe in a little way I had, because I wasn't screaming or shaking. But it was still a shock. A loss, even if Weber had it coming, but I . . .

I had never smiled at it before.

"Your intervention . . . was unnecessary," the Lord said, drawing my gaze to him. Kneeling, he wiped the gore from his hand on Weber's shirt. He turned his head toward me, and I thought I could see the beginning of an actual eye in the right socket. "You should've . . . stayed back."

It took me a moment to find words. "You were injured. You're still injured." And he was. His chest was moving in short, shallow pants. Even in the moonlight, I could see that his skin had lost a lot of its color. The violence had cost him.

"And you are . . . a mortal barely able to defend yourself . . . or another." He rose, his movements shaky. "But you're brave—braver than . . . many stronger than you."

A laugh rattled out of me. "I'm not brave."

"Then what . . . do you call your actions tonight?"

"Foolish."

"Well, there is such a thing as foolish bravery," he said, sighing as he moved toward me. "He . . . struck you."

I inched to the side, away from him. "I'm fine."

The Hyhborn lord halted.

"My nose isn't even bleeding anymore," I rambled. "It was barely a hit."

A moment of silence passed. "I'm not going to hurt you." His shoulders tensed. "I . . . I won't hurt you again."

At least he had the self-awareness to realize that he had, even if his actions had been accidental.

"You knew . . . the man?" He dragged a hand up his face, through his hair.

"Yes. He worked at the bakery."

"He was . . . waiting around outside when I left the tavern. He was with . . . two others. The one . . . at the tavern . . . and another who was there drinking."

I opened my mouth, then closed it. He was speaking of Porter and likely Mickie.

"They've done this before," he continued, voice becoming hoarse.

I shuddered. For them to know what Fool's Parsley would do to a Hyhborn and to have the *lunea* blades, they'd probably done this more than once.

He then looked down at himself, pressing his finger just below the wound on his chest.

"Does it hurt?" I blurted out yet another incredibly pointless question.

His head lifted, and now all I saw was the straight line of his nose. "It feels like a . . . hole was carved . . . through my chest cavity."

Bile rose. "I'm sorry."

The Lord went still again. "You do that a lot? Apologizing . . . for something you've had nothing to do with."

"I'm empathizing," I told him. "You didn't do anything to deserve that, right? You were just at the tavern, for . . . for whatever reason. That is all. No one deserves what was done to you."

"Including a Hyhborn?"

"Yes."

He made a noise that sounded like a dry laugh.

I took a small breath. "I need to leave. So do you. The others involved in this will come back."

"And they will die too." He turned, swaying.

My heart lurched with alarm. "My lord?"

"I need . . . your help. Again." A ragged breath left him. "I need to clean up. The *lunea*—it contaminates the body. It's in my blood and sweat, and the Fool's Parsley . . . is making it hard to . . . flush it out. I need to bathe. I need water. If not, I won't be able to heal completely. I'll pass out again."

I looked around. There was no water here, surely not enough to bathe him or for him to actually ingest.

Tension poured into my muscles as I stared at him. The logical part of my brain was demanding I tell him that I could be of no more help, that I wished him well, and then get as far away as I could. But the other part, the one that I was born with and that always, always won over anything my mind was telling me, demanded I do the exact opposite of what was smart and reasonable.

But it was more than my intuition. It was also because it was *him*. My Hyhborn lord—no, he wasn't mine. I needed to stop with that.

I looked to the door and then to Weber, hands closing at my sides. "Can you walk?"

He didn't answer for a long moment. "Yes."

"Good," I whispered, taking a step toward him. I spotted the milky-white blade in the moonlight. Bending, I picked it up and glanced beyond him, to the darkened aisle. "Stay here. For real this time."

The Lord didn't answer as I inched past him and hurried back to the stall he'd been held in. The gas lamp was still on. I walked forward, hand tightening around the *lunea* blade as I kicked over the buckets of blood.

CHAPTER 5

I was concerned.

The Hyhborn lord was strong, obviously, but he'd been able to take only a few steps outside of the stall before his breathing became labored. He stumbled. I shot forward, folding an arm around his waist, and held on to him as best as I could. My own strength was quickly cracking under his weight, but the wound on his chest was bleeding again and no longer just seeping. It also looked larger. I didn't think his other injuries fared any better.

"Just a little further," I assured him, hoping that Finn was right and Jac would be occupied till dawn, because if not . . .

It would be bad.

He nodded, the hair now hanging in stringy clumps around his face. That was the only response I got as we made it out of the barn. As we crossed the uneven ground, I looked to the woods and spotted Iris's shadowy form grazing.

Gritting my teeth, I forged forward, fingers slipping over his now-slick waist. It felt like an eternity by the time we reached the back door of the blacksmith's home. The Lord leaned against the cement siding typical of buildings of this age, head hanging limply on his shoulders. "Who lives . . . here? The blacksmith?"

"Yes. He shouldn't be back for a while," I assured him. "This isn't a trap or anything."

"I would . . . hope not," he said, tipping his head against the wall, exposing his throat to the moonlight. "You've gone to . . . a lot of unnecessary . . . trouble if so."

Biting the inside of my lip, I turned the handle. Or tried to. My shoulders slumped. "It's locked."

"That's . . . an inconvenience." He angled his body toward mine. Lifting a fist, he punched the door, just above the handle. Wood cracked and splintered, exploding as his fist went straight through.

My jaw dropped.

He reached into the ragged hole and turned the lock. "There you . . . go. No longer locked."

I blinked as my fingers fluttered to my throat. That same hand he'd just put through a thick wooden door had been around my throat.

"If I weren't . . . weakened," he said, eyeing me from behind a curtain of hair, "I would've killed you the moment I had . . . your throat in my hand. You're lucky."

My hand lowered as my heart skipped. I wasn't feeling very lucky at the moment. Instead, I was feeling like I'd really gotten myself in over my head this time.

The Lord pushed open the door, all but stumbling aside at the faint stench of sour ale and decaying food. I gave the space a quick look, making out a small table and unwashed pots and pans stacked in a sink. My gaze lifted to the archway and narrow hall that appeared to lead toward the front, which Jac likely used to meet with clients. Many of the buildings in this area of Archwood were several hundred years old, having survived the Great War. So, they were larger, and had a lot of chambers and were built entirely differently from the way they were today. I turned, spying another door on the other side of the table.

Figuring that led to bedchambers and hopefully a bathing space, I helped the Lord around the wooden table.

"You . . . you weren't at the tavern," he rasped.

"How do you know?"

"I would've seen . . . you."

I arched a brow. "I was out for a walk when I overheard what had happened."

"Where?"

I didn't answer as I nudged the door open and led him down the narrow hall.

"You've . . . been somewhere near . . . a garden," he said.

My head whipped toward him. "How do you know that?"

"I smell . . . the earth on you," he said, and I frowned, having no idea if that meant I smelled bad or not. "Hints of . . . of catmint and . . ."

Surprise flickered through me. I had been messing around with the catmint earlier that day. I stared at him. "How do you smell that?"

"Just can," he mumbled as he slipped from me, swaying. I reached for him, but he waved me off. "I'm okay."

I wasn't so sure about that as I glanced ahead. Another door, left ajar, loomed.

His breath was ragged as he used the wall as support. "The catmint?"

"I was trimming some earlier today."

He made a sound sort of like a hum. "I . . . like the smell . . . of them."

"As do I." Blowing out a breath, I pushed the door open. Moonlight streamed in from the window, casting silvery light over a bed and a surprisingly tidy chamber that smelled of fresh laundry.

The Lord shuffled into the chamber. Closing the door behind him, I threw the tiny hook-and-eye lock, as if that would stop a rabbit from getting in, let alone another person.

He sat down heavily on the edge of the bed. I halted, hand pressing against my chest as he grasped his knees, bent slightly at the waist. I started to ask if he was okay, but stopped myself. He wasn't. At all. Seeing anyone like this caused my stomach to jump all over the place.

Pivoting away from him, I found a lamp near the bed and turned it on. The buttery light lit the space as I crossed the chamber, pushed open the next door, and stepped inside. Relief hit me when I saw the type of shower stall found in the oldest buildings. It wasn't very large, but it would do. "You can get cleaned up in here."

"I'm going to need a minute," he slurred. "The chamber seems to be moving."

Returning to the bedchamber, I looked around, and spied a cupboard. Hurrying to it, I pulled the *lunea* dagger from the pocket of my cloak, half surprised I hadn't stabbed myself with it. I placed it on the cupboard as I spotted a closed jar of what appeared to be water on a small table opposite the bed. I lifted it to my nose, taking a sniff, and when I smelled nothing, I poured a glass and took a drink. "Will this help? It's just water, but warm."

"It should."

I handed him the glass, stepping back. He took just a small sip at first and then downed the entire glass.

"More?"

"I think I . . . should let that . . . settle first."

Taking the glass from him, I placed it on the table. "Is the room still moving?"

"Unfortunately." His hands fell to the edge of the bed. "Legs don't feel attached at the moment and the light—my eyes . . . aren't quite ready for it."

I cursed, not having thought of that. "Sorry," I mumbled, quickly turning the lamp off.

The Lord had gone quiet as I faced him. Trepidation rose as I inched closer to him—one of the most powerful beings in all the realm, and he was . . . he was shaking. His legs. Arms. "Is it the hemlock or the . . . the blood loss?"

"Those things . . . and the *lunea*. That alone weakens us—sickens us," he explained. "When any . . . *lunea* blade is left in us or its wound goes untreated, it turns into a toxin, breaking down our tissues. . . ." His large shoulders curled inward. "Another of my kind would need far more than water and time to heal."

Meaning that if he weren't a lord, the injuries would've likely ended his life. I felt the need to apologize again but managed to stop myself.

I needed to get him cleaned up and safely out of here before others came to check on him . . . or Weber. "What would they need?" I asked, just in case the water wasn't enough, as I knelt before him. "To heal?"

"I . . . I would need to feed."

"Um." I glanced at the door. "I can probably find you something to eat."

"I'm not talking . . . about food."

My brows lifted as I fumbled in the darkness, running my hands over his boot until I found the top. For the short period of time things had been intimate between Claude and me, I'd gained quite a bit of experience undressing a half-conscious man, but I still felt a little out of my element as I grasped the shaft of the boot and yanked it off. "What are you talking about?"

A sudden soft glow sparked to life, drawing my gaze up as I moved on to his other boot. I looked up to see that he'd picked up a candle from the nightstand and had lit it . . . with his touch. My lips parted with a soft inhale at the reminder of exactly what he was. "How . . . did you do that?"

"Magic."

My brows inched up. I'd never actually seen a Hyhborn use the elements. "Really?"

"No."

I stared at him a second, then shook my head. Unnerved, I grabbed ahold of his other boot. "Does the candlelight hurt your eyes?"

"No," he answered.

I wasn't sure if I believed him as I dropped his boot. I glanced at the bathing chamber, then took the candle from him. "I'll get the shower ready for you." I rose. "But I can't promise it will be warm."

"It'll . . . be fine."

Nibbling on my lip, I reentered the bathing chamber, placing the candle on a shelf. I spared a glance at my reflection and winced. The skin had split along the bridge of my nose and there was already a puffiness beneath my eyes. My nose didn't appear broken, but I had no idea how I was going to explain this to Grady.

Going to the shower, I quickly cranked the knobs on the wall. Steady streams of water pounded off the porcelain floor of the stall. I thrust my hand beneath the stream. Blood ran between my fingers, splattering off the floor as I tested the temperature. It wasn't exactly hot, but it wasn't freezing. I washed the blood from my other hand, then turned.

The Lord leaned against the doorframe. How he moved so quietly while injured and so . . . well, so large, was beyond me.

"Should you be standing?" I asked.

"The chamber stopped moving."

"That sounds like good . . ." I trailed off as he swayed away from the doorframe.

His head hung weakly as he reached for his pants. Realizing he was about to undress, I started to turn away. His fingers fumbled, though, nearly useless as he stumbled. "Fuck."

I snapped forward, catching the Hyhborn. His weight was immense, the bare flesh of his chest hot as I kept my arms around him. "You okay?"

He steadied a little. "Yeah."

I started to let go, but he began to wobble. "You are not okay."

"Yeah," he repeated, reaching around me to plant a hand on the rim of the sink basin.

Throat dry, I looked over my shoulder at the running water, mind racing. I then glanced down at the length of cloak I wore and finally at his pants. I sighed. "Can you hold on to the sink for a moment?"

Head bent, he nodded.

Sliding my arms away, I waited to make sure he wasn't going to fall. When he didn't, I toed off my boots and kicked them back into the bedchamber. I unhooked the clasps beneath my neck.

"What are you doing?" he rasped, voice hoarse.

"You need to get cleaned up, right?" I let the cloak fall to the floor. "And it doesn't look like you're going to be able to do that on your own."

"And here I thought . . ." He shuddered, muscles along his arms spasming. "I thought you were planning to take advantage of me."

I froze. "Are you serious?"

"No." He seemed to shudder. "The room is moving again, *na'laa*."

Damn it. I went still, thinking that it might help if I didn't move. Wait. What did he call me? "'*Na'laa*'?"

"It's Enochian." One arm dropped to rest on his bent knee. "A phrase . . . in our language."

I knew Hyhborn had their own language, but I'd never heard it spoken before. "What does it mean?"

"It . . . has many meanings. One of them is . . . used to describe . . . someone who is brave."

My cheeks warmed for some reason.

"There . . . must be . . . a lot of conjurer activity in your city," he said after a moment.

Thinking of all the times in the past I'd been accused of being such a person, I glanced at him. "I honestly don't know if there is," I answered. "I'm not even sure I believe any of what is said to be done with bone magic is possible."

"Oh, it's real." His arms trembled as he held himself there. "Ingesting our blood would kill a mortal, but smooth . . . it over a wound? A scar? It will be healed. Sprinkle it on barren land and crops will flourish. Bury a hand . . . in freshly plowed soil, and crops will flourish there too, ones insusceptible . . . to drought or disease." His chin dropped even farther. "Our teeth dropped into water can create coin."

"Really?" Doubt crept into my tone as I realized his blood had seeped through my cloak and stained the nightgown.

"Really," he confirmed. "But that's not all."

"Of course not," I murmured.

"Keeping an eye of ours . . . near will warn the wearer of anyone . . . who approaches," he continued, and I didn't even want to know how one wore an eye. I could go my entire life not knowing that. "Our tongues will force the truth . . . from anyone who speaks, and weaving strands of our hair . . . among yours? It will ensure one remains . . . in good health as long as the hair stays in place. Our bones . . . can restore one's health."

"Oh," I whispered, somewhat transfixed.

"Burying our fingers and toes . . . will bring water from deep within the land," he went on. "Strips of our . . . of our skin hung above a door will ward off the *nix*."

"That's disgusting." A chill swept through me, though, at the mention of the creature. The *nix* were related to the Hyhborn in some fashion and were found in the woods where usually only long game hunters entered, especially in the Wychwoods—the vast sacred forest rumored to have trees that bled. The woods skirted the territories of the Lowlands and the Midlands and traveled all the way to the Highlands. The creatures found within them didn't look remotely mortal and were more frightening than birdeaters—ridiculously large and horrifying spiders with claws. I'd never seen one, either a birdeater or a *nix*.

"What do . . . they look like? The *nix*?" I asked.

"Have you . . . seen a Rae?"

I shuddered, thinking of the Hyhborn riders that were more bone than flesh. "Once."

"Imagine that . . . but thinner, faster, and with sharp teeth and claws," he told me. "And they can get in your head, make you think you're seeing and experiencing . . . what is not there."

I stiffened, breath catching.

"So perhaps . . . knowing what they look like no longer makes hanging our skin at the doors too disgusting," he remarked. "Then there . . . are our cocks."

"I'm sorry," I choked. "What?"

"Our cocks, *na'laa*," he repeated. "Being in possession . . . of one will ensure that the owner . . . has a very . . . fruitful union."

I opened my mouth, but I was at an utter loss for words for several seconds. "There is a part of me—a huge part of me—that regrets having this conversation."

"There is more," he said, and I thought his tone had lightened. Almost teasing. "I haven't . . . even gotten to what our muscles—"

"Great," I muttered. "Is the chamber still moving?"

"No."

Thank the gods. I reached for the straps on my nightgown.

"Our come," he said, and I halted. "It's known to be a . . . powerful aphrodisiac. Some mix it with herbs to rub . . . on themselves. Others drink—"

"I get it," I cut him off, having heard of potions that promised to increase the pleasure of those who used them. "Just to make it clear, I'm not after your blood or . . ."

"Or my come?" he finished.

"Definitely not that," I snapped.

"What a shame."

Shaking my head, I shimmied out of my nightgown. I refused to think about what I was doing as my bare skin pimpled in the damp heat. "I'm undressed, by the way."

"That sounded oddly . . . like a warning," he murmured. "As if knowing you're naked would somehow prevent . . . me from looking."

"It's not a warning. It's just to let you know so you can be polite and not look."

"I know we . . . don't know . . . one another, but you . . . should know, I'm not known . . . to be polite."

"You can try." I knelt beside him, and hesitated, the reality of what I was doing striking me.

I was undressing a Hyhborn—a Hyhborn lord.

Naomi would be so jealous.

Biting back a laugh, I reached for the flap on his pants and began to unhook the buttons. The back of my hands brushed along something I also refused to think of, causing him to suck in the deepest breath I'd heard him take that evening. "Hold still."

"I am holding still, but . . . you're on your knees, your fingers are near my dick, and you're currently gloriously nude, so . . ."

Undoing the final button, I rolled my eyes. "You can't even stand on your own two feet and you're currently regrowing eyeballs. The last thing you need to be thinking about is me on my knees, your dick, or my nudity."

"I've regrown my eyes, na'laa."

My chin jerked up. The mess of hair shielded his face, but his head was turned in my direction. My gaze dropped to his hands—to his long fingers pressing into the rim of the sink.

"That's how . . . I know you're gloriously nude," he continued.

Muscles curled low in my stomach, stealing the breath I took.

Good gods, that was the utter last thing I needed to be feeling now.

I quickly finished with the last button, maybe a little too roughly because his low groan burned the tips of my ears. I reached to pull his pants down—

"I got this," he muttered.

I wasn't sure he actually did, so when I rose, I stood behind him. I kept my gaze trained on his back as he unsteadily shucked off his pants, and I stepped aside once he finished and pushed off the sink. He took a step and began to sway again. I caught him, folding an arm around his waist. My hand flattened against his stomach, and I tensed.

There were no voices.

No images.

Would it be like with a *caelestia*, where I would have a few blissful minutes of being able to touch them? Though I still had to concentrate to avoid slipping into their minds even in those brief minutes.

"I was wrong." The Lord leaned into me, his hip pressing into my stomach. "I don't have it."

I helped him toward the stall, unable to ignore the feel of him. His skin was incredibly warm.

"There's a small ledge to step over," I warned him.

He nodded, lifting his foot over the ledge as I followed, keeping my arm around him.

And keeping my eyes trained up, on the white tile of the stall.

The fall of water was a bit of a shock as we stepped under the stream, his body taking the brunt of it. I held on, closing my hand into a fist as he turned and braced a hand against the tile, facing the stream. I looked up and found his head tipped back, exposing his face and chest to the shower.

His groan was . . . it was downright sinful-sounding as water streamed over his face and through his hair. Heat returned, creeping up my throat as my stare followed the water coursing down the corded muscles of his back, cutting trails in the dried blood there and the, well, rather firm curve of his ass.

Squeezing my eyes shut, I ordered myself to get a grip. Hyhborn were nice to look upon. I already knew that. Everyone did. It didn't matter that it was a nice ass. An ass was an ass. There was nothing spectacular about any ass, including his.

Opening my eyes, I wanted to smack myself as the water swirling around the drain became tinted red. "How are you feeling?"

"Better."

My gaze lifted to the hand on the tile. His arm still trembled. Blue and purple blotches marred his flesh. Anger slithered through me. "They really did a number on you."

"The Fool's Parsley had . . . kicked in just as I walked out of the tavern. I think they expected it to have a greater effect more . . . quickly."

He stiffened as I reached around to grab the soap I spotted. The effort brought my bare chest against his back. The contact was brief, but long enough to send a shiver of awareness through me. I grabbed the bar and leaned back.

"That one . . . jumped me."

"Weber?"

He nodded. "Then the other two joined in. There were two others . . . I didn't recognize."

Figuring he might be speaking of Finn and Mickie, I slowly drew my arm from him. When he remained upright, I rubbed the soap between my hands. "When you were jumped—you fought back?"

"Killed one of them . . . before I passed out."

My breath caught as I halted, suds running down my arm. Okay. Maybe he wasn't speaking of Finn and Mickie. How many people in Archwood were involved in this? The Baron needed to be warned. Dragging my lip between my teeth, I placed my hand on his back. His muscles bunched under my palm, but he didn't pull away. I drew my hand over his back, washing away the blood there.

"Those you overheard speaking earlier tonight?" he asked. "Did you . . . hear them say anything else?"

I thought over what I'd heard. "Actually, I did. They spoke of someone they called Muriel."

The Lord stiffened.

"Do you know who that is?"

"I do," he said, and didn't elaborate further.

My nose stung a little as the stream of water reached me. "Has this happened to you before?"

A rough, dry laugh rattled from him. "No. But I should've been more careful. Not like I'm unaware of hemlock and its effect on my kind. I was just . . ."

I shifted, running my soapy hand down to his hip and back up, mindful of the bruises as I focused on the feel and texture of his skin. It reminded me of . . . of marble or granite. "What?"

"I was just careless," he revealed after I lifted my hand.

"Well, it happens to the best of us, right?" I soaped up my hand again and moved to the other side of his back.

His head tipped back again, causing the edges of his hair to tease my fingers as I drew my hand lightly over his shoulder. There seemed to be a . . . a faint glow in his skin, but I wasn't sure if that was what I was seeing. "Right."

In the silence that fell between us, I found myself getting a little lost in just touching someone—touching him. I heard and felt nothing. No violent futures or whispers of knowledge—detailed things impossible for me to know. Their names. Ages. If they were married or not. How they lived. Their innermost secrets and desires, which were what Claude found most valuable.

There were just my own thoughts. Even with Claude, I would've had to be careful, and by now I would've started to hear his thoughts. The only time I experienced this nothingness was when I drank enough to dull my senses, but doing so also dulled everything else, including my memories. When I touched someone, there was no need to picture that mental string, but with this lord, there was nothing.

A shudder rolled through me. Maybe I was just too distracted— too overwhelmed for even my intuition to kick in. I didn't know, and at that moment, I didn't care. Closing my eyes, I let myself . . . I let myself enjoy this. The contact. The feel of another's skin beneath my palms. The way muscles tensed and moved under them. I could do this forever.

But we didn't have forever.

"What . . . what were you even doing at the Twin Barrels?" I asked, clearing my throat. "It's not a place frequented by the Hyhborn of Primvera."

"I'm not . . . from Primvera," he said, confirming what Mickie believed. "I was meeting someone. They suggested the place."

I glanced up at the back of his head. "Did you meet with them?"

"No." He tipped his head to the other side. "And I don't think they will be looking for me."

I didn't need my intuition to figure that whomever he was to meet there might've set him up. Could've even been this Muriel. "Will anyone be looking for you? Like a friend?"

He nodded. "Eventually."

That was a relief.

Until he turned in the small stall, and I was suddenly at eye level with the wound in his chest.

My lips parted as I saw that the wound had shrunk again, this time to about the size of a small golden coin. Most of the blood had washed away, except for a few patches here and there, but there was this . . . I squinted. There were these tiny whitish dots scattered about his chest and his stomach—

I didn't let myself look farther as he shifted slightly. More of the lukewarm water reached me. "What is . . . coming out of your skin? Is it the hemlock?"

"Most of that is gone now," he said. "You're seeing the aftereffects of what a *lunea* blade does. Once the blade hits our flesh, it too acts as a poison. It eats away, reaching our blood, and then . . . burns us from the inside, much like a fever would a mortal. My body is pushing it out."

"Oh," I whispered, somewhat fascinated and disturbed by it. By all of this. Everything felt too surreal. The conversation I overheard and the mad flight into the city. Discovering that it was him my intuition had guided me to. Being in the shower with him. . . . His body.

I'd seen a lot of naked men in various different situations. Some like Grady, whose frame was honed from training and handling a sword, and others who were softer than myself, and some even like Claude, who was naturally slender. But this lord was . . . he was different.

Slowly, I lifted my gaze to his. His eyes . . . They were definitely regenerated, and exactly how I remembered them. A burst of swirling blue, green, and brown. They were so strange and so beautiful. I glanced over his features. The bruising had nearly all faded from his face. That wasn't the only thing now absent.

"The markings on your face," I said, brows furrowing. "They're gone."

His head tilted slightly. "Markings? I'm not sure of what you speak."

"You . . . you had these marks on your face, along your jaw and temple. Looked like a tattoo," I told him. "But it appeared to come from within your skin."

The colors of his irises slowed, then stilled. "I believe you've mistaken what you saw," he said, chin dipping. "It must've been blood or dirt."

"Maybe." Tiny goose bumps appeared on my flesh, responding to the sudden coolness of the bathing chamber. I took a nervous step back. "I think—"

"Will you touch me?" he asked.

The breath I took went nowhere as my gaze shot back to his. "What?"

"To continue to bathe me," he clarified, thick lashes lowered. "I find myself thoroughly enjoying this." There was a pause. "And I believe you also enjoy it."

I *was* thoroughly enjoying this—touching him. I swallowed as I stood there. Strands of wet hair had slipped free, clinging to my cheeks as my grip on the soap tightened. Aiding him didn't seem all that necessary at this point. His voice was stronger. Based on the rise and fall of his chest and how he was taking fewer breaks between his words, his breathing was no longer labored. He could likely finish cleaning himself, especially if he was capable of thoroughly enjoying this.

But I . . . I was . . . reckless, I was more than a little foolish, and I had an extremely long history of making bad life choices despite knowing better.

And I . . . I could touch him.

Stomach dipping, I placed a soapy hand on his chest. He seemed to inhale deeply, or maybe it was me. I wasn't sure as I drew my palm over his skin, watching the white beads disappear in the suds. I stayed clear of the wound in his chest and the ones on his arms even though they looked far better, almost completely closed. Lathering the soap once more, I glided my palm over his stomach.

Holding my lip between my teeth, I brought my hand near his navel. My pulse was ticking rapidly, and my skin felt hot despite the cooling of the water and the air. I closed my eyes as my hand slipped over his hip, along the inside and over the taut muscle there. I didn't go farther. I wanted to, but that seemed highly inappropriate, all things considered.

The muscles beneath my fingers tensed, and I opened my eyes to see what my hard work had accomplished. The blood was gone, and I no longer saw those tiny specks appearing where the suds had trailed off. Other than the wound, he looked much better. His skin tone had even deepened, more tan than sandy now, and his body . . .

There was still not a single strand of body hair to be seen. It was as if he'd been carved from marble, every line and muscle perfectly defined. My gaze lowered, drawn irresistibly to the . . . the thick, hard length of him.

My gods, I . . . I'd never really thought a man's cock was all that attractive to look upon, but his was just like the rest of him. Stunning. Breathtaking. Brutally beautiful.

"Na'laa?"

A rush of damp heat flooded my core. "Yes?"

"You're staring at me."

My chest rose sharply. I so was. There was no denying it.

"It's okay." His breath danced over the top of my head, and my own snagged. Was he closer? He was. "I'm staring at you."

He spoke no lies. I could feel his eyes on me. I had felt his gaze moving over my brow, down my nose, and over my lips as mine had traveled over his chest. The intensity of his stare was like a caress, gliding lower. The tips of my breasts tingled as his perusal continued, just as mine had, coasting over the curve of my waist, my hips and thighs, and between them, where I ached—where I wanted . . . I wanted him to touch.

"You shouldn't be," I whispered. "You're injured."

"So?"

"So?" I repeated. There was a dipping, whirling motion in my stomach. "I don't know what you're thinking about—"

"I think you're quite aware of what I'm thinking about."

A heady breath left me. "You should have other things on your mind."

"Not when a beautiful woman stands before me, one who has been brave and kind, giving me aid in my time of need, endangering herself, and asking for nothing in return."

My laugh sounded shaky. "There is no need for flattery."

"I only speak the truth." His words coasted over my cheek, igniting a flutter deep inside.

Each breath I took felt labored. For the hundredth time that evening, I wondered what in the world I was doing. But I was still standing there, pulse racing as my eyes returned to his hand and his fingers, now bent. The tips were pressed into the ceramic—

Air leaked from my lips. His fingers were *denting* the ceramic tile.

The Lord lifted his hand then, cupping my chin. A strange sound rumbled up my throat, one I didn't think I'd ever made before. I was barely able to bite back the moan. His touch was featherlight, barely there, but my senses went haywire. I felt it in every part of my being. He tipped my head back. His eyes . . . those colors were a dizzying kaleidoscope, and spots of white appeared in his pupils. Our gazes connected, and I braced myself out of habit, but I . . . I still saw and heard nothing.

His fingers—the same that had just dented ceramic—grazed my cheek, catching the strands of hair there. Soapy bubbles seeped between my fingers as I stood there, heart racing out of control. He tucked the hair back behind my ear, hand then sliding to my jaw, and I swore I felt that light touch throughout the entirety of my body. His other hand found the soap I currently had in a death grip. He pried it from my fingers, placing it on the ledge.

Heat returned, flushing my skin and invading my blood. My chest ached, becoming heavy. Desire, hot and dark, pulsed through me. He barely touched me. Just a featherlight brush against my jaw, and my entire body throbbed. I'd never in my life been so . . . so viscerally affected.

The Lord stepped in closer, as if I had willed him to, and that was just a silly thought, but somehow, I'd moved too. His cock brushed my belly, and I shuddered, the very core of me tightening. Tiny tremors racked my entire body. My fingers practically ached with the want to touch him.

The need to touch him.

CHAPTER 6

I truly had never felt such need before. I *ached* as I lifted my hand—

Then it struck me.

The why behind such need.

Hyhborn exuded sensuality, in their voices and in their touch, and that carnal lushness spilled into the air around them, influencing even the most pious of lowborn to be a little bit wicked. It was why the upcoming Feasts became exactly what I'd said to Naomi earlier—a decadent indulgence in all things carnal.

That had to be the cause of my reaction to him.

That and the fact that he was, well, more than just pleasant to look upon, and we both were completely nude.

My heart beat so fast I thought it might actually give out on me as my gaze lowered, falling to the wound on his chest.

The sight of the nearly healed wound brought forth a semblance of common sense.

Sucking in a sharp breath, I took a step back. His hand slipped from my jaw, leaving a swirl of tingles behind.

"I need to dry off. Excuse me." I left the stall, quickly grabbing one of the towels. I wrapped it around me, then gathered up my clothing and quickly left the bathing chamber.

Water dripped from me as I entered the unfamiliar bedchamber. I dried off hastily, my mind a mess as I went to the wardrobe. I searched until I found a suitable shirt. There was no way I could put that nightgown back on. I was going to have to burn it. Maybe the cloak too—something I would've never considered during my time before Archwood. Bloody. Soiled. It hadn't mattered. Clothing had simply been clothing.

The shirt I pulled out was soft and worn, reaching my knees. It was completely inappropriate to be dressed as such, but it was shapeless and provided the same amount of coverage as the night-gown I had worn and half of my gowns. And besides, I had just been completely nude.

I just . . . just felt different.

As did the near-raw reaction to him—my want of him. It was entirely too animalistic, too primal.

Rooting around in the wardrobe, I found a pair of clean breeches that looked like they could fit the Lord. I pulled them out and another shirt, this one white, draping both over the corner of the bed.

Hearing the water turn off, I tugged the loose strands of hair free from the collar of the shirt. Making my way to the small table, I turned on the lamp and then poured a glass of water for him and one for myself. I downed the liquid, but it was of no help in calming my heart or nerves. I sat on the edge of the bed, thinking I probably should've taken the time to bolt.

I had no idea what time it was, but the city streets outside the home were quiet. Morning must be only hours away. I touched the bridge of my nose and winced at the flare of dull pain. How was I going to explain this?

Hearing the bathing chamber open, I lowered my hand to my lap. "There is water on the table," I told him. "I poured you a glass and found you some clothing that might fit."

"Appreciated."

I peeked up then, my gaze traveling over the corded muscles of his back as he walked toward the cupboard. He wore nothing more than the towel wrapped around his hips, and that was, well, simply indecent in the most delicious way I certainly wasn't acknowledging.

The Lord was silent as he drank the water, filled a third glass, and finished that off too. That was good—him drinking so much water. I watched him place the glass on the table, then turn for the clothing. He picked up the black breeches.

"These will do," he said.

"Good."

He undid the towel, and I quickly looked away, face warming despite all that I'd said. When I was sure he was at least partially clothed, I glanced over to find that he had donned the breeches. They were loose at his waist, hanging low on his hips.

I blinked in surprise. The wounds on his arms and in his chest appeared to be almost gone. I looked up at his face. The faint traces of bruises that had remained while he'd been in the shower were completely gone. A tingling sensation swept through me as I took in the Lord's high, angled cheekbones and the straight, proud nose. His jaw cut a hard, carved line, and his mouth was wide and lush. There was a faint, almost feline quality to his features now visible without the bruising. It was like looking at a work of art that one feared to appreciate because the beauty was unsettling.

"Your wounds," I managed.

"They're healing," he answered. His hair was slicked back from his face. "Thanks to you."

There was an unsteady flutter in my chest. "I didn't do much."

He eyed me for a moment. "Do you know why Hyhborn have such a sensual effect on mortals?"

His question caught me off guard, and it took me a moment to answer. "I know some . . . things about what helps strengthen a Hyhborn."

One side of his lips curved up. "And do these things you know involve pleasure?"

"I know that Hyhborn . . ." I struggled to find an accurate word to describe what I'd heard.

The Lord, however, did not. "Feed?"

I nodded, feeling my skin warm a bit. "I'm not sure how I've been of aid to you in that area."

"Na'laa," he murmured, chuckling. "You found great pleasure in aiding me in the shower. Not that you are unaware of that."

Snapping my mouth shut, I looked away. I wasn't unaware of that. I'd just forgotten in the moment that my pleasure in the simple act of touching him was something that could help him.

"We don't just feed on the pleasure of others," he added after a moment. "We also feed on our own pleasure. I too enjoyed the shower."

I peeked at him, for some idiotic reason pleased that he'd enjoyed it.

"But you did even more than you realize," he continued. "You saved lives tonight."

Lives? Namely his. Uncomfortable with that idea and even more that I was disquieted by that fact, I squirmed. "You don't know. You could've escaped."

"Oh, I would've definitely escaped once I came to," he said. "My purpose for being here wouldn't matter. I would've leveled half this town. I would've left nothing but ash and ruin behind."

My chest clenched. "You . . . you would've done that?"

"Yes. I wouldn't have been pleased with what I'd done. I take no joy in the killing of innocents, but my guilt wouldn't have undone my actions or made up for them, now would it have?"

"No," I whispered, unsettled by what he was sharing—by how close Archwood had come to destruction.

"Interesting."

"What?" I tensed as he started toward the bed.

"This whole time, you haven't been afraid of me. You're still not." His head inclined to the constant movement of my fingers, opening and closing in my lap. "But you're nervous. Unless you're normally this fidgety?"

I bit down on my lip, stopping myself from immediately denying it. "I am normally this fidgety," I admitted. "And you do make me nervous. If you said there was no reason to be, I'd still feel that way."

"But I wouldn't tell you that," he said. "You should always be nervous around one like myself."

"Oh," I whispered. "That's . . . that's reassuring."

The Hyhborn lord smiled. There was this razor-sharp, almost predatory edge to it. "But you don't have to fear me. There is a difference between the two."

"How would you know if I'm nervous or afraid?"

"It's in the quickening of your breath and your heart."

My brows lifted. "I . . . I didn't know you could hear that?"

"It's not so much hearing, but if we're focused on an individual, tuned in to their essence, we can. It's how we can feed." A hint of smile briefly appeared. "And I'm focused on you enough that I can tell exactly what causes that hitch in your breath—when it's not fear that causes a change in your breathing and when it's pleasure." A pause. "Arousal."

I inhaled sharply. "I'm not—"

"Going to lie to me? Because I'd know better."

"I don't think you do," I countered as I scooted back, the shirt snagging around my thighs.

"But please do lie. It amuses me."

I frowned at him, thinking that was odd.

He planted a knee on the bed. Our gazes locked, and the urge to ask if he recognized me hit hard. He obviously hadn't. If so, he would've surely said something, but for some ridiculous, pointless reason I wanted to know if he even remembered.

"Do you—" Something stopped me. I wasn't sure what it was. Why would it matter if he did? Or if I told him that we'd met before?

Then it struck me.

It was my intuition. The heightened level of instinct. There had to be a reason for that, especially since my intuition rarely worked to my benefit. My intuition was stopping me. Why, I didn't know, but my heart turned over heavily.

"Are you all right?" the Lord asked.

"Yeah. Yes." I cleared my throat. "I'm just tired. It's been a strange night."

He stared at me for a moment. "That it has."

The nervousness he sensed earlier returned. "We should be leaving before—"

"I know," he said, and then the Lord moved so unbelievably fast. He was above me before I took another breath.

His mere presence forced me onto my back. Our bodies didn't touch, but he was caging me, his large frame blocking out the quarters—the entire realm—until it was only him. Only us. He brought his fingertips to my cheek. My entire body jerked at the touch. The blue swirled completely into the green of his eyes as he drew his fingers down my cheek, catching a strand of hair. He tucked it back, his gentleness shocking.

"You're not afraid of me now," he noted.

"No." I sucked in a small breath as the pads of his fingers made another pass over my bottom lip. "Are you trying to make me afraid?"

"I'm not sure."

A shiver of apprehension tinged with something I couldn't acknowledge skated over my skin.

His gaze swept over my face and then lower, across my throat. "I know you said you were fine earlier, but in a few hours, the skin beneath your eyes and nose will darken, joining the bruises I left upon your throat. Let me change that."

I stared at him. "You . . . you can do that?"

"There are many things I can do." That half grin returned as my eyes narrowed. "Let me do this for you."

Not having to worry about how I would explain the bruises would be a relief, but it was more curiosity than anything. I wasn't sure how he could do this.

"You need to close your eyes," he said.

"Really?"

"Really." The starbursts in his pupils brightened.

Holding his stare for several moments, I nodded and then did as he requested. I closed my eyes. A heartbeat passed, then another, and nothing happened. I started to open my eyes but stopped. The fingers along the curve of my jaw . . . *warmed*. I felt his breath on my chin. Against my parted lips. I didn't take more than a shallow, quick breath then. His breath moved up, and another tense second passed. Then I felt the soft press of his . . . his lips against the bridge of my nose. My entire body jerked.

"Stay still," he ordered, his breath coasting over my cheek.

I tried to, but a tremor started, coursing through me. His mouth lifted. There was nothing . . . and then *something*—a strange tingling warmth. His breath played over the side of my throat and his lips followed. He kissed just below the wildly beating pulse. I sucked in a stuttered gasp as his hair grazed my chin, then his lips pressed against the other side. The shivery warmth blossomed to life there, and in a few moments, the aches I had forced to the back of my mind faded.

But the Lord didn't move away.

His head remained bent, his lips pressed so softly against my throat, and a wholly different kind of warmth came alive once more, sending an aching pulse deep. This . . . this felt far more dangerous than being in the shower stall with him, but then his lips lifted from my skin. He drew back, and I wanted to feel immense relief. I should.

I didn't.

Slowly, I opened my eyes. He remained above me, eyes half closed, and I thought . . . I thought I saw a faint golden glow around him, like I had thought I'd seen in the shower. Was it the lamplight? I didn't think so. "Your kisses . . ." My voice sounded far too reedy. I cleared my throat. "Your kisses heal?"

"Some injuries." The right side of his lips quirked. "Sometimes."

I had the distinct impression he wasn't being all that truthful. "I'm not sure if you realize this or not, but I think you're kind of glowing."

"It happens."

"When . . . you're feeding?" I guessed.

"Yes."

I glanced down. My eyes went wide. "The wound on your chest is closed." I glanced at his arms. Shiny, pink skin had appeared where the wounds had been in his biceps.

His fingers danced along the neckline of my borrowed shirt, while my own fingers were pressed flat against the bed, behaving themselves. They practically itched with the urge to touch him.

And why couldn't I?

Well, there were a lot of reasons, likely ones I hadn't even thought of yet, but I lifted a hand. Out of habit, I hesitated before placing my palm against his chest.

The Lord . . . he *purred*.

Skin warming, I drew my fingers over the carved slabs of hard muscle. Never could I become accustomed to the feel of a Hyhborn's skin.

Never would I become used to being able to touch someone so easily.

He held still above me as I drew my hand down his chest, lips parted. I knew this couldn't continue. We needed to get out of here. I needed to return to the manor, but . . . but my fingers drifted down, over the tightly packed muscle of his abdomen. I reached the loose band of his breeches. The tips of my fingers brushed over a hard, rounded—

A dark, shadowy sound rumbled from the Lord as he caught my wrist, stopping my exploration. "As much as I'd enjoy allowing you to continue, I fear we don't have time for that."

My gaze lifted. He was right. My fingers curled inward. "I know."

He dipped his head as he lifted my hand to his mouth. I inhaled softly as he pressed a kiss to the center of my palm. Our gazes locked once more. The blue had covered all the other colors, becoming an intense shade of sapphire.

Then he was gone from above me, standing several feet away. His head cut sharply toward the window.

"Stay here," he said softly.

Swallowing hard, I sat up, feeling dizzy doing so. "Is everything okay?"

"Yes." His attention shifted back to me, the greens and brown becoming visible once more. "A . . . a friend has arrived."

Frowning, I strained to hear anything that could've alerted him to such a presence, but heard nothing.

"I'll be right back."

I blinked, and the Lord was *gone* yet again. Stunned by how fast he moved, I rose on shaky legs. I didn't let myself think about anything as I went into the bathing chamber to gather my ruined clothing. After toeing on my boots, I stepped into the bedchamber, waiting until the very last minute before I donned my cloak.

The Lord wasn't gone that long; it was maybe a few more moments before I felt a stirring of air in the chamber. I turned, finding him standing in the doorway of the bedchamber. He held something black in his hands.

"Is your friend still here?" I asked.

The Lord nodded. "The horse tethered in the woods? Is it yours?"

I glanced at the lone window. "If it's the one eating everything in sight, then yes."

"She is." There was a pause. "That is a fine horse."

I nodded.

"I brought you this. It is a cloak—a clean one."

"Oh, than—" Remembering one of the bizarre customs surrounding the Hyhborn, I stopped myself from thanking him. Supposedly they felt it tainted their act or something. "That is kind of you."

He said nothing as he came to me, taking my soiled clothing, dropping it on the bed. "This will need to be destroyed," he said. "Hyhborn blood will not wash from the items."

That was something else I hadn't known.

"How far do you have to travel to return home?" he asked.

"Not that . . ." I trailed off as he draped the cloak over my shoulders. The backs of his hands grazed my chest as he drew the halves together. The material was heavier than what was worn this time of year, but it more than reached the floor, hiding my bare legs.

"How far?" he repeated, securing the clasps at my throat.

"Not a great distance."

He eyed me. "Good."

"And you?"

There was something hard about the Lord's smile, and it was completely at odds with the gentleness of his touch. He brought his hand to my cheek. The tips of his fingers glided over my skin. "It's safe for you to leave. You should do that and do so quickly."

A shiver erupted along my spine. "What are you—"

"You don't want me to answer that." He palmed my jaw, causing my breath to catch as he ran his thumb over my lower lip.

His gaze held mine for several more moments; then he dropped his hand and stepped to the side. I didn't move, though, not for several moments, and it was hard to make myself do it. "Will you be okay?"

There was a faint softening to his features. "I will."

"Okay." I swallowed. "Goodbye then."

The Lord said nothing.

I briefly closed my eyes, then forced myself to walk. I went for the door.

"*Na'laa?*"

I stopped as something . . . something like hope swelled inside me. Hope for what? I really couldn't say as I looked over my shoulder at him.

The Lord stood with his back to me, shoulders a tense straight line. "Be careful."

CHAPTER 7

Leaning over the neat row of fiery-pink dianthus, I curled my fingers around the base of a dandelion. Feeling a bit guilty, I tore the little sucker from the soil. With all their medicinal benefits, the weeds wouldn't go wasted, but I still felt bad for tearing them out for purely cosmetic reasons.

It didn't help that my mind conjured up woeful shrieks every time I yanked out a weed.

As I tossed the weed into the basket of its cohorts, my attention shifted to the purplish-blue spikes of catmint. At once, I saw *him*—heard his voice and felt him.

My Hyhborn lord.

Last night . . . it felt like a fever dream, but the grisly memories of seeing him impaled to that table were all too real, as was the shower. Touching him. The feel of him beneath my palms. The brush of his lips against my bruised skin.

Still, none of it felt real—I'd known I would see him again, but never in two lifetimes would I have expected what had happened. My reaction to him. My want. *Need.* Any of it.

A faint shudder rocked me as I reopened my eyes and looked up, past the stone walls of the manor, toward the city of Archwood. Dual streams of smoke still filled the air near the wharf.

I swallowed, skin chilling despite the warmth of the early-morning sun.

When I had woken after only a few hours, if that, of sleep, I'd found myself staring at the *lunea* dagger lying on the nightstand beside my bed. I'd snatched it from the cupboard as I left the black-smith's house. Taking it wasn't something I'd consciously thought of doing. I'd just done it, guided by intuition.

And as I'd stared at that strange blade, I'd thought about what I needed to do. Claude had to be made aware of the apparently very active shadow market in Archwood, and the fact that at least two of his guards were involved in not only the trade but the harvesting.

Knowing that Claude wouldn't be awake until later, I'd headed out to the gardens in hopes of stilling my mind. The gardens and having my hands in the soil would've helped if not for the smoke I'd spotted as soon as I stepped out of the manor. I didn't need my gifts to know what the cause of the fires was.

Him.

It was why he'd said I didn't want him to answer the question of what he was going to do.

He'd sought revenge. But could it even count as revenge when whatever his actions were likely prevented another Hyhborn from being used in such a manner? Sounded more like justice to me, as harsh as that was.

I hadn't seen Finn or Mickie that morning, but I hadn't exactly looked for them as I entered the gardens. I thought—no, *I knew*— there was no reason to. They were no longer of this realm.

And I didn't feel an ounce of sympathy for them, not even Finn and his nice smiles. What they were a part of was wrong, horrific even. It was nothing like the stories I'd heard of people digging up Hyhborn graves to use what was left of their remains. They were committing torture and murder, and if they had succeeded in drain- ing the Lord of all his blood? Harvesting his . . . his parts and selling them on the shadow market? Eventually, those kinds of deeds al- ways came to light. I needed no intuition to tell me how King Euros would respond if he learned of what had been attempted against one of his lords. He'd send the dreaded Prince of Vytrus to handle Archwood, and whatever unrest was happening at the border would be the least of our problems.

But it wasn't even that terrible reality that caused my heart to seize. It was the idea that . . . that *he* could've died. The mere thought made me sick to my stomach, and I shouldn't have *that* kind of reac- tion to it, no matter the brief past I wasn't sure he even remembered.

Was he still in Archwood?

I remained still, silencing my thoughts, but nothing came.

But I hoped—

"No," I whispered, cutting that particular idiotic thought off. I would not hope to see him again. Besides the fact that he was a lord, there was always the risk of a Hyhborn discovering my abilities and accusing me of being a conjurer.

It would be best if I never saw him again.

No, that voice whispered in my mind, *it would not be.*

A shadow appeared beside mine, blocking out the early-morning glare of the sun. I looked over my shoulder, spotting Grady.

"Been looking for you," he announced. "You hear about the fires early this morning?"

"No, but I've seen the smoke." I nibbled on my lower lip. "Do . . . do you know what happened?"

"The Twin Barrels and Jac's—the blacksmith's place—burned. That's what Osmund told me," he said, referring to another guard. "He was on the wall early this morning when the fires started."

I tensed.

"When I first heard of the fires, I was hoping it was the Iron Knights—"

"Gods, Grady," I cut him off, stomach twisting. "You shouldn't even be thinking that, let alone speaking it out loud."

"What?" Grady rolled his eyes. "There isn't anyone out here."

"You don't know who could be near and overhear you," I pointed out. "If someone did and reported you?" My heart stuttered. "You'd be tried for treason, Grady, and by tried, I mean executed without a trial."

"Yeah, and you can't tell me that's not wrong," he shot back. "The fact that the mere suspicion of being sympathetic to the Iron Knights ends in death or worse? Like what was done to Astoria?"

"It is messed up, and so is hoping the Iron Knights had something to do with the fires since you know exactly what happened to Astoria."

"Again, you can't tell me that's not also wrong."

"I'm not saying it isn't. . . ." I trailed off, staring at him. Ever since news of Beylen and the Iron Knights first reached Archwood, Grady had shown more than a passing interest in what was being said about the rebels. And how could he not? Both of us were products of a kingdom that cared very little for its most vulnerable, but we had a life now. We had a future, and I had already risked that enough for the both of us. Worry gnawed at me as I looked away.

"Anyway," Grady said with a heavy sigh. "It wasn't the Iron Knights. Osmund said the flames were *golden,* and you know only one thing can create that kind of fire." Grady continued, "But that's not all."

Knots formed in my stomach. "It's not?"

"No. There were bodies found. Two at the blacksmith's and three at the Twin Barrels."

I shouldn't feel relief, but I did. The death toll could've been higher just at the Twin Barrels, where rooms were always rented. And it could've been catastrophic if the Lord had done as he said he would have, leaving half the city in ruins.

"That's terrible news," I mumbled, because I honestly didn't know what to say.

"Yeah." Grady's brows knitted as he looked at the sky. "You don't seem all that surprised."

"I don't?"

He was quiet for only a moment. "What do you know?"

My head swung back to him. "What do you mean?"

He searched my eyes, trusting that if I lost my grip on my intuition, I would look away. Or if I did see something, I wouldn't tell him. Grady, like Naomi, didn't want to know what the future held for him, and I could respect that. "How long have we known each other?"

I raised a brow. "Some days it feels like forever."

"Yeah, this is one of them," he retorted, and I wrinkled my nose. "You tried to lie to me earlier and you're doing it again. When have you ever been able to successfully lie to me?"

"If I had, you wouldn't know." I gave him a cheeky smile. "Now would you?"

There was no smile. There were no dimples. "Osmund saw you last night, Lis, leaving the manor grounds."

"And?"

"He also saw you returning hours later, riding like a bat out of hell."

"I'm not sure where this is going?"

"You were wearing a different cloak upon your return."

My mouth dropped open. "How could he tell that?"

Grady shrugged. "I guess he has really good eyes."

"Gods," I muttered.

"So? You going to be honest with me now?"

I opened my mouth, but words abandoned me. I was such a pathologically *terrible* liar. Especially when it came to Grady, because he knew me well enough to know that my lack of response to the news about the fires meant something. He knew me better than I did some days.

And lying to Grady, or trying to at the very least, always felt wrong. If he'd managed to peel me off when I first latched on to him, I wouldn't have made it out of the first orphanage I'd been sent to after the Prioress of Mercy had died and no successor replaced her. I'd been weak. A hindrance. I didn't know how to fend for myself— how to move about without making a sound. The streets we were left to roam were an unfamiliar and scary maze to me, nor did I know how to avoid the caretakers' careless hands and fists.

Grady had been kind, even then. Or he'd simply taken pity on me. Either way, eventually I was no longer shadowing him but he was making sure I was right behind him. He made sure I survived.

Grady still made sure I survived.

Sighing, I crossed my arms. "I couldn't sleep after leaving the Great Chamber and I went into the stables to spend time with Iris. While I was there, I overheard two people talking—Finn and Mickie. They had captured a Hyhborn."

"Fuck," he murmured.

I nodded slowly. "And I had to do something about it."

Grady's head tipped toward mine. "What?"

"I got this urge—you know, this need to do it. I had to—"

"Are you about to tell me that you went by yourself to free this Hyhborn?"

I cringed. "I didn't want to involve you—"

"Are you out of your mind?"

"Yes. Completely."

Grady sighed, scrubbing a hand over his face. "Dear gods."

I took a deep breath, and then I told him what had happened—well, almost everything. One of the things I left out was the whole shower situation. He didn't need to know that. "So, those fires? It has to be this Hyhborn lord."

"I couldn't give two shits about this lord at the moment," Grady exclaimed, his gaze roaming over my face. "Are you sure you're not hurt? Should I summon one of the physicians and have you checked over?"

"Nothing hurts. Seriously. I'm fine." And I was. There hadn't been a single bruise or even a dull ache when I looked myself over this morning.

"This Hyhborn lord you talked to?" Grady drew my attention back to him. "Was he from Primvera?"

"No, but I don't know where he is from." My stomach dipped and twisted. I hadn't told Grady that the Lord had been *my* Hyhborn lord. Grady didn't like to talk about that night in Union City. That wasn't a good enough excuse for not saying anything, but I'd also never told him that I knew I'd see the Lord again.

Glancing at the horizon, I saw that the faint traces of smoke remained, and it happened again. The coldness between my shoulder blades and the hollow in my stomach. The whisper returned, repeating the same two words it had said in the Great Chamber.

He's coming.

⇛

Upon returning, I found the Baron in his study, seated at the settee with a cloth draped over his forehead and eyes, thankfully alone.

Straw hat in hand, I pushed the door all the way open. "Claude?"

He lifted a limp wrist. "Lis, darling, do come in."

I closed the door behind me and went to the matching forest-green settee across from the one he sat in. "How are you doing this morning?"

"I'm feeling quite well." He leaned back, crossing one long leg over the other. "Can't you tell?"

I smiled a little, sort of amused by the fact that even *caelestias* could get hangovers. "Yes, you look energetic and ready to seize the day."

"You are too kind, pet." A wan grin appeared beneath the pale blue cloth. "What brings you to me this morning?"

"There's something I need to tell you."

"I do hope it's good news." When I didn't answer, he peeled the cloth back from one half-open eye. "What in the gods' name are you wearing?"

I glanced down at myself, confused. I wore an old threadbare blouse and a pair of breeches that I found a few years back, left behind in the laundry chambers. Granted, the pants had seen better days, but they were perfect for when I was outside. "I was in the gardens."

An eyebrow rose. "Whose pants are those?"

"I have no idea," I said, and his lip curled like the idea of wearing someone else's clothes made him want to vomit. "I . . . I know something that could potentially be a bad thing."

Claude sighed, removing the cloth. He dropped it on the end table. "Hopefully it's not more strange, golden fires."

"You've heard?"

"Hymel woke me with the news." He picked up what I hoped was only a glass of orange juice. "Is it about that?"

"I'm not sure." I chose my words wisely. "Last night, I came across Finn and Mickie—two of your guards."

The look on his face told me he had no idea who I was talking about.

"And I learned something about them," I shared. "They are involved in the shadow market."

Claude lowered his glass. "In what way?"

"The worst way," I said. "Harvesting . . . parts for bone magic."

He stared at me for a moment. "For fuck's sake, are you sure?"

I stared at him.

"Yes. Of course you are." He set the glass aside as he dropped his boot to the floor. The dark shirt he wore moved like liquid silk over his shoulders as he dragged a hand through his hair. "Those fires? Hymel said the magistrates had heard from witnesses that the flames were golden."

"That's what Grady told me." My fingers curled along the rim of my hat. "They weren't successful in their harvesting."

"I wouldn't think so based on the charred remains found after the fires were put out," he remarked, and my stomach soured. "Porter? The owner of the Twin Barrels? He was engaged in this business?"

I nodded. "I don't know how many are involved, but . . ."

"But at least two of my guards are?" His jaw tightened. "Or were, if they were among the bodies discovered."

"There was another name that I've heard. A Muriel."

Claude frowned. "Muriel?"

"Yes. I'm not sure who that is."

He eyed me for a moment, then sat back. A moment passed. "The last thing we need is for Prince Rainer to believe Archwood is a haven for those seeking to use bone magic."

Prince Rainer oversaw the Court of Primvera. I had never seen the Hyhborn, but Claude said the Prince was a friendly sort. Hopefully he continued to be that way.

"I can try to see if any other guards are involved," I offered.

Claude's chest rose with a heavy breath. "Thank you for coming to me, and for your aid. That would be appreciated."

I nodded, beginning to rise. "Hopefully they were it."

"Yes," Claude murmured, squinting as he stared out the window. "Hopefully."

"I'll let you know if I find anything." I started to leave, then stopped. "Would you like something for your headache? I have some peppermint—"

"No, that won't be necessary." His smile turned wry as he looked up at me. "The headaches are deserved."

They probably were, but I didn't think that meant he needed to suffer. "You sure?"

"Yes, pet. I am."

Hesitating for a moment, I then turned. I made it only a few steps.

"Pet?"

I faced him. "Yes?"

He'd picked up the cloth. "Are you happy here?"

"Yes, of course. Why do you ask?" At once, my stomach dropped as my mind went to the worst-case scenario. For him to ask something similar twice in the span of twenty-four hours unnerved me. "Are you not happy with me?"

"No—no. That's not why I asked," he was quick to say. "I'm lucky to have you." He twisted at the waist, toward me. "I just want to make sure you know that."

"I do," I whispered.

Claude smiled, but there was something off about it. Tired, even brittle, but I imagined that had more to do with the ache in his head.

"Feel better," I said, crossing the study. Something struck me then—about this Muriel.

I didn't know . . . anything about him. Nothing came to me, which could mean only one thing.

Muriel was a Hyhborn.

But that made little sense. Why would a Hyhborn be involved in bone magic?

CHAPTER 8

Sultry music drifted down from the balcony above the solarium, masking some of the sounds radiating from the various couches and nooks. Beneath the music and the clink of glasses, there were thicker, heated sounds mingling with the hum of conversation. Teasing laughter. Low groans. Breathy gasps as bodies moved against one another.

The evening festivities were in full swing—an excess in all forms of lasciviousness, whether it be imbibing too much drink or indulging in the flesh.

I shifted on the couch I sat upon, my chest feeling too tight as my thoughts circled the general sense of unease that had been building since I'd spoken to Grady and had left Claude's study. The cause of it could be several things. The raids along the border. The shadow market in Archwood. Claude. A Hyhborn potentially being involved in harvesting. *Him.*

He's coming.

My skin felt too cold despite the balmy warmth of the solarium, and the sweet-tasting wine I sipped did little to warm me. I knew that whisper was for him—my lord—but what I didn't understand was why I could sense that and yet nothing else when it came to Hyhborn.

I eyed where Claude was currently holding court with his closest peers—sons and daughters of Archwood's most elite, those desperate to be close to anything Hyhborn, even a *caelestia*. They laughed and carried on while Claude held Allyson in his lap.

The Baron had disappeared more than once to step outside, and I feared he'd also been indulging in the Midnight Oil—a powder derived from poppies grown in the Lowlands and often smoked. *Caelestias* had a higher tolerance, but they didn't seem to know exactly when they exceeded that tolerance. He had that unsteady way about him that always followed smoking the drug. Had he reached out to Prince Rainer?

I didn't know, but I'd spent a good part of the day strolling near the wall, peeking into the thoughts of the guards who were on duty. Thankfully none of them had sent up any red flags, but then again, they would have to have been thinking about the shadow market for me to pick up on it.

However, I did learn that Hendrick, one of the guards, was thinking about proposing to the girl he'd been seeing.

Not sure what I could do with that piece of information.

I took another drink of the wine as I peeked over at the nearby divan, and nearly choked at the sight of Mrs. Isbill. The wife of a wealthy ship merchant was likely unrecognizable to most, since half her face was obscured by a jewel-encrusted domino mask. She was sprawled across the red cushion, the bodice of her gown exposing one breast. The skirt of her gown was hiked up to her knees, doing very little to hide the fact that it was most definitely not her husband's head between her thighs. I knew this, because he was currently seated beside her, and whoever was between her legs also had his hand on Mr. Isbill's cock.

My gaze flickered over those in attendance. Like the Isbills, most wore masks that covered half of the face, from the forehead to the nose. Some wore elaborate constructions of flowers and streaming ribbons, topped with crowns or garlands. Others were less dramatic in their approach, simply settling for one made of satin or brocade. The aristo used these masks to conceal themselves, as if keeping their identities hidden was the permission they needed to behave as they wished.

I glanced at Claude again. Like me, he wore no mask, and neither did Grady or the guards who stood behind him.

Grady and I had been studiously avoiding eye contact all evening, pretending that we weren't witnessing all that was occurring in this chamber at the same time. No matter how many times the nights devolved into this, it was still awkward as hell.

I fixed my gaze on the floor, since it was the only safe place to look at the moment. The behavior of the aristo amused me. Claude never made any attempt to hide his desires. He wouldn't be ashamed come morning, like some of the aristo in attendance surely would. Most of them would never behave in such provocative, wanton ways in public, but here at Archwood, when they were assured of not being recognized and among those who wanted the same thing as they did, there appeared to be no pretense of modesty.

I supposed their behavior wasn't as amusing as it was sad. However, it was the aristo, not the Hyhborn, who had not only established but reinforced these rules of what they felt was appropriate behavior. These aristo were stifling themselves, and for what?

A groan of release echoed from the nearby divan. The head that had been between Mrs. Isbill's thighs was now in the lap of Mr. Isbill. Gods, I really hoped this man ended up well rewarded for all his . . . hard work this evening.

Sighing, I turned my head to a nearby glass wall that overlooked the yards of the manor and the gardens.

I'd rather be out there.

The space between my shoulder blades began to tingle.

I *needed* to be out there.

I was moving before I realized what I was doing, muscles tensing to stand, when a man wearing dove-gray pants suddenly filled my view, his linen shirt left unbuttoned. Leaning back against the thick cushions of the couch, I looked up to see a white mask shielding all but the lower half of his face.

"You look like you're in need of company," the man announced.

"I'm not."

"You sure about that?" He stepped forward, moving to where my legs took up the remaining length of the couch.

I did nothing to hide my sigh. This man wasn't the first to make it past Naomi, who was doing her level best to lure would-be pursuers away. I was beginning to feel as if the solarium were a henhouse full of foxes. "I'm positive."

"I can change your mind," he said with all the confidence typical of a man who was used to turning nos into yeses. My senses opened, reaching out to him. Or with the confidence of a man who was used to *forcing* nos into yeses. "You won't regret it."

Knowing I should just ignore the man, I instead smiled up at him and did exactly what I shouldn't.

Because apparently, I was in the season of making bad life choices.

I extended my hand. He didn't hesitate, taking it. The moment my skin connected with his, I felt his voice in my mind, as clear as if he were speaking, but it was my voice that whispered, telling me things unknown till that very moment. His name. How he made his living. His *wife*, who was not here. I saw what he wanted—his intentions. He wanted to get off. Shocker. But there was more to that, something that brought on a bitter bite of disgust.

I tugged on his arm, guiding him so we were at eye level, and then leaned in. "I have no interest in choking on your cock tonight," I whispered, my mouth inches from his. "Or any night, *Gregory*."

His jaw went slack with surprise. He went to jerk his hand free, but I held on, letting him watch my smile grow—watching the blood drain from the skin beneath his mask. I released him. Eyes wide, he backed away from me and turned without saying another word. Laughing under my breath, I wiped the hand he had touched on the cushion as I once more spotted Naomi moving about the crowd, her long legs and arms shimmering from a dusting of gold body paint. She had lingered close to me most of the evening before I shooed her off. While her watchfulness was kind of her, it wasn't . . . it wasn't right.

I wasn't her responsibility.

But she was coming straight for me.

"Scoot over," she instructed, leaning over my legs.

I kept the glass of wine steady, watching Naomi as I grinned. It was clear Naomi was up to something as she all but prowled up the length of my body. The seductive, fluid movements of her body were a bit exaggerated. I knew she knew it too, because one eye winked. She wore no mask. None of Claude's paramours felt the need to hide their faces.

"I thought you might want company." She stretched out behind me, propping her elbow on the arm of the couch. She dipped her head close to mine. "Keep those special hands of yours to yourself," she reminded me.

"I will," I promised, knowing that her coming to me about Laurelin was atypical of her. She preferred that I remain unseeing to her future and to her thoughts. Sometimes that was impossible, though, even without touching her. I just didn't let her know when that accidentally happened. "You know I don't need the company, right?"

"Oh, but you most definitely do." Her hand curved around my hip and squeezed gently as she flicked her gaze toward Claude. "The longer you're alone, the more interesting you become to those around you."

My jaw clenched. "You should be enjoying yourself."

"I am."

"Sure." I shivered as the edges of her hair fell over my arm. "You must be thrilled to be lying behind me."

"I am."

"Naomi—"

"Come now, you know I like to play with you." She slid her hand down my hip as I rolled my eyes. Her nails slipped over the slit in the gown, skating over the bare skin of my thigh. "You know damn well my motives aren't purely altruistic."

I did know her actions weren't solely out of the goodness of her heart. Naomi liked to play, when it was only her doing the touching and caressing. And because she knew that, no matter what, I wouldn't forget what she asked of me and touch her, she had complete control. A part of her got off on that.

A part of me did too.

But I still couldn't help but feel a bit guilty and . . . I glanced at Grady. And like a weight around the necks of those I cared for.

"I'm annoyed, though."

I returned my attention to her, offering my glass of wine. "With what?"

"That Grady is here," she said, taking the glass and finishing it off before placing it on the small end table by the couch. "Which means unless I want to see him pass out from the horror of seeing you come, I won't get to really play."

A strangled laugh left me. "He absolutely would pass out."

"He's such a bore." Her chin dipped and she pressed a kiss to the curve of my shoulder.

"He's really not." My gaze swept over the chamber—over those talking, drinking, and eating, and those who were using their hands and mouths for other things. "I would be equally horrified to see him in the throes of lust."

"I know. I'm just being petty because I must behave myself." Pouting, she ran her fingers back over my stomach. "But in case you are curious about what he's like in the throes of lust, all you need to do is ask me—"

"Please stop." My nose wrinkled. "Because I really don't want to ever know what that looks like."

"You both are as boring as Laurelin." Naomi's laugh faded.

My heart ached. "How is your sister?"

"A little better."

I could tell her truth about what lay in store for Laurelin past the fever, but I didn't want Naomi's relief at Laurelin's improvement to be taken from her. And I was also selfish. I didn't want to be the one to take that relief from her. "I'm sorry. I don't know if I said that before, but I'm sorry for what she's going through—what you're going through."

"Thank you."

I nodded, staying silent while Naomi likely quieted those thoughts and emotions surrounding her sister. My gaze swept over the chamber, landing on Claude. Allyson was still in his lap, those around him continued to laugh and chat, but he was silent, his expression pinched as he stared at something only he could see.

"I think something's going on with him," Naomi said quietly, having followed my gaze. "Claude."

"Really?" When she nodded, I asked, "Why do you think something's going on?"

Her nails scraped over the thin material of the bodice, causing my back to arch. "I'm not sure." She lowered her head, resting her chin on my shoulder. "But he's been acting off—nervous and morose one moment and then overly joyful—and he's been drinking a lot more of late."

"That I've noticed." I thought of his question this early afternoon. "You heard about what happened in the city last night?"

"Yes. Terrible news." She shuddered. "But he's been acting differently for weeks."

"This is recent too, but there was news—" My breath caught as she toyed with the peak of my breast. My own fingers pressed into the cushion of the couch in front of me. "You have a very skewed view of behaving yourself."

"I do?" She winked at me. "You were saying?"

I shook my head at her. "I was saying there has been news concerning the Westlands."

"What?" she asked, and as I told her what Ramsey had said, she slid her hand from my now far too sensitive breast. "What in the world could be causing this? Why would a princess turn against the King?"

"I don't know," I murmured. I hadn't paid much attention to Hyhborn politics. Most of us lowborn didn't, since it rarely impacted us, but that . . . that was changing, wasn't it?

"King Euros has to do something about it," Naomi mused. "Don't you think?"

"The Iron Knights are suspected of being responsible for the raids along the border, right? And if that is true, that means they are doing so on the orders of the Princess of Visalia, but the King hasn't done anything about the raids, so . . ."

"True." She paused. "He's a bastard."

My shoulders shook with laugher. "I'm pretty sure all of those who are in power are bastards."

Naomi grinned as her hand skated over my thigh.

My gaze flicked to the Baron. He was focused once more on Allyson. Was he at all worried about the raids encroaching farther into the Midlands? Or how close to utter devastation Archwood had come?

"What are you thinking about?" Naomi asked, and I gave a little jump as her hand made its way to the opening in the panels. "You look entirely too serious for someone in the midst of an orgy."

I laughed, but worry gnawed at me, if not Claude. I glanced at Naomi. "Why do you stay here?"

She went still behind me for just half a second. "Why not?"

Sighing, I looked away from her.

"What?" She nipped at my throat when I didn't answer, causing me to gasp at the dual stroke of pain and something entirely different. "*What?*"

I shot her a narrowed glare over my shoulder. "*Ouch.*"

"You liked it," she retorted with a saucy grin. "What was that sigh for?"

"It was for the hand on my thigh," I replied.

"As if that were true. You never make a sound when it comes to that, not even when I do that thing with my fingers that I know you like, because everyone likes it."

I knew exactly what she was talking about. "I just . . . I just don't get why you stay here," I said finally, tucking my foot between hers as her arm slipped deeper between the panels of gown.

"Do you think I'm not happy?"

"Are you?"

Naomi didn't answer right away, instead contenting herself with drawing her fingers over my navel and lower. She made no comment when no undergarments met her adventurous fingers, knowing that Maven had dressed me. "I stay because I want to. Because I am happy here."

It was now I who went quiet.

"You don't believe me, do you?"

I tipped my head into the crook of her shoulder. "I hope you speak the truth."

"You should." She looked down at me, brown eyes serious. "Look, I've heard you say it before. Archwood is like any other city in any other territory, but it's pretty here. The air is clean and not clogged with smoke like the towns near the mines. I have a roof over my head and as much food as I can eat, and I don't have to break my back for that."

"You sure you aren't breaking your back?" I quipped.

Naomi's stare turned droll, and I giggled. "It's not my back I break," she said, and another small laugh left me. "*Anyway*, as I was saying, I don't have to work myself to death in the mines or cleaning up after others. Nor do I have to marry to feel secure. I choose what I do with my days and with whom. Besides, I like fucking and being fucked," she told me, hand slipping between my thighs.

"Never would've guessed that," I stated.

Naomi's laugh tugged at my lips, and my own crawled up my throat. That was the thing about her laughs. They were infectious.

"I'm not like my sister, you know? I never wanted to be married and be used as nothing more than a broodmare," she said, the corners of her mouth tensing. "That's why this life with Claude is perfect for me. There are no expectations. No boundaries. I like what I am." Her gaze briefly met mine. "I wish you could like what you are."

My breath caught. "I do," I whispered.

"And I want to believe that." Naomi kissed my shoulder. A moment passed; then she changed the subject. "I heard a rumor."

"About?"

"The fires," she said. "That the Hyhborn were involved in it."

"Oh?" I didn't tell her what I knew. Not because I didn't trust her. Obviously, I did. I just . . . I didn't want her to worry. She already had enough on her mind with Laurelin.

"I wish I had seen the Hyhborn—not the burning of the buildings part," she amended, and I snorted. "It's too few and far between that we get to gaze upon their magnificence."

I knew Naomi was being silly, but his features were too easy to conjure forth—the curve of his jaw, the slant of his teasing mouth, and those stunning eyes.

"Lis?" Naomi whispered, her lips at the curve of my cheek.

I fixed my stare to the stone floor in front of the couch. A flutter started in my chest, joining the one much, much lower as her touch elicited a fine, tight shiver. "Yes?"

"I asked if you wanted me to get you something to drink." Her fingers danced over my lower stomach, inching their way below my navel.

"I'm—" My words ended in a gasp. My gaze flew to Naomi's and narrowed.

"What?" she said innocently. "Did my fingers grow too close to a very sensitive part of you?"

"Possibly."

Her grin was pure devilish wickedness. "I do hope you partake in the Feasts this year."

I raised a brow. "I think the only reason you're looking forward to the Feasts is so you can wrap a Hyhborn around your finger."

"What else would look better around my finger?" The tips of her fingers made their way down my lower stomach once more, stopping a mere inch, if that, above the junction of my thighs. "Besides you?"

I laughed.

Her eyes glittered. "Did I tell you that Hyhborn are . . . *magnificently* endowed?"

She was speaking only the truth. "Can we stop saying 'magnificent'?"

"Never." Her lips curved in a faint smile as her fingers swept back and forth, almost—*almost* brushing against the too-sensitive bud of flesh. "We're being watched, by the way."

"There's not a single part of me surprised to hear that," I muttered, but I looked to see the man who'd been with the Isbills watching, as was a woman across the way. They weren't the only ones eyeing us. Luckily Grady wasn't. Especially since Naomi's hand was on the prowl again. "And you still have a very strange understanding of behaving yourself," I said.

Naomi ignored that. "It's hard when I know there's an audience. I've always found it a little unnerving." Her fingers began to move again in slow, teasing circles. "And a little arousing."

"There's something wrong with you," I stated.

"Please, as if I don't know that you too like to be watched."

My hips shifted restlessly. "That's beside the point."

"Tell me something." Naomi's lips curled against my cheek. "Exactly how wet are you right now?"

My face heating, my eyes narrowed on her.

"If I wasn't behaving myself out of respect for our poor Grady's emotional and mental well-being, I bet I'd discover that you are." Her nose touched mine as she whispered, "Don't even try to lie, because the way your hips keep squirming will tell a very different story."

"It's telling the story your fingers are writing."

She made a throaty sound in the space between my lips. "Oh, I bet my teasing got you nice and warm," she said. Her gaze turned shrewd. "But I'm also willing to bet the fact that your thinking of magnificently endowed Hyhborn has got you *soaked*."

Muscles tightened as my toes curled, but she was wrong. And she was right. While Naomi was technically behaving herself, I did . . . I did *ache*, but it wasn't just me. I could feel the quickening in her breath. I felt her restless movements against my thigh. It was partly her touch, and she was also right. I was thinking of magnificently endowed Hyhborn, except I was thinking of him.

My Hyhborn lord.

CHAPTER 9

Knowing that Naomi wouldn't enjoy her evening when she felt she had to run interference, I told her I was going to call it a night. In all honesty, I should be tired, considering what little sleep I'd gotten the night before, but a nervous sort of energy coursed through me even after I changed into a slippery soft nightgown, leaving me restless and amped-up.

I was going to blame Naomi and her idea of behaving herself for that.

As I lay down on the bed, my mind was absolutely no help, deciding to alternate between the memory of the soft, teasing touches of Naomi's and the . . . the feel of my lord's hard, slick skin.

Skin flushed, I rolled onto my side, pressing my thighs together. A sharp pulse echoed throughout me. I bit down on my lip as I trailed my hand over my chest. The breath I took was shaky. His voice was so clear to me, as if he were beside me, whispering in my ear. My fingers spread, grazing a hardened nipple through the cotton nightgown. Except they weren't my fingers. They were Naomi's. They were *his*.

Heat sluiced through my veins, reigniting the ache deep inside me. I sucked in a gasp as my nails dragged over the peak of my breast. I moved restlessly, hips rocking. The tips of my breasts had never been all that sensitive, but they tingled then, becoming almost painful as damp heat gathered low, between my thighs. My pulse thrummed as I shifted onto my back, closing my eyes as I slipped my hand down over my stomach and lower, drawing the nightgown up as I went. Cool air kissed the heated space between my legs, wringing a soft gasp from me. I jerked as my fingers touched the bare skin of my upper thighs, burning me—burning through me, because it was *their* touch I conjured up.

I spread my thighs, my breaths coming in short, shallow pants as my fingers grazed the sensitive, taut flesh. I jerked again, toes curling as I dipped my fingers lower. Pressing my head back, I moaned as I lifted my hips. I teased just as I knew Naomi would have, just as I imagined my lord would if I had stayed in that shower. It wasn't my fingers that plunged through my slippery wetness or curled around my breast. It was Naomi's and then his, working me until I was thrusting up. I arched, wanting more. Needing more.

Touch me.

The memory of his voice tumbled me over the edge, into ecstasy, and I was swept away by the tense but too-short waves of pleasure. I was left panting and . . . and still aching.

Still unfulfilled.

Because it hadn't been Naomi's touch. It hadn't been his. It had only been my own fingers.

I dragged in a deep breath, and my eyes flew open as I caught a faint woodsy, soft scent.

His scent.

I turned my head to the settee across from the bed, where I had left the cloak he had given me. I should do something with it. Donate it. Trash it. Maybe burn it.

I sighed, my gaze flicking to the ceiling, and then I sat up, going to the bathing chamber. I splashed cool water over my face, the restlessness still there, the—

The urge returned, the one from the solarium.

The want.

The *need* to be out there.

I padded barefoot to the window and looked out. Immediately, I spied the floating, glowing balls of light that appeared in the night sky somewhere between the end of spring and the beginning of summer, in the weeks before the Feasts, and then disappeared shortly after.

A smile raced across my face at the sight of them. I pushed away from the window and slipped my feet into a pair of thin-soled shoes. Grabbing a midnight-blue, short-sleeved robe from the bathing chamber, I slipped it on and belted it at my waist as I glanced at the *lunea* dagger on the nightstand, reminding myself to ask Grady if he had an extra sheath for it.

Leaving through the terrace doors, I crossed the back lawn, avoiding the partygoers as I made my way to the narrow footbridge that crossed the small stream and entered the gardens. I followed the winding path of the Baron's gardens, focused on the bright spheres drifting down from high above like stars to float among the sweeping loblolly pine. The magical lights cast a soft glow as they filled the sky. They'd always fascinated me, even as a child. I couldn't remember if the Prioress had ever told me why they appeared when they did. I'd asked Claude once, but he'd shrugged and said they were just a part of the Hyhborn.

That really hadn't told me anything.

My steps slowed as one of the spheres, about the size of my hand, floated down from the trees to hover a few feet in front of me, surprising me. I'd never been this close to one, not even before I came to Archwood. I took a hesitant step forward, half afraid the orb would flutter away or disappear.

It didn't.

The ball of light remained close enough for me to see that it wasn't just one central light. My eyes widened. It was actually a series of tiny lights clustered together. The orb pulsed, then drifted away, slowly returning to the trees above. I watched the lights dip and rise as if they were joined in a dance before they fluttered back into the trees.

Toying with the edge of my braid, I started walking again, trailing after the lights as night birds sang from the trees. The peace of the gardens calmed my mind. I wondered if Claude would be against me setting up a . . . a hammock out here? I doubted I would have any problems—

Stop.

I jerked to a sudden halt. Brows knitting, I slowly turned and faced an archway to my right. My fingers twitched as an acute sense of awareness washed over me, pressing between my shoulder blades.

Intuition had sparked. It had done so well over an hour ago, I realized. There had been that urge to leave the solarium and enter the gardens.

"You have got to be kidding me," I muttered, staring into the darkened pathway.

I held myself still, my heart kicking unsteadily in my chest. Only the gods knew what my intuition wanted to lead me toward tonight. I didn't even want to know. My fingers gave a spasm, muscles trembling as I fought the pull of intuition.

"Damn it." I blew out an aggravated breath and crossed under the archway.

Very little moonlight pierced the large wisteria trees and their heavy vines, and only a few glowing spheres glided high up in the trees, their soft glow illuminating the pale blue trailing stems. Brushing aside the low-hanging limbs, I continued along the path, traveling deep within the wisteria trees.

Then I felt it, a sudden change to the air. It had cooled, but there was a thickness to it. A heaviness. *Power.* I'd felt this before—

"Like I just said, I have no idea what you're talking about." A man was speaking up ahead. There was a . . . a cadence to his speech, where certain letters were trilled, that was uncommon to the Midlands region, but his voice also did something to me. It felt like thistle weeds against my skin, and it opened that door in my mind.

I *saw* red.

Dripping against stone.

Splattering pale blossoms.

Blood.

I halted, breath catching.

I saw nothing of those who spoke beneath the shadows of the wisteria trees, but I *knew* something bloody was about to happen.

Which meant I should be hightailing my ass out of there. The last thing I needed was to get caught up in whatever drama was about to go down. Whatever this was, especially after last night, it wasn't my business.

But I saw blood.

Someone was going to be hurt.

My fingers curled around a stream of blossoms as I dragged my teeth over my lower lip. I should've just stayed in the solarium and drunk half my weight in liquor tonight. The *sight*, the *voices*, the *knowing* would've been silenced for a little while. I wouldn't be standing here, on the verge of doing something very ill-advised—and my gods, just last night accounted for a year's worth of foolishness.

I ordered myself to turn around, but that wasn't what I was doing.

Inching forward, I gritted my teeth. There was nothing wrong with not wanting to get involved, I told myself. It didn't make me a bad person. I'd proved that last night. Besides, what was I going to do to stop whatever was about to happen? Grady had taught me how to throw a pretty mean right hook, but I didn't think that was going to be of much help.

"And I don't like the accusations you're making either," the man continued. "Nor will he, and you should be concerned by that. You're not untouchable, despite what you think."

Knocking a wisteria vine aside, I plowed forward—

A dryly amused chuckle answered, causing tiny goose bumps to break out along my bare arms. That sound . . .

My eyes went wide as my foot immediately snagged on an exposed root. "Fuck," I gasped, stumbling. I planted a hand on the rough bark of a nearby tree, catching myself before I planted my face into the ground.

Silence.

Utter complete silence surrounded me as I slowly lifted my head, face burning. I started to speak—to say what, I had no idea, because every single thought fled my mind as I saw two men standing beneath those damn spheres of light that seemed to have appeared out of nowhere to bear witness to my absolute fuckery. They both had turned toward me, and I zeroed in on the one my senses warned against.

He was blond and pale-skinned. Tall and attractive, his features so perfectly crafted that one would believe they'd been carved by the gods themselves, and I knew what that meant before I saw what was strapped to his hip. My blood immediately went cold at the sight of the dull, milky white of a *lunea* blade.

I didn't know what shocked me more—that my intuition had

actually worked with something that involved Hyhborn or that it had led me to . . . to *him*.

Fingers tangled in the vines, I could feel my heart pumping icy shock through my veins as my gaze shot to the other man, and I knew. I knew the moment I heard the soft, smoky chuckle.

Air leaked out of my lungs. He was standing mostly in the shadows and wearing all black. He would've blended into them if not for the glimpses of sandy-hued skin. I thought I might've forgotten how to breathe as he stepped more fully into the soft light of the orbs. I was sure the ground rolled beneath my feet.

It was *him*.

My Hyhborn lord.

The hard, carved line of his jaw tilted as his wide, lush lips curved into a half grin. "This is becoming a habit."

"What is?" I heard myself whisper.

His features fell back into the shadows. "Meeting like this."

"Who in the fuck is this?" the other Hyhborn demanded, jerking my attention back to him.

"I'm n-no one. I . . . I just was following the little balls of light—I like the balls . . . of light," I blurted out, and my entire brain cringed. *I like the balls? Gods.* Untangling my fingers from the wisteria, I started to take a step back. "Sorry, please just forget that I was here—that I even exist."

A slice of moonlight cut across the lower half of my Hyhborn's face—and gods, he wasn't mine. His grin had deepened. "One moment, please."

The "please" stopped me.

Because a Hyhborn lord, even him, saying that? To me? A lowborn? That was . . . that was unheard of. He hadn't even said that last night, when he asked for my help.

Then everything happened so fast.

The other Hyhborn cursed, darting backward as he withdrew the *lunea* dagger, but the other lord was faster. He caught the Hyhborn by the wrist and twisted. The crack of bone was like thunder. I smacked my hand over my mouth, silencing a scream.

The Hyhborn hissed in pain as the blade fell to the ground. "You do this"—his lips peeled back—"you'll regret it. With your very last breath, you will."

"No, Nathaniel," the Lord replied, and he sounded bored. Like Grady did whenever I started to talk about the different types of daisies. "I will not."

I caught only a glimpse of the Lord's fist. Just a second before it slammed against the Hyhborn's chest—*into* his chest.

The one called Nathaniel threw his head back, his body jerking as my hand fell from my mouth.

"Just one more moment," the Lord said, rather casually.

Golden fire erupted from Nathaniel's chest—or from the Lord's hand, which was still plunged deep inside said chest. The fire spread over Nathaniel in a rippling, violent wave of vibrant gold flames, and I suddenly knew exactly how the blacksmith's and the Twin Barrels had been incinerated. Within a few heartbeats, all that remained of Nathaniel was . . . was a pile of ash and a few strips of charred clothing beside the fallen *lunea* blade.

"Holy shit," I whispered, horrified . . . and a little awed by the display of power, but mostly horrified as I lifted my gaze. Behind where Nathaniel had stood, the pale blossoms were splattered with blood, just as I'd seen.

I lifted my stare to the Lord, who . . . who could barely walk on his own last night, whom I had just fantasized about while pleasuring myself, and he'd . . .

And he'd incinerated another with his *hand*.

If he could do that to one of his own, what in the whole wide realm of *nope* could he do to a lowborn?

I took a shaky step back, reminded once more of exactly what this lord was. Somehow, I'd forgotten that.

"*Na'laa*," the Lord called softly.

My entire body jolted.

A strand of hair slipped forward and fell against his jaw as he bent, wiping his hand on one of the pieces of burnt clothing. "You should come closer."

I inched back another step. "I don't know about that."

"Are you finally afraid of me?" the Lord asked, picking up the fallen *lunea* blade.

I wasn't sure, but I knew I should be. I should be terrified.

His head cut in my direction. "Don't move any further—"

I moved several more feet. Somehow the fire he'd created was more unnerving than seeing him tear out Weber's windpipe. I wasn't even sure why, but—

Something snagged my braid, jerking me back. I cried out as pain radiated down my neck and spine. My feet slipped out from underneath me as I was spun. A hand clamped down on my throat. Dragged back against a wall of a chest, I gripped the hand upon my throat, and I heard absolutely *nothing* as I saw the tall Hyhborn lord through the swaying wisteria vines.

"Muriel," the Lord drawled, and shock rolled through me. I knew that name. Finn and Mickie had spoken it. "I've spent all day looking for you."

"Don't come any closer," the one holding me warned as I clawed at his hand, breaking my nails on the hard flesh of another Hyhborn.

The Hyhborn lord prowled forward slowly, the trailing vines lifting and swinging out of his way before his body even came into contact with them. "Correct me if I'm wrong," the Lord said, ignoring Muriel. "But didn't I tell you not to move?"

"I—"

"Stop," Muriel growled, cutting me off. His grip on my throat tightened. Panic threatened to seize me. "Or I will snap her fucking neck."

"That neck is a pretty one," the Hyhborn lord responded. "But why, Muriel, would you think I'd care if you did snap it?"

"Bastard," I hissed before I could stop myself, disbelief having loosened my tongue.

The Lord cocked his head. "That wasn't very nice of you."

I gaped at him. I'd helped him last night. Got him to safety. Risked my own life, and he didn't care if my neck was snapped. "You just said—"

Muriel dug his fingers into my throat, ending my words in a strangled gasp. "What did you do to Nathaniel?" he demanded.

"Put him in a time-out." Another stream of blossoms fluttered out of his path. "Permanently."

Muriel inched us back, forcing me onto the tips of my toes. "Why in the hell would you do that?"

"You know better than to ask that question, but since I'm feeling generous tonight, I'll explain it to you. Besides the fact he was boring me," the Lord answered, "he set me up. So did you."

Muriel halted as I strained against his hold. "Yeah, I do know better." He cursed again. "I should've known better than to trust lowborn to get the job done."

"You should have." The Lord paused. "And *you* should stop struggling while Muriel and I have our little chat. If not, you're only going to harm yourself."

Stop struggling? While Muriel crushed my windpipe?

"And you should be more worried about your own neck," Muriel spat.

"Your concern for me warms my heart."

"Yeah, I can see that." Muriel yanked me harshly to the side as I struggled to break free. Nothing worked. His hold remained firm. "You know, you brought this onto yourself."

"And how did I do that?"

"Play coy all you want. It won't work for much longer," Muriel snarled. "There's only one reason why you were willing to risk your ass to get that information from us."

"Speaking of that information," the Lord replied. "Was any of it true?"

"Fuck you," spat Muriel.

The Lord sighed.

"How do you think the King's going to respond when he learns of what you were looking for?" Muriel shot back. I truly had no idea what they were speaking of. "The King's going to have your head."

"Doubtful." The Lord chuckled again, and the sound raised the hairs on the nape of my neck. "I'm one of the King's favorites, in case you've forgotten."

"Not after tonight," Muriel promised. "Not when he learns the truth."

The truth of what?

The Lord had stopped coming closer. He now stood a few feet from us. "I'm curious, Muriel, as to why you actually believe the King would hear of anything that has occurred this night? Or even last night?"

Muriel stiffened behind me, seeming to sense the not-so-veiled threat in the Lord's words. A stuttered heartbeat passed. "I'm leaving."

"Okay?" The Lord cocked his head.

"I mean it," Muriel said, and I thought I heard a tremor in his words. "You come after me, I'll rip her heart out."

"Does it look like I'm trying to stop you from leaving?" the Lord asked.

It didn't.

It really didn't.

I didn't know why I expected anything different from the Lord. Even my Hyhborn lord. He'd needed my aid last night. He clearly didn't need it tonight. I was a fool, because a feeling of . . . of betrayal settled in deep, which even I could admit made no sense. Just because I had helped him last night didn't mean he was obligated to me.

Gods, I really wished I hadn't thought of him when I touched myself.

My heart sank as Muriel moved us back through the wisteria vines. The fragrant limbs fell in place, forming a curtain that quickly obscured the Lord. Muriel was dragging me farther into the trees— away from the manor, and that was bad, because I seriously doubted this Hyhborn would let me go once he was clear of the Lord.

Panic exploded. I struggled wildly, kicking at Muriel's legs as I beat on his arm. Each blow I landed sent a ripple of pain up my arm and leg. I gagged, eyes widening as he spun us around. I flailed against his hold, throwing my weight in every direction.

A guttural sound of warning echoed from Muriel as he lifted me off my feet. "Keep it up and I'll—*Fuck*."

Something large and dark crashed into us, knocking Muriel back several feet. He slammed into a tree, the impact shaking him first, then me. He grunted, his grip remaining as my legs started to cave.

A blur of movement whipped the loose hairs around my face. I saw a glimpse of a hand coming down on Muriel's arm, then a flash of the milky-white *lunea* blade. The pressure lifted from my neck, but there was no time to feel any relief, to even catch my breath. Another hand clamped down on my arm. I was flung sideways—*thrown*. For a moment, I was weightless among the sweetly scented blossoms. There was no up or down, sky or ground, and in those seconds, I realized it was over. The running. The loneliness. It was all over. The Baron was going to be so sad when he found my broken body.

I hit the ground hard, rattling every bone in my body as my head snapped back. Stunning, brutal pain whipped through me.

Then there was nothing.

CHAPTER 10

Out of the fog of nothingness, I felt . . . I felt fingers drifting along the sides of my neck and under the thick twist of my braid, along the back of my skull. The touch was featherlight, but warm—almost hot, moving in soothing, barely there circles. I felt the touch of something softer against my brow.

"Is she going to make it?" a man asked.

I didn't recognize the voice, but I thought his had the same inflection of speech of the other Hyhborn's. I couldn't be sure, because I slipped into the nothingness again, and I didn't know how long I stayed there. It felt like a small eternity before I became aware of that featherlight touch along my arm—a thumb moving in the same slow, gentle circles just above my elbow. The touch wasn't hot this time, just comforting and . . . and disarming, stirring up a prickly sense of awareness I couldn't make sense of. I was too warm and comfortable to even try. I heard that same voice again, sounding as if it were on the other end of a narrow tunnel.

The man spoke again. "Want me to sit with her until she wakes up?"

"Offer is appreciated, Bas, but I'm fine where I am."

Some of the fog cleared then as that acute sense of awareness increased. That voice was closer, clearer. It was *him*. My Hyhborn lord who . . . What had happened? Flashes of memories broke through. The gardens full of softly glowing orbs. My intuition. Blood splattered along the pale blossoms—

"You sure?" Bas's voice was louder now. "Your time is better spent elsewhere."

"I know it is," the Lord responded. "But I'm quite enjoying the peace and quiet."

"And the scenery?" Bas remarked.

"That too."

A low, rough chuckle came from this Bas, and then there was the silence of unconsciousness again, and I welcomed it, feeling . . . feeling cared for.

Safe.

So I let myself slip away.

⤜⤜⤜

Slowly, I became aware of a pleasant scent. A woodsy, soft one. I also became aware of my head resting on something firm, but not nearly as hard as the ground, and then the distant singing of night birds and insects. My heart kicked up. I was still in the gardens, lying half on cool grass, but my head was—

The thumb on my arm stilled. "I think you're finally waking up, *na'laa*."

My eyes fluttered open and my breath caught. The Lord's face was above mine, cast mostly in shadow. Only a thin slice of moonlight cut through the canopy of limbs above us, glancing off his jaw and mouth.

He gave me a faint smile. "Hello."

Bits of what had happened came back in an instant, propelling me into action. Jackknifing upright, I scurried onto my hands and knees, backing away several feet.

"You should know by now." The Lord's hands fell to his lap—the lap my head had been resting in. "That I'm not going to harm you."

"You said you didn't care if my neck was snapped," I panted, arms and legs trembling with the rush of leftover adrenaline.

"That is what I said."

I stared at the shadows of his face, dumbfounded. "I helped you last night and you let him take me—"

"But I didn't let him take you, now did I?" He crossed an ankle of one long leg over the other. "If I had, you wouldn't be alive. He would've snapped your neck or ripped out your heart as he threatened."

He had a point. I could recognize that, but the fear and anger, the sense of betrayal and the icy panic, were flooding my system, chasing away that strange and completely idiotic feeling of safety, of being cared for.

I lifted a shaking hand to my throat, still able to feel Muriel's grip pressing in, bruising and crushing.

"Are you in pain?" the Lord asked.

"No." I gently prodded the skin as I rocked back on my haunches. The skin there was a little tender, but nothing extreme, which made no sense. I clearly remembered falling—no, being thrown aside and my head hitting something hard, then sudden, violent pain before the nothingness. I lifted my gaze to the Lord once more, recalling the warmth of his touch and the brush of something softer against my forehead.

"Contrary to what I led the dearly departed Muriel to believe, and unfortunately, you to also think, I didn't allow him to continue to use you as a shield," he said. "I stopped him, and you were caught in the middle of that."

The memory of something hard crashing into us—a flash of a hand landing on Muriel's arm—rose. "He . . . he threw me."

"Actually, that was me," the Lord corrected. "I was attempting to get you to a safe distance. I may have done so a bit too enthusiastically." His chin dipped, and the moonlight hit one high, sweeping cheekbone. "My apologies."

My heart hammered as I lowered my hand to hover a few inches above the plush grass. A bit too enthusiastically? I remembered that feeling of weightlessness—of flying. He'd thrown me aside as if I weighed nothing more than a small child, and there was nothing small about me. I swallowed hard as I started to look around us.

"Muriel is no more," the Lord shared.

That I figured. "There was another who was here. A . . . a Bas?"

"That was Bastian—Lord Bastian. He's left," he said. "We're alone, *na'laa*."

There was a skip in my breath. "I should be hurt. I should be . . ." I couldn't bring myself to say it. That I should be dead. I sat back on my ass. Or fell on it, landing in a puddle of moonlight. "Did you . . . did you kiss me again?"

"Excuse me?"

"Heal me," I clarified. "Did you heal me again?"

Across from me, the Lord uncrossed his ankles and drew one leg up. He lifted a shoulder. "I told you that *na'laa* means several things in my language."

I blinked, pressing my hand into the grass. His unwillingness to answer my question didn't pass by me. "I remember. You said it means 'brave one.'"

"It does." One arm dropped to rest on his bent knee. "It can also mean 'stubborn one.'" There was a hint of a smile in his voice. "Which makes the nickname all the more fitting."

My lips turned down at the corners. "And why would you think that?"

His fingers began to tap against the air. "Is that a serious question?"

"I'm not stubborn."

"I beg to differ," he said. "I clearly remember telling you to come to me. You didn't. Then I told you not to move and you then ran."

I stiffened, indignant. "I ran because I had just seen you put your hand into another's chest and incinerate them."

"But it was not your chest my hand went into, was it?" he countered.

"No, but—"

"But you ran anyway," he cut in. "Then when I told you to cease struggling since you would only harm yourself, you continued to do so."

I couldn't believe I had to explain any of this. "That's because he was crushing my neck."

"I wouldn't have allowed that."

"You had just said—"

"That I didn't care if he snapped your neck. I know what I said," he interrupted. *Again.* "And I didn't care about what he claimed, because I knew I would not allow that."

"How was I supposed to know that?" I exclaimed.

"Well, you gave me aid last night. What would that make me if I allowed you to become hurt? Oh, I know. A bastard."

My eyes narrowed.

"And because I'm a Deminyen," he said, as if that meant anything. "And we are your protectors." There was another pause. "Mostly."

I squelched the laugh threatening to escape. Yes. *Mostly.* "Muriel was going to harm me. He was—"

"Muriel was an idiot."

Irritation loosened my tongue, but I caught myself, snapping my mouth shut. This was a Hyhborn lord I was speaking to and he wasn't injured now.

His head tilted again. "You were going to say something?"

"No, I—"

"Yes, you were."

"Oh, my gods," I snapped. "I was going to ask you to stop interrupting me; however, that would be impossible because you keep doing it, so I'm trying to be respectful."

"Unlike . . . ?" Those fingers still danced at the air. "Unlike me?"

"You know? I think I liked you better when you didn't have the energy to speak."

"So, you liked me?"

"That's not what I said."

"That's exactly what you said."

"For fuck's sake," I hissed. "That wasn't what I meant."

The Lord laughed—and the sound was deep and . . . and nice. Unexpected. He hadn't laughed like that last night. "Did you know that *na'laa* has another use? For one who is . . . outspoken?"

Stubborn? Outspoken? "I think I prefer the 'brave' meaning."

"There is a fourth meaning," the Lord added.

"This word of yours has a lot of meanings," I muttered.

"Many," he murmured. "But the fourth is also used to describe someone who is ungrateful. That is also rather fitting, don't you think? I saved your life, and yet, you find me impolite."

I gaped at him.

"And I also sat here and waited until you woke up, just to make sure you were okay. Watching over you. Even let you use my body as a pillow." There it was again—the hint of the teasing smile I couldn't see but heard in his voice. "I think that was quite polite of me, especially since I didn't get to use your body as one last night."

"I clearly recall you asking for my help last night," I shot back. "Meanwhile, I didn't ask you to do any of those things."

"You would've helped even if I hadn't asked," he said, and I pressed my lips together. "Just as I did without you asking, even though I do have far more important things to attend to."

Anger hit my blood in a hot rush, loosening that *mouth*. "If you have far more important things to do, no one is stopping you. Your presence is not needed nor welcomed, *my lord*."

Those fingers stilled in the space above his knee as he shifted a little bit farther into the stream of moonlight. His mouth, the curve of his jaw, and his nose became more visible. His smile was wolfish.

My stomach hollowed as I became very still. There was a good chance I'd overstepped myself.

"You're right, *na'laa*. I don't *need* to be here," he said, almost as softly as when he had spoken to the Hyhborn in those mere seconds before he ended their existence. "I *want* to be here."

I felt it then. His gaze. Even though I couldn't see his eyes, I could feel his stare drifting over my features, then down. A tingling wave of warmth followed.

"After all," he said, voice thicker, smoother. "The scenery is quite lovely."

I glanced down, seeing that the midnight-blue robe had come unbelted at some point and the ivory nightgown was visible underneath. It was basically translucent in the moonlight, leaving much of my breasts clearly visible beneath the wispy gown.

"I'm staring. I know," the Lord said. "And I'm also aware of how *impolite* I'm being now."

Slowly, I lifted my gaze to him. It was known that the Hyhborn enjoyed only two things equally. Violence and . . . and sex. I shouldn't be surprised, especially when I had seen how he was the night before, but he was a Hyhborn lord, and now, with him uninjured and in the gardens, I . . . I was just some lowborn—

Come to think of it, what were he and the other two doing in these gardens? Hyhborn tended to interact with lowborn more freely and . . . intimately during the Feasts, even Hyhborn lords, but the Feasts were quite a ways off from beginning.

"Muriel?" I said. "He was the one I heard Finn and Mickie speak of."

"He was."

I dragged my teeth over my lower lip. "And Finn? Mickie?" There was a beat of silence. "The fires? That's where they ended up?"

"I think you know the answer to that."

I did. "How did you end up in the gardens?"

"I'd sent a message to Nathaniel to meet, knowing Muriel is never far from his brother," he answered. "As luck would have it, this is where Nathaniel requested to meet."

Then that had to mean the Hyhborn brothers were from Primvera.

"You said you liked those little balls of light?" he said, drawing me from my thoughts, and it took a moment for me to realize he was responding to what I'd said to him and Muriel. "I assume you were speaking of the *sōls*."

"Souls?" I whispered, surprised enough to ask.

"Not souls of mortals." That faint grin appeared again. "But *sōls* of all that is around you. The tree we sit beneath. The grass. The blooms of the wisteria currently in your hair."

"Oh." My hand lifted out of reflex. I ran my hand down my braid until I felt something soft and dewy. I pulled the petal free, cringing. "I didn't know that."

He chuckled again. The sound was still nice, which seemed completely at odds with, well, everything. "I'm sure the blossom was pleased to find itself being attached to such a lovely mortal. Though, I can think of far more interesting places I would've *attached* myself to."

I blinked once.

Then twice.

And then my mind decided to take a quick jaunt where it shouldn't go, conjuring up all those interesting places. A sudden aching twist curled deep in my stomach. I shifted on the grass, left unsteady by the intense pulse of desire—by yet another stark reminder of *what* he was.

"So, were you looking for the *sōls?*" the Lord questioned, lifting a hand. He made a soft humming noise—a gentle, melodic sound.

A heartbeat later, a buttery glow appeared in the tree above us, slowly descending through the branches and vines. Then another. And another. My lips parted. A little over a half dozen floated through the trees.

"You can call them to you?" I asked.

"Of course," he answered. "We are a part of everything that surrounds us. They are a part of us."

I watched as one of the *sōls* drifted above me. "They're beautiful."

"They appreciate you saying so."

A brow rose. "They can understand me?"

"They can." He lifted his chin, gesturing to one of the *sōls.* "See how their lights have grown brighter?"

I nodded.

"That's how you know."

"Oh." My fingers tingled with the urge to reach out and touch one without the gloves, but I figured that was pushing it. I peeked at the Lord, wishing I could see more of his face. His eyes. But it was probably a blessing that I couldn't at this point. "What . . . what is your name?"

"Thorne."

There was a strange whooshing motion throughout my chest. After all these years, I finally had a name for him. I didn't know how to think of that, but it felt strangely life-altering.

I cleared my throat. "I . . . I should probably be on my way."

He inclined his head. "Probably."

Relieved yet unnerved that he'd agreed, I rose.

"But I would be bereft if you did," he added, and I seriously doubted that. "I have so many questions."

I halted. "About?"

He stood so quickly, I hadn't seen him move. One minute he was sitting and then he was standing. "About you, of course."

My heart gave a sharp lurch. "There's not much to know about me."

"I cannot believe that's true." He was nearly in the shadows of the wisteria now, but somehow he seemed closer. "I'm willing to bet there is, starting with how we met."

A fine shiver skated across the back of my skull and down my spine. The ground felt like it was shifting again. "How . . . how we met?"

"Tonight," he clarified. "Is this how you normally spend your nights? Alone, chasing *sōls* when you're not rescuing those in distress?"

"Yes," I admitted. "I normally don't travel this part of the gardens at night."

"But tonight was different."

I nodded, once again deciding to err on the side of half truth. "I heard voices and was concerned that something bad might happen."

"So you decided to intervene? Again?" The surprise was evident in his voice. "With no weapon, and still, apparently no knowledge of how to defend yourself?"

My lips pursed. "I suppose so."

There was a moment of silence. "Once more, you've proven just how brave you are."

"I just . . . I just did what I thought was right."

"And that often takes the most bravery, doesn't it?"

I nodded, telling myself I needed to shut down this conversation. There was a whole slew of reasons why. It had to be late, but I hesitated. . . .

That smile of his appeared once more. The slight, tight curve of his lips, and again, there was a sharp, taut curl low in my belly. My mouth dried a little.

"I'm assuming you call Archwood Manor your home?" Lord Thorne asked, and although I hadn't seen him move, he was closer.

I nodded. "I . . . I spend a lot of time in these gardens," I shared, and I wasn't even sure why except for the edgy nervousness that always led to me rambling. "That's why you smelled catmint on me."

"I wouldn't have even entered them if it had not been for Nathaniel," he said, head turning as he scanned the gardens. "Strange how that worked out." His gaze returned to me. "With you."

Yes, it was strange.

"I'm sorry about your . . ." Friends? It was obvious that neither Muriel nor Nathaniel had been a friend. "I'm sorry about what happened with them."

His head turned back to mine as he went quiet. It was the same reaction he'd had the night before when I apologized for what was done to him.

I swallowed. "There's something I've been wondering all day about Muriel. He set you up, didn't he?"

Lord Thorne nodded.

"Why would a Hyhborn be involved in the shadow market?"

He was quiet for several moments. "That's a good question. One I would like to know the answer to, but I do have another question for you."

"What is that?"

One of the vines moved to the side as, this time, I saw him step forward. He hadn't touched the vine, but as he'd said, he was part of the realm in a way lowborn could never be. "How did you spend your day wondering why a Hyhborn would be involved in the shadow market when you did not know until tonight that he was a Hyhborn?"

Shit.

My heart tripped over itself. "I . . . I just assumed he was." My thoughts raced. "You said you were to meet him at the Twin Barrels. I figured it would be another Hyhborn."

"Ah." Another wisteria stem spun without his touch. "It should be I who apologized, for what you had to witness and experienced these last two nights. I'm sure that's not something you see every day."

"I . . . I wasn't expecting to find Hyhborn on the verge of killing one another."

He let out a dry laugh. "You may be surprised to know that isn't all that uncommon an occurrence."

My brows rose. I *was* surprised. Then again, I knew little of what occurred in the Hyhborn Courts.

"You must think I'm a monster now?"

"No, that hasn't changed. I mean, he was going to stab you,

which seemed like a really poorly thought-out decision based on how that turned out for him. And well, Muriel was going to kill me, so fuck him," I went on, flushing at his low chuckle. "Why did he set you up?"

"Besides the fact he was a fool? He was scared."

"Of?"

"Me." One of the *sōls* moved over his shoulder, nearly grazing mine as it passed us by. "So, he thought it best to have me dealt with."

I didn't really know Lord Thorne at all, but he didn't strike me as the type one attempted to force into anything. "I guess both were making more than one poorly thought-out choice tonight."

"You've guessed right." His fingers drifted over one of the wisteria stems once more.

However, it seemed to me that it was more than Muriel just being afraid of Lord Thorne. Granted, that would be enough reason for most, but they'd spoken in those brief moments as if they were alluding to something else—something that was likely not my business, but I was curious.

"Well, I . . . I hope you find whatever it is you were looking for," I told him, and his head tilted again. "It sounded like you were looking for something that he claimed to have information on."

"Yes, but now I'm not sure if he spoke the truth or not."

I started to ask what it was that would possibly anger the King, but Lord Thorne touched a wisteria blossom, drawing my gaze as his fingers drew them down the length of the vine, not dislodging a single blossom.

Another *sōl* appeared, joining the other as they floated over us, casting enough light that when Lord Thorne turned his head toward me fully, I finally saw his face clearly once more.

A tingling sensation started at the base of my neck and spread throughout the entirety of my body as my gaze lifted to the golden-brown hair brushing against powerful shoulders and a throat the color of warm sand.

As a young girl, I'd found him to be beautiful and terrifying.

And that hadn't changed.

A lock of hair fell across his cheek as an eyebrow a shade or two darker than that wavy lock of hair rose. "Are you all right?"

I gave a small jerk. "Yes. I'm just tired. It's been a strange two nights."

He stared at me for a moment. "That it has."

I swallowed. "I think I . . . I need to return to the manor."

Lord Thorne was silent, watching me closely. Intently.

Heart thumping, I took another step back. "I appreciate that you made sure I . . . I didn't die back there and, um, that you watched over me."

His head straightened. "So, you *are* appreciative of the aid you didn't ask for?"

"Of course—" I cut myself off, seeing the teasing lift of his lips. "You still didn't have to."

"I know."

I held his stare for a moment, then nodded. "Good night," I whispered.

I started to turn away.

"Na'laa?"

I twisted toward him, gasping as I jerked back, bumping into a nearby wisteria. Lord Thorne stood less than a foot before me, the trailing blossoms behind him still, completely undisturbed. I hadn't even heard him move. He towered over me in the darkness of the tree, blocking out all traces of moonlight. My hands fell to my sides, palms pressing against the rough bark.

"There is something I must ask of you before you go," he said.

The shallow breath I took was full of his woodsy, soft scent. What was that scent? I jolted at the unexpected touch of his hands on my shoulders. "What?"

"What you saw here tonight?" His hands coasted down my arms. The touch was light, but immediately sent my pulse racing. He reached my wrists. "With Muriel and Nathaniel? Do not speak of it."

I shivered as his hands slid to my hips. The nightgown was no barrier against the warmth of his palms. His touch . . . it felt branding. "O-Of course."

"To anyone," he insisted, his hands leaving my hips and going to the halves of my robe. I sucked in a heady gasp of air as his knuckles brushed the curve of my stomach. He folded the robe closed, then found the sash.

I held my breath as he tied the sash just below my breasts. "I won't."

Remaining completely still as he finished with the sash, I felt my pulse pound as he then took ahold of my wrist and lifted it to his mouth. I couldn't move. It wasn't fear or distress that held me in place, and it should be.

Yet I wasn't afraid.

It was . . . was an emotion I couldn't name or describe as he turned my hand over, pressing his lips to the center of my palm, just as he had done the night before. The feel of his lips against my skin was a shock to the senses. They were soft and gentle, yet firm and unyielding, and when he lowered my hand, his breath traced the curve of my cheek until our mouths were mere inches apart.

Was he going to kiss me?

For one chaotic moment, an array of sensations assailed me— disbelief and wanting, panic and yearning. My heart hammered in confusion. I didn't want to be kissed by a Hyhborn lord, especially one who currently felt vaguely threatening.

But I didn't turn my head away when his breath danced over my lips. I knew in that moment what I'd discovered several times throughout my life: there had to be something seriously wrong with me. My eyes started to drift shut—

A cool wind kissed the nape of my neck.

Lord Thorne stilled.

Eyes opening, I felt that chill travel across my body. The night birds no longer sang. The entire garden was eerily silent, and as I glanced around, I saw that even the *sōls* seemed to have abandoned the area as that earlier feeling returned—the icy thickening of the air.

"Return to your home." Lord Thorne's voice was cooler and harder, falling against my skin like frozen rain. "Do so quickly, *na'laa*. There are things moving in the garden now that will find your flesh as tasty as I find it lovely."

My stomach lurched. "Will you be okay?"

Lord Thorne stilled, and I supposed my question had rendered him speechless. It had also shocked me. Why would I be worried when I'd seen him incinerate another Hyhborn? Or why would I even care if he was okay? Because he had helped Grady and me once before? It felt like more than that, though.

"Of course," he promised. "You need to hurry." His hand firmed against my neck, then he let go.

I stumbled back, heart thundering. I opened my mouth—

"Go, na'laa."

Trembling, I backed away and then I turned—I turned and ran, unsure of what unsettled me more. If it was the sounds of heavy wings beating at the night sky or if it was the inexplicable feeling that I shouldn't be running.

That I should be standing at his side, facing what was coming.

CHAPTER 11

"How many?" the Baron demanded as he paced the length of one of the numerous receiving chambers near the Great Chamber. Only one tail of his crisp white shirt was tucked into the tan breeches he wore. His dark hair appeared as if he'd run his hands through it several times that morning, leaving it sticking up in different directions. "How many of my men were killed last night?"

"Three are confirmed to be deceased," Magistrate Kidder responded from where he sat, his hands gripping his knees until his knuckles were bleached white. "But there were . . . pieces found along the outside of the manor wall that have led us to believe there may be two or more yet unconfirmed."

Behind the gray-haired magistrate, Hymel frowned.

"Pieces?" Claude spun toward the Magistrate as my gaze flickered to the doorway, briefly meeting Grady's. "What do you mean by *pieces?*"

"Well, to be more exact, there were additional limbs that outnumbered those accounted for." Magistrate Kidder's complexion was nearly as pale as the Baron's shirt. "One leg and two additional arms."

"Fuck," Hymel muttered, lip curling.

The bite of cold meat sandwich I'd swallowed mere minutes ago immediately soured in my stomach. I slowly placed the fork and knife onto the table, immensely regretting not having taken my lunch in my quarters. But I hadn't been prepared for Claude to storm into the space with the Magistrate in tow. Nor had I been prepared to learn that three of the Baron's guards had been killed last night. Or four. Or five.

Claude grabbed a decanter from the credenza and drank straight from it. "How long before your people can find and clean up the remains that belonged to those additional arms and legs?" He set the decanter down heavily. "Guests have already begun to arrive for this evening's festivities. The last thing I need is for any of them to stumble upon a random head or torso among the roses."

I briefly closed my eyes, more disgusted by the Baron's somewhat surprising utter lack of care regarding who those pieces belonged to than I was with the grotesque topic of conversation.

"I have several men out there right now, searching for possible remains," the Magistrate assured him. "But I would suggest you close the gardens for the next several hours."

"No shit," Claude muttered, dragging his hand through his hair again. The water in my glass began to tremble as he started pacing again. "You've seen the bodies, right?"

Magistrate Kidder's throat bobbed as he nodded. "And I won't unsee any of it."

Claude crossed in front of the window, momentarily blocking the sunlight. "What do you think caused this?"

"Likely what your cousin thinks and what the others reported seeing." The Magistrate glanced back at Hymel. *"Ni'meres."*

A shudder ran through me as I recalled the sound of wings beating against the air. I had to agree with what Hymel and the other guards were saying.

Ni'meres were another type of Hyhborn, the kind lowborn rarely dealt with or saw. I'd only ever seen them once before, when Grady and I were just kids, after leaving Union City. The stagecoach driver had spotted them on the road, circling a portion of the Wychwoods. They were something straight from a nightmare—a creature with a wingspan of over seven feet and talons longer and sharper than the claws of a bear. From the neck down, they resembled extraordinarily large eagles that stood nearly four feet tall.

But their head was that of a mortal.

"But why the fuck would *ni'meres* attack my men?" Claude demanded. "Don't they only attack when someone comes too close to where they're nesting?"

"I don't think they were the target." Grady spoke up from where he stood at the doors. "That's what Osmund said this morning. That the *ni'meres* were heading for something in the gardens, and those patrolling the wall were unfortunately in the way. Grell and Osmund were on the ground when they hit."

Claude passed by my table. "Then do you know what could've been in the gardens, that drew them?"

Now my stomach churned for an entirely different reason. Something had been in the gardens. My Hyhborn lord—no, he wasn't mine. I really needed to stop with that. I picked up the glass of water and took several gulps.

"That I can't answer," Grady responded, his gaze briefly flicking to mine. I shrank a little in my seat. "None of the others saw anything out of the ordinary before they swarmed the gardens."

Swarmed.

My hand shook slightly as I placed the glass down. A Hyhborn lord was a powerful being, but there had to be at least a dozen or more *ni'meres*. How could Lord Thorne have fought them off? But he had to have, because if not, they would have found him.

Unless those extra limbs belonged to him.

Worry festered, knotting in my chest as I set my glass down.

"Gods damn, *ni'meres*," Claude muttered, shaking his head. "What next? The *nix*?"

I shuddered. Gods, I hoped not.

"*Ni'meres* behaving like that?" Hymel spoke up, frowning. "It's rather unheard of, isn't it?"

"A lot of unheard-of things have been happening," Magistrate Kidder replied.

Claude stopped, looking at the older man. "Care to add more detail to that?"

"I've been hearing rumors of Hyhborn fighting," the Magistrate began. "There've been reports of it happening in other cities. Just the other week, I heard that there had been quite the skirmish between them in Urbane last month."

My brows knitted in a frown. Urbane was in the Lowlands territory, not all that far from the Hyhborn Court of Augustine, which also served as the capital of Caelum. I thought of what Lord Thorne had said when it came to Hyhborn on the verge of killing one another. Apparently it wasn't out of the ordinary in their Courts, but it was rare to hear of it happening in front of the lowborn.

"Several were killed," Magistrate Kidder added. "As well as a few lowborn who were unfortunately in the wrong place at the wrong time."

"Do we know what they are fighting about?" Claude asked.

"That I haven't heard." The Magistrate scratched at his jaw. "But if I do hear anything, I will let you know."

"Thank you." Claude glanced over at me, his expression un-readable. He crossed his arms. "I want the gardens cleared by this evening." He faced the Magistrate. "I don't want anything left be-hind, not even a fingernail."

"Will do." Magistrate Kidder got to his feet and strode stiffly out of the chamber, not looking in my direction. He hadn't once since he'd entered. I didn't need intuition to know that he thought I was nothing more than a well-kept whore that he'd have to pay for the pleasure of even looking upon.

Whatever.

The moment the door closed behind the Magistrate, the Baron turned to me. His features were so tensed that his mouth was noth-ing more than a slash. The Baron was clearly in a mood, and right-fully so. There *were* body parts in his gardens.

"Tell me, my pet, with all your intuition and second sight," he said, arms at his sides, "you didn't see a horde of *ni'meres* descending to wreak havoc on my gardens?"

"For her to have seen that, she would have to actually be useful," Hymel remarked, crossing his arms over his chest. Over his shoul-der, I saw Grady eyeing the back of his head like he wished to knock it off his shoulders. "And beyond parlor tricks and good instincts, she isn't good for much, cousin."

Claude's head swung toward Hymel. "Shut up."

A ruddy flush hit Hymel's cheeks. He liked to run his mouth, but he knew that what I did had nothing to do with parlor tricks or illusion. He was just being an ass, as per usual.

So I ignored him, *as per usual.*

Claude faced me. "Lis?"

"It doesn't work like that," I reminded him. "You know—" I jumped as Claude lunged forward, swiping his arm across the table. The glass of water and plate of tiny triangle-sliced sandwiches went flying onto the hardwood floors.

My jaw unlocked in surprise as I stared at the mess on the floor. Claude had a temper. Most *caelestias* did. I'd seen him throw a glass or two before. Expensive bottles of wine had hit the ground more than once, but he'd never acted that way toward me.

"Yes," Claude hissed inches from my face as he planted his hands on the table. I saw Grady start to step forward, but he stopped himself when I gave a curt shake of my head. "I know it doesn't work that way. You can't see anything dealing with the Hyhborn, but . . ." His gaze locked on to mine. "But I also know that isn't always the case. Sometimes you get vague impressions, and I also know you can't see what you are a part of."

My fingers dug into the skirt of my gown as something occurred to me. Last night I had seen what was about to happen regarding Muriel and Lord Thorne—the blood splattered on the wisteria blossoms. It hadn't occurred to me then. Was it because it involved Lord Thorne?

"So, tell me, my pet." He smiled, snapping me out of my realization. Or tried to. It was more of a grimace. "Were you involved in this?"

"No!" I exclaimed. Shock rolled through me as I stared at him. It wasn't even because I was, *somewhat*, involved in what happened last night. But because he would even think I had anything to do with freaking *ni'meres*. "I had nothing to do with that. I didn't even know there were *ni'meres* in Archwood."

The Baron eyed me for several moments and then pushed off the table, rattling the remaining utensils. "There aren't *ni'meres* in Archwood," he said, nostrils flaring as he took a step back, nearly stepping in the food. "But there are some in Primvera. That is where they likely came from." He stared down at the mess he'd created, pink spreading across his cheeks. "Either way," he said, shoving the untucked tail of his shirt into his breeches. "Those *ni'meres* were obviously unhappy with something in that garden."

More like unhappy with *someone*.

"Make sure that magistrate does his job," he said to Hymel before stopping and coming back to where I sat. His throat bobbed as he stared down at me. "I'm sorry for losing my temper. I shouldn't have done that. It's not because I was angry with you."

I said nothing, eyeing him warily.

He exhaled roughly. "I can retrieve a fresh plate of food for you."

The Baron sounded like he was truly sorry. Not that it made his outburst justified. "It's okay," I said with a smile, because it had to be.

The Baron hesitated. "No, it's—" He stopped himself and took a deep breath. "I am sorry," he repeated, and then he started toward the door, stopping to speak to Grady. "Can you make sure this is cleaned up?"

Grady nodded.

I rose as the door closed behind the Baron and his cousin, turning to the disaster on the floor.

"I got it," Grady said roughly, approaching the table.

"It's my food." I knelt, beginning to retrieve the scattered slices of ham and cheese.

"Doesn't mean I can't help." Grady knelt across from me, picking up the plate. "What a waste of good food."

I nodded as I dropped a few of the pieces onto the plate he held, thinking there was a time when neither of us would've batted an eye at eating food that had fallen on the floor and been stepped on.

Finding a tomato, I cringed at the slimy dampness. "He's in a mood, isn't he?"

"Understatement of the year, Lis." His jaw worked as he picked up the cup and set it on the table. "That wasn't okay."

"I know." I briefly met his gaze. "He's not my lover," I reminded him.

"What is he to you? Your boss, who randomly gets far too friendly with you?"

"No, he's my boss who pretends to be more than he is." Probably wished he were, too—wished he felt more for me, that is.

"Still doesn't make it okay."

I nodded, scooping up the last piece of food, placing it on the plate as I rose. "But it's not every day you have *ni'meres* swarming your gardens."

Grady snorted. "Thank the gods." He picked up a piece of bread. "I would've pissed myself if I had been out there, on the wall, and saw them coming."

"No, you wouldn't have."

He pinned me with a stare, brows raised.

"Okay." I laughed. "You would've done that and then fought them off."

"No, I would have done that and then run, or pissed myself while running, which is the only sensible thing when faced with something like a *ni'mere*."

Shaking my head, I picked up the last bit of food and dropped it on the plate Grady was holding. I started to rise when I noticed an angry, shiny reddish-brown patch of skin on Grady's arm, just below his wrist. I reached for his hand, but caught myself. My gaze flew to his. "What happened to your arm?"

"What?" He glanced down. "Oh. It's nothing. I was making a new blade and my hand slipped. Got too close to the heat."

"Gods, Grady. That looks painful. Have you put anything on it?" Immediately, I started thinking of the different poultices that could be used. "I can—"

"I already used the stuff you made last time. See?" He tilted his arm toward the light. "The sheen? It's from the aloe stuff you made."

"You need to use more than that." I took the plate from him, placing it on the table. "And you should cover it when you're outside, especially when you're working in the shop."

"Yes, Mother," Grady replied dryly.

Eyeing his wound, I was reminded of something. "Have you talked to Claude about taking over for his blacksmith? Danil should be retiring soon, right? And with what happened to Jac . . ."

"I haven't." Grady turned away.

My eyes narrowed. "But you will, right?"

One shoulder lifted.

"I can ask him—"

"Don't do that." Grady faced me.

"Why not?" I crossed my arms. "You're good at that—"

"I'm good at what I do now."

"Yeah, but you actually enjoy working with iron and steel. It's rare that someone is good at something they enjoy doing." I watched him fiddle with the leather strap across his chest, holding one of the blades I knew he had crafted himself. "You need to ask Claude. He's not going to tell you no."

"I know. I will." He was quiet for a moment. "You're going to hate what I say next, but you should probably stay out of the gardens for a little while."

"Yeah, probably." I crossed the chamber, the gown snapping at my heels. I stared out the window, my thoughts drifting back to that odd feeling I had last night. That I should've stayed by his side.

It was still there, like a shadow in the back of my mind. That I should be out there.

With *him.*

Where I belonged.

CHAPTER 12

In the days that followed, things had calmed around the manor and within Archwood. There had been no more *ni'mere* attacks or word concerning the Iron Knights and the Westlands' princess, nor had I found any more guards involved in the shadow-market trade.

Things were normal.

I spent time in the gardens and with Naomi, sat with Grady in the evenings. I joined Claude for his suppers and rode Iris through the meadows between the manor and the city, and I found pleasure in these things, like a good little lowborn.

But each night, I went into the gardens, and I tried to convince myself that it wasn't because of him. That I wasn't out there because I hoped to find the Hyhborn lord among the wisteria blossoms. That it had nothing to do with the odd feeling that haunted me as days turned into weeks.

Lord Thorne hadn't returned, but that feeling I'd had the first time we met remained. I knew I would see him again.

Tonight I'd stayed in my quarters, not feeling up to socializing. I was in a weird mood; one I couldn't quite decipher. Alone, I'd spent much of the evening watching the *sōls* drifting across the lawn and into the gardens while the hum of music from the lawn followed the warm breeze. I'd even gone to bed at an unreasonably early time, but I'd woken suddenly, sometime before midnight, heart racing. It was like waking from a nightmare, but I wasn't even sure I'd been asleep long enough to dream.

That had been half an hour ago, and unable to fall back asleep, I returned to my chair, a book unopened in my lap as I watched the *sōls*. I revisited that odd feeling that remained, like I'd done so many times since I'd last seen Lord Thorne. I just couldn't figure it out, and it preyed upon my mind. Why would I think I needed to remain by his side when the *ni'meres* arrived? Wasn't like I would've been much help, unless screaming frightened them away.

Why did I feel like I . . . I no longer belonged where I was, more so than normal? I was beginning to think that was the source of my mood tonight—

A loud series of raps caused me to give a little jump. I twisted toward the door as I heard Grady call out, "Lis? You in there?"

"Coming." I rose, tightening the sash on my robe. Worry sprang to life as I crossed the narrow space, opening the door. I could think of only two reasons Grady would come to my chambers at this time of night. Sometimes it was just to share the same bed when he was having trouble sleeping—a comfort born out of the years of doing so, and which helped, since neither of us slept all that well. The other reason was, well, potentially stressful.

Grady stood alone in the dimly lit hallway. "The Baron has summoned you."

My shoulders tensed. "Hell," I muttered, not wasting time changing into more suitable clothing. I stepped out into the hall and closed the door behind me as I glanced up at Grady. "Do you know why?"

"I don't," he answered. "All I do know is that he was in the solarium when Hymel came to get him. He left for about a half an hour, then came back and told me to retrieve you."

I drew my lower lip between my teeth. The options were truly limitless when it came to Claude, but I seriously doubted he'd want me to take part in whatever celebrations were occurring at this hour.

Grady led me through the back halls of the manor, the ones traveled only by staff and those who didn't want to risk the chance of running into anyone. We ended up at the small antechamber that sat behind the Great Chamber.

There were a few people in the antechamber, but my attention focused on Claude. I hadn't seen him since his earlier temper tantrum, and I wondered if he too was thinking of that when our eyes met, because his cheeks flushed. I didn't think it had anything to do with the blonde half sprawled in his lap. Her eyes were unfocused as

Claude tapped her on the hip, urging her to rise. She half slid onto the empty portion of the settee, and I had a feeling she'd been enjoying the laudanum-laced wine that was often served for the Baron's closest friends.

"How are you feeling, pet?" the Baron asked as I approached him.

Immediately, I caught the sickly sweet stench of Midnight Oil, and I had to stop myself from launching into a tirade. "Well. What is going on?"

"I'm not sure. We have unanticipated guests," he shared as he guided me away from the settee, his steps sluggish. He kept his voice low as Grady approached us. "It is a member of the Royal Court that has requested shelter for him and three others for the evening."

Every part of my being tensed. Members of the Royal Court were often chancellors. "That is uncommon."

"My sentiments exactly." We stepped back from those in the chamber. "He isn't saying why he's here, claiming that he'll speak with me in the morning when . . ."

"When what?" I asked when he trailed off.

"When, as he said, 'I'm of clear mind' or some other variation of that." Claude's cheeks deepened in color, and I suddenly understood his flush. I too would be embarrassed if a chancellor arrived with potentially important business to discuss and I was too intoxicated or high to do so. He cleared his throat, chin lifting. "I would like for you to go to him and see if you can ferret out his reasoning for being here."

Aware of others around us, I kept my voice low. "You can't wait to find out yourself in the morning?"

"It's not the waiting that will keep me up all night stressed. It's not knowing what he wants by the time we meet. I need to be prepared for this meeting." He sounded positively aghast at the notion. "You already know how hard it is for me to sleep."

It was hard for all of us to sleep, but I didn't think the Baron was aware of that.

"I am . . ." He dipped his head as he brushed a strand of hair back from my shoulder. "I am worried that he brings word from the

Royal Throne—the King. I may be a . . . tad bit late on the quarterly tithes."

"For fuck's sake," I muttered.

A rather high-pitched giggle escaped Claude, and my brows shot up as I stared at him. "Sorry," he murmured, lips twitching. "I need your special aid, pet."

What Claude needed was to indulge less in his party favors and stop spending coin on frivolous bullshit.

But what none of us, those who relied on him keeping his shit together, needed was for Claude to get himself even more worked up. That would likely result in him smoking more of the Midnight Oil and being a complete mess by the time he was to speak with the chancellor of the Royal Court. And if this was because he'd failed to pay his quarterly taxes, Claude would need to be in top form to plead for any necessary forbearance *and* forgiveness.

"Okay," I sighed. "I will do this."

A toothy smile appeared. "Thank you—"

"*If* you promise me that you will go to bed," I interrupted. "You need to rest."

"Of course," he agreed too quickly. "That is the plan."

I eyed him.

"I swear," he added, a flop of dark hair falling over his forehead. "I want to be fresh as aired laundry—" He giggled again, this time at himself. "I will be sleeping very soon."

"You better," I warned.

"You are a rare jewel," he exclaimed, pressing a quick kiss to my forehead. "Enjoy yourself, Lis."

The Baron patted my shoulder again, and I turned from him before I did something reckless, like knocking him on his ass.

Followed by Grady, I crossed the antechamber, catching sight of Naomi. Her gaze briefly met mine as I passed. I glanced pointedly in Claude's direction, and she rolled her eyes, but nodded. This wasn't the first time she was tasked with making sure the Baron made it to his bed *alone*. She wheeled toward Claude, a laugh spilling from her lips—beautiful, but I caught the hint of annoyance in the sound.

For some reason I recalled the first time I'd been asked to do whatever it took to ensure I could gain what Claude wanted, which required me to behave as a courtesan. It had been Naomi who had taken me aside, took what limited knowledge I had when it came to the various degrees of intimacy, and prepared me for what was to come. After all, I had been a virgin before meeting Claude, having experienced only a few hasty gropings that ended with me hearing things I'd wished I hadn't.

But Naomi had also prepared me with something even Claude was unaware of. Knowledge of how the Long Night could be used. Grady always carried a small pouch of it in the breast pocket of his tunic. With it, I could choose exactly how far I wished the evening to progress.

Sadly, I'd used the Long Night more often than not, and tonight would likely be no different.

"I need to see Maven," I told Grady when we left the antechamber.

Grady's shoulders tensed, but he nodded. Entering another narrow, even less traveled hall, we stopped in front of a rounded, wooden door set within an alcove. Like always, the robed figure of the silver-haired Maven answered at the sound of the knock. I walked into her candlelit chamber, leaving Grady in the hall, his jaw so hard I wouldn't be surprised if he cracked his molars.

One look around the space and I saw that she had been expecting me, meaning that either Claude or Hymel had already alerted her. Annoyance flashed. What would Claude have done if I had said no?

But why would he have thought that I would? I didn't tell him no. Doing so rarely crossed my mind, because this was how I made sure I was invaluable to the Baron. This was how I ensured that Grady and I would never end up back on the streets. So, I wasn't sure whom I should be more annoyed with. Me or him?

Maven's space was more of a preparation chamber, outfitted with all the necessities—a clawfoot tub filled with steaming, scented water, brushes and racks of clothing. There was a narrow table where more intense preparation occurred—the waxing and plucking of all the hair on my body except for what grew from my scalp. Claude preferred that long, so it reached my waist now. I didn't mind the length of hair on my head, but if I ever decided to leave, I was never going to touch a single piece of hair anyplace else again. Thankfully the removal of body hair had already routinely taken place.

I went to the tub, disrobing in the silence. Maven wasn't known for being talkative. She didn't speak. Not once as the nightgown slipped from my shoulders and slid over my hips, or while I stepped into the tub and bathed myself. She just waited, a towel held in those crooked fingers, her gaze rheumy but alert.

Naomi had once told me that Maven was the Baron's grand-mother on his father's side, but Valentino, one of the other par-amours, said that she was the widowed wife of one of the past groundskeepers. Lindie, a cook at the manor, claimed that Maven had been a mistress of one of the past Barons, but I was of the opin-ion that she was a wraith that somehow had managed to keep the flesh on her bones. I glanced at the papery thin skin of her forearms. She *barely* kept the flesh on her bones.

Once I'd finished in the tub, she dried me off as roughly as hu-manly possible. Maven also wasn't known for her gentleness. I stood naked, toes curling against the floor as she shuffled to the rack. The hangers clanged off one another as she flipped through the clothing, eventually pulling out a robe that was the color between cyan and blue. The shade of the Midlands' cloudless sky.

I shoved my arms into the wrapper and stood still as she knotted the sash so tightly the fabric cut into the soft skin of my waist. One glance in the standing mirror confirmed what I already knew. The vee of the neckline was absurdly deep and the robe was more gossa-mer than cloth. If I walked in brighter light, the exact shade of the skin surrounding my nipple would be known.

Swallowing a sigh, I went to the stool, sitting so Maven could undo all the pins holding up my hair. She then brushed out the tan-gles, jerking my head back with each stroke. My nails dug into my palms throughout the whole process; I was sure I'd be half bald soon. When she finished, no more than an hour had passed. She opened the door, leaving me to rejoin Grady in the hall. She didn't follow. Her task was done for the night.

Neither Grady nor I spoke until we entered the silent hall leading to the various wings of the manor. Only the soft light of the moon streaming in through the windows lit our way, thank the gods.

Twisting my fingers around the sash, I stared ahead, breathing in the air scented with honeysuckle that flourished along the walls of the manor as I thought of other times I'd been asked to use my abilities. Usually it was a visiting baron or another member of the aristo. My intuition usually was able to warn whether the visitor could be trusted or if they were up to something. I could even sense more, if that was what Claude wanted. He liked to know what made the others tick so that he could use that in potential dealings.

"Here," Grady finally said, reaching into the breast pocket of his tunic, dropping a small coin-sized pouch into my palm. The laughter that usually filled his deep brown eyes was nowhere to be seen, nor were those boyishly charming dimples that had gotten him out of so much trouble when we were younger. "Find out what you need to know and get out."

I glanced down at the black pouch containing the Long Night. Claude's targets were never aware that they'd been drugged. The Long Night was odorless and tasteless. "Did you see who has come?"

"No. I only know of the chamber, but I'm assuming it's a chancellor." His nostrils flared. "I don't like this, Lis."

"I know." Curling my fingers around the pouch, I slipped it into the pocket of the robe, where the material was thankfully thicker. "But you shouldn't worry. I'll have it under control."

Lips pressed together, he shook his head as we walked a little farther, his hand clutching the hilt of his sword. We neared the east wing, which overlooked the courtyards and the sections of the gardens where the roses bloomed. The chambers here were stately, reserved only for those the Baron sought to impress.

I glanced up at Grady. The muscle along his jaw was ticking. "You understand that I don't have to do this. That I'm choosing to do this."

Grady's brows flew up. "Really?"

"Yes. I could've said no. Claude wouldn't have made me do it, and if I don't want things to progress, I'll use the Long Night once

I find out why this chancellor is here. Hopefully, it's not because Claude is late on his tithe, because we really don't need that on top of everything else to worry about," I said. "Tonight is no different than any other night."

The muscle continued to pulse at his jaw. "You speak as if this is not a big deal."

Folding my arms over my chest, I looked away. The thing was, these meetings were complicated, because sometimes it wasn't a big deal. Sometimes I *enjoyed* the touching. It wasn't like those I met under these circumstances were always bad, odious people. Often they were charming and interesting, and I . . . could touch them without the guilt of seeing or sensing what they likely wanted to keep hidden. I could shovel that blame onto Claude, and yeah, I knew how messed up that was. Deep down, I knew I still shared some of that guilt. Either way, I walked away from these encounters unharmed, and there had been only a few times I sensed things I felt like I'd never be able to erase the memory of.

Walking once more, there were just the sounds of his boots and my robe whispering against the stone floor until we came to a set of double doors.

"We're here," Grady said quietly. "If anything happens . . ."

"I scream," I told him—something I'd yet to have to do.

Grady stepped in to me, his hand moving to my arm. "Be careful," he whispered. "Please."

My heart squeezed. "I will be." I smiled at him. "It'll be okay."

Grady stiffened. "You keep saying that."

"And maybe you'll start believing me."

"Or maybe *you'll* start believing it."

I tensed. A weird mixture of sensation hit me—confusion and an emotion that scalded my insides, making me wonder if I shouldn't be okay with any of this. If I already knew the answer to that and my words were all false bravado and deflection. I turned from him, more than just a little unsettled. But now wasn't the time for deep introspection.

Because I was already a bit nervous. I was every time I did this. I liked to think anyone would be, because I never knew what was waiting on the other side of the walls. I wasted no more time, reaching for the gold ornate knobs. Unlocked as expected. I stepped inside an antechamber lit by a lone lamp placed by a deep-seated settee. The doors made no sound as I closed them behind me. I hesitated for only a few seconds as I scanned the space. It was empty except for the rich furnishings draped in lush fabrics and carved out of smooth, glossy wood, but there was . . . there was a presence here.

A tangible energy that coated my skin, eliciting a wave of goose bumps. My mouth dried as I turned to the rounded archway that led to the bedchambers. Fingers still twisting the sash nervously between them, I started forward even as unease resurfaced.

I assumed that whoever was here would be expecting company. Surely, Claude would've made sure of that. After all, the doors were unlocked. But I heard nothing as I entered the darkened bedchamber. My steps slowed as I allowed my vision to adjust to the darkness. I inched closer, making out the door leading to the bathing chamber left slightly ajar. Power also drenched the walls and floor. Tiny shivers coursed over my skin. My heart began to pound even faster. I knew this feeling, and there was a scent here. A soft, woodsy aroma that reminded me of—

Suddenly, I could no longer see the door of the bathing chamber. The room had become pitch black, leaving me blind, and that . . . yeah, that wasn't normal. I started to take a step back.

A rush of warm air stirred the edges of my robe. My fingers slipped away from the sash as I went completely still, holding my breath. The nape of my neck tingled. The air of the chamber shifted, thickened and became electrified, reminding me of the atmosphere right before lightning struck.

I wasn't alone in the utter, unnatural darkness. The breath in my lungs left me in one ragged exhale as an acute awareness pressed against the entire right side of my body. It was like I was suddenly standing too close to open flames. Instinct kicked in, not the kind fueled by my abilities but the kind fueled by pure need to survive. It screamed that I flee.

My trembling lips parted to speak or maybe scream, but before a single sound could escape, an arm came around my waist, jerking me back against a hard wall of muscle. I was lifted until my feet no longer touched the floor—until they dangled several *inches* from the floor.

There was no mortal I knew who could lift me so easily, and that could only mean—

"I have two questions, and each answer better be honest," a deep voice drawled, his cadence of speech almost relaxed but the tone low in warning, at the same instant a warm, callused hand pressed on the expanse of skin above my breasts, forcing my back against a . . . a chest. "What are you doing in my quarters?" Breath stirred the wisps of hair at my temple. "And do you have a death wish?"

CHAPTER 13

A Hyhborn.

The Baron had sent me to the quarters of a freaking *Hyhborn*.

And not just any Hyhborn. Him.

Lord Thorne.

I grasped his forearm. My fingers met smooth, crisp linen. The hold on me was nothing like when Muriel had grabbed me, but it still caused panic to ripple through me.

"That's not an answer," Lord Thorne chided softly.

Then he moved.

In two steps, he had me pinned, my cheek plastered against the wall and my arms trapped. His strength was terrifying, sending my pulse into a frantic pace. I pushed back against him, trying to lower my feet to the floor. He pressed in, the full length of his body encaging mine.

"I suggest that you try again," he said, his cheek grazing mine. "You're getting a very rare, very generous offer. I suggest you don't throw it away."

"It's me," I said. "We've—"

"I know it's you," he interrupted, and my eyes went wide. "But that doesn't answer my questions, *na'laa*."

It took me a heartbeat to remember. "I was sent to you."

"By?" The arm at my waist shifted, and I felt his hand open along the side of my waist and his fingers press into the thin robe.

"Baron Huntington. He said you were expecting company."

Lord Thorne went incredibly still behind me. I didn't even feel his chest rise against my back. "I was expecting no one."

My eyes slammed shut as anger boiled. *Fucking Claude.* Was he that high or drunk that he hadn't thought to warn me that he was sending me to a Hyhborn lord and not a chancellor? Or to even prepare him for my arrival? If I didn't end up dead tonight, I very well might kill Claude for this.

The hand above my chest moved—the same hand I'd seen incinerate a Hyhborn—and slid to the base of my throat. "And?"

I blinked, toes curling in the empty air. "And . . . what?"

His thumb and forefinger began to move along the sides of my throat in soft, almost . . . *gentle* sweeps. "And there is one more question, *na'laa*."

"Don't call me that," I snapped.

"But it's still so fitting and I enjoy how annoyed you get when I call you it," he murmured, and my mouth dropped open. "What's your answer to my second question?"

One more question? What was he—*Do you have a death wish?* My lips peeled back as that anger flamed deep in me. "No, I don't have a death wish." What came out of my mouth next weren't my wisest words. "But perhaps you do."

"Me?" Those fingers still moved, creating a warm friction that was . . . that was oddly and distressingly soothing. "I'm curious as to how I have a death wish."

"I'm a favorite of the Baron's," I said. "He would be most displeased if you were to break me."

Lord Thorne was silent for what felt like a small eternity, and then he laughed. He actually *laughed*, and it was a deep, husky sound that reverberated through me much like that animalistic sound he'd made. "Well." He drew the word out, those fingers stilling at my throat. "I wouldn't want to displease the honorable baron."

In any other situation, one where I wasn't being held what had to be at least a foot off the ground, I would've appreciated the mockery dripping from his tone.

"I'm interested though. What would the Baron do?" The fingers slipped from my throat to just below the shallow indent between my collarbones. The feel of his touch there and the palm that rested just above my still wildly beating heart was a jolt to my already scattered senses. "If I did break a . . . *favorite* of his?"

My mouth opened but nothing came out. What *could* the Baron do if he decided to harm me? Even as a *caelestia*, there was absolutely nothing, which was why Claude sending me to the Hyhborn lord like this was so unbelievable.

"He would . . ." I sighed. "He would pout."

That deep laugh came again, rumbling along my back and rear, causing my toes to curl even further. He was holding me entirely too close. "I wouldn't want that to happen."

Then Lord Thorne released me, but he did so slowly. *Painstakingly* slowly. I slid down the entire length of him, and it was a whole lot of length. I was uncomfortably aware of how the robe had snagged, catching between our bodies, and . . . and the feel of him. There was simply a lot of him. By the time my feet hit the floor, my legs were exposed all the way to the thighs. Luckily, the chamber was still dark, but not as fathomless as before.

"We keep meeting under the strangest circumstances," he noted. "I'm beginning to think fate is afoot."

"Fate?" I laughed. "You believe in fate?"

"You don't?"

How could I when I knew that the future wasn't always set in stone—that every decision, no matter how small or unimportant, could have a domino effect? "No."

"Interesting." His arm between my breasts vanished, but the one at my waist still held me against the front of his body.

Seconds ticked by, and I became aware of that hand along the curve of my waist moving in slow, tight circles that tugged on the sash. "Are you . . . are you going to let me go?"

"I don't know," he said after a moment.

I stared at the dark wall. "You don't?"

"I like the feel of you against me."

Okay, that . . . that was not what I was expecting. "I'm not sure how I'm supposed to be of service to you if you continue to hold me."

His chin grazed the top of my head. "This is servicing me."

"I'm not sure how that's possible."

"If you're one of the Baron's favorites and he sent you to *service* me," he said, "then you know exactly how you are servicing me at the moment."

I bit down on my lip, at once recognizing that I was in trouble, big trouble, and I didn't think the Long Night was going to help get me out of it. It worked on a *caelestia*, but I had no idea if it worked on a Hyhborn. Naomi had never used it on one. She'd never wanted to. Either way, attempting to drug Lord Thorne was far too much of a risk. If it didn't work on him and he somehow realized what I'd attempted to do, I wouldn't have to worry about ending up on the streets. I'd be dead.

Hell, I didn't even know if my abilities worked on Hyhborn. I hadn't even tried to read him last night and I had picked up nothing from the first night, but then again, I had been distracted. I managed to quiet my thoughts and empty my mind. I reached down, finding his hand in the darkness. My mind was an open, blank field.

I saw . . . I saw nothing but white.

And I heard nothing but static.

But I felt relief—a burst of my own *relief*, because I was really beginning to think that I could still touch him without being bombarded with anything. I spread my fingers along the top of his hand, following the elegant stretches of bone and tendon. This was . . . this was bad and yet good—but good in a very short-term manner.

Knots of unease formed in my stomach. Perhaps I had to try harder. Or maybe it was because I wasn't looking upon him. The tips of my fingers slipped over his knuckles. His hand had gone still beneath mine. His skin . . . it was so hard. I'd known that it wouldn't feel like a mortal's. A Hyhborn's flesh was different. It was why most weapons couldn't penetrate their skin, but I hadn't expected it to feel this hard and smooth. Was all of him like this? Like *all* of him—

"Did I hurt you?" Lord Thorne asked.

"What?" I withdrew my hand from his.

"Did I hurt you just now? I was rough with you."

He'd asked that question after grabbing me in the barn, but it still caught me off guard. "You only startled me." I told the truth. "If you knew it was me, why did you grab me? Or do you always grab women who enter your chambers?"

He snorted. "At one time, I welcomed soft and shapely women

entering my chambers, expected or not, but that was before more than one had come into possession of a *lunea* blade and entered my chambers with the intentions of drawing my blood and enriching themselves."

I supposed after what he recently experienced, I too would react first and ask questions later. "At this point, you have to know that I have no interest in your blood, body parts, or—"

"My come?" Lord Thorne tacked on. "I think that has changed since we first spoke of it."

I briefly closed my eyes. "Are you ready to release me so that I can better service you?" I asked. "And perhaps turn on a light?"

His chin grazed the top of my head once more. "I believe I'm ready to be serviced."

I didn't know what I should be more concerned about in that moment. That his arm remained around my waist or that he made "serviced" sound like the most decadent, wicked word ever to be spoken.

His lips suddenly brushed against my temple, causing an unexpected hitch in my breath. "But just to be clear, *na'laa*, I trust your baron less than I do the ones who created the *nix*. No matter what aid you have given me, if you try anything, I won't hesitate to retaliate." His arm tightened around me. "Do you understand me?"

CHAPTER 14

My skin had gone cold as my thoughts flashed to the small pouch in my pocket. This was the kind of Hyhborn lord I expected. Icy. Deadly. Not teasing and laughing, claiming to be a protector. It was a good reminder of exactly what I was dealing with. "I understand."

"I'm relieved to hear that." His mouth touched my temple again. "I'd hate to have to end you when I've been quite . . . enthralled by you."

He sounded like that surprised him, as it did me. I wasn't sure I liked the idea of enthralling anyone, let alone a Hyhborn who'd threatened my life. "I think you've confused being enthralled with amusing yourself by irritating me."

"Possibly," he remarked. "I do find pleasure in that." He paused. "Na'laa."

I sighed.

Lord Thorne then released me, and the sudden freedom caused me to stumble. His hands curved briefly around my upper arms, steadying me. When he let go this time, I was expecting it, but I could still feel the . . . the heat of him standing behind me as the wall sconces flickered to life, the two framing the doorway and one near the bathing chamber.

He'd done that without moving, instead using the very air we breathed to flip a switch on a wall several feet away.

I sucked in a shallow breath. Even though I knew he was a Hyhborn lord and I'd seen what he was capable of, his power was still as shocking as Claude expecting me to gain information—to manipulate it out of such a powerful being.

Panic threatened to take root and spread, but I couldn't allow it. I needed to pull myself together. It wasn't just my life riding on it.

Taking a moment to calm my heart and mind, I fixed a smile on my face. "It's a good thing I cannot turn lights on without touching them," I said, turning around. "I would never rise from a . . ."

Words failed me as my gaze crawled up long legs and strong hips encased in supple dark brown leather, the loose dark tunic and the leather of his baldric crossing the broad chest I had already known he had. A dagger I hadn't felt was sheathed and strapped flat. Seeing him now in the light of the chamber, where I could get a better look at him, left me unsteady.

"You're staring." One side of those full lips rose as he walked toward a narrow table by the entry to the bedchamber.

Feeling my cheeks warm, I ordered myself to pull it together. "You're . . . nice to stare at, as I'm sure you're well aware."

"I am," he said without an ounce of arrogance. It was just a statement of truth. He withdrew a dagger from the baldric and then another from a sheath above his hip. There were dual flashes of milky-white blade before he placed them on the table. *Lunea* blades.

"That wasn't the only reason I was staring," I admitted after a moment. "I was . . . I was worried about you."

An eyebrow rose as his hands halted along the other side of his waist. "For what reason?"

"I heard there was a violent battle in the gardens the night I last saw you. The *ni'meres*." I watched him slide another blade from his other hip. "A few of the guards were killed."

"Their loss was unfortunate. A damn shame that shouldn't have happened," he said, and he sounded genuine. "But I was not harmed." A pause. "And I would not call that a battle, *na'laa*."

"Then what would you call it?"

"An inconvenience."

I blinked, thinking that something which resulted in scattered body pieces could not be considered just an inconvenience. But what I thought didn't matter. I focused on him, opening my senses. I pictured that string connecting us as I asked, "Why . . . why did they come? Was it because of the other two Hyhborn?"

Nothing.

Nothing but the hum of the white wall.

He eyed me for a moment. "What do you know about the *ni'meres, na'laa*?"

His nickname severed the connection. The only knowledge that I gained was that he seemed unaware of what I'd been trying to do. "Not much. To be honest, I didn't know there were any in Primvera. I only knew that they tend to leave people alone as long as we don't go near where they are nesting."

"That's true, but they can also serve as guards of Hyhborn, even become loyal to some, which appears to have been the case for either Nathaniel or Muriel."

"Did the *ni'meres* travel with them or . . ."

"Both were from Primvera," he answered, brows knitting.

My stomach tumbled a bit. Lord Thorne had killed two Hyhborn and likely many *ni'meres* from the Court that could be seen from some parts of the property. "I imagine Prince Rainer will be displeased."

"Actually, I imagine he'll be quite the opposite." He continued before I could ask why that would be. "So, your baron didn't advise you of whose chamber you'd be entering?"

His change of subject not only failed to pass me by, but also frustrated me as my senses were currently proving to be of no help. "No." I was momentarily distracted as he pulled free another dagger that had been strapped along his waist. My lips parted as he reached back, sliding a . . . a silver-hilted steel sword, the kind with the slight curve to the blade and often carried by the lawmen who patrolled the Bone Road that traveled all five territories.

"You're lucky, you know." Lord Thorne bent, his long fingers reaching for straps I hadn't seen along the shafts of his boots. He unhooked another dagger, tossing it onto the table. It landed with a thump, rattling the other weapons.

"I . . . I am?"

"Yes." He moved to the other boot, and yet another sheathed dagger came free. "You're lucky that my men weren't here when you entered. You would've never reached this space."

I glanced into the antechamber.

"They're not here. They arrived roughly around the time I had you pinned to the wall," he said, and my gaze darted back to him. They had? "They're gone now. We're alone."

"Oh." That was all I could say as I watched him shove up the sleeve of his left arm, revealing yet another sheath along the top of his forearm. "How many weapons do you have on you?"

"Just enough," he remarked, placing that smaller, sheathed blade on the table.

"But why? You're a lord. You can—" I stopped myself from pointing out what he obviously already knew. "Why would you need so many weapons?"

He laughed softly.

"What?" I asked. "What's funny?"

"A better question to ask was how I was foolish enough to not realize I'd been drugged and impaled to a table in a dirty barn."

I snapped my mouth shut.

A wry grin appeared as he moved to the bed, sitting on its edge. "No being is so powerful that they cannot become weak. Not even a lord, a prince, or a king."

"Okay." I thought over what he said. "Could you not just do the whole fire thing with your hand again?" I asked, and immediately recognized that was a question I never thought I'd ever ask.

"The whole fire thing with my hand?" He chuckled, watching me as he reached for his boot. He'd watched me this entire time. Not once had his gaze strayed from me as he unloaded his small arsenal. "I could summon the element of fire, but that takes *divus*."

"*Divus?*" My nose wrinkled. "That is . . . Enochian? What does it mean?"

"It can be loosely translated into 'energy,' and spent energy must be replenished," he explained, and it seemed logical that he spoke of feeding. "Plus, that would only kill one less powerful than the summoner."

Meaning it wouldn't have been so lethal against another lord.

"The mortal weapons aren't necessary," he continued. "But sometimes it's more interesting to fight the fairer way when it comes to mortals."

"Versus ripping their throats out?"

"That is also interesting." He straightened, now barefoot.

I wet my lips nervously—

Lord Thorne's gaze fixed on my mouth. White stars flickered through his pupils, and much like hares did in the gardens whenever I grew too close, I froze. His stare was . . . it was intense and . . . and *heated*. A flush crawled up my throat. I'd never been looked at like that before, not even by those who believed they were moments from joining their bodies with mine.

He came forward, his steps slow and measured. Precise in a wholly unsettling way. A shiver coursed down my spine. His gaze dropped. The sash at my waist had either loosened during our struggle or when he'd been moving his fingers over it, causing the cut of the neckline to be deeper, wider. The inner swells of my breasts were clearly visible, all the way to the darker shade at the peaks. Slowly, his gaze returned to mine. The blue of his irises seeped into the green.

"When you said the manor was your home, I figured you were a member of the aristo," he noted.

I snorted. "Why would you think that?"

"Your clothing. Both times I've seen you, you've been draped in the kind of expensive cloth a member of a less fortunate class wouldn't spend coin on."

"You're right about that," I said. "But I'm no aristo."

"I see." His head tilted as his gaze flicked over my face. "And I can also see why you'd be a favorite of the Baron. You are very . . . interesting."

The corners of my lips tipped down. "Was that supposed to be a compliment?"

"It should be," he said. "I've never found a mortal to be all that interesting or enthralling." His head tilted. "Or amusing."

My brows shot up. "Then I don't think you've met many lowborn."

"I've known far too many," he replied as he went to a small credenza situated near a window. I wondered what his age was. He appeared as if he couldn't be more than a decade older than me, if that, but Hyhborn didn't age like lowborn, and there was a heaviness to his words—an ancient weight to them.

"So . . . you find lowborn boring?" I asked.

"That's not what I said." He picked up a crystal decanter and poured himself a glass of the amber liquid. "Would you like a glass?"

I shook my head.

He picked up his glass. "I find your kind's natural instinct for survival in the face of insurmountable odds admirable. To be honest, I'm fascinated by how every second of every minute counts in a way I don't believe they ever could for one of my own. Life is a bit of a bore for a Hyhborn. I doubt the same could be said about a mortal." Facing me, Lord Thorne took a drink. "But one has never interested me beyond that fleeting fascination."

I wasn't sure what to say to that as I let my senses reach out to him once again. There was nothing but that humming white wall. What if my abilities didn't work on a Hyhborn?

He watched me from above the rim of his glass. "I realize I don't know your name."

"Lis."

"Is it short for something?"

I didn't know why, but I nodded. "Calista."

"*Calista*," he murmured.

My breath snagged at the sound of my name. Possibly because it was so rare to hear it spoken, as only Grady knew it, but the way he said "Calista" . . . He twisted his tongue around my name in a way I'd never heard before.

He took a drink. "It too is fitting."

"It is?" I murmured, utterly confounded by the fact that I'd shared that piece of information—something that I'd kept to myself because it was the only thing that was purely mine, as silly as that sounded.

"Yes. Do you know what it means?"

"The name has a meaning?"

"All names do." A faint smile appeared. "Calista means 'most beautiful.'"

Warmth crept up my throat. "Oh."

He inclined his head, then finished off the whiskey and set the glass down. "I would like a bath since I have such . . . fond memories of how we met."

But that wasn't how we met. Not really. "Okay?"

A faint grin appeared. "You have been sent to service me, correct?" He faced me fully. "Would drawing my bath not be a part of that?"

Yes. Yes, it would, and I felt foolish for not realizing that immediately. I opened my mouth as he reached back, grasping the neckline of his linen shirt. Whatever I was going to say died on my tongue as he pulled the shirt over his head and cast it aside.

I inhaled softly as I eyed his chest, the slabs of tightly coiled muscles of his abdomen, and the tapering of his waist above the band of his pants. There wasn't even a faint scar from where the *lunea* spikes had pierced his skin. Instead, power vibrated from every inch of muscle. Energy coated those defined lines.

"Or we can skip the bath and go straight to far more enjoyable forms of service if you want," Lord Thorne offered, snapping my gaze to his face. "I will not mind at all."

I pivoted, hurrying into the bathing chamber without saying a single word.

His low, husky chuckle followed.

Good gods, what kind of favored courtesan dashed out of the chamber at the mere suggestion of sex? And that was obviously what he believed me to be. After all, it was how I presented myself to all of Claude's targets, but I was acting like a bashful virgin.

What was wrong with me? It wasn't like I hadn't seen him nude before. It just . . . Everything felt different now.

Cursing my reaction, and well, everything, I reached to flip on the light only to realize there were no powered lights in this space. I quickly set about lighting the numerous candles spaced on the stone ledges circling the oval-shaped chamber. Willing my hands to stop trembling, I went to the deep and wide tub in the center of the room. I cranked the water until it poured into the porcelain basin, using these moments to collect myself.

Who Lord Thorne was to me—not that he was anything to me—didn't matter. Neither did the fact that he'd yet to recognize me. Nor did how . . . nice he was to look at, but that was rather a small blessing, wasn't it? Or large blessing. The only thing that mattered was that I needed to get it together, to find some level of calm. Concentrate. Either Claude was too stoned to consider that my abilities wouldn't work on a Hyhborn or he obviously believed my abilities could, and maybe he would know that, being that he descended from them, but . . .

But wouldn't that also mean he knew another who could do the same as me? Which I was positive he didn't.

Either way, I needed to get my intuition to work, to continue to prove how indispensable I was to the Baron. That keeping me comfortable was a priority, because if not . . .

The ever-present fear of returning to that desperate kind of life threatened to take root in my chest, but I squashed it. Giving in to it wouldn't help. I shifted focus. There was this . . . this sense that I could get inside the Hyhborn's mind. A knowledge I couldn't back up but was there nonetheless. It was intuition telling me that I could. I just needed to figure out how.

But I did know what he'd shared with me already. That he was here because he'd been looking for something he'd believed that Muriel knew how to locate. However, I wasn't sure if that was why he was here, at the manor. That was what I needed to discover.

Testing the water, I hoped Lord Thorne liked it warm as I cut off the faucet. I rose to retrieve a towel, to place it on the nearby stool as I said, "Your bath is ready, my lord."

"Thorne," he corrected.

I gave a little jump at how close his voice was. How one of his size could move so silently still was beyond me. Picking up a fluffy towel, I turned and nearly dropped it.

A wicked sense of déjà vu swept through me. Once more, Lord Thorne stood in the doorway, and he was completely, utterly naked, and I was transfixed by the display of smooth, sandy skin and taut muscle as my gaze lowered to his cock. My breath caught. He was thick and long, yet not even fully aroused. How could one fully take him—

All right. I needed to stop thinking. And staring. Maybe even breathing. Perhaps dying would be a good choice at the moment.

"Keep looking at me like that and I don't think a bath will be what I'll need."

Heat exploded in my cheeks as I forced my gaze to his, hoping that in the candlelight he couldn't see how red my face felt. I didn't think courtesans blushed at a nude man.

Then again . . .

I glanced quickly at the thick length between his legs and decided that even Naomi probably would right now.

"Are you sure this is what you wish?"

Sucking in a sharp breath, I looked up at him. "I'm sorry?"

"To be of service to me?" Lord Thorne clarified. "When I'm not injured?"

"Yes." I fixed a smile on my face. "Of course."

"And you understand what that entails? That I will seek pleasure and I will feed on it?"

The way he said that made this sound like a business arrangement, and perhaps that was the appropriate way to think of this. After all, wasn't that what this was? But it didn't feel like that at all as I nodded.

He eyed me for several moments, his stare piercing, as if he could see right through me—through what was partially a facade. My heart was pounding so hard, I was sure he could hear it. I didn't dare look away or let my smile falter, didn't want to give away how nervous I was.

Then he strode forward, completely at ease with the fact that not a single stitch of clothing covered him. He briefly caught my gaze again as he stepped into the tub and sank into the water, giving me a nice view of a rather firm rear.

His ass truly was extraordinary.

Lord Thorne hummed a sound of pleasure, drawing my gaze down. He'd let his head rest against the rim of the tub. With his eyes closed, I let myself take in the elegant features of his face and the display of his body. It was truly unfair that any being could look as . . . as decadent as my—*Nope*. Damn it, he was not my anything. I really, *really* needed to stop with that nonsense.

Refocusing, I glanced around the chamber and spied the soap. "Would you like me to bathe you?"

"It would please me greatly if you would."

I placed the towel back on the stool.

"And I know it will please you greatly to do so," he added.

It would, and the fact that he remembered that annoyed me. Also excited me as I went to one of the numerous shelves. I picked up a bar of soap that carried the faint scent of lemongrass. Turning, I saw that his eyes were open to thin slits and both arms lay on the edge of the tub. He watched me closely as I approached him. I could feel this . . . this tension crackling between us, electric and alive. A flutter of unease and . . . and something else started in my chest and moved lower.

"Is the water to your liking?" I knelt on the marble floor behind the tub.

"Very," he replied, and the flutter moved again at that one word.

I placed the soap on the small metal caddy beside me. Hands lathered, I reached for his arm.

He gave a little jerk when my hands touched him, like he'd done in the shower. Or I did this time. Maybe we both did. I wasn't sure as he lifted his arm for me and I drew my hands up, hoping he didn't notice the faint tremor in them.

Silencing my own thoughts was harder than before, but I managed. Like before, I . . . I heard none of his thoughts. There was a good chance I was simply too distracted once more by how hard and smooth his skin was. It was almost like granite. Did all of him—

Nope.

Was not going there.

"Tell me something about yourself," Lord Thorne said, the roughness of his voice drawing my gaze from his arm. His head was still resting against the rim, eyes closed.

"Like what?" I asked.

"Anything," he answered. "The silence allows my mind to wander to what your hands will feel like on my dick."

My hands halted at his elbow for half a heartbeat as a sudden sharp, twisting motion pulsed through me. A little breathless, I resumed tracing the length of his strong arm. "Is that something you wish to prevent your mind from wandering to?"

The corners of his lips tipped up. "Not normally; however, I've come to learn that I enjoy you bathing me, and I do not wish to rush it."

Skin flushing with a heat that now came from within, I slipped my hands over his shoulder and then down one side of his chest. "I'm not sure what to tell you, my lord."

"Our paths have now crossed three times," he said, and I mentally corrected him. Four times. Our paths had crossed four times. "Yet, I know little about you. You can start with something easy. Like are you from Archwood?"

"No." My slippery fingers slid over the stonelike skin of his upper stomach.

"The Midlands at all?"

I considered lying but decided against it as I re-lathered my hands. "I'm from the southern lands."

"The Lowlands?"

"Close about." That was somewhat of a lie. Union City existed on the border of the Lowlands and Midlands. I dragged my teeth over my lower lip. "Where are you from?"

"Vytrus."

My heart skipped over itself. Vytrus was the Hyhborn Court nestled deep in the Highlands, the northernmost territory of Caelum and incredibly far from the Midlands, and yet, we all knew of *the* Prince of Vytrus. He was said to be one of the most dangerous of Hyhborn, unpredictable and volatile as the lands that he protected, and the hand of the King's wrath. The King's . . .

I'm one of the King's favorites, in case you've forgotten.

The breath I took went nowhere as I stared at the back of his head and a sudden sense of knowing filled me. "The Prince of Vytrus?" I whispered. "What is his name?"

He turned his head slightly. A moment passed. "You already know it."

CHAPTER 15

A faint tremor ran through my arms. "You're not a lord."

"No, I am not."

Heart leaping, I jerked my hands back as if I'd been scalded while one chaotic thought crashed into another. I'd been touching a Hyhborn prince. *The* Prince of Vytrus was *my* Hyhborn. The dangerous, deadly being I'd rescued and was currently *bathing* was a prince. Oh my gods, Finn and those fools had bled and tortured a prince, almost—

"Finally," he . . . Prince Thorne murmured.

I jolted. "Finally what?"

He faced forward. A moment passed. "You're afraid."

I blinked rapidly. Was I afraid? Who wouldn't be, but . . . "You let me believe you were a lord."

"I did." His shoulders had tensed. "Is that why you're now afraid? Because you know who I truly am?"

"I'm . . . I'm a little uneasy. You're a prince and you have quite the . . ."

"Reputation?" he finished for me.

"Yes."

His fingers tapped along the rim. "You shouldn't believe everything you hear, *na'laa.*"

"Sure," I replied. "I mean, you can take a lowborn's soul."

"Just because I can, doesn't mean I have."

My brows shot up. "You've created no Rae?"

"Not in a very long time."

I frowned at the back of his head. The way he said that . . . "Exactly how old are you?"

He chuckled. "Older than I look. Younger than you're probably thinking."

Well, that was also incredibly vague, but as the shock of his actual identity lessened and my heart calmed, I realized I . . . I wasn't afraid of him. I was more afraid of *what* he was and *why* he was here. There was no way the King would've sent the Prince of Vytrus to collect tithes. He was here for another reason that I wasn't sure had anything to do with the information he'd sought from Muriel. My heart started pounding again. When the Prince of Vytrus acted on the behalf of King Euros, violence and destruction almost always followed.

My throat dried as I forced myself to pull it together once more. I resumed servicing him, giving a fine shiver as my hands once more made contact with him. "Why have you not created any Rae in a long time?"

"Because it . . . seems unfair to do that to a soul."

I didn't know what to say to that. It wasn't fair. Frankly, it was disturbing, but I hadn't expected any Hyhborn to think that, let alone a prince. "I'm relieved to hear that."

He said nothing to that.

I eyed the tense line of his shoulder and arms and decided to change the subject. "You're very far from home."

"I am."

Opening my mind to his, I saw and felt that white wall. It was like standing with my face to the sun on a warm summer day. "This information that you sought from Muriel? Is that why you're here?"

That wall—that shield of sorts—kept his mind silent as he said, "Partly."

"That . . . sounds mysterious."

One side of his lips tipped up. "Does it?"

"Yes," I murmured. Could he feel the pounding of my heart against the back of his shoulders as I leaned into him? "Your appearance is also mysterious."

"How so?"

"One would think with us being so close to Primvera, you would simply request lodging there," I pointed out.

"One would think that," he said. "However, my needs are better met outside of the Court."

My brows knitted. What could those needs be? Whatever vague

answers I gained from him only led to more questions. I leaned in, biting down on my lip as I drew my hands over his flesh.

"I'm curious, my—" I caught myself. "I'm curious, Your Grace."

"Thorne," he corrected. "And I'm sure you are."

I arched a brow at that. "What could your needs be if they cannot be met within Primvera?"

"Right now? I wouldn't have your hands on me if I were there, would I?"

"As I said before, flattery is not necessary."

"But appreciated?"

I cracked a grin. "Always."

He chuckled roughly. "How did you end up here?" he asked.

I glanced down at him, seeing the thick fringe of lashes along his cheeks. The sleeves of the borrowed robe floated along the water as I ran my sudsy hands over his lower stomach. The muscles were tauter there, as if he'd tensed. "Archwood seemed as good a place as any."

"I didn't mean the city," he expanded. "But here, in this manor and in this chamber, a . . . favorite of a *caelestia*."

Air thinned between my teeth. He wanted to know how I ended up a courtesan, which I wasn't. None of the paramours truly were, but I was sure the reasons one chose such a profession varied, so I decided to keep the answer simple. "I needed a job."

"And this was all that was available to you?" A pause. "This is what you chose?"

Heat burned the back of my throat as my eyes narrowed on him. Did he look down on such a profession? Irritation flared to life, and whether I was a courtesan or not, the idea that he thought less of the trade needled my temper. I started to lift my hands. "Is there something wrong with choosing to do this?"

His hand moved faster than I could track, closing over mine and trapping it against his chest. My heart stuttered at the feel of his hand around mine, and there being no thoughts, no images. He kicked his head back, his eyes meeting mine. "If I thought there was something wrong with that, I would not be where I am and nor would you."

I nodded, watching his pupils expand and then shrink back to their normal size.

The Prince's gaze held mine. "I only ask because of the way you speak. Your dialect and words. It's not what you typically hear from one who is not of the aristo class," he noted. "Or within those of . . . your trade. You've been educated."

I had been educated. Kind of. It wasn't a formal education like Grady had received before his parents died of a catching fever, leaving him an orphan. Nor had it been one sanctioned by the Hyhborn, but the Prioress had taught me how to read and write and to do basic math, and the Baron had insisted that I speak properly.

But Naomi spoke properly too . . . unless she was angry. The same could be said about Grady and me, and then we'd slip into a less formal way of speaking.

"My education and how I speak don't make me better than anyone else, nor less than an aristo," I said.

He huffed. "What a novel thing for a mortal to say."

I frowned. "What's that supposed to mean?"

"From my experience, mortals seem preoccupied with who is better and who is less than."

"And the Hyhborn are different, *Your Grace?*"

His lips twitched at the emphasis on his title. "We once were."

Now it was I who huffed.

"You don't believe me?"

I shrugged, thinking it was rather ridiculous since they were the ones who created the class structure.

"You do know that Hyhborn cannot tell a lie." A smile played over his lips.

"So I've heard."

He chuckled, releasing my hand as he faced forward once more. I remained as I was for several moments, my palm still flat to his chest, to where his heart should be located, but I . . . I felt nothing.

My brows furrowed. "Do you . . . have a heart?"

"What?" He laughed. "Yes."

"But I don't feel it," I told him, a little unnerved. "Is it because your skin . . . is so hard?"

"It's not that," he said. "My heart hasn't beat in a long time, not as it would for a mortal."

I opened my mouth, but I was at a loss as to how to respond to that—at the reminder of how different we were. Drawing in a soft breath, I shook my head as I slid my hand from his chest. I didn't know why I said what I did next. The words sort of spilled out of me. "This is not what I always want to be," I shared, and goodness, that was the truth if there ever was one. "This is not the future I planned as a child."

The finger of his right hand began to tap idly along the rim once more. "What's the future you planned?"

"I . . ." I had to really think about that. "I don't know," I admitted, my voice sounding small to my own ears.

"You said you had a plan, *na'laa.*"

Brow creasing, I shook my head. I had no idea why I'd even said what I had. I had no future planned beyond this day, this night. I couldn't when living simply meant surviving to the next day or dreading what could come, which wasn't really living at all. But that was all I knew. The same for more lowborn than not, even if they weren't in my situation.

But Hyhborn—especially those like Prince Thorne—didn't live that way. I knew that because even though I'd never entered their Courts, I saw their gold-tipped roofs hidden behind their fortified walls. I'd seen their richly tailored clothing, their well-bred horses and finely crafted coaches from a distance. I'd never heard of a starved Hyhborn or seen one with shadows of worry staining the skin beneath their eyes. Hell, you barely saw that in the face of a *caelestia.* I doubted any of them knew what it was like to sleep with mice scurrying over them or found themselves on the verge of death due to some sickness they'd picked up from poor living conditions.

But none of that mattered right now . . . or at all, it seemed, so I shoved those thoughts aside as I soaped up my hands again. "I like plants."

His head tilted. "Come again?"

I cringed, thinking I could've said that a bit more eloquently. "I mean, I have always had an interest in plants—in gardening. I have a bit of a green thumb and basic knowledge of how many plants can be of aid. I know, a botanist is not the most lucrative of careers," I rambled on. "But that would be a plan."

"If it is something you enjoy then it is lucrative in a way that means more than coin."

Said the person who obviously had more coin than they would ever need.

I wisely kept that to myself, though, and neither of us spoke for several moments. In the quiet, I took a moment to remind myself of what I was supposed to be doing, which was not touching him for the sake of doing so. I focused on him until all I saw was the expanse of sandy skin and all I felt was his flesh beneath mine. The wall of white light appeared in my mind. It was endless, one as tall as the sky and wide as the realm. In my mind, I saw my fingers brushing against it. Nothing happened as I brought my hands back up his chest and reached for the soap, noticing the faint glow around his shoulders.

He was feeding.

On my pleasure? I was enjoying this even though I couldn't read a thing from him. Or was he feeding on his own pleasure—pleasure derived from my touch? I tried not to feel, well, special. Hyhborn were beings of pleasure. I didn't think it mattered who they were with.

"Is that why you were taking such a late-night walk in the gardens?" Prince Thorne asked. "Your enjoyment of plants?"

"Yes. I find gardens to be . . ." I trailed off, searching for the right word.

"Peaceful?"

"Yes, but more than that." The feeling of being in a garden or outside ran deeper than that. "It's more like, I don't know, being at . . . at home."

His head turned slightly as he looked back at me, his expression unreadable.

"What?"

He gave a shake of his head. "Nothing." He cleared his throat. "Are you often in them late at night?"

"When I can't sleep, yes."

"And it's safe for you to do that?"

"Usually," I remarked. "Normally there aren't Hyhborn fighting in them or *ni'meres*."

The steam of the water dampened my skin, causing the sheer robe to cling to my body as I reached around him, washing the other side of his chest. I kept my eyes trained on what existed above the waterline. Which was difficult enough because his skin was fascinating. Did Hyhborn not grow hair anywhere but from their head? Man, that would be so convenient.

Dragging my lip between my teeth, I placed my hand on his back. His muscles bunched under my palm. I withdrew my hands. "Did I—"

"It's fine." His voice roughened. "Please continue."

Suds ran down my arms, but I did as he requested. I focused on the feel and texture of his skin, pushing with my mind against what I was really beginning to believe was a shield. A mental one. The only similar thing I could think of was what I saw when I tried to read Claude or Hymel. Theirs was gray, though. I knew of no low-born who could do that, so this had to be some kind of Hyhborn ability, a weak version of which had passed down to the *caelestias*.

Shields could be cracked, though. Broken. But one had to be strong to break a shield. Was I that strong?

I shifted my attention to the feel of his skin beneath my hands. It really did remind me of . . . of marble or granite as I washed his shoulders. This area of him couldn't get cleaner at this point, but I was enjoying this—touching him and just feeling his skin beneath my palms without images or thoughts intruding upon mine, and that was wrong, so very wrong, because discovering his intentions was the whole point of this.

But other than the night I helped him in the shower, I . . . I couldn't remember the last time I touched someone out of . . . of sheer enjoyment instead of doing so to gain information or because my gifts forced me to. Sometimes the intuition compelled me to reach out to touch someone—to see or hear—and I'd never been able to deny the urge.

Like a handful of years ago, when Grady and I had been in Arch-wood for only a few weeks, barely scraping by when a handsome young man passed by me. I'd been waiting for the baker to turn his back so I could make a grab for the bread I knew he was going to throw out, but my intuition had seized control of me. I'd followed the young man outside and grabbed his hand before I could stop myself. He'd whipped around, those handsome features contorting with anger as he demanded that I explain myself, but all I could see was him walking down the street, where a man with a dirty brown cap waited—a man who would grab for the chain of the gold time-piece hanging from the pocket of his vest. I *saw* this man fighting back. I heard his screams of pain as the thief's blade sank into his stomach. I'd told him what I'd seen in a rush and watched the anger fade into surprise when I warned him not to continue down the street.

That young man, only a few years older than me, had been Claude Huntington, the newly titled Baron of Archwood.

Pulling myself out of the past, I leaned back and let my hands rest on the rim of the tub. "Is there anything else you need my assistance with?"

"Need? No." His head turned to the side. A lock of bronze hair fell against his cheek. "Want? Yes. But that would be selfish of me. I prefer to be greedy."

"Are they not the same thing?"

"Not in my opinion. Greedy is not necessarily a solitary act," he replied. "Join me while the water is still warm."

"I've already bathed, Your Grace."

"Thorne," he corrected, and that curve of his lips deepened, sending my stomach tumbling in a way that wasn't entirely unpleas-ant. "I didn't have bathing in mind, *na'laa*."

Oh.

Oh.

Of course he wouldn't have bathing on the mind when he be-lieved me to be a favored courtesan. I should've known that too, but I had never felt more in over my head than I did at that moment, and it quickly struck me as to why.

By this point, I should already be well on my way to discovering whatever it was that Claude had requested to know, whether it be ferreting out a certain piece of information or not. I was nowhere near that point, and I couldn't even think of the fact that Grady waited for me at a discreet distance in the hall.

Prince Thorne's chin dipped, causing several more strands of hair to fall against his jaw. "Are you not here to service me, *na'laa?*"

My breath hitched. "I am."

"Then surely you understand what I would want from you."

"You want to . . . to feed more?" I surmised.

"I'm always hungry," he said, sending a shiver dancing down my spine. Thick lashes lifted. Those maddening eyes met mine. "But that is not the sole reason behind why I would like for you to join me, Calista. It is your choice to do so."

Thinking I might've hallucinated those words, I stared at the Hyhborn prince. He could make me to do whatever he wanted, stripping my will like Lord Samriel had done to Grady all those years ago. He could do it and see absolutely nothing wrong with doing so, but he wasn't. Instead, he was asking and he was giving me a choice. That mattered even if it shouldn't matter *enough.*

And it also mattered that he wanted me to join him not to solely feed him. It shouldn't. Because that really didn't make this feel like a business transaction, but it too mattered.

A series of fine tremors moved through me as I rose from the back of the tub, my thoughts colliding into one another. What was I doing? Thinking? He wasn't even a lord. He was a *prince.* I wasn't sure as I picked up the soap and returned it to the shelf, not really feeling my legs. My trembling hands went to the loose sash at my waist. I didn't need to do this. I could find another reason to linger, to discover his secrets, or he could send me away. I was already failing at reading him, so leaving now wasn't going to change that.

Or I could join him.

And I would have a higher chance at cracking that shield of his if I was able to touch him, but . . .

I stopped, unable to keep lying to myself.

Getting in that tub with him had nothing to do with aiding my abilities or proving how valuable I was to the Baron.

It was the fact that I could touch him and not see or hear anything. I could just *feel*. It was because I . . . I liked touching him.

It was because it was *him*. The Hyhborn that had been nothing but a ghost for the last twelve years, but now was very real and very much here.

A sweet, heady warmth invaded my blood at the mere idea of touching more of him. Of being touched by him.

Still, I hesitated. I wasn't worried about consequences. I knew there were no diseases that could pass between mortal and Hyhborn, and I took precautions, an herb to prevent—what had Prince Thorne called it? A fruitful union? Besides, it was incredibly rare that a *caelestia* was even born. I halted because if I got into the tub with him, things could quickly spin out of control, like they almost had in the shower. Or, more out of control than things already felt. But that was it. The part that sent my heart racing. I didn't know if I would want to put an end to things if they did progress.

And it had been a fairly long time since I'd done more than touch—felt more than my own fingers or another's inside me.

Long enough that I had begun to wonder if it were possible to become a virgin once more.

But he was the Prince of Vytrus—it was said that no lowborn lived within a hundred miles of his Court. That those who trespassed were never seen again. But I didn't get the impression that he despised lowborn. Or at the very least, he didn't speak as if he did. Perhaps what was said of him was only partly true.

It didn't matter, though.

My fingers undid the sash, my body and mind clearly knowing what they wanted. What I wanted. The robe parted and I let it slip past my shoulders, down my arms, and then to the floor, where it pooled at my feet. Warm, damp air teased already sensitized flesh. Dark strands of hair clung to the damp skin of my breasts and back as I turned.

The Prince was watching me through half-open eyes, his lips

parting as I approached him. I thought I . . . I saw surprise flickering across his features, but it was gone before I could be sure. It very well could've been my imagination, but I did see that faint golden glow. My gaze tracked over the radiance outlining his shoulders. The soft light was beautiful—and a stark reminder of how otherworldly he was.

"I find pleasure in looking upon you," he said, having noted what I was staring at.

I felt a strange, silly jump in my chest. I didn't know if he could detect the shivers that came and went, but he didn't blink. Not once as he lifted his hand to mine.

My pulse hammered as I placed my palm in his. Long, callused fingers closed around mine. The simple act of our hands joined together was a shock. His grip was steady and firm as I stepped over the side of the tub and into the warm, sudsy water, placing my feet on either side of his legs.

I began to lower myself, but he let go of my hand and clasped my hips. The feel of his hands against my bare flesh was a shock, a branding. I didn't move.

Prince Thorne tipped his head back, and though I could see only a hint of those stunning eyes, I could feel his stare hot and hungry against my skin. Hadn't he said he was always hungry? But I thought it was more than just the need of all Deminyens. The slow slide of his perusal felt like a physical caress over the width of my jaw and mouth, down my throat and across the tingling skin peeking between the strands of my hair. And lower still, over the curve of my stomach, the flare of my hip, and . . . and between my thighs.

Little air seemed to make it into my lungs as I stood there, letting Prince Thorne look his fill, and he did so greedily.

A flush stained my skin. I could feel it, and I was sure he could see it. It wasn't brought on by embarrassment. I'd had men and women look upon my body, but I'd never had any look at me like Prince Thorne did. He gazed upon me as if he . . . he wanted to devour me.

I didn't think I would mind being devoured.

His fingers pressed into the flesh of my hips as he leaned in. He was so damn tall that even seated, he had to bend his neck to press his lips to the skin below my navel. I gasped at the feel of his mouth there. The bridge of his nose grazed my skin as his head lowered and lowered. Spread as my legs were, there was nothing preventing his attention from dipping between my thighs. The muscles in my legs locked as I felt his warm breath against my center. I held my breath, staring at the top of his head. I didn't know what he was about to—I mean, I had a whole litany of things he could do, but—

Prince Thorne's lips grazed the sensitive flesh there, and then I felt his tongue slipping over me, *in* me for the briefest second. Air left my lungs as a bolt of desire swept through me. His mouth closed around the tightened nub of nerves, and he sucked—sucked *hard*. A sound came from me. A cry I'd never made as another dart of blade-shaped pleasure sliced through me.

His mouth left me. He leaned back, and thick lashes swept up, and I truly couldn't get enough air to return to my lungs then. Dots of white appeared, sprinkled throughout his pupils, as he left me aching, throbbing.

"Beautiful," he said, voice smoky.

My chest rose and fell heavily. "That is . . . that is kind of you to say."

"It's not kind of me." He tugged on my hips. I grasped the edges of the tub, legs unsteady. Water sloshed against the sides as he guided me down so that I straddled his thighs. I shuddered as I felt the thick length of him brush my thigh. He slid his hands up my waist. Shivers followed his hands over my ribs and then across my chest, just below my collarbone. "I am simply speaking the truth."

I held still as he gathered the strands of hair in his hands. A reedy breath left me as he lifted the hair, dragging it back behind my shoulders, and then there was truly nothing between his gaze and me.

The stars in his eyes turned luminous as his fingers lingered in my hair, as I looked over his features. I thought of the markings I'd seen on his face when he'd been unconscious—the trailing design that had been slightly raised. He'd said it had been blood and dirt, and it had to be true, because there was no sign of them now.

"When you first entered my quarters," he said, "I wasn't all that pleased by it, even though I enjoyed parts of our time in the gardens and before."

"And now?" I asked.

"Very pleased." His fingers made their way from my hair and danced across my arms, leaving a fine wake of tremors behind. Several seconds passed. "But I should've sent you from my chambers."

"Why?"

"Because I have this distinctive feeling this isn't exactly wise," he said, and my stomach dipped. "Touch me, *na'laa*."

I was caught between the unease his statement created and how his demand caused my pulse to spin. I released my grip on the tub, placing my hands on his chest. His back arched slightly, much like a cat's when petted.

"I like being touched," he said when my gaze lifted to his. "Do you?"

More than he could ever realize. Heart thrumming, I nodded as I dragged my fingertips down, under the water and over the corded muscles of his stomach.

I opened myself up as I explored his lower stomach, but there was just that shield of white as my fingers slipped beyond his navel. I glanced down. The faint glow edged his chest and waist, but I was unable to see through the suds. However, I knew what my hands were near. I could feel him resting against my thigh.

His thumbs swept over the tips of my breasts, causing me to jerk. "How long have you been in Archwood?"

It took me a couple of moments to answer. "For a few years."

The Prince made another swipe over the center of my breast as his right hand followed the same direction as mine, slipping down my stomach and then under water. I sucked in a heady breath as his palm stopped just below my navel. His hand was so large that when that thumb began to move, it dipped between the crease of my thigh and hip.

"And in those few years that you've been here," he said, the thumb at my breast moving in the same slow sweeps as the one along my inner thigh. His touch created a heat that spread across my skin and seeped into my blood. "How often have you proved to be quite the decadent distraction?"

I grinned, letting myself explore a little further, brushing my fingers against the thick, impossibly hard flesh between his legs. He made a sound, a deep one that came from his chest as I traced his rigid length. The flesh there was smooth yet gently ridged. Toward the base, he was thicker and rounder, almost as if the flesh was more . . . round there. I hadn't looked close enough to notice that, and I'd never felt anything like it, nor had Naomi mentioned anything of the sort. I had no idea what that would feel like in . . . inside me, but my imagination . . .

Goodness.

My fingers floated away. I swallowed as muscles low in my stomach clenched. "That I cannot answer."

"Interesting," he remarked, and my hips jerked as his knuckles brushed the very center of me. The corners of his lips tipped up. The stars seemed to pulse in his eyes as his fingers dipped deeper along my thigh.

Feeling breathless, I shuddered as his fingers closed around my nipple. I tried to focus on anything other than what he was doing with his hands, but his touch was increasingly distracting, as was the feel of his flesh beneath my hands.

Prince Thorne's head tilted to the side as I spread my fingers. Beneath them, the muscles of his stomach seemed to tighten and relax. "How did you become a favorite of the Baron's?"

My heart turned over heavily as my gaze shot to his. "As one typically does."

A tight smile reappeared as I lowered my head to his neck. I pressed my lips there, kissing him softly and slowly working my way down, nipping at the skin at the curve of his shoulder.

"Like this?" he asked, brushing the back of his hand along the center of me once more.

"Many ways," I murmured against his chest, the salt of his skin and the faint flavor of soap gathering against my lips.

The hand on my thigh slid an inch or two down. I tensed, pulse skipping as one of his fingers drifted along the slit. It was a barely there touch, but my entire body jerked in response.

My fingers curled against his skin as I dragged my hands up. I licked at the hard line of his chest. I knew I should be using my hands elsewhere, but I was already distracted enough. Possibly too much, because I could barely see the white wall now. "What other—" I gasped as a finger of his pressed down on the sensitive center of nerves.

"You were saying?"

What was I saying? Oh, yes. Why he was here. "What other reasons could've brought you to the manor?"

His finger swirled around my clit, causing me to tremor. "You ask many questions, *na'laa.*"

"I'm known to be very curious."

"And stubborn?"

"Maybe that—" I gasped as his head dipped suddenly. His warm breath on my skin was the only warning I had before his mouth closed over my nipple. I trembled as his tongue teased, sending shivers of pleasure racing through me. His hand came up to cup my other breast, thumbing the sensitive peak. A breathy moan escaped me. He then drew my nipple into his mouth, sucking deep and hard. I shook, crying out. He chuckled low in his throat, and the sound vibrated in the most wantonly delicious way.

He slowly released the throbbing flesh from his mouth. "Sorry," he said, brushing his lips over the skin. "I wanted to know what your skin tasted like."

My nails scraped against his hard flesh as I slipped my hand over his navel and underwater. "And what does my skin taste like, Your Grace?"

"Thorne," he sighed, trailing a path of hot, wet kisses to my other breast. His tongue flicked out, tantalizing and wicked. "Your skin tastes of hunger and smells of . . ." His lips then coasted along the side of my throat, coaxing my head back. He didn't need to. I was already giving him whatever he sought. "Cherries."

"*Cherries?*" My fingers brushed against his cock. It had been a while since I finished a man. From previous experience, I judged that it wasn't all that difficult; most men seemed rather easy to please. But this was a Hyhborn prince. I hesitated as I wrapped my hand around him, unsure.

"Your skin smells of the cherries that flourish in the meadows of Highgrove." His other hand slipped from my breast and found mine beneath the water. "I bet your lips taste just as sweet."

My breath snagged as his hand closed over mine. He tightened my grip on him and began to move my hand up his length. I exhaled a shaky breath as he throbbed against my palm.

"This is how I like it," he told me, sending a shivery wave of heat through me as he drew my hand back down him. "Tight. Hard. You won't hurt me."

Swallowing, I nodded. His lips brushed my cheek as he let go of my hand. I kept going, my own breath coming in short, shallow pants as I moved my hand in tune with his fingers' slow, idle caresses, gaining confidence in what I was doing.

Prince Thorne nipped at my lower lip, but didn't kiss me as he drew his finger over the throbbing heat. "Have you ever done this?"

"Done what?"

"This." His finger made another pass. "*Serviced* another."

"Of course," I answered.

"Then how long have you been servicing others?"

"Long enough."

That faint smile returned as more specks of white crowded his pupils. The effect was startling enough that I found it difficult to look away from. "You know what I think?"

My hips jerked again as his hand cupped me between the thighs. "What?"

His palm pressed against me, and my body reacted without thought, rubbing against him. "I think you're lying to me."

CHAPTER 16

In a very distant part of my brain, warning bells rang. They'd probably been ringing this whole time but I'd been too distracted to notice.

Prince Thorne's fingers kept moving idly between my thighs and at my breast. *"Na'laa?"*

"I . . . I've never seduced a Hyhborn," I managed, thighs trembling. "Or been seduced by one."

"Both of those things aren't necessarily true," he said. "You seduced me in the shower, and you were so very close to being seduced then."

"I don't believe that counts."

"It doesn't?" His fingers closed over the peak of my breast, sending a bolt of pleasured pain through me. "So . . ." He drew the word out as the finger he ran along me didn't make an idle pass, but stopped, slipping into me. Not deep, but the shallow intrusion still was a stunning, acute shock, wringing a soft cry from me. "If it was my cock inside you instead of my finger?" That finger retreated until he nearly left me, and then he reclaimed the scant fingertip length. "Moving through this tight, hot heat of yours?"

Each breath I took felt like it went nowhere as his finger moved slowly, steadily—as his hand shifted and his thumb brushed over the nub of flesh just above his finger.

"Going deeper? Harder? Faster?" The blue and green churned wildly through the brown of his irises. His pupils were nearly white. "Would the sounds you make be those of a well-practiced and skilled lover as I fuck you? Or would your cries be those of one who has little experience in such pleasure?"

The moan that left me was one I'd never made before. I shuddered. I'd been *fucked* before, but I'd never felt these almost too-intense sensations he was creating inside of me, drawing out of me.

He dipped his head, lips glancing off my cheek. "I don't think you're a skilled courtesan."

My heart thundered as I said the first thing that came to mind. "Perhaps the Baron believed you would not want one so *experienced*?"

One single brow rose. "Are you suggesting that your baron thought I would prefer debauching an unpracticed potential virgin who one day wants to become a botanist?"

A wave of prickly warmth hit my skin, loosening my hold on my tongue and common sense, but tightening my grip on his cock, just above that knot of flesh. He *was* even harder there than the rest of his body. "You don't?" I asked, watching him as I moved my hand along his length just as he said he liked it. Tight. Hard. Those tiny sparks of light appeared in his pupils. "I'm no virgin, Your Highness, but truth is not nearly as important as perception. So, if you believe me to be an unpracticed virgin, it didn't stop you from engaging in said debauchery, did it?"

The corners of his lips twitched as if he wished to smile. "It did not."

Knowing *that* ground I was treading on was getting even thinner, more dangerous, I glanced down at where his hand was still between my legs, his finger *still* inside me. My eyes returned to his as I stroked him from the base to the tip, marveling a bit at the ridged feel of him. "And still hasn't?"

The Prince didn't respond for a long moment, but I felt his chest rise sharply under my other hand. "Am I to believe the way you all but ran into the bathing chamber upon the suggestion that we'd skip the bath was an act? That the flush of your skin when I entered the chamber was a trick of the eyes? Your hesitation in joining me? Your nervousness? All an act?"

I leaned in until our mouths were inches apart, summoning every ounce of bravery I had. "I'm not here to make you believe one thing or another."

His hips jerked and the fingers at my breast pressed into my flesh. "Then what are you here for?" he asked, voice thick and soft.

I swirled my thumb over the tip of his cock, smiling when air hissed between his clenched teeth. "If I have to explain that, then obviously I'm doing something wrong." I squeezed him, feeling a surge of satisfaction at the roll of his hips that sent water splashing against the sides of the tub. "But I don't think that I am."

Prince Thorne's lips parted, but he said nothing as I continued to stroke him, just as slowly as his finger moved inside me. Through half-closed eyes, I watched him closely. His breathing picked up, coming in short, shallow pants. So, I alternated between smooth slides and tighter, slower tugs, but the controlled plunges of his finger made it difficult to focus on anything but that.

"I think you owe me an apology," I panted, muscles low in my stomach quivering.

"For what?"

"For being wrong about me."

"Perhaps." He groaned, cock twitching in my hand. His fingers splayed across my breast and then found their way to the nape of my neck.

Each thrust of his finger, he went a little deeper, a little faster. Then it was his *fingers*, stretching me as his thumb swirled around my taut clit. I tried to rein it back. All of it. The way I moved. My reaction to him. The soft, breathy sounds I made. My body. The pleasure, and my hunger for it. My need. This wasn't what I was here for. I slowed, throat dry as I struggled to remember my whole purpose for being here, but I was so thrown by the . . . the realization that I wanted this. Badly. Wanted more.

I shouldn't. At least, I didn't think that I should, but I . . . I did. I *was* enjoying that it was I who was the cause of his breath quickening. That it was *my touch* that brought forth those deep, rumbling sounds from a Hyhborn prince as I worked his flesh—as he did the same to me. A fluttering sensation low in my stomach and even lower. I *wanted* to be doing this.

Just as I had wanted to get in the tub.

To be touched.

To *touch*.

It had to be because I was simply touching another—giving pleasure and experiencing it without taking their thoughts or prying into their futures. And it was that, but it also felt like something more. I didn't know what or understand it, and that scared me. I could feel it building inside of me, a rising tide of desire that threatened to overwhelm my senses—every part of me. I tried to hold back, to rein myself in, but it was like trying to hold back the ocean.

"Don't fight it. Give in to what your body wants," he coaxed. "Give in to me."

I shuddered, surrendering to his demands—to the demands of my own body. I gave myself over to the moment, rocking against him, my hand *faster* now, his fingers *harder* now. Muscles coiled low inside me, tauter and tauter until the tension bordered on pain. Until I began to tremble.

"That's it," he growled, his body straining—his body *humming* against mine. "I want to feel you come on my fingers, *na'laa.*"

His pupils . . . they went completely white as I began to tremble. Then all that tightening, swirling pressure erupted. I came, crying out as all that tension unfurled in a molten hot flood of desire as his shaft swelled against my palm. The release was sharp and stunning. Waves of sensation crashed through me as . . . as his body seemed to heat against mine, so much so that my eyes fluttered open even as the swirling pleasure rippled throughout me.

His pupils glowed intensely, like polished diamonds. They were so wide that I couldn't see any of his irises, and his body *was* humming, lending an almost blurred effect to the outline of his shoulders. He dragged me against his chest, his arm going around my waist, holding me tight as I gasped into the crook of his neck. The feel of his flesh against my breasts sent a myriad of unexpected sensations darting through me. I lost my rhythm on his cock, but he didn't seem to notice as his hips pushed against my grip, sending water splashing over the rim of the tub. His cock jerked, spasming, and the sound he made as he came heated my blood, leaving me feeling as hot as his body now felt against mine.

The aftershocks of pleasure left me limp against his chest, my breathing ragged. Resting my cheek on his shoulder, I followed the lead of his body, slowing my movements as the spasms eased and then finally lifting my hand from him. I didn't move away from him, though. His fingers still danced and teased, coaxing out a fainter ripple of pleasure before he slowly withdrew his fingers from me. Eyes closed, I still didn't move as he folded his other arm around me. I didn't know why he did this, but I . . . I relaxed into him. There was something unexpectedly soothing about his warm embrace, comforting. It made me want to . . . to *snuggle* closer, into the heat of his body.

The quiet ticked by, and I was unable to hold back my questions. "Your body . . . it seemed to increase in temperature and vibrate? Is that because you were feeding or was I imagining that?"

"You weren't." Prince Thorne cleared his throat.

"Does it hurt when it does that?"

"It does not." His hand moved up and down my back, tangling gently in my hair. "It feels quite the opposite."

Trying to picture my body heating and vibrating, I was unable to imagine how that would feel pleasant. "I'll have to take your word on that."

His chuckle was low and rough. The quiet returned then, and for a little while, I just let myself feel it all. How tight he held me. The weight of his arms around me and the warm, hard flesh pressing against mine, and the way it felt . . . it felt right.

Gods, that was such a silly thought, but that's what I felt. I didn't understand how it could feel right. It shouldn't, but it did, and I soaked it all in, committing every second of it to memory.

Because I had never felt any of this before.

And I had no idea when I would feel it again.

I didn't attempt to get past his shields, and that was, well, not good. I could've tried again, especially while we both were so quiet, but doing so felt as if it would . . . taint this.

Whatever *this* was—which was nothing, absolutely nothing.

I couldn't linger, though. Grady had to be beside himself with worry, and I . . . I needed to figure out what the hell I was going to tell Claude, because what few answers I'd gained were vague at best. All I could tell him was who this Hyhborn prince was and what I already knew.

"*Na'laa?*"

"Hmm," I murmured.

"I'm never wrong."

It took me a moment to get what he was referencing. When I did, a chill slithered down my spine. Opening my eyes, I lifted my head and started to pull back. His embrace held firm. I gained only a scant inch or two of separation. My gaze met his. The stars were gone from his eyes. The colors had slowed until they were blots of green, blue, and brown. Nothing could be gained from the striking angles of his face.

I gathered up all that bravado it had taken to enter the chambers, sensing that now was not the time to finally feel the terror I should've felt from the moment we crossed paths in the gardens the night before. "Besides the fact that the idea that anyone, Hyhborn or not, can never be wrong seems implausible to me, I'm not exactly sure what you're referencing."

His lips curved, but the smile was tight and cool. "You said you were sent to service me, correct?"

I nodded.

One of his hands slid up my back, tangling in my hair. "I don't think that was the only reason you were sent to me."

The tips of my fingers pressed into the hard flesh of his shoulders. "I—"

"While I find your little lies and half-truths to be strangely amusing, this is not one of those moments." His fingers found their way to the nape of my neck and stayed. "Trust me when I say it would be very, very unwise to do so."

CHAPTER 17

I tensed, every part of my being focusing on the feel of his hand at my neck. He put no pressure there, but the weight of his hand was warning enough.

The arm still around my waist tightened. Our chests were flush once more as he drew my body against his. I gasped, feeling him against my core. He was *still* hard. A pounding pulse of sharp desire renewed a throbbing ache, shocking me, because now was so not the time to be feeling any of that.

Prince Thorne's smile lost some of its coldness. "Please don't lie, Calista."

Please.

That word again. My name. Hearing both was unnerving. I didn't think "please" was something he often said, and it made me want to be truthful, but even if he hadn't said it, I was smart enough to know that lying now would likely end very badly for me.

Telling the truth was also likely to end badly. I knew Claude wouldn't send me away, but he could become angry enough that he banished Grady from the manor—from Archwood. But if I lied now, and the Prince reacted in anger? If I screamed and Grady came in? He wouldn't survive going toe-to-toe with the Prince.

So, it was a no-win situation, except that lying ended in violence, and the truth—or at least a part of it—ended in the loss of security and, at the least, the sense of safety.

I swallowed, knowing I couldn't endanger Grady. "The Baron was . . . he is worried about your unexpected appearance."

"Does he have a reason to worry?" Prince Thorne asked.

"He's apparently behind on his quarterly tithes," I shared, stomach churning. "He feared that you were sent by the King to collect them."

His head tilted slightly. "Your baron saw me. Do I look like some-one the King would send to collect tithes?"

"No." I almost laughed, but nothing about this was funny. "But I also don't think the Baron was in the . . . um, right frame of mind at the moment to recognize who you were."

"That's vastly understated." His fingers began to move at my neck, pressing into the taut muscles there. "He was as high as the mountains of my Court."

"True," I whispered.

"So, he sent you to ferret out why I was here," he surmised. "In-stead of waiting till the morning, as I advised?"

"Yes."

Tension bracketed his mouth, but the motions of his fingers re-mained gently, oddly soothing. "Are you even a courtesan?"

"Why does that matter?"

"Because it does."

"It didn't matter when you led me to believe you were a lord," I pointed out, which a part of me fully recognized I probably shouldn't have, but it was absurd and . . . and unfair for him to be questioning me when he too hadn't exactly been forthcoming.

"We're not talking about me, *na'laa*."

"I have a feeling you're calling me stubborn instead of brave when you call me that," I muttered.

"Right now, it's a mixture of both." His gaze swept over my fea-tures. "Did you have a choice in coming to me tonight?"

"What?"

"Were you forced to come to me tonight?"

His questions knocked me off-kilter. I couldn't fathom why he'd care if that was the case. "Yes."

He stared at me for several moments; then his lashes swept down, shielding his eyes. "Your baron is a fool."

I opened my mouth, but I couldn't really disagree with that state-ment. Claude was a fool and so was I for going along with this. My heart pounded unsteadily in the silence that followed. I didn't know what to expect, but then he let me go. Confused, I remained where

I was, my body pressed tightly against his, my hands flattened on his shoulders, and . . . the rigid length of him still nestled against my core.

"You should dry off," he said quietly.

"You . . . you're not going to punish me?" I asked.

"Why would I punish you for the idiocy of another?" Those lashes lifted then, and the faintest burst of white was visible in his eyes.

More than a little surprised, I rose on shaky legs, causing water to splash over the sides as I stepped out of the tub. I quickly dried off and then retrieved my robe. Sliding it on, I hastily secured the sash and made sure the pouch had remained in the pocket. If that fell out . . . good gods.

I turned back to the Prince, startled into taking a step back. He'd already left the tub. I hadn't heard him or a single sound of the water being disturbed. Meanwhile, I'd sounded like a small child splashing in a puddle when I had risen. I picked up a fresh towel, offering it to him.

He didn't take it.

Instead, his hands went to my throat. I tensed, nearly losing my grip on the towel.

Prince Thorne's lips quirked as he slipped his hands beneath my hair. His fingers grazed the nape of my neck, sending a series of shivers down my back. I stood there as he . . . as he tugged the heavy length of hair free from the robe.

"There," he said.

My breath . . . it *skipped*. Thrown by his gesture, I went completely still again.

"You behave as if you expect violence from me at every turn," he commented, taking the towel from me. "I know my kind can be . . . unpredictable, but have I behaved in a way that would give you pause?"

I swallowed.

He looked over at me as he drew the towel across his chest. "It's an honest question."

"Well, you did take me to the ground that night in the barn and threaten to drown me in your blood."

"I was not quite aware of myself at that moment."

"And when I first entered your bedchamber, you held me against a wall," I continued.

One eyebrow rose. "The bedchamber you entered uninvited and unexpected."

I shifted my weight from one foot to the next. "You asked why I'd expect violence. Those were just two examples."

"Just two?" he replied. "There's more?"

I glanced at the tub. "I did come here under false pretenses."

"Yes," he said. "There is that. Are you to speak with the Baron upon leaving my quarters?"

"I'm to meet with him in the morning, before he speaks with you."

"What will happen if you have no real information to provide him?"

"Nothing."

He lowered the towel, his stare piercing straight through me. *"Na'laa."*

"I do not like that nickname."

"You would if you knew all the meanings."

I gritted my teeth as he continued to wait for an answer—for the truth. "He will be . . . disappointed."

"Will he punish you?"

"No." I looked away, uncomfortable with the idea that he would think that. Uncomfortable with the fact that I'd expected it from him. "He might not even remember sending me to you, to be honest." That was unlikely, but there was a sliver of a chance. "He was quite intoxicated."

A low rumble radiated from the Prince. My gaze shot back to him, my eyes widening. There was nothing remotely human about that sound. It resembled that of a . . . a wolf or something far larger.

"Tell him I'm not here to collect tithes," he said, turning from me as he drew the towel around his waist. "That I'm here to discuss the situation with the Iron Knights. That should be enough to tide him over until I can speak with him in more detail. Do not tell him you confided in me. I will not speak a word of it."

My mouth dropped open in shock. His pardon—and that's what his silence regarding telling him the truth truly was—was unexpected. Yet again, he was unknowingly saving Grady and me.

He nodded, walking from the bathing chamber. "You seem surprised."

"I suppose I am." I trailed off, following him. "I didn't expect you to tell me or . . ." Or for him to cover for me. I cleared my throat. "I also hadn't expected it to involve the issue with the Iron Knights." I watched him pour himself a glass of whiskey. He looked back at me, and I shook my head at the offer of a drink. "Is that the kind of information you were seeking when you were here before?" I asked, heart lurching as I thought of Astoria. "Does the King believe that Archwood is somehow sympathetic to the Iron Knights?"

"What I came for before is unrelated to why I'm here now." He faced me, the towel knotted at his waist and the edges of his hair damp. Tiny drops of water still clung to his chest, drawing my gaze as they traveled down over the dips of his stomach. "And the situation regarding the Iron Knights has changed."

I started to ask why, but my eyes met his and I fell silent. My skin tingled with awareness. The sense to drop the conversation slammed into me, and this time I listened to it. I glanced around his quarters, my hands going to the sash on the robe. I wanted to thank him for making sure I bore no consequences for what I had taken part in this evening, but I had to choose my words wisely. "I . . . I appreciate you telling me why you have come to Archwood."

Prince Thorne inclined his head in what I assumed was acknowledgment.

A keen sense of nervousness invaded me as he stared. "If there's not anything else I can do for you, I should be on my way."

He stood silent, watching me.

Taking his lack of answer as a good enough response, I gave a quick and terrible curtsy. "Good night, Your Grace."

He didn't correct my use of the honorific. He was still quiet, watching me with an expression I couldn't quite make out. Passing him, I made it to the door of the antechamber.

"Stay."

I whipped toward him. "Excuse me?"

"Stay," he repeated, his grip on the glass tightening. "Stay the night with me."

I opened my mouth, but I found no words. He wanted me to stay? The night with him? I glanced at the bed, stomach clenching and dropping at the same time.

"To sleep," he added, and my attention swung back to him. My eyes had widened slightly. Cracks had formed in the glass he held. Not deep enough to spill the drink, but I could see the fragile spiderweb-like lines racing throughout the glass. "That is all, *na'laa.*"

My mind went in two vastly different directions as I stared at him. One part of me couldn't even believe he was asking for such a thing, because why in the five realms would he want to just sleep with me? The other part of me was foolishly wondering what it was like to sleep beside another who wasn't Grady, and thinking about that caused the skipping of my breath to repeat itself in my chest and stomach.

And that . . . that was unacceptable for various reasons.

"That I cannot do," I said.

His head cocked. "Cannot or will not?"

There was a difference between the two. "Cannot" wasn't a choice. "Will not" was. The problem was I didn't know which it was.

"Both," I admitted, shaken. "Good night."

I didn't wait. Turning, I left the bedchamber and reached the main door. I turned the handle. It didn't budge. Frowning, I glanced up, seeing that it was unlocked. What the—? *Prince Thorne.* He was stopping me from opening the door. I stiffened, feeling his intense stare on my back, and for a wild moment, a wicked thrill went through me, leaving me breathless. The idea that he'd stopped me sent a hot, tight shiver through me.

I didn't want him to let me go.

That damnable feeling—the one of belonging with him—surged through me, and dear gods, there truly was something wrong with me.

My hands flattened against the wood. In my chest, my heart raced. Then the door cracked open beneath my palms. He was letting me go. Something akin to . . . to disappointment flashed through me, leaving me even more confused, with him—with myself.

⇒⟫

"All right, I'm officially . . . flabbergasted." The soft glow from the lamp near the bed I sat upon lit Grady's profile. He sat on the edge of my bed, his sword resting against the chest at the foot of the bed, more relaxed after most of his anger at learning that the special guest hadn't been expecting me had passed.

"Flabbergasted?"

"Dumbfounded and every other unnecessary adjective you can think of. The Prince of Vytrus came to discuss the Iron Knights? Who wouldn't be surprised." Grady dragged a hand over his face. "And you're sure he's not going to say something to the Baron about you telling him the truth?"

"I'm pretty sure." I tipped my head back. It was late, about an hour after I'd left Prince Thorne's chambers. I'd just finished telling Grady what had happened—well, not *everything*. I didn't want to traumatize him with unnecessary details. "But I can't know for sure since I can't read him. I tried several times to get inside his head, but I couldn't."

He scratched at the faint growth of hair along his cheek. "You have to tell the Baron that you got the information at least partly that way, though. If he thinks the Prince simply told you because you asked, he's not going to believe you."

"I know." Which meant I really hoped Prince Thorne held to what he said, and that he wouldn't speak a word of it.

Tugging the edges of the black robe—*my* robe, one made of comfortable cotton that wasn't transparent—around me, I smothered a yawn as silence filled the large, fairly empty chamber.

There wasn't much to the immaculate space. A wardrobe. The bed. A settee near the terrace doors. A nightstand and chest. The antechamber, though, was outfitted with more than the necessities—a deep-seated settee and chairs arranged upon a thick plush rug of ivory chenille, a small dining table and credenza made of white oak, and various odds and ends the Baron had gifted over the years. The space was beautiful, well maintained, and leagues above any other place I'd have ever slept in, but it wasn't home.

I wanted it to feel like that.

I'd yet to know what that even felt like, but I thought it would be a lot like what I felt when I was in the gardens, my fingers sunk deep in the soil, and my mind quiet. There was a sense of belonging there. Peace.

"You were with this prince for a while." Grady tentatively broached what he'd yet to bring up.

My toes curled against the sheet. "Not that long."

"Long enough."

Stay the night with me. My stomach made that idiotic dipping motion again. I shook my head. Why in the world did he want me to stay the night with him? I wasn't sure I had pleased him beyond providing a release. Except, he had said I'd interested him, enthralled him.

"What happened?" Grady prodded.

Immediately, the memory of the Prince and me in that damn bathtub flashed in my mind. His hands on me. His finger inside me. Holding me. And it was the last bit that stuck with me. The *holding me* part. I dragged my teeth over my lip as I swallowed. "Not much."

"Lis . . ."

"Grady?"

A muscle ticked at his temple. "You can talk to me about anything. You know that. So, if something happened that's got you feeling—"

"Nothing happened that I didn't allow to happen," I cut in.

"That's the thing, though." Grady scooted closer. "You didn't really choose to go to him tonight, now did you? You felt like you had to, so were you ever in the position to not allow whatever it was that happened?"

I wiggled a little, discomfited with that being the second time I'd been asked that question. "He gave me a choice, and I did choose to go to him—something we've already established."

Grady stared at me as if I had sprouted a third eye in the center of my forehead.

"Seriously. He gave me a choice in what we did—and we didn't have sex," I told him. "And so what if we had? I'm not a virgin, Grady."

His lips curled, and though I couldn't see the flush in his brown skin, I knew it was there. "I really didn't need to know that but thank you for sharing."

"You're welcome." Dipping my chin, I giggled at the glare he sent me. "He really did give me a choice, Grady, and I get that the whole idea of me wanting to do anything that I did is a complicated mess. Trust me. I know, but . . ." I thought of what Naomi had once told me when I confided in her that I sometimes enjoyed it when Claude sent me to find out information for him. *Few things are black-and-white, Lis. Most of life exists in that messy gray area in between, but if you wanted what was happening—you enjoyed it and so did the other—then there's nothing wrong,* she'd said. *Anyone who tells you different either hasn't been where you've been or they're just living a different life. Doesn't make either of you right or wrong.* I exhaled slowly. "But this Hyhborn . . . he's different."

"Different how?"

I shrugged.

"They're all the same, Lis. Nice to look at and charming on the outside but demented assholes on the inside. Just because one of them made sure you didn't get hurt and didn't compel you into doing something against your will doesn't mean they can be trusted, especially this one. You know what has been said about the Prince of Vytrus."

"I know."

"Do you?" He raised his brows. "He led the army that laid siege to Astoria."

I found myself nodding again, but it was difficult reconciling the Prince Thorne I knew with the one who had been spoken about for years. Then again, I didn't really know the Prince, did I?

But that didn't feel right.

It did feel like I knew him, and he did seem different from what we knew of the Hyhborn, even before I knew his name. When I saw him in the gardens and farther back? My mind went all the way to the night in Union City. "There's something I haven't told you," I began. "We've met this Hyhborn before."

Grady stared at me for a moment, then sat straighter. His brown eyes widened the moment he clearly realized what I was speaking of. "Union City?"

I nodded.

He leaned back, then pitched forward. "And you're just now telling me?"

I winced. "I just . . . I don't know why I didn't say anything earlier."

"That's a shit excuse, Lis."

"It's not meant to be one at all," I told him. "I'm sorry. I should've said something before."

He looked away. "It's not that one who grabbed me, is it?"

"Good gods, no. It was the other one," I assured him, frowning as I realized then that Prince Thorne had also led the Mister to believe he was a lord that night. "He hasn't recognized me, by the way."

Grady seemed to let that bit of news sink in. "Are you sure it was him?"

I shot him a look. "It's really annoying when people ask me that question."

He held up his hand. "Of course you're sure. I was just asking because that's . . . that's a hell of a coincidence."

It was, except I didn't believe in coincidences, and neither did Grady.

Grady became silent as his gaze trailed to the terrace doors. Some time passed before he spoke. "I think about that night a lot, you know? Trying to figure out why the Hyhborn were there in the first place. They were looking for someone—like one of their own? Like a *caelestia* or something?"

"Maybe." It wasn't impossible, I supposed. Claude and Hymel were several generations removed from whatever Hyhborn they descended from, but I imagined there were ones born recently. Though I had no idea if the Hyhborn cared for that child or not. I didn't know if any *caelestias* lived in their Courts.

"I have something I want to talk about that you're not going to like," Grady started after a moment.

"What?"

Grady took a deep breath, and I tensed, because I had a feeling that this was going to be a conversation that we'd had before. One that would add yet another thing for me to worry about. "We don't have to stay here," he began, and yep, I was right.

"Yes, we do." I shoved the blanket off my legs, already feeling my body heat.

"No, we don't. There are other cities, other territories—"

"And what would we do in these other places that would be better than this?" I challenged, scooting off the bed. I needed to be standing for this conversation. "Do you think you can get a position like this—one that not only pays you but gives you shelter? Nice shelter at that?" I began pacing. "A job that doesn't require you risking your life every day, like the miners or the long hunters do?"

Grady clamped his jaw shut.

"And what will I do? Go back to playing fortune teller at markets, risking being called a conjurer? Or find work in some tavern, where I'm likely to be on the menu along with ale that tastes like horse piss?"

"And you're not on the menu now?" he fired back. "To be sampled by whoever, whenever?"

"I'm on the menu because I want to be." My hands balled into fists. "And I'm not even really on the menu. I'm like a barely chosen . . . appetizer."

Grady stared at me, his brows climbing. "What . . . the fuck?"

"Okay, that was a poor analogy, but you know what I mean. We have it made here, Grady. Gods." Frustration rose. "You really aren't even planning to ask Claude about apprenticing to the blacksmith, are you?"

"Honest? I don't give a fuck about apprenticing to the Baron's blacksmith."

I slammed my eyes shut. "Grady, you're good at that. You actually enjoy it—"

"Yes, I am good at it and I do enjoy it, but I'd rather use my talent forging weapons for the Iron Knights than for some fuck-boy *caelestia*."

"Grady," I gasped, eyes flying open as I crossed the short distance between us. "My gods, will you please stop saying stuff like that? Especially now? When the Prince of Vytrus is here to discuss them?"

"I'm not worried about that when it comes to him."

"Really?" I challenged.

"Really." He glared up at me. "Look, I know it freaks you out when I talk about the Iron Knights, but damn it, you can't tell me that you're happy here. That you're happy with all of *this*." He swept his arm out. "And I'm not just talking about this manor and the Baron, but the way we lived. The way we've had to live."

"Oh my gods." I pressed my hands to my face.

"And I know you're not. I know you think the same way I do about the Hyhborn—that they do nothing for us lowborn," he said, and I peeked between my fingers, seeing his nostrils flared with anger. "You know, one day I'd like to marry."

I lowered my hands to my sides.

"And maybe have a kid or two," he continued. "But why the fuck would I do that? Why would I want to bring a child into this world? There's no real opportunity for that kid to be anything of value when the Hyhborn control everything—who can get an education, who can own land—" He cut himself off. "They'll just keep putting *caelestias* like the Baron in control, and yeah, I know he's not that bad, but I could spend all night naming others who would be better suited but would never get the chance. We are basically just cattle for them, working in the mines, feeding them, keeping the realm running, and for what? So yeah, we have it better than we did before, but we don't have it good, Lis. None of us do."

"I . . ." I lifted my shoulders, but the weight of his words—of the truth—pulled them back down. I went to the bed and sat beside him. "I don't know what to say."

"You can just think about it, you know."

My breath caught. "Think about what, exactly?"

"Leaving here."

"Grady—"

"I know of a place," he cut in. "It's a town in the Eastlands."

Slowly, I twisted toward him. I heard the name of the city whispered in my mind before he even spoke it. "Cold Springs." Then I heard more, and it terrified me. "You're talking about a town," I said, lowering my voice to a whisper, "that is basically becoming a stronghold for rebels. A town that will inevitably end up like Astoria? You think there'll be a future *there?*"

"You don't know that." His eyes narrowed as his shoulders went rigid. "Unless you *do* know that."

"I don't know that as in I've seen this town get destroyed, but I don't need special gifts to know that will eventually happen."

Grady relaxed. "Maybe not. Maybe Beylen will make sure it doesn't."

Shaking my head, I let out a short, rough laugh. "You have a lot of faith in someone you've never met and who's only succeeded in making a lot of people homeless or dead."

"It isn't different from any of those who have faith in a king they've never met," he pointed out. "Who hasn't done a damn thing for the lowborn."

Well, he was right about that. I folded my arms over my waist as I pressed my toes against the floor. He was right about a lot of stuff when it came to the Hyhborn and how the realm was ruled. It wasn't like I hadn't thought these things myself, but Grady wasn't just suggesting that we leave Archwood. He was suggesting that we leave to join the rebellion, which would likely put us in a worse position than we'd ever experienced before. Even if I couldn't see it, the chances it would end in our deaths were high. "Would we be having this conversation if Claude hadn't summoned me tonight?"

"Eventually," Grady said. "But it sure as hell makes now seem like a better time than ever. What's going on in the Westlands? The Prince of fucking Vytrus being here?"

I looked at him. "The Prince . . . he's different," I repeated.

"And what makes you think that, Lis? Honestly?"

"Well, starting with what he did to the Mister."

"*That* makes you think he's different?" Grady coughed out a short laugh. "Lis, he left the Mister looking like a gods-damn human pretzel."

I cringed. "I wasn't talking about that. He—Prince Thorne—he asked about the bruises on my arms."

"What?"

"Mister's pinching. It always left bruises—"

"Yeah, I remember that fucker always pinching you," Grady cut in. "But what do you mean by the Prince asking about that?"

Frowning, I looked over at him. His expression mirrored mine. "That night? After he looked into my eyes, he glanced down at my arms and asked how I got them."

Grady stared at me, his brows inching up his forehead.

"You don't remember?"

"I remember everything about that night—even when I couldn't move a damn muscle or blink an eye." His jaw tightened. "What I do not remember is that prince asking you that."

"But he did. He saw them and asked what had caused them. I didn't answer but I glanced at the Mister. That's why he did that to . . ." I trailed off. "Are you serious? You really didn't hear him ask that?"

"Yeah, Lis, I'm serious. I didn't hear him say anything of the sort, and I was right there."

I opened my mouth, but I didn't know what to say as I sat back. I knew that I'd heard him. That he had spoken to me as he held my arm, and then he'd put his fingers to his lips and grinned, but how could Grady not have heard him?

And how could I have?

CHAPTER 18

Between everything that had happened with Prince Thorne and what I'd discussed with Grady afterward, I didn't think I'd be able to rest. Especially with how my mind kept going back and forth on whether I had actually heard Prince Thorne's voice all those years ago or it was just a product of a scared child's imagination. The latter seemed the likeliest explanation, but was also one that didn't sit right with me.

But I'd ended up falling asleep after Grady left, and I didn't toss and turn, waking up every hour like I normally did. I slept like the dead, and somehow, I was still tired in the morning, wanting nothing more than to return to bed, but I knew better than to show that as Hymel escorted me through the halls of Archwood Manor.

Large bouquets of jasmine now lined the halls, filling the air with a sweet and slightly musky aroma, likely being displayed to impress Prince Thorne. The flowers' sultry scent wasn't the only thing new to the halls. There was a . . . a distinctive charge to the atmosphere. I'd noticed it this morning while I forced myself to dress. I'd kept getting a staticky charge every time I touched something, and I felt that here, flooding the hall.

It was the Hyhborn's presence. I'd felt it that night in Union City, in the gardens, and last night. I knew it was said that the change in the air occurred if a Hyhborn was feeling a lot of powerful emotions like anger or joy or if there were several in one space.

I glanced out one of the open archways, spying the stables in the distance, where there was more activity than normal. Grooms and stable boys brushed down and fed glossy black and pure white horses beneath the run-ins—horses whose withers, the point where the body met the neck, had to stand at least six feet from the ground. That was . . . that had to be a good half a foot above our shire horse.

"They belong to the Hyhborn that have arrived," Hymel said, following my stare. "Huge, aren't they?"

Staring at the horses, I counted four of the beasts. Was Prince Thorne moving about the manor? My heart skipped a bit. It was still very early, but . . .

"You know," Hymel said from where he walked a few steps in front of me, drawing my gaze to the sword strapped to his back, "it wouldn't kill you to say good morning. Make a little conversation. Respond to a comment or two."

I bit back a sigh. This wasn't the first time he'd given me grief about not *chatting* with him. It was a rather routine thing, just as was my silence. I didn't like Hymel. He knew that.

"Might make things a bit more enjoyable for you," he added as we turned a corner.

The only thing that would make these walks more enjoyable was if there were a cliff involved and he walked off it.

"And just in case you need reminding," Hymel was saying as we neared the pillared archway of Claude's study, "you're no better than me. At the end of the day, you've become little more than a whore who can sometimes see the future."

I rolled my eyes so hard it was a surprise they didn't fall out of the back of my head. I wasn't sure if he actually thought that offended me as he stopped to open the door. Likely he believed he'd delivered some sort of cutting blow with his words. Most little men thought they were capable of such. He looked over his shoulder, the stare in his pale eyes challenging.

Meeting his gaze, I smiled, and that smile deepened as I saw his jaw clench. Breaking eye contact, I walked into the study.

Claude sat on the edge of his desk, his long, lean legs encased in black breeches. He looked up from a piece of parchment he held as we entered. A loose smile appeared on Claude's handsome face, and I was struck by how there wasn't a single hint of last night's indulgences there. It had to be because of what he was. If I behaved like him, I'd have permanent shadows beneath my eyes.

"Good morning, pet." He lowered the parchment to the white oak surface of his desk. "Please have a seat."

"Good morning." I sat on the settee as Hymel closed the study door, folding my hands in the lap of my plain, cream-hued gown.

"Would you like some coffee?" he asked as he picked up a small cup.

"No, thank you." The last thing my jumpy stomach needed was caffeine.

"You sure?" Claude took a small, rather delicate sip of coffee. "You look tired."

"It was a . . . late night," I said.

Claude raised a dark brow. "And a tiring one?"

I watched Hymel cross over to the credenza, a smirk plastered across his lips. "Somewhat. I . . . I didn't expect to meet a Hyhborn when I entered his chambers."

"Oh." He frowned. "Did I not tell you he was a Hyhborn?"

"No," I stated flatly.

"Good gods, I thought I did. I was . . ." He exhaled slowly. "I was a bit deep in my cups last night."

And then some.

"My deepest apologies, Lis. I truly thought I had told you he was a lord." He sounded genuine, but at the moment, I didn't care. "But did you enjoy yourself?"

"I did," I answered, feeling a bit of warmth creep up my throat.

"Of course you did." He drank from his cup. "Tell me, is it true what they say? Are Hyhborn lords hung like—" He glanced at Hymel, brow scrunching. "What do they say?"

"They say they're hung like their stallions," Hymel told him, having poured himself a glass of whiskey.

"Ah yes." Claude's brow smoothed out. "That. Dying to know."

I wasn't sure why Claude needed to ask for clarification on that saying. Besides the fact that it was a rather common, crass one, he was part Hyhborn. *Caelestias* were quite well-endowed in that area. "I believe it would be a somewhat close comparison."

Pale skin crinkled at the corners of his eyes as he laughed. "Look at you," he purred. *"Blushing."*

Forcing a slow breath in and then out, I pictured one of those stallions crashing through the study and trampling the Baron. And Hymel. Just a little. My smile returned.

"As much as I would love to hear all about what brought that blush to your cheeks, that will have to wait," Claude continued. "What did you two speak of?"

"We spoke of where he was from, but not in any great detail."

"And?"

I eyed him. "Do you know *who* he is? More than just his name?"

Claude raised a brow. "All I know is his name, which is why I sent you, my pet. I assume he's some lord the King keeps close at the capital."

"He's not just some lord," I told him. "He's not even a lord, Claude. He's the Prince of Vytrus."

"Holy shit," Hymel rasped, eyes widening.

The Baron lowered his mug to his thigh. "Are you sure?"

Why did everyone keep asking *me* that? "Yes, I'm positive. He is the Prince of Vytrus."

"My gods, why in the realm would he come here?" Claude exclaimed.

"He's not here to collect any tithes," I shared.

"No shit," Claude murmured, settling the mug onto the desk, likely staining the wood with a ring. I didn't even know why I was thinking about that, but it was a shame to damage such beautiful wood.

"I thought you'd be more relieved," I ventured.

"I would be, but I'm far more concerned about having such a brute in the manor." His throat bobbed. "When the King is displeased, it is usually the Prince of Vytrus who is sent to rectify the situation, and by rectifying, I do mean spilling copious amounts of blood."

My chest tightened. "Prince Thorne may be many things, but a brute, he is not."

Hymel's brows rose as he leaned against the credenza.

"Is that so?" Claude remarked.

"Yes." My fingers tightened around each other. "I'm not sure if what's said about him is all that true. He was a . . ." Gentleman? That didn't sound like the appropriate descriptor. I shook my head. "He's not a brute."

The Baron went silent.

"Someone sounds like they had the common sense fucked out of them," Hymel remarked.

I shot him a nasty look.

Hymel smirked.

Pulling my gaze from Claude's cousin, I resisted the urge to pick up one of those heavy paperweights from the Baron's desk and launch it at his head. "He's here to discuss the situation along the border with you."

Claude's shoulders straightened. "The Westlands? The Iron Knights?"

I nodded.

"Does he believe that this issue will spill over into the rest of the Midlands? Archwood?"

Balls of anxiety plopped from my chest into my stomach. "That I don't know," I said. Here was where things would get tricky. "It was very hard to read him, even when I . . . when I was touching him."

Claude was silent as curiosity crept into his expression. "What do you mean?"

"When I try to, you know, connect to him?" My nails dug into my palms. The story I was fabricating was flimsy at best. "I saw white— like a white wall, which made it hard for me to get a lot of information out of him."

"Huh." Claude appeared thoughtful, and for some reason those balls of anxiety started to knot even further in my stomach. "This shield you saw was attempting to block you?"

"Yes. I thought if it was that, it could be broken." My stomach churned upon me admitting that out loud to Claude. It left a foul taste in my mouth.

Claude said nothing for a long moment. "A prince would be far harder for you to read than a lord." He then looked to Hymel as I frowned. "I'll speak with you later."

The dismissal was clear. So was Hymel's irritation. He slammed his glass down on the credenza before stiffly exiting the study.

Claude arched a brow as Hymel shut the door behind him. "He's a prickly fellow, isn't he?"

"He doesn't like it when you pull rank and he's reminded that you're the baron."

"And that he is not?"

"Yes." I watched Claude stand. "But you know that."

"I do so love to needle him when I can." He flashed a quick grin, motioning me to him. "Come."

The danger of Claude somehow figuring out I'd admitted to being sent to the Prince to gain information seemed to have passed. Curiosity rose in its place as I stood, coming toward him.

He moved aside, extending a hand to the side of his desk free from letters. "Sit."

I hopped up on the desk, wrapping my fingers around the edge of the smooth wood. My feet dangled a few inches from the floor.

Claude looked me over slowly, starting with my face and then moving lower, as if he were searching for signs of something.

Having no idea what he was up to, I held still as he brushed the strands of hair over my shoulder.

"Did you have a good evening?" he asked abruptly. "Truly?"

"Yes."

There was a brief smile. "I want all the details of what transpired between the two of you."

"Well . . ." I drew the word out, quickly thinking of what I could or should share. "It appears that you may have also believed you told him that I would be joining him, but actually didn't."

"Fuck." His fingers halted along the strands of my hair. "Seriously?"

I nodded.

"I am sorry. Really." His eyes briefly met mine. "I wouldn't have sent you if I'd known it was the Prince of Vytrus."

I wasn't sure I believed him. Claude was capable of making any unwise decision while intoxicated.

"How did he respond to your appearance?"

"He was . . ." My brows lifted as he touched my chin, turning my head to the left and then the right. "He was caught off guard by it."

"Did he harm you?" he asked, a lock of hair falling across his forehead. "In any way?"

"No." I realized he was looking for a sign—a mark or bruising. "He didn't, Claude."

He said nothing for a long moment. "Did you service him?"

"He requested that I aid him with his bath." I gave a little jerk as the back of his thumb brushed over my lower lip. My gaze flew to him. Claude . . . he hadn't touched me like this in well over a year. Maybe even two years, and there was a time when I wanted him to. When I looked forward to him visiting my quarters or summoning me to his, maybe even desperately, because I could touch him without guilt, because he knew what I could do—he understood the risks to his privacy, and I had to really concentrate to read him. My intuition wouldn't stay quiet long, though. He could always tell when that happened. I would stiffen, pull away. That's when Claude would prevent me from returning his caresses, his touches, and there was a tiny part of me that had gotten off a little on that. Well, there was a part of me that still did.

"And?" Claude pressed.

"Then he asked for me to join him in his bath and I did."

One side of his lips curled up. "I'm sure all baths will now be dull in comparison."

"Perhaps," I murmured.

"What else?" His gaze flicked to mine.

"He . . . he touched me."

"Like this?"

I nodded as he cupped both breasts, dragging his thumbs over the peaks of my breasts. A wisp of pleasure slowly curled through me, a simple reaction to touch—to any touch, and not necessarily Claude's. I slid my hands over the desk, leaning forward a little. His gaze dropped once more. His lips parted as his fingers pressed into the flesh. Claude had always been a breast man. I watched him slip a finger along the neckline of my bodice, his skin paler than my own—paler and so much cooler than Thorne's. My breath snagged again, but it wasn't the Baron's touch that caused that.

"Did he fuck you?"

There was a sharper twist of desire that had nothing to do with what Claude's hands were up to. It was his words. It was the image of . . . of Prince Thorne that those words conjured up that caused me to squirm a little. "No."

"Really?" Doubt filled his tone as he looked up at me.

"He used his fingers and I my hand." The all-too-clear memory of that thickened my voice and my blood. "That was all."

"Well, that is somewhat disappointing."

A laugh bubbled out of me, drawing his sea-green gaze. "I'm sorry. It's just that you seem genuinely disappointed."

"I am." A small smile appeared as he kneaded my skin. "I don't like that you spend so many nights alone."

Neither did I, but . . . "I enjoyed myself."

"Good." His attention once more returned to my chest. If he could spend the rest of his life fucking breasts, he'd be a happy man.

My gaze dropped to his groin, and I could see he was semi-aroused. I could reach for him. Touch him for at least a little bit before he'd stop me. He was obviously in some sort of playful mood this morning. I could guide him into me, urge him to take me right here on his desk. It wouldn't be the first time, but . . .

Neither of us really wanted it from the other. Other than the breasts, I wasn't his type. He preferred lighter hair and slimmer frames, even when it came to the men. And me? I wasn't sure what my type was. There was nothing in any particular trait of a man or woman I fancied more than another.

Still, if I reached for him, he wouldn't reject me. Not just because I was a warm body. I did *know* Claude's intentions. He would give me what I wanted because he wished he could give me more.

But that seemed like too much effort, and for what? A few seconds of pleasure easily forgotten.

And gods, wasn't that telling? Especially when seeking pleasure was as common as one who sought to quench a thirst?

"Did you learn of anything else?" Claude asked, catching my attention.

My thoughts raced. Claude likely expected that I had learned more about the Prince than why he was here. He knew exactly what I could ferret out of an individual. "He hasn't created a Rae in a long time," I said, the first thing that popped to my mind.

"Well, that's unexpected," he commented, drawing his thumb back over the tip of my breast.

I nodded. "And he's also searching for something—or was."

Claude's touch stilled. "What?"

"He was searching for something he . . . he believed that another Hyhborn had information on," I said slowly, relying fully on what the Prince had shared with me.

Light blue-green eyes met mine. "Do you know who he was looking for?"

I shook my head. "That I couldn't read from him."

His lashes lowered, and he was quiet for several moments. "The Prince of Vytrus rode out this morning at dawn," Claude said, running his hands over my breasts once more, and then his hands went to the table, beside mine. "He told one of the guards he'd be back by supper. I figure that is when he plans to discuss things with me."

I searched myself for a hint of disappointment over him ceasing to touch me and found nothing but apathy. I didn't want that. I wanted to find more. "Do you wish to inspect anywhere else, like between my thighs, for signs of the Prince's brutality?"

Claude snorted. "Maybe later. I'm expected to join the Bower brothers."

The Bowers were a pair of aristo sons who were as often reckless as the Baron. I really hoped he planned on keeping his mind clear.

"I want you with me when he does speak with me."

My stomach dipped. "Why?"

"Because I want to make sure he is telling me everything," he said, fixing the lace on my bodice. "And that he has no ill intentions when it comes to his presence."

Shit.

I would be as much help to him as a crystal ball. He stepped back, and I slipped from the desk. The gown pooled against the floor as panic threatened to spiral.

"I'll have Hymel summon you when he returns, so stay close." He bent, kissing my cheek. "I'll see you later."

I stood motionless as Claude strolled out of the study, and I remained there for several moments. "Fuck," I moaned, letting my head fall back.

"No, thank you."

My head jerked upward and twisted toward the sound of Hymel's voice.

He stood in the open doorway, the ever-present smirk plastered across his features. "I'm sure my cousin already took care of that for you today." He paused. "Then again, that would've been unimpressively quick."

Rolling my eyes, I ignored him as I headed toward the door.

Hymel didn't move. "What did he want to talk to you about in private?" he demanded. "Was it about Prince Rainer?"

I stopped then, but I didn't respond.

"He just asked me in the hall to send a message to the Prince of Primvera requesting to meet but wouldn't tell me why," Hymel said.

Surprise flickered through me. Could it be about the shadow market? If so, was he just now getting around to doing that? Weeks later?

"I'm betting you know why he's requested a meeting," Hymel surmised.

I honestly didn't, but what I found interesting was the fact that neither did Hymel. I doubted it was something that had simply slipped Claude's mind. I said nothing as I brushed past him.

He turned quickly, grabbing my wrist. Grip tight, he yanked me back. I stumbled, catching myself as my furious gaze shot to his. I yanked on his hold—

Hymel twisted his wrist sharply. I yelped at the sharp, sudden pain radiating up my arm. His eyes lit up and the tilt of his smile was sickening. "I asked you a question."

"I know," I seethed, watching his eyes widen in response to me actually speaking to him. "And I'm ignoring you, so let me go."

His lips peeled back. "You think you're so special, don't you? Yet you're—"

"Nothing more than a whore. I know. I heard you the first five hundred times you said that. At least I'm getting off." I held his stare, knowing I was about to deliver a low, mean blow that was as cruel as he was. "Can't say the same about you though."

The back of Hymel's other hand cut through the space between us, aiming straight for my face, but somehow, I was *faster*. I caught his arm, my fingers curling into the crispness of his tunic. "Do not ever think to strike me."

Hymel's jaw loosened, his face paling as he dropped my aching wrist. Our stares locked, and for a moment, I would've sworn I saw fear in his eyes. Real, primal fear. Then his expression smoothed out.

"Or what, Lis?"

A series of tingles ran along the back of my head as images flooded my mind—horrific images of Hymel taking his own sword, impaling himself on it. My grip tightened on his arm. A coldness ramped up inside me. An energy. A power. What I saw was no future set in stone. It was what I wished to make Hymel do—

I dropped his arm, taking a step back. My heart thumped unsteadily.

Hymel eyed me for several seconds. "It's funny, you know? You. Your abilities. One touch and you can know a person's name and their desires. Their future. Even how they die." His lips curved into a smirk behind the neatly trimmed beard. "And yet, you don't know shit."

"Maybe," I said softly. "But I do know how you die."

He went rigid.

"Do you want to know?" I smiled at him. "It's not pleasant."

Inhaling sharply, Hymel took a step toward me, but stopped himself. Without another word, he pivoted and stalked out of the chamber.

"Okay then," I murmured, glancing down at my wrist. The skin was already turning red. "What an asshole."

But so was I.

I'd lied. I'd never touched Hymel or pushed hard enough to see his future. I had no idea how he died. And because karma was about as real as the idea of fate, he'd probably outlive us all.

I left the Baron's study, and it wasn't until I was halfway to my quarters, while I pictured myself repeatedly kicking Hymel between the legs, when something about Claude struck me. It brought me to a complete stop by the windows facing the stables.

Claude hadn't asked what Prince Thorne had been searching for information on but *who*.

⇛

I paced the length of my quarters, thinking over what Claude had said. It was likely just a slip of the tongue, saying who when he meant what, but . . .

My intuition told me that wasn't the case.

But what could it even mean—if Claude knew that the Prince had been in search of information on someone? Why did that matter?

My intuition was no help there.

What I really needed to be stressed about was how I was supposed to be of aid to the Baron when he spoke with Prince Thorne. My stomach twisted as I all but stomped into my bedchamber. The lazy churn of the ceiling fan kept the room cool, but it was still far too warm. I undid the buttons of my bodice and shimmied out of the gown. I left it on the floor, too tired and, well, too lazy to hang it up.

Dressed only in a thigh-length chemise, I plopped down on the bed and lay flat on my back, resting my aching wrist on my stomach. I tentatively turned it. It was definitely going to turn a lovely shade of blue by the day's end, but it wasn't sprained or broken.

I *was* lucky for that.

There had been times in the past, when I'd been caught stealing food or being where I wasn't supposed to be, when I hadn't been so lucky.

I stared at the ceiling, thoughts returning to this supper. I couldn't read the Prince. Unless I cracked the shield. Something that Claude seemed to think I could do, and I wasn't sure if that was because I'd led him to believe that or if he already knew.

Gods, maybe I should've just told the truth. Too late now. Now, I was just going to have to . . . figure something out.

I snorted, wanting to smack some better life choices into myself, because it was unlikely that I would think of something less idiotic than lying.

Gods, I was going to be seeing him again.

An edgy nervousness swept through me. It wasn't a bad feeling, nothing like the anxiety of dread. It felt a lot like . . . like anticipation, and that did worry me. I had no business being excited when it came to any Hyhborn, especially one such as the Prince of Vytrus. Even if I hadn't seen him incinerate a Hyhborn with his hand or rip out a lowborn's throat, the very last thing I should feel was anticipation.

Any interaction with a Hyhborn was potentially dangerous when they could learn of my abilities and assume I was a practitioner of bone magic. Especially within Archwood Manor, where there were one too many who knew of my gifts. What I should be anticipating was the moment the Prince left Archwood.

But I wasn't.

Maybe Hymel had been somewhat right, and I'd had the common sense *fingered* out of me.

Sighing, my mind found its way back to Claude. I thought back to the first time I'd met him, and how his features had turned from anger to surprise as I warned him about the man who was set on robbing him.

But that surprise hadn't lasted long. He didn't doubt or question what I told him like many did when I first warned them about something. He'd simply accepted that what I knew was true. He wasn't the first to do that, but he was definitely the first aristo that believed me without question. Maybe that should have raised some questions, but I was just too damn grateful when Claude showed his appreciation by offering a place to work and stay, not just for me but also for Grady. I wanted a warm, safe bed and I didn't want to have to steal stale bread to not starve. I didn't want to ever again have to watch Grady sicken and have there be nothing I could do to help him.

But maybe I should've asked questions?

Instead, I had confided in Claude, telling him a lot. How Grady had gotten so sick when we were younger. The orphanages that were more like work homes. Even about Union City. And he had told me about his family, the Hyhborn blood that came in from his father's side and how Hymel had believed he would be named baron upon the elder's passing. But I didn't ask questions.

That was another thing that was too late, but if Claude knew something, like if he had met another like me in the past, why would he keep that from me? Claude sometimes went to extremes to make sure I was happy. Would he really run the risk of me finding out he knew something and kept it from me? Eyes drifting shut, I rolled onto my side.

My thoughts finally floated their way back to last night as I lay there—to Prince Thorne and the time with him. Not the pleasure he gave me or the release I provided him, but those brief moments where he'd . . . he'd simply held me.

I tucked my legs close to my stomach in a sad attempt to re-create that feeling of being held, of . . . of *belonging*.

Of *rightness*.

It was a silly feeling, but I dozed off to it, and when I opened my eyes again, the dappled sunlight had shifted from one side of the wall to the other, signaling that it was the afternoon. I lay there for several moments, my eyes heavy, and I was close to falling back to sleep when I realized that the change in sunlight wasn't the only thing that had *shifted* into the chamber.

The air was different.

Thicker.

Charged.

A shivery wave of awareness danced down the curve of my spine. The cobwebs of sleep cleared from my mind as my heart stuttered.

I wasn't alone.

Slowly, I straightened my legs and rose onto my elbow as I looked over my shoulder to see what I already sensed—already knew on some sort of primal level—and saw Prince Thorne.

CHAPTER 19

All I could do for several moments was stare at Prince Thorne, thinking I must be hallucinating that he sat on the settee by the terrace doors, the ankle of one long leg resting on top of another. A beam of sunlight cut across the dark tunic stretched across his chest, but from the shoulders up he was cast in shadow.

"Good afternoon." Prince Thorne lifted a glass of amber-hued liquid. "Did you have a restful nap?"

As I blinked rapidly, a rush of disbelief snapped me out of my stupor. "You seem not to be aware of this, but you appear to have lost your way to your own chambers."

"I'm exactly where I intend to be."

I could practically hear the smile in his voice, and it made me bristle. "Then what are you doing here?" And how long had he been sitting there? My gaze swung back to the glass he'd taken a drink from, then lowered to the arm of the settee, then narrowed. "Did you help yourself to my whiskey?"

"I'm sightseeing," he answered. "And I needed refreshment while doing so."

The pounding of my heart slowed. "There is nothing of interest to see in my private quarters, Your Grace."

"Thorne," he corrected, and though his eyes were hidden to me, I felt his heated stare move over the curve of my hip . . . to the length of my leg, and a whole lot of my legs was exposed to him. "And I disagree. There is an . . . abundance of interest to look upon."

Whatever modesty I previously lacked decided to rear its head. I sat up, pressing my legs together. My wrist ached as I tugged on the chemise, which did very little to cover me. Even in the low light of my bedchamber, the material was basically transparent. Something I had a feeling he was well aware of as I glared at him.

A deep chuckle radiated from the sun-streaked shadows, sending an odd mixture of sensations rippling throughout me. Wariness. An acidic burn of unease. Worse yet, a sweet trill of *anticipation*, which I would blame on being half asleep. There was a hefty dose of curiosity, though. I couldn't fathom why Prince Thorne would attempt to seek me out in private like this unless . . . unless he was in need of being *serviced?*

Logically, that made no sense. He didn't believe that I was a courtesan. Still, my body had no plans to listen to common sense. A pulse of desire lit up my veins, causing several parts of my body to throb to life—

Good gods, what in the whole realm was wrong with me? Actually, I knew the answer. It was *what* he was that was wrong with me. A Hyhborn's presence and their sensual effect on lowborn. It made sense that a prince's presence would be even more . . . hard to ignore and stronger.

In reality, if he had sought me out to service him, it was likely only because, as he had said, he was always hungry. So, there was no reason to allow myself to be controlled by my apparently easily influenced hormones. I lifted my chin. "I'm not . . . *working* right now."

His head tilted to one side. "It pleases me greatly to hear that."

My mouth puckered. "And why would it please you?"

"Because I'd rather our interactions going forward be between you and me," he said. "And not dictated by a third party."

"There will be no interactions between us going forward," I said, which was a lie since there would be, but his uninvited presence irked me . . . and thrilled me, which also served to really irritate me.

"I wouldn't count on that."

My chest rose with a deep, short breath. There was something different about him. I didn't know if it was his unexpected visit or the fact that I couldn't see his face, or if it was his words. It could've been all those things, but a different kind of instinct came alive then, one that had nothing to do with my abilities and was purely mortal. Primal. It urged that I rise slowly and leave this space—that I didn't run, because if so, he would give chase like any predator would.

In the shadows, the starbursts in his eyes brightened. Prince Thorne's entire body appeared to tense, as if he sensed I was about to take flight. His chin dipped into the stroke of sunlight. The curve of his lips was full of predatory intent.

A skipping motion went through my chest as I quickly looked away, feeling a little breathless.

"You didn't answer," Prince Thorne said, drawing my attention back to him. He took another sip of *my* whiskey. "Did you have a restful nap?"

"It *was* quite restful until I was woken up to find someone un-invited in my chambers," I pointed out. "Why are you here? Honestly?"

Those long . . . devilish fingers of his tapped along the arm of the settee. "Would you believe me if I said I missed you and wanted to see you?"

I snorted. "No."

"Your lack of faith in my intentions wounds me, *na'laa*."

"I don't know you well enough to have any knowledge of your intentions or faith in them."

"Really?" Prince Thorne drawled, then leaned more fully into the sunlight. My chest felt too tight as he tilted his head to the side. His hair was pulled back from his face and only a wavy strand glanced off his cheek. Multicolored eyes locked on to mine. "You feel you don't know me well enough after I had my fingers inside you and your hand on my cock?"

Another sharp burst of desire darted through me. That was the absolute last thing I needed to be reminded of. "As if that has any-thing to do with knowing you."

"True," he murmured, an amused half grin forming on his mouth.

I folded an arm over my waist. "How did you even know which chambers were mine? Better yet, how did you get in here? The door was locked."

One side of his lips curved up. "Do you think a simple lock can prevent me from being where I want to be?"

My stomach dipped. "Well, that is somewhat . . . creepy."

"Maybe." He was clearly unbothered by that fact. "As to how I knew which quarters were yours, I have my ways."

I stared at him. "At the risk of sounding repetitive—"

"What I just said was also somewhat . . ." The tilt to his lips was now daring. "Creepy."

"Yes." My fingers went to the little red bow at the neckline of my chemise. "But I can see that even though you're aware of being creepy, that hasn't stopped you."

"It hasn't."

"Well, I suppose being aware of your troublesome behavior is one half of the battle."

"It would only be a battle if I found my behavior to be troublesome."

"At least you're honest," I muttered, twisting the ribbon.

"One of us has to be."

My eyes narrowed. "I'm not sure what you're insinuating."

"You're not?" He set the glass of whiskey he'd helped himself to onto the small end table.

"No." I feigned a yawn as I eyed him. His body was reclined in an almost arrogant sprawl. My gaze went to his hand, and immediately I thought of his hand slipping beneath the water. A taut curl low in my belly followed.

"What are you thinking about, *na'laa?*"

"Stop calling me that. And I wasn't thinking of anything."

"Would you get mad if I said you were lying?"

"Yes, but I have a feeling that's not going to stop you."

"It's not." That half smile remained. "Your pulse picked up and it was not fear or anger that caused it. It was arousal."

Inhaling sharply, I resisted the urge to pick up a pillow and throw it at him. "And so what if it was? You should be used to it, being what you are. It's just a . . . a natural reaction to your presence, not one I can control."

"Oh, *na'laa,*" he chuckled. "I do enjoy your lies."

"What? I'm not lying."

"But you are. What you speak of sounds more of a compulsion, and that is not what this is. Our presence doesn't incite what's not already there," he told me. "It doesn't force you to feel pleasure if you were not already open to doing so. It simply heightens whatever is already there."

I snapped my mouth shut.

He raised a brow. "Your response to me isn't something to be ashamed of."

"I'm not." I shifted again, putting weight on my right hand. Wincing at the flare of pain, I jerked my hand from the bed.

"Sure." He rose to his full height.

I tensed, fingers stilling on the ribbon. My pulse was pounding, every part of me wholly aware of how his stare hadn't left me from the moment I'd awakened. "You shouldn't be in here."

"Why?" he questioned as he approached the bed. He didn't so much walk as he did prowl. "Would your baron become upset?"

"No, he would not, but that's beside the point. I didn't invite you in here."

"I did knock," he said, stopping at the side of the bed. "You didn't answer, and I'm glad to hear he wouldn't be displeased."

I ignored the last comment. "Then you decided—what? To come right in?"

"Obviously," he murmured, gaze dropping to the length of my leg. "Then I decided to allow you to sleep. You looked . . . so peaceful." His stare lifted to mine. "I'm assuming that you want me to apologize for entering without permission. To recognize that I've overstepped boundaries."

"That would be a good start," I retorted. "But I have the distinct impression that you're not going to."

His answer was a close-lipped grin. "I'm going to let you in on something you're not quite willing to admit. You don't find my behavior to be all that troublesome."

I swallowed. "You're wrong."

"I'm never wrong, remember?"

"I remember you saying that." Heart thrumming, I watched him sit on the edge of the bed, beside me. "But I also remember finding it unlikely that anyone can never be wrong."

"You might be annoyed that I let myself in," he said, planting his hand on the other side of my legs.

"Might?"

One side of his lips curled up. "Okay, you *are* annoyed, but you do not find my presence here troublesome at all."

The breath I took was full of that soft, woodsy scent that I still couldn't quite place. "I must admit, Your Grace, that I'm disappointed in you."

"Thorne," he corrected yet again. "And how have I disappointed you?"

"I would've thought a Hyhborn of your power would be better at reading people," I said. "Apparently, I gave you too much credit."

He laughed softly as his chin dipped. Another lock of golden-brown hair fell, but to his jaw this time. "I do believe you have forgotten something very important that I shared with you in the gardens. I'm tuned in to you. I know exactly what has caused every catch of your breath and race of your pulse. You're not troubled by my appearance." Thick lashes lowered as his gaze swept over me. "You're excited by it, *na'laa*."

Heat hit my cheeks. He was right, but I *was* troubled by the truth in his words.

Prince Thorne lifted his brows. "You have nothing to say to that?"

I twisted the ribbon tightly around my finger. "No."

He chuckled deeply. "I see you helped yourself to something that doesn't belong to you."

"What?" I frowned; then he glanced pointedly at the dagger resting on the nightstand, beside the sheath and harness Grady had found for me. "Are you going to take it?"

"Should I?"

"I don't know. Aren't you worried about me using it against you?"

"Not particularly," he replied, and irritation flared. "That bothers you."

"Yeah," I admitted. "It's kind of insulting."

"It's insulting that I don't fear you trying to harm me?"

I thought that over. "Kind of."

Prince Thorne laughed then, deep and smoky, and I decided I

also found those kinds of laughs to be insulting due to how nice they were.

"Maybe if you did, you wouldn't barge into my space unannounced or invited," I reasoned.

"No, that probably wouldn't stop me either."

"Nice."

"I do have a reason for being here."

"Other than annoying me?" I countered.

"In addition to that." His gaze dropped to my finger. I stopped messing with the ribbon as his eyes returned to mine. "I wanted to see how things went with your baron."

I started to speak, somewhat relieved . . . and dismayed that he actually did have a reason to be here, but my gaze locked with his, and I suddenly wanted to ask if he ever thought of the young girl he'd found in the orphanage. I wanted to know if he had spoken to me like I believed he had, but Grady said was impossible. I wanted . . .

Clearing my throat, I looked away. "I did speak with him this morning. He was relieved that you were not here due to the King being displeased with him."

"I never said the King wasn't displeased with him."

My head jerked back to him. An unsteady rush of breath left me. He was closer somehow; now less than a foot separated us. "What—?"

Prince Thorne's hand curled around my elbow, and before I knew what he was about, he lifted my right arm. The line of his jaw tightened. "You're bruised." The colors of his eyes had stopped moving, but his pupils had expanded. He carefully turned my hand over, exposing the inside of my wrist to the thin slice of sunlight. "I know I didn't do this last night. Who did?"

I shook my head. "I didn't even know it was bruised," I lied, because there was absolutely no way I would speak the truth, not even to Grady. It was . . . it was just too embarrassing, and I knew it was wrong to feel that way, but it didn't change how I felt. "I have no idea how that happened."

"The bruises look like fingertips." His voice was low, and a chill hit the air.

Tiny goose bumps appeared over my flesh as I glanced nervously around the chamber. "It must be an illusion." I pulled at his hold.

Prince Thorne held on, sliding his long fingers over my wrist. They moved in slow, smooth circles. "Your skin is far too lovely to be bruised," he remarked, some of the ice easing from his tone. "Tell me, *na'laa*, does your baron not treat his *favorite* . . . whatever you are well?"

"I . . ." I trailed off as he lifted my wrist to his mouth. He pressed his lips to the skin—lips that were hard and unyielding, and yet somehow soft as satin. My own parted as a strange tingling warmth spread across my wrist, easing . . . then *erasing* the ache there. I lifted my gaze to his as he lowered my hand to my lap. The bruises were gone. He'd done it again.

Maybe his kisses did heal?

His fingers glided up my arm. "Who bruised you?"

"I told you already. No one."

He tilted his head, sending a wave of hair across his jaw. "Has anyone told you that you're a terrible liar?"

"Has anyone told you that you know not what you speak of?" I snapped.

"Never." His chin lifted, a quizzical look to his expression. "And no one has ever spoken to me like you do."

That should've been a warning to watch my tone, but I huffed. "I don't believe that for one second."

"And I don't believe you."

"I think we've already established that," I retorted.

White streaked across the blue of his eyes, then spread into the green. "Does the Baron treat you kindly?"

"Yes, he does."

Another starburst exploded along the blue of his eyes. "What little I know already tells a different story."

"How so?"

"I don't think I need to explain how reckless he was with your life last night," he said, a muscle thrumming at his temple. "But just in case you haven't realized this—the Baron sent you into the quarters of a Hyhborn prince that was unaware of your arrival. My men could've killed you. I could have. Another of my kind *would've* done that and more."

My skin chilled, not at his words but because I knew he spoke the truth.

"And he did this when it is clear that you're not as experienced as you wanted so badly for me to believe," he continued, and I jerked at the graze of his fingers along the curve of my arm. His featherlight touch kicked off a riot of confusing reactions. I should be angered that he was in my chambers, touching me and demanding answers of me.

Except I didn't feel anger.

All I felt was the tight, shivery wave that followed the path of his fingertips over the curve of my elbow. How my skin suddenly felt hot as he caught hold of the loosened sleeve of my chemise, and . . . and anticipation.

"So, I already know the answer to my question," he said. His eyes never left mine as he paused to brush the strands of my hair back. Nor did they lower as his fingers drifted down my chemise, straightening the dainty lace there.

I struggled to gather my scattered thoughts. Without my intuition to guide me, I had no idea why this prince cared about how I was treated. I also didn't know what he'd do to the Baron, and while Claude sometimes behaved as an overgrown man-child who had made more bad decisions than even me, he was the best many of us had. "The Baron treats me kindly." I held his gaze, not even allowing myself to consider telling him it had been Hymel. Not because I sought to protect that bastard, but because I knew Claude would react very unwisely to his cousin being harmed. "He treats all of us kindly."

"All?"

"His paramours. Ask any of them, and they will tell you the same."

"So, that's what you are? A paramour?"

I nodded.

"He sends his favorite paramour to the chambers of other men?"

"We are not exclusive." We weren't really anything, but that seemed like a moot point at the moment. "None of his paramours are."

"Interesting."

I raised my brows at him. "Not really."

"We will have to disagree on that." Prince Thorne's head dipped, and my breath caught at the feel of his mouth beneath my ear, against my thundering pulse. He kissed the space there. "Who bruised you, *na'laa?*"

Pulling back, I gained some distance between us. "No one," I said. "I likely caused it while . . . while gardening."

Slowly churning eyes lifted to meet mine. Several seconds passed with neither of us saying a word, as if we both had fallen prey to a sudden trance. It was he who broke the silence. "Gardening?"

I nodded.

"I didn't realize that was such a violent activity?"

My lips pressed together. "It's normally not."

"And how did you bruise your wrist while gardening?"

"I don't know. I already told you I wasn't even aware that it had happened." Frustration rose, and I scooted back, away from him. Swinging my legs off the bed, I stood. "And why do you even care?"

Prince Thorne angled his body toward me, and the moment he faced me, I realized that standing wasn't exactly the brightest move. I stood in the filtered beams of sunlight, and I might as well be nude.

His gaze strayed from mine then and drifted lower, over the sleeves and lace he'd straightened. The tips of my breasts tingled, hardening under his stare. A heated shiver followed his gaze over the curve of my waist and the swell of my hip.

I could've moved to cover myself, but I didn't, and it had nothing to do with him already seeing me without a stitch of clothing twice now.

It was the same reason as last night. I . . . I wanted him to look.

And he did as he tipped forward and rose. He looked for so long that muscles all along my body began to tighten in . . . in heady anticipation.

The urge came again, the one that goaded me to turn and take flight, knowing that he would chase. But it was more. I wanted that. Him to chase.

The colors of his eyes were moving again, the stars brightening. Shadows formed in the sudden hollows of his cheeks, and it could have been my imagination, but I thought he *wanted* to give chase.

All of that sounded . . . insane to me. I didn't want to be chased or . . . or *captured* by anyone, especially not a prince.

Trembling, I held myself completely still. When I spoke, I barely recognized my voice. "I asked why you cared?"

Prince Thorne didn't respond for a long moment, and then he inhaled deeply, the tension leaking from his body and . . . and then mine. "Why would I care about some lowborn girl who pretends at being a courtesan—"

"I'm not a *girl*," I interrupted, irritated by him—by me. "And that is something you should be well aware of."

"You are correct." His gaze swept over me in a languid perusal, and the right side of his lips curved up. "My apologies."

I stiffened at the low, sultry drawl. "That sounded more like innuendo than an apology."

"Probably because the flush in your cheeks when perturbed reminds me of the same flush of when you come," he said, and my mouth dropped open. "I would apologize for that also, but I have a feeling that too would sound like an innuendo."

"Oh my gods," I hissed. "You are . . ."

"What?" The colors of his eyes were churning again. "Captivating to you? I know. There's no need to tell me."

"Wasn't planning to."

"Whatever you say, *na'laa*," he murmured.

My hands curled into fists.

His faint grin faded as he glanced at the terrace doors. A moment passed. "You asked why I care?" His brows knitted. "There is this . . . feeling that I know you. It's this strange sensation that we've met before."

The words *we have* crept up my throat, but I couldn't get them past my lips. The want for him to know that we had battled with the warning that doing so could be a mistake. I froze in confusion, not understanding either response.

"Other than that?" The line of his jaw tensed. "I really don't know. You shouldn't matter."

I blinked. "Wow."

"You misunderstand."

The Prince wasn't the only one feeling strange sensations. Currently, there was something akin to the sting of . . . of rejection burning at my insides. "No, I think that was pretty clear."

He turned to me. "I don't mean that personally, Calista."

I shivered at the sound of my name.

He tilted his head, seeming to catch that response. "I am a Deminyen. Do you understand what that means?"

"Uh, that you are a very powerful Hyhborn?"

A low, dark laugh left him. "It means that I am the furthest thing from a mortal—from humanity—you can get. I care about mankind as a whole, but that is only because of what I am. How I was created."

"Created?" I whispered.

His stare held mine. "Deminyens are not born like the *caelestia.*"

"I know." Something struck me then as I stared at him. "You were—" I stopped myself from saying he'd appeared a little younger when we first met. He had appeared younger to me then in comparison to Lord Samriel, but his features hadn't really changed in the twelve years since. "What are you saying? That you cannot feel compassion or caring?"

"Some Deminyens can. Lords and ladies, if they choose to do so."

"But not you?" I looked him over. "Or not princes and princesses? The King?"

"Not us."

"Because you're more powerful?"

"It's more . . . complicated than that, but yes."

My forehead creased. "From what I know of you, I don't believe that you're incapable of such."

"I thought we didn't know each other at all."

I narrowed my eyes. "I know enough about you to believe that."

The Prince stared at me in silence before murmuring, "Precious."

"What is?"

"You."

Crossing my arms, I rolled my eyes. "Okay. Whatever—"

"I've shown *you* compassion, *na'laa*. That doesn't mean I am a compassionate being."

Little of that statement made sense to me. "I think you're wrong."

"Really?" That tight smile resurfaced. "And why do you think this?"

"Because you said you would've been disappointed if you had destroyed Archwood," I pointed out. "And it's not like our city represents all of mankind."

"And I also said that wouldn't have stopped me from doing so."

My stomach dipped. "Yes, but you also said that you thought turning a soul into a Rae was unfair. If you were incapable of feeling compassion, wouldn't you also be incapable of feeling remorse or guilt or even fairness?"

Prince Thorne opened his mouth, but he said nothing as he stared at me. Seconds ticked by, and I thought . . . I thought he paled a little.

"You're right," he said hoarsely.

Then he turned and left the chambers without saying another word, leaving me to wonder why the idea of him having compassion would cause him such obvious unease.

⇛

Prince Thorne's strange response to the idea that he had compassion lingered with me throughout the day, but as the evening neared, my confusion was replaced by anxiety.

As I walked into the bathing chamber, I thought I really should've mentioned the dinner to the Prince when he'd been here. I turned the water on in the sink, dipped my head, and splashed cool water over my face.

Grabbing a towel, I patted my face dry as I lifted my chin and began to turn. I stopped, something in the mirror snagging my attention. My hand lowered to the rim of the vanity as I leaned in closer. My eyes . . . they didn't look right.

They were *mostly* brown.

"What the hell?" I leaned in closer to the mirror. The inner part closest to the pupil was a . . . shade of pale blue, and that wasn't normal at all.

Slamming my eyes shut, I felt my breathing pick up. It had to be the light in the bathing chamber or . . . my mind playing tricks on me. There was no other logical reason for my eyes to suddenly change color. I had to be seeing things.

I just needed to open them to prove that.

My heart fluttered like a caged bird. "Stop being ridiculous," I scolded myself. "Your eyes didn't change colors."

A knock on the chamber doors startled me. It had to be Hymel, and knowing him, he would be impatient as usual, but my heart still pounded. Forcing a deep breath into my lungs, I opened my eyes and leaned in close to the mirror.

My eyes . . . they were indeed brown. Just plain old brown.

The knock came again, this time louder. Tossing the towel into the basin, I hurried to the chamber doors.

"The Baron Huntington has requested your presence," Hymel announced.

My stomach toppled so fast that it was a wonder I didn't vomit all over Hymel's polished boots.

I was expecting this, and still, anxiety surged through me as I joined Hymel in the hall.

Hymel looked at me as we walked, his stare challenging. "You going to tell my cousin about earlier?"

"Are you worried?" I countered, instead of ignoring him as I normally would.

The man laughed, but it sounded forced. "No."

I rolled my eyes.

Hymel was silent until we neared Maven's chambers. "I wouldn't say anything about it if I were you," he said, staring straight ahead. "You cause me problems—"

"You'll cause me problems?" I finished for him. Gods, Hymel was a walking cliché.

"No." Stopping at Maven's door, he faced me. "I'll cause your beloved Grady to have very significant issues."

My head whipped toward him as my heart lurched.

Hymel smirked, pushing open the rounded wooden door. "Don't take too long."

Anger and fear crashed together as I forced myself to walk away from Hymel. I entered the darkened chamber, chest filling with so much hatred I was barely aware of Maven ushering me toward the tub. As her gnarled fingers undid the buttons of my gown, I willed my heart to calm. Hymel had some level of authority in the manor, but there was no way Claude would allow Hymel to banish Grady from the manor or something like that. Not as long as Claude was satisfied with what I could do for him.

That was what I reminded myself of as I bathed and then was dried off. Maven's hunched form shuffled along the rack of clothing, pulling free a gown of diaphanous black.

After I donned a piece of fabric that could barely be considered an undergarment, Maven dressed me in the gauzy material. A series of delicate lacy straps crisscrossed loosely at my chest, and I was sure my breasts would make an impromptu appearance if I bent in the wrong direction. I glanced down at the skirt of the gown. There were slits on both sides, all the way to my upper thigh. The gown could barely be called that, but it likely cost far too much coin.

Brush in hand, Maven urged me to sit on the stool. She began to work the tangles out of my hair, jerking my head back. Once she was satisfied with the results, the paint came next. Red for the lips. Dark kohl for the eyes. Pink rouge for the cheeks. Her hands smelled of soap, the kind used to launder clothing. She then limped toward the deep shelves lining the wall, retrieving a headpiece from a chest.

Strings of small, oval rubies nearly as long as my hair hung from a circlet. The jewels glimmered in the flickering candlelight. Maven placed the headpiece upon the crown of my head. It was far lighter than the diamond one.

After straightening the strings of rubies in my hair, Maven

stepped away, turning her back. I knew what that meant. She was done, and I was dismissed to return to Hymel.

But I was slow to move as I stood, my gaze flicking from the curved line of Maven's back to the standing mirror. I walked to it, half afraid to get closer and to see my eyes, but I did.

They were still brown.

What I'd seen in my bathing chamber had just been my imagination.

That was all.

CHAPTER 20

In between the numerous lit candelabra, platters full of roasted duck and plump chicken breast lined the long dining table, placed among the plates of grilled salmon and bowls of steaming carrots and stewed potatoes. Trays of desserts were already on the table, tiny square chocolates and fruit-filled pastries. There were enough baskets of bread to feed an entire family for a month.

As long as I lived, I would never grow accustomed to seeing so much food on one table, in one home.

And it was far too much, but Claude wanted to impress the Prince with a feast. I didn't even want to think about how much this cost as I made a mental note to let the cook know to send the leftovers to the local Priory, who would know which families were most in need. At least what was left untouched wouldn't go to waste.

"Where in the fuck is this prince?"

Across from me, the red-haired Mollie nearly dropped a bottle of champagne before placing it on the table. Her gaze darted from mine to the man seated next to me while the rest of the staff waited along the wall as if they were trying to become a part of it.

Slowly, I looked at Claude and took a deep breath that did very little to calm my temper.

He was sprawled in his seat, one booted foot resting on the edge of the table, mere inches from his plate. A diamond-studded champagne flute dangled precariously from his fingertips, glittering in the candlelight. At any given moment, the contents of his glass or the entire flute was going to end up on the floor. Or his lap.

I squeezed my hands together until I could barely feel my fingers. All my other many, many concerns had fallen to the wayside the moment I'd seen Claude.

He had not made wise choices during his afternoon spent with the Bower brothers.

My jaw ached from how tightly I was clenching it. I didn't even want to think of what would go through the Prince's mind if he walked in the dining hall and saw the Baron seated as he was. At least he wasn't as bad as he had been the night prior. Luckily, no stench of the Midnight Oil clung to his white dress shirt or fawn breeches, but he couldn't be that many glasses of champagne away from being three sheets to the wind.

"They should be here momentarily." Hymel cleared his throat from where he sat on the other side of the Baron. He was paler than normal, and I thought that he actually appeared concerned. "At least that's what I was told by one of the Hyhborn that had traveled with him."

Claude huffed, lifting the flute to his mouth. "Momentarily?" He took a drink. "As if we have all the time in the world to wait for them."

I wasn't quite sure what Claude had to do after the dinner that was so pressing. Well, other than joining the aristo who had already begun to gather in the solarium and Great Chamber. But he could survive one evening being late to festivities or not taking part in them.

Reaching for the pitcher of water, I poured a glass and then slid it toward the Baron. "Perhaps you would like some water?"

He lowered the flute as he gave me a wide smile that showed way too much teeth. "Thank you, darling."

I returned his smile, praying to the gods he would take the hint. But of course he didn't.

"You look lovely this evening, by the way." He reached over, tugging gently on a strand of rubies. Dark lashes lowered. "At least I have something lovely to look upon while I wait."

I widened my eyes as I reached for my own glass of water. Maybe he was closer to being completely useless than I suspected. My gaze fell to the floor. My gaze fell to the gold veining of the marble tile. It was the same flooring throughout the dining and receiving hall, as well as the Great Chamber. I turned to where Grady stood guard between marble and gold pillars.

"They're coming," Grady announced.

My stomach dropped, and I wasn't sure if it was what I'd seen in the mirror earlier, Claude's current state, or the fact that it was *he* who was coming.

"About damn time," Claude muttered, thankfully drawing his foot off the table. He set the champagne aside.

The sound of chair legs scratching across the stone snapped me into motion. I rose, having momentarily forgotten that one was to stand upon the arrival of a Hyhborn.

My skin pimpled with the charge of energy entering the dining hall as Grady gave a curt bow, then stepped aside. The air thickened around us.

The first Hyhborn to enter was one with skin a rich shade of brown and dark hair shaved to a fade along the sides, leaving the short dreads along the top shaped into a mohawk of sorts. His broad, stunning features were highlighted by the neatly trimmed beard framing his jaw and mouth. Flames flickered above the candles before going completely still as he crossed the space. His eyes were like Prince Thorne's, the blue and green more vibrant, though, as his gaze swept to where we stood, slipping past me and then darting back.

A slow half grin tugged at his full mouth.

Before I could even consider that smile, another entered. One as tall as the first, but not as broad. The sharp, striking features were a cool shade of fawn, a startling contrast against the onyx-hued hair that fell over his forehead and into wide-set, narrow eyes—eyes that were such a pale shade of blue and green, they were nearly luminous in the candlelight. There was no brown that I could see in his irises, nor did he have the same almost frenetic aura of energy as the one who entered before him, but there was an undeniable keen sense of power as he gave us a once-over.

Then . . . then the air felt as if it were sucked out of the hall.

Prince Thorne entered as the flames went wild above the candles, dancing rapidly. Like a coward, I averted my gaze to the table. I didn't see his expression, but I knew the very moment he saw me. Tiny shivers erupted over my skin. I felt his stare drilling into me, straining my nerves until I was a second away from making some sort of absurd noise like a squeak. Or a scream. Heat crept up my throat as I *still* felt his stare. Good gods, why in the holy fires was no one speaking? And how long were we supposed to—

"Please be seated," Prince Thorne finally said, shattering the silence with his deep voice.

I all but collapsed into my chair as Claude surprisingly took a steadier seat. "It is an honor to have you at my table, Prince Thorne," he said, and I felt a laugh bubbling up. *Honor?* He hadn't sounded honored moments ago, but at least he sounded genuine. "Though, I do hope there will be no need for the armor between the servings of duck and fish."

Armor? What?

"One can never be too prepared," Thorne replied.

I peeked up, finding the three Hyhborn seated at the table and the staff in the midst of placing diamond-encrusted plates and glasses before them. The Hyhborn were indeed armored, a fact easily missed with a quick glance. The chest plates were covered in black leather, causing the armor to blend into the sleeveless black tunics beneath. There was something etched into the leather—a sword with a cross handle framed by . . . by wings—wings outlined in thread of gold.

"I was unaware that we would have company," Prince Thorne stated.

My pulse skittered, and before I could stop myself, my gaze lifted to him. He was, of course, somehow seated directly across from me, and he . . .

Prince Thorne was devastating in the glow of the candles, his hair unbound and resting softly against his cheeks. He didn't look remotely mortal then. I couldn't seem to get my throat to work on a swallow as my eyes locked with his. The swirls of colors in his irises were still, but his regard was no less intense and piercing.

"Ah, yes. I figured since you two have already met, you wouldn't mind her presence," Claude said, champagne flute once more in hand. "I hope I'm not faulty in my assumption?"

"No." Prince Thorne smiled, his stare not leaving me as he relaxed into his seat. "I do not mind her presence at all."

I sank about an inch in my chair.

"In fact," Prince Thorne continued, "I welcome it."

My heart gave a strange little skip that I would need to smack myself for later as Claude cocked his head to the side. That terse silence fell again. After a small eternity, the Prince's gaze shifted away, and I was finally able to swallow before I choked on my own saliva.

"And who may this be?" Prince Thorne asked.

"My cousin Hymel," Claude answered, placing his flute by his plate. I hoped that glass stayed there. "As the Captain of the Guard, he is an integral part of Archwood Manor and the city."

"Your Grace." Hymel bowed his head respectively. "It is a great honor to have you and your men at our table."

Our table? I barely contained my snort.

Prince Thorne eyed him, the curve of his well-formed lips nothing like the smiles I'd seen him give. His smile was cold. Dispassionate. My skin prickled.

"I don't believe I've been introduced to those accompanying you," Claude stated as the glasses of champagne were filled by the staff and plates generously loaded with a helping of all that was on offer.

"Commander Lord Rhaziel." Prince Thorne extended a hand toward the Hyhborn who'd been the second to enter and then nodded at the other. "And Lord Bastian."

Bas.

My gaze shot to the other Hyhborn lord, and I suddenly understood his smile when he had spotted me upon entering. He had been in the gardens that night, the one who had spoken to Prince Thorne while I slipped in and out of consciousness.

Lord Bastian caught my stare and winked. "Your city is most peaceful," he said, shifting his attention to the Baron. "As are your manor grounds. Very . . . lovely scenery you have, especially in the gardens."

Oh gods . . .

Would it be considered dramatic for me to wish that the floor would open up beneath my chair and swallow me whole?

"That is most kind of you. Archwood is the jewel of the Midlands." Claude reached for that damn glass of champagne. "Please, enjoy our food. It has all been prepared in your honor."

"It is much appreciated," Prince Thorne acknowledged.

"Archwood is more than just the jewel of the Midlands," Commander Rhaziel stated as the Prince picked up a knife, cutting into the chicken. "It's a vital trading port, situated at a central point in the kingdom, and by far the most easily accessible city along the Eastern Canal," he said. That was true only because the remaining cities along the Eastern Canal were isolated by the Wychwoods. "Archwood is very important to the . . . kingdom."

"It is a relief to hear that King Euros recognizes the importance of Archwood in regard to the integrity of Caelum," Hymel responded, and then launched into a declaration of Archwood's successes in the organization of the ships transporting goods and the funneling of such throughout the other five territories.

I was barely listening as, from the corner of my eye, I saw Claude motion for his glass to be refilled. I tensed, doubting it went unnoticed by Prince Thorne or the others. Claude picked up a buttery roll, tearing it apart before eating it piece by piece as niceties continued to be exchanged. I hoped the bread soaked up some of the alcohol he was consuming. I glanced at the Prince—at his hands as he carved into the chicken.

There was this distinctive edge creeping into how everyone spoke, an increasing thinness to the words of the Hyhborn as the Baron continued to drink. And I was fascinated with watching the Hyhborn eat, which I could admit was a bit odd. It was just strange to see them eat with such impeccable manners while in their armor, with the brief glimpses of sheathed daggers each time they moved in their chairs. Meanwhile, the Baron continued to pick at his food like a small child.

"Would you like something else?" Prince Thorne asked.

When there was no answer, I looked up from the Prince's hands, slowly realizing he was speaking to me. My cheeks warmed. "Excuse me?"

He gestured at my plate with this fork. "You've barely eaten."

My normally robust appetite had been all but vanquished by my nerves and what was going on around me. "I ate a small meal not too long before dinner," I told him.

One brow rose, and he looked at me as if he knew I was lying, which I was.

"Are you tired?" Claude glanced at my plate before looking over at the Prince. "She has been quite tired of late."

I bit down on my lip. That was extremely unnecessary of him to share.

"Is that so?" Prince Thorne's fingers tapped idly.

"She's been spending a lot of time outside," Claude went on as I inhaled deeply through my nose. "In that garden of hers."

Interest sparked in Lord Bastian's features. "The garden?"

"Not the garden you're likely thinking of," I quickly explained. "There's just a small patch of the Baron's gardens that is mine."

"If I can't find her within these manor walls, I always know where to find her," Claude said with a touch of fondness. "She has quite the green thumb."

Feeling Prince Thorne's gaze on me, I speared a steamed carrot with my fork.

"So I've heard," Prince Thorne murmured.

"You've told him about your garden?" Claude asked with a deep chuckle. "Did she speak to you about the various breeds of sedum? Stimulating conversation, I assure you."

"Different *species*," I muttered under my breath.

"Not as of yet." Prince Thorne took a bite of his chicken. "How many different species of sedum are there?"

Surely, he couldn't seriously want to know, but he placed his fork beside his plate and waited. "There are . . . there are hundreds of different species, Your Grace."

"Thorne," he corrected.

Beside him, Commander Rhaziel turned his head to him, his brows lifting.

"Hundreds?" the Prince questioned, either unaware of the Commander's stare or ignoring him. "How can anyone be sure of that? I imagine they all look the same."

"They don't look the same, though." I tipped forward in my chair. "Some grow to over a foot while others hug the ground. Their stems can be rather delicate and easily snapped, but they can choke out even the most persistent of weeds—especially a type called Dragon's Blood, which spreads rather rapidly. They're a genus of succulent that . . ." I trailed off, realizing that everyone, including the staff, was staring at me.

Lord Bastian had that curious little smile on his face.

Commander Rhaziel appeared as if icepicks were being driven into his ears.

But Prince Thorne . . . he looked *engrossed*. "And what?" he insisted.

I cleared my throat. "And they come in almost every color, but I . . . I prefer the red and pink kinds. They seem to be easier to cultivate and last the longest."

Prince Thorne flexed the hand that tapped. "What is the most common then?"

Aware of the other Hyhborn's gazes bouncing between the Prince and me, I felt warmth creep into my cheeks. "Likely a type known as Autumn Joy. It reminds me a bit of cauliflower in appearance throughout summer, and then blooms a bright pink starting in September."

"I believe we have them in the Highlands," Lord Bastian said, drawing his fork over what was left of the duck on his plate. He grinned at me. "I only know this because I too think they resemble cauliflower."

I tentatively returned his smile.

"Speaking of the Highlands," Claude chimed in, drinking from his glass. "All of you have traveled from Vytrus?"

Nearly positive that that was the second time he'd asked that, I glanced at him. Was there a slight glaze to his eyes? I swallowed a sigh.

Lord Bastian's fork stilled, his lazy grin fading as Mollie came to my side of the table with a fresh pitcher of water. "We have."

I leaned toward her, keeping my voice low as I said, "Can you make sure the cook knows to not let what food is left go to waste?"

Understanding what I requested, Mollie nodded, her brown eyes briefly meeting mine.

"Thank you," I whispered, once again facing forward.

Prince Thorne watched, the blue of his eyes darkening. I wiggled a little in my chair.

"Did you travel by horse or ship?" Hymel asked, shattering the ensuing silence.

"Horse." Commander Rhaziel held the stem of his glass, but I hadn't seen him drink from it.

I thought of what Claude had said that morning. That the Prince was harder to get through but the others wouldn't be. There was a chance he was simply speaking nonsense, but I could find out now, couldn't I? Rhaziel was a lord, but I thought about what I felt when he first entered the dining hall. He didn't carry with him the same . . . aura of power.

"Horse?" Claude laughed, eyes widening. "That must have been an incredibly long trip. To be honest, I'm not sure I would've survived such a journey," he prattled on. "I'm far too impatient. I would've taken a ship."

"One would be unable to take a ship from the Highlands," the Commander pointed out as I worked up the nerve to try reading him.

Over the rim of my glass, I focused on the dark-haired Hyhborn. Quieting my mind, I opened up my senses. I created that string in my mind, connecting us. That white wall became visible. The shield. I pictured my hand stretching out, brushing against it, and then I pictured my fingers digging into the light, scouring the wall.

The shield *split*, and at once I *heard* what the Commander thought. *How in the five lands has this man kept this city afloat?*

My own shock pulled me from the Commander's mind before I could sense any more. Claude *had* been right. My gaze darted to the Baron.

"Of course. You're surrounded by mountains and the Wych-woods." Champagne dripped as he flung his wrist toward the Hyhborn, causing me to give a little jump. "Yet, the Eastern Canal is accessible within the Wychwoods, is it not?"

Then again, perhaps I needed no intuition to know what these Hyhborn thought of the Baron.

I focused on Lord Bastian this time, creating that string and finding that white wall. It took several moments, but his shield cracked just enough for me to hear *Exactly how much has he drunk this evening?*

Severing the connection, I shifted with unease. Claude had been right about being able to read Hyhborn, but had he been intentionally correct? Because this wasn't something he would know simply because he was *caelestia*. He could know only if he had experience with someone like me in the past.

The Commander raised a brow, appearing unaware of my intrusion. "It would be several days' ride to reach the Eastern Canal."

"Is it? Then again, geography was never my strong suit." Claude's glass moved wildly again, and this time, I caught his sleeved arm before he ended up dumping half the champagne into his or my lap. He glanced over at me, his smile loose. "Apologies, my pet. I do get a bit animated when I speak. Got it from my mother."

"'Pet'?" Prince Thorne queried softly.

The back of my neck tingled, and it had nothing to do with intuition.

"Is there an animal in the hall that I'm unaware of?" the Prince continued. "A hound or even a cat?"

A snort came from the general direction of Hymel, and I found myself suddenly staring at my knife. Oh, how badly I would enjoy stabbing Hymel with it.

"Goodness no." Claude laughed, tipping his head back. "It's a term of endearment for Lis."

"Is that so?" murmured Prince Thorne. "What a . . . fitting endearment."

Muscles along my spine tensed as my gaze collided with the Prince's. There was no mistaking the derision in his tone. One needed only an ear to hear it. "Far more fitting than other *endearments*," I said.

The corners of his mouth twitched. "I can think of at least one that is better suited."

"You can?" Claude leaned forward, far too eager. "I am dying to hear what you'd think would be more fitting after spending such a short time with her."

Prince Thorne opened his mouth.

"How have you all been enjoying the late-spring Midlands weather?" I jumped in, glancing among the Hyhborn. "I hear the weather of the Highlands is quite temperamental."

"One could say that." Lord Bastian leaned back in his seat, that grin of his having returned at some point. "It is far cooler than here." He glanced at Prince Thorne. "What other terms of endearment are you thinking of?"

Oh, my gods. . . .

Prince Thorne's lips curved up in a slow, smoky smile. *"Na'laa."*

The Commander sounded like he choked.

"What does that mean?" Claude asked.

"It has many meanings," Lord Bastian answered. "I am curious as to which is meant in this case."

"He thinks I'm stubborn," I said, meeting the Prince's gaze.

"Well," Claude drawled. "That I can agree with."

"And ungrateful," I added before Prince Thorne could.

Claude frowned.

"I was going to say brave," Prince Thorne said instead.

My lips pursed as I felt my cheeks heat again.

Prince Thorne's attention was fixed on me, hand curled loosely around the stem of his glass while his other fingers tapped on the surface of the table. He hadn't eaten much but appeared to be done eating. Tentatively, I opened my senses and let them stretch out to him. I met the white wall almost instantaneously. The hand I pictured did nothing.

"The humidity here is quite unbearable," the Commander added just then, almost reluctantly, as if he thought he needed to add something to the conversation that had veered so off track.

"Yes, we don't escape the humidity that bleeds out from the Lowlands," Claude was saying as his glass was topped off once more. "You'll be relieved to learn that the worst of the humidity doesn't arrive until the Feasts. I imagine you all will be gone well before then."

"That I cannot answer," Prince Thorne answered. "We will be here for some time."

CHAPTER 21

I stiffened, caught between a wave of dread and . . . relief, and about a dozen other emotions I couldn't even begin to figure out.

"Excuse me?" Claude choked.

Turning to him, I picked up the glass of water he had yet to touch. "Here."

"Thank you, pet." His smile was brittle as he refocused on the Hyhborn. "When will you be gone?"

"That is hard to answer," Prince Thorne stated coolly, and I would've sworn the temperature of the hall dropped by several degrees.

"I believe there are matters best discussed in private," Lord Bastian advised.

Claude jerked his head at the staff. They peeled away from the shadowed walls, quiet like spirits. Hymel remained seated, but I stood, ready to run from the room despite wanting to hear these matters myself, which I figured had to do with the Iron Knights.

"Your *pet* can stay," Prince Thorne said.

I froze for half a heartbeat. Hands curling into fists at my sides, I slowly turned to the Prince. Our eyes locked once more.

He winked.

My nostrils flared as a rush of irritation swamped me.

The Prince's smile *warmed*.

"Good," Claude said, and before I could take a seat in my own chair, he tugged me down, *into* his lap. "I have a strong suspicion that I will be in need of her comfort during this conversation."

Prince Thorne's fingers stopped tapping. A fine shiver broke out over my skin as the candle flames rippled as if a wind had whipped into the hall, but there had been no such thing.

As soon as the staff had exited and the door closed, Prince

Thorne spoke. "You appear . . . unnerved by the prospect of host-ing us."

"Just surprised. That is all." Claude cleared his throat, tensing a bit. "I'm not at all displeased by the news."

I glanced between the Hyhborn. I didn't think anyone in the room believed that.

"I'm relieved to hear that," Prince Thorne said. "I'm sure you're aware of what is happening along the border with the Westlands. We've come to determine what course of action needs to be taken."

"We have heard some news regarding this." Claude kept an arm around my waist as he reached around, picking up his godsforsaken champagne.

Prince Thorne's unflinching gaze made it hard to sit still. "The Westlands have amassed quite the army and it is believed that they will soon be marching across the Midlands. We suspect that the Princess of Visalia has her sights turned to Archwood and the Court of Primvera."

My breath stalled in my lungs. A siege of Archwood? That was what Ramsey Ellis had feared, but to hear the Prince say it was some-thing entirely different. My mouth dried, and I suddenly wished I could reach my champagne.

"But that isn't the only development," Lord Bastian stated. "There is the Iron Knights."

"Yes, we've heard that they have possibly joined forces with the Westlands," Claude said. "However, I've found that news to be most confounding. Vayne Beylen, who wants to see a lowborn on the throne, joining forces with the Westlands Hyhborn army? It makes little sense."

"From what we've learned, Beylen has decided that his revolt is more likely to be accomplished through aiding the Westlands," Commander Rhaziel shared.

Claude let out a strangled sort of laugh. "I understand the Court politics are usually none of our business," he began.

"They are not," Prince Thorne agreed.

"But whatever strife there is between the Hyhborn is involving us." Claude downed the rest of his champagne. "What is the issue with the Princess of Visalia? What is the cause of this? I'm sure it's complicated, but I should know what is driving the Westlands to jeopardize the safety of my home."

"It's actually not complicated," Prince Thorne replied. "The Princess believes that it is time for a queen instead of a king to rule."

My brows shot up as my lips parted. A queen instead of a king? There had never been one, not since time had started to be recorded—not since the Great War. Could there have been queens before then? Possibly?

"I think the lovely Lis may not be against such an idea," Lord Bastian pointed out.

Prince Thorne inclined his head. "Do you think a queen would rule better simply because of the gender?"

"No," I said without hesitation. "I don't think it makes a difference."

"And how would you feel if it were a lowborn who ruled?" Commander Rhaziel asked.

His question caught me off guard, and I swallowed.

"Your answer will go no further than this room and will be heard without judgment," Prince Thorne advised. "Please. Share what you think."

"I . . ." I cleared my throat, wondering exactly how I ended up being the one asked this question. Oh, yeah, my facial expressions, which likely had betrayed my thoughts. "Things could possibly be different if a lowborn ruled. There are more of us than Hyhborn, and logically, a lowborn would be better at understanding the needs of their own, but . . ."

"But?" Commander Rhaziel pressed, his stare just as hard.

"But it probably wouldn't be better or worse," I said. "You gain that kind of authority and wealth? You no longer represent the people, lowborn or Hyhborn, king or queen."

"Interesting point," Lord Bastian said, dragging his fingers along his mouth.

"But it's an irrelevant point," I added. "If the Iron Knights are now backing the Westlands, then that means they are backing yet another Hyhborn."

"Indeed," Prince Thorne murmured. "It seems Beylen believes that the Princess will rule differently."

I almost laughed, but I thought of Grady—thought of all the lowborn who'd joined or supported Beylen's cause. Did they know that Beylen was now supporting another Hyhborn? Those who risked their lives and died for Beylen's cause? I doubted they would be happy to hear this.

"So, you've come to tell me that war is not only brewing?" Claude lowered his glass to rest on my leg. His grip was tight, knuckles white. "But has also come to my doorstep?"

"I have," Prince Thorne confirmed, and my chest went cold. "But also to inform you that Archwood will be defended."

Relief poured through me, pushing out a rough exhale, because there was a moment something I didn't even want to acknowledge had begun to creep into my thoughts. But the Hyhborn were going to—

"Defended? With just the three of you?" Claude sputtered.

Whatever short-lived relief I'd felt had already vanished, and it now felt like it had never existed. "The Baron means no offense," I quickly said, forcing a weak smile. "Right?"

"Of course," Claude drawled.

"We know the Hyhborn are quite powerful." Hymel spoke up, and I had never thought I'd think this before, but thank the gods he'd said something. Hell, I would've been happy if it were only to insult me. "But three of you to hold back an army?"

"You'd be shocked by what the three of us can do," Prince Thorne remarked. "However, I believe you would prefer that your city remains standing?"

My next breath went nowhere. Immediately, I thought of Astoria and . . . I looked at the Prince. Saw his smile. It was pure ice. Maybe I had been wrong about him being compassionate. If it was he who had destroyed Astoria, innocents had to have lost their lives in the process. At the very least, thousands had been displaced, turned into refugees over the acts of a few.

Something about that didn't sit right, though. He was my—Gods damn it, if smacking myself wouldn't have drawn attention, I would've done it. He was not my anything.

"Since it's been decided, we will have an army ourselves," Commander Rhaziel said, and I focused on one word. *Decided.*

As if there had been another option.

"Unless invisibility is a talent of a Hyhborn army . . ." Claude made a show of looking around the hall. ". . . I'm assuming this army has yet to arrive?"

Oh my gods. . . .

Silence fell in the dining hall. It was so quiet I was sure I could hear a fly cough.

"The army is waiting on my orders." Prince Thorne's tone was frigid. "We have several hundred Hyhborn warriors, in addition to five hundred of the Crown's Regiment"—the lowborn and *caelestias* who served as knights. "There are also Primvera's forces." He glanced at the Commander.

"I believe they have roughly three hundred Hyhborn warriors," the Commander answered.

"So, that's what?" Claude's chest pressed against my back as he leaned forward. "A little over a thousand who will defend Archwood against *several thousand* of the Iron Knights and the armies of the Westlands? And five hundred of them are lowborn and *caelestia?*"

"Five hundred trained by *us,*" the Commander countered, his lips thinning.

"Several hundred Hyhborn has to equate to several thousand lowborn," I assured Claude, gently squeezing his forearm. "That is enough."

His stare met mine, and then he relaxed into his chair, likely thinking that it was my intuition speaking, but it wasn't. My intuition was silent. I was just trying to keep him from saying one more idiotic thing and getting himself killed.

"Your *pet* is correct," Prince Thorne stated.

My head swung in his direction, and I also had to remind myself to not say something idiotic as that irritation sparked deep within me once more. Claude's term of endearment was often annoying, but he never said it the mocking way Prince Thorne did.

For once, Thorne was looking past my shoulder, to Claude. "Any of age who wish to defend their city, or can, should be preparing for such an event."

"We have guards," Claude murmured absently. "Trained men."

My chest tightened as my gaze shot to the closed doors, toward where Grady waited in the halls.

"*Any* of age who are able can be given basic training," Prince Thorne restated. "That would include you, Baron Huntington."

Claude went still behind me; then the laugh that was crawling up my throat spilled out of his lips. "I haven't picked up a sword since I came into my title."

Nothing about the Hyhborn's expressions said that surprised them.

"Then I would suggest you do that as soon as possible," Prince Thorne advised. "After all, one cannot ask others to fight for their homes and lives if one is not willing to fight oneself."

Prince Thorne spoke the truth, but what good was a soldier who was more likely to stab themselves than the enemy?

"As Commander Rhaziel stated before, Archwood is a vital port," Prince Thorne continued after a moment. "Seizing Archwood and then Primvera would cause a catastrophic ripple effect throughout the entire kingdom. It would give the Westlands an advantage in the form of leverage, and the King will not tolerate that. Archwood would then be considered a loss."

The dining hall fell silent. All I could hear for several moments was the pounding of my heart.

It was Hymel who broke the silence. "You mean, Archwood would fall into the hands of the Westlands, therefore becoming a part of this open rebellion of lowborn and Hyhborn?"

My intuition told me no, that wasn't the case, and then it went silent on me, and I knew what that meant. That the answer lay with the Hyhborn, which I could not see, but could guess.

The icy finger of unease pressed against the nape of my neck.

"You wish to speak." The Prince's attention was fixed on me. "Please do so."

I stiffened, knowing it wasn't my place to ask questions, at least not in such a public setting, and I was already pushing it with my thoughts on the whole king and queen business. It was the Baron's place, or at the very most, Hymel's. But neither did. No one did.

The Prince waited.

I cleared my throat. "If the Westlands or even the Iron Knights alone succeeded in seizing Archwood, what would happen?"

"The ports and trading posts would all be destroyed." Prince Thorne's eyes met mine, the colors frighteningly calm. "As would be the entire city."

CHAPTER 22

The diamond-crusted plates and the platters of uneaten food had long since been removed from the table, and only a few trays of desserts remained. Hymel had left with Commander Rhaziel and Lord Bastian to discuss preparations for the arriving regiment—something that the Baron should be taking part in. However, a bottle of brandy had replaced the champagne and only the three of us were now in the dining hall.

By this time of the evening, the Baron would already be in either the solarium or the Great Chamber, surrounded by his paramours and cronies, but the Prince had shown no indication of preparing to leave the hall. Therefore, the Baron remained.

And so did I.

"Tell me something, Your Grace," Claude began, and I briefly closed my eyes, having no idea what level of absurdity was going to come out of his mouth.

And there had been a lot of ridiculousness already, everything from Claude asking whether or not Prince Thorne believed the cold grain cereal often eaten upon waking could be considered a soup, which the Prince had answered only with a stare that was part confusion, part disbelief, to him regaling the Prince with tales of his time spent at the University of Urbane, just outside of Augustine.

Or attempting to.

Prince Thorne didn't appear regaled by any of what the Baron was saying.

However, he did appear to be quite interested in where Claude's free hand was. He'd tracked how the Baron's fingers had first toyed with the string lacing between my breasts, and his stare had followed Claude's eventual path down my stomach, to my hip. He was aware of the exact moment Claude's wandering palm made it to my thigh, exposed by the high cut of the skirt. Tiny bursts of white had appeared in the Prince's eyes.

Claude seemed not to realize what the Prince was so attentive to, but I was aware—too aware. The Baron's touch was cool, but the burn of the Prince's perusal scalded my flesh, creating warring sensations that made it impossible to ignore.

Honestly, I could've left at any point. I wasn't even trying to read Prince Thorne. Claude might have been disappointed, but he wouldn't have tried to stop me. I feared that if I left Claude alone with the Prince, he would get himself in trouble or worse.

Killed.

But was that the only reason?

My gaze briefly met the Prince's, and my breath snagged.

"I've heard something utterly fascinating about Hyhborn that I've always been curious about but never got the chance to ask," Claude went on, his fingers sweeping back and forth along the curve of my upper thigh. "I once heard that a Hyhborn could . . . regenerate severed limbs."

I nearly choked on the champagne I'd been nursing.

"Is that true?" Claude asked.

Across from us, the Hyhborn prince sat as he had in my bedchamber earlier. A short glass of whiskey in hand, his posture almost relaxed, *almost* lazy; but the coiled tension, the barely restrained power, was there.

"Depends," Prince Thorne answered, tracing the rim of his glass, the amber-hued liquor nearly the same color as the hair resting against his jaw.

"On?" the Baron prodded.

Prince Thorne's jaw tightened. "On exactly how . . . strong one may be. Healing such an injury would take an extraordinary amount of energy, even for a Deminyen." His gaze tracked Claude's fingers as they slid beneath the panel of my gown, and I bit down on the inside of my lip. "Energy is not infinite, no matter the being."

"Interesting." Claude swallowed another mouthful.

"Is it?" Prince Thorne inquired. "Should I be concerned about such interest?"

I pressed the side of the flute against my chest, skin prickling at how deceptively soft his tone was.

"Well, I'm half tempted to chop off an arm just to watch it grow back," Claude said with a loud laugh. "Must be a bizarre thing to witness."

My eyes went wide. I told myself he didn't just say that to a Hyhborn—to *the* Prince of Vytrus.

The Prince's finger stilled on the rim of his glass. Flames rippled suddenly above the candle.

"He's only joking, Your Grace." I smiled, stomach twisting. "There is no need for worry. He just has quite the unique sense of humor."

"I'm not worried," Prince Thorne replied, returning to tracing the rim of his glass. "After all, he hasn't picked up a sword since when? He came into his title?"

I doubted Claude had handled a sword before then.

"And one would have to wield a sword made of *lunea* if they thought to pierce the skin and bone." He paused, taking a small drink of his whiskey. "They are quite . . . heavy."

I took a rather large gulp of my champagne then, knowing damn well Claude couldn't lift a *lunea* sword. Prince Thorne knew that.

So did Claude. "Touché." He laughed, reaching for the bottle of brandy. His pour was surprisingly steady. "Though, there are *lunea* daggers that I imagine are less unwieldy."

Dear gods. . . .

"I would like to know something," Prince Thorne stated. "What will you do if the Iron Knights breach Archwood?"

"That shouldn't happen with you and your regiment guarding the city." Claude's fingers slid under the panel of my gown once more. "But if there were to be a . . ." Claude drank, and I tensed. "If there were to be a failure? I have my guards."

Prince Thorne smiled faintly. "And if your guards are killed?"

My stomach knotted, gaze shooting to the door. I didn't even want to think about that.

"Then I suppose I would be up the river without a paddle, as they say," he said, sliding his hand over my thigh. His palm grazed my stomach.

Prince Thorne smirked. "Well, let us hope it doesn't come to that."

"Let's." Claude's fingers returned to the lacing, as did the Prince's regard. "But in all seriousness? If that were to happen? I would defend what is mine in any way I possibly could. Even if I haven't picked up a sword in many years."

Halting with his whiskey halfway to his mouth, Prince Thorne tilted his head. "And what do you consider yours?"

Claude's fingers brushed over the swell of my breast. "Everything that you see."

"Everything?" Prince Thorne pressed.

"The city, from the Eastern Canal to the Wychwoods, and her people. Their homes and livelihoods," Claude said, and it was the first time I'd heard him sound, well, like a baron should. Which was a stark contrast to his fingers dragging over the tip of my breast. I jerked, a small breath escaping me. The thin material was no real barrier against the coolness of his touch. "The grounds and gardens, this very home and everyone inside it."

"Your staff?" The Prince's gaze was latched on to the Baron's hand. "Your paramours?" Taking a drink, he didn't blink. "Your *pet?*"

I jolted again, and this time it had nothing to do with Claude's touch. My eyes narrowed on the Hyhborn prince, but he didn't see. How could he when his attention was fixed to the Baron's hand and my breast?

"Especially her." Claude's cool, damp lips pressed against the side of my neck. "She is the most valuable of all."

My brows shot up.

Prince Thorne lowered his whiskey as his gaze lifted to Claude's. "I do believe that is something we can agree on."

I stiffened. "I am sitting—" My breath caught as Claude rolled the sensitive peak of my breast with his fingers. My grip tightened on the flute stem as the flames above the candles flickered once more.

"You were saying?" Prince Thorne questioned, one side of his lips curving up.

"I was saying, I'm sitting right here." I ignored Claude's hand as it trailed back down my stomach—ignored the Prince's heated gaze that followed, and that heightened, dual sensation of hot and cold. "In case you two have forgotten."

"Trust me," Prince Thorne drawled, leaning back. The stars were even brighter in his eyes. "Neither of us has forgotten."

"That is the second thing we can both agree on." Claude drew his fingers down, past my navel and between my thighs, his hand further widening the gap in the panels.

"I'm glad to hear that you two have discovered something to bond over," I said, lifting my chin. "I hope I can provide a third thing."

"And what is that?" Claude asked, retrieving his glass.

"I am not a possession." I waited till the Prince's gaze returned to mine. "I am owned by no one."

"Agreed," Claude murmured, his fingers pressing into the skin of my inner thigh, drawing my leg a few inches to the side until there was no doubt that the Prince could see the scant black lace between my thighs.

Prince Thorne's gaze hadn't missed a second, and I thought that . . . that his lips had parted just the slightest as he seemed to soak in what the Baron had revealed to him—purposely revealed. My skin flushed hot beneath his stare, but not with shame. A part of me thought that maybe I should be embarrassed. That if I was *good*, I should put a stop to whatever it was that Claude was currently up to, because I was really beginning to wonder exactly *how* drunk Claude truly was.

He was either far more intoxicated than I suspected, or he was handling his drink better than I believed, because his actions and words had become entirely precise and clear.

The Baron was often playful, especially when he drank, even with me when it led nowhere, but I was beginning to think I'd been wrong about Claude being unaware of what the Prince was paying such close attention to. There was a taunting edge to Claude's actions now. As if it was not his own desire that drove him, but what he saw in the Prince's stare.

But I made no move to stop Claude. I couldn't . . . or I didn't want to as the Prince watched, as heat in my skin flooded my veins.

And maybe I had drunk more champagne than I had thought, because I was suddenly emboldened.

"How about you, Your Grace?" I challenged. "Do you agree?"

The dancing flames cast interesting shadows across his features. "I would, except that would be a lie."

"How—" An unsteady rush of air left me as Claude's hand folded over me. A sharp twist of pleasure followed. "How so?"

"No one in the Kingdom of Caelum is truly free." He watched as Claude's hand moved. "All are owned by the King."

Claude chuckled. "He has a point there, pet."

The Prince did, but I said nothing. My pulse was thundering. I felt a little dazed and maybe a bit crazed. I wasn't sure how we'd gone from talk an impending siege to this. I didn't think it was even possible to figure out.

"I have another question for you," Prince Thorne said. "When you were at the University in Urbane, did you spend any time at the Royal Court?"

"I did."

"And what did you think of it?"

"It was an . . . experience," Claude said. "Partly as I expected."

"Partly?"

I was curious to hear the Baron elaborate. I hadn't known he'd been at the King's Court. Only the *caelestias* and a few aristo entered the Hyhborn Courts—well, them and those the Hyhborn *collected*. But I was finding it difficult to listen. I was now watching the Prince as avidly as he watched the Baron's hand. His fingers traced the rim of his glass in nearly perfect synchrony with the ones between my thighs, and it was far, far too easy to imagine it was his fingers I felt.

My hips twisted restlessly as I focused on the Prince's fingers, my breathing quickening. Could the Baron feel the rush of damp heat through the silky undergarment? Did he believe it was my body responding to his touches, or . . . ? I shifted in the Baron's lap, chest rising sharply as he pressed into the lacy undergarment, but I . . . I didn't feel *him* beneath me.

The Baron knew.

Claude was rubbing me like he sought to draw forth an answer from a crystal ball. Not the most arousing technique, nor what I knew he was capable of. He was . . .

He was putting on a show.

"It's as opulent and beautiful as I believed it to be," Claude answered after a moment. "But I didn't expect it to be so . . ."

"So?"

I bit down on my lip at the sound of his voice, at the one word. It washed over my skin like heated silk, and my toes curled in their slippers.

"Cruel," Claude said.

And that one word cooled some of the heat in my blood.

"I have a question for you, Your Grace."

The Prince inclined his chin.

"Are you as cruel as the rumors claim you are?" he asked, causing my heart to turn over heavily.

Prince Thorne didn't answer for several too-long moments, only watching as Claude's fingers continued to move. "Only when necessary."

Claude seemed to understand whatever that meant. "Would you like something other than whiskey to drink? You haven't touched what you have in some time."

"It's not what I'm thirsty for."

"I suppose not." Claude had gone quiet, and that flipping motion repeated. "Pet?" he said against my flushed temple, his thumb sweeping over the throbbing juncture of nerves. "Why don't you go to the Prince."

My gaze collided with the Prince's. The air stilled in my lungs as my body locked up, but my heart hammered.

"He does look lonely," Claude whispered. "Does he not?"

Prince Thorne didn't look lonely.

His entire body appeared taut, features sharper in the violently dancing flames. He looked . . .

Prince Thorne looked *hungry*.

"Go," urged Claude, slipping his arm from my waist and his hand from between my legs.

I hesitated despite the stunning pulse of desire that echoed in response to the Baron's . . . what? Order? Permission? I didn't know which it was. I knew Claude liked to be watched and liked to watch, but this was a prince. Not one of his paramours and another aristo.

But I slipped from his lap and stood, placing my glass on the table. Prince Thorne said nothing, but he tracked me as I walked on legs that felt weaker than they should. I looked at the door, knowing I could leave. Claude wouldn't stop me. I didn't *think* Prince Thorne would. I could easily walk out and put a stop to whatever madness this was beginning to feel like.

I didn't.

If this were anyone else, I would've, but it was *him*.

I went to the Prince's side, heart pounding and hands tingling. He looked up at me, still silent, and suddenly I thought that it might have been a good idea to leave. Clearly, if the Prince wanted company, he would've said so. A different kind of burn hit my skin. I started to take a step back—

Prince Thorne extended his arm as he leaned back. I froze.

Swirling eyes met mine. "Sit."

Feeling as if I couldn't breathe deeply enough, I slipped between him and the table. That was as far as I made it. His arm came around my hips and he tugged me down into his lap.

I felt *him* immediately.

He was thick and hard against my bottom. My gasp likely echoed through the too-silent hall. Across from me, Claude smiled.

Prince Thorne's chest was flush against my back. One hand just below my chest, fingers splayed across my ribs, he was sitting straighter than the Baron had been as his fingers left the glass of whiskey. "What do you think of the Princess of Visalia's intentions to rebel?" he asked of Claude.

"I'm not sure I know enough about her intentions to have an opinion." The Baron lifted his glass.

"You know she wants to rule," Prince Thorne said as I watched that hand slip across the smooth surface of the wood, my heart still pounding. "Is that enough?"

"I suppose, but if what drives her is simply a desire to overthrow King Euros?" Claude snorted, taking a drink. "Then I don't hold her intentions in very high esteem."

The Prince's hand left the table and went to my thigh. I gave a little jump as his warm skin came in contact with mine. He didn't stop there. There was no teasing or . . . or taunting. His hand slid under the gown and between my legs, fingers delving beneath the scrap of lace and against the damp flesh there. My body reacted, back arching and hips lifting to his touch. His chest vibrated against my back, the low rumble scorching my skin. I didn't know what caused that sound—if it was my reaction or his to the slickness.

"The hunger for power seems to be something that plagues both lowborn and Hyhborn equally," Claude was saying. "You can't really fault one for doing what has become second nature."

"I suppose not," Prince Thorne said, slipping one finger through the throbbing dampness, and then inside me. My hips rolled as I gripped the arm of the chair. The sound he made then was unmistakable. A low chuckle. "Can you, *pet*? It's only nature for any species to assert dominance," he added as his finger plunged deep.

My head snapped toward his. Our mouths were inches apart. "Do not call me that."

The blue of his eyes raced across the other colors. "What am I supposed to call you?"

"Not that—" I gasped as his finger hooked, finding a . . . a *spot*.

His gaze roamed over my face, seeming to catch the heightening in color. "What do you say then? Can you blame another for attempting to dominate what they want?"

"I . . ." I had a feeling he wasn't just speaking of the leader of the Iron Knights, but I couldn't be sure, because he touched that spot again. A riot of sensations arced through me. I leaned into him. "I . . . I suppose it depends."

"On?"

"On what one is attempting to dominate," I said, looking away. "And why they want it."

Claude was now who watched, but . . . but I realized that how Prince Thorne sat, my lap and his hand were shielded by the table.

Unlike the Baron, he didn't want another watching that closely, which was surprising. I would've thought . . .

My thoughts scattered as the Prince's thumb joined in. I trembled as all those acute curling motions rapidly built. The Prince's body—his hand and his fingers warmed, heated against me and inside me. Oh gods, I'd never felt anything like that. The edge of the wood dug into my palm.

"But I doubt simply a hunger for more power could drive one, even a princess, to be so bold and reckless as to attempt to seize a city that would draw the ire and the might of the King," Claude continued. "Surely, there must be more than a port that she finds valuable enough to risk being destroyed for."

Something . . . something about how Claude spoke caused my skin to prickle with awareness. Breathing too fast, I tried to focus.

"I do believe that is the third thing . . ." Prince Thorne's finger thrust, his thumb swirled, and it was . . . it was too much. The pleasure building bordered on pain. I started to push away. The arm around my waist prevented that. "That we agree on."

The tension erupted without warning. I came, crying out—

Prince Thorne's hand covered my mouth, muffling the moan of release. "Not here," he whispered in my ear. "Not for anyone else's ears but mine."

My eyes closed as I shuddered, lost a little in the waves of raw pleasure—in the feel of his hard flesh and the tendons of his forearm that I had clutched at some point—and I heard and saw nothing. All I felt was the rippling tremors of pleasure and the heated presence of his finger as it slowed.

I was panting as I settled in his lap, body limp and relaxed completely into his. I watched through half-opened eyes as he slid his palm over my thigh and lifted his hand.

Prince Thorne's eyes snagged mine as he brought his glistening finger to his mouth and . . . and sucked deep.

Oh gods, my entire body tensed once more.

"Thank you," he said, then his gaze flicked to the Baron. "I do enjoy dessert."

Claude laughed deeply, finishing off his glass of brandy. "Don't we all?"

"There is something I require from you, Baron," Prince Thorne said after a moment, his other hand returning to my waist while I focused on slowing my breathing and my heart. "I want her."

I went stiff.

"I want her," Prince Thorne repeated. "For the duration of my time here, she is mine."

CHAPTER 23

The unexpected and possibly inappropriate orgasm had likely addled my mind, because there was no way I'd heard Prince Thorne correctly.

Claude slowly lowered the bottle of brandy. "Why?"

"Does there have to be a reason?" Prince Thorne countered.

Disbelief coursed through me. I *had* heard him correctly.

Jerking out of my stupor, I snapped forward, but I didn't make it very far before the Prince's arm tugged me back against his chest. My head whipped toward him. "Let me go."

Swirling eyes locked with mine. A tense heartbeat passed; then his arm slipped away as a faint grin appeared. "Your command is my will."

I stood, bumping into the table and rattling the glasses that remained as I slipped away from him. "I don't know why you're smiling, Your Grace. What you ask for, you cannot have."

"Thorne," he corrected. He picked up his whiskey. "This should come as a surprise to no one, but just so we all are clear, what I want? I get. And what I want is for you to keep me company during my stay here."

I inhaled sharply. "Well, I suppose this will be a first for you then."

He took a drink as he looked up at me. "I already had a first. Just once when I didn't get what I wanted. There will not be a second time."

Anger welled up inside me so quickly that I forgot *what* he was and *who* I was. "You are out of your mind if you think you can just demand to have me."

"Lis," Claude warned.

"No," I snapped, chest rising and falling heavily. "It will be over my dead body."

The Prince only raised a brow. "That's a bit dramatic, *na'laa*."

"Don't call me that." My lips thinned. "I am not an object that you can simply take possession of or collect."

"I didn't suggest that you are an object."

My nails bit into my palms. "Exactly what are you suggesting then? Because I didn't hear you ask me what I wanted."

"I already know what you want." Something far too close to amusement danced in his churning eyes.

"You have no idea what I want."

"We'll have to disagree on that."

"There's no disagreeing—"

"I'm only asking this once," he said to the Baron, cutting me off. "I will not ask again."

"In other words, you're not asking for permission," I shot back.

He lifted a shoulder. "You can choose to see it that way."

"Choose?" I exclaimed. "There is no other way to see it."

"Once more, we will have to disagree."

"Why her?" Claude demanded again, surprising me.

Prince Thorne didn't answer for a long moment. "I will need to feed, and I prefer to do so with her."

He wanted me so he could feed? The anger nearly choked me, but it was tinged with something akin to . . . to disappointment? Which made no sense. Furious, I turned away from the Prince, fully intending on leaving the dining hall. I was done with this absurdity.

"You asked if I was cruel." Prince Thorne spoke again, focusing on the Baron. "I ask the same question of you. Are you cruel?"

I stopped, turning back to the Prince. He wouldn't . . .

"I'm sorry?" Claude stood, planting his hands on the table. "I'm not sure why you would ask that question of me."

"You're not?" Prince Thorne spoke softly, sending a chill through me. "You claim that she is most valued and yet you have treated her with such reckless disregard. You sent her to my quarters, apparently either too forgetful or too intoxicated to inform me of her arrival. She could've been killed."

"But I wasn't," I hissed. "Obviously."

Prince Thorne ignored me. "Not only that, she has been treated cruelly. When I saw her earlier, she was bruised."

My head jerked back. "I was not bruised."

The Prince eyed me. "I do enjoy your lies."

Claude turned stiffly toward me. "What is he speaking of?"

"Nothing—"

"Her wrist was bruised," Prince Thorne interrupted. "She said she got it while gardening."

"I did." I shot him a glare that should've set him afire.

He was unfazed. "It was such a strange bruise to obtain while gardening, considering it clearly resembled fingerprints."

"What happened, Lis?" Claude asked, pressing his hands flat to the table.

I lifted my chin. "As I said, nothing."

Claude's jaw hardened as he leaned forward. "Hyhborn cannot lie, but *caelestias* and mortals can. I want the truth."

"I'm not saying he is." The tips of my ears burning, I crossed my arms. "I didn't even realize I was bruised, so I assumed it happened while I was gardening."

"Huh." Prince Thorne inclined his head. "I didn't know plants had fingers and were able to grab someone hard enough to leave a bruise."

"No one asked you for your opinion," I retorted.

Slowly, the Prince turned his gaze upon me.

"*Lis,*" Claude hissed this time. "You know better."

I did.

I did know better as I stared at the Prince of Vytrus, my heart slamming against my ribs. I'd overstepped, more than once, but this time, I'd belly-flopped over that line. I froze. Tiny hairs lifted along the nape of my neck as the air thickened and the flames stilled. That *mouth* of mine had surely gotten me in trouble this time.

But Prince Thorne . . . he *smiled.*

My stomach dipped.

The smile he bestowed was not tight or cold. It was wide and real, showing a hint of teeth and softening the icy, unreal beauty of his features.

"She meant no offense. That I can assure you," Claude promised, and I almost laughed at the irony of him having to defend me. "She sometimes speaks passionately and . . . without thinking."

"No offense taken." The blue of the Prince's eyes had brightened once more. "Quite the opposite, to be honest."

I shook my head in disbelief, but he did seem . . . *pleased*, and that was just, well, somehow more disturbing.

"Your understanding is appreciated." Claude took his seat. "I swear to you that my treatment of her is not what left her skin bruised." A muscle flexed along his jaw. "But I will get to the bottom of it."

"Glad to hear that." Prince Thorne's fingers tapped along the table again. "And my request?"

His request? More like his demand.

"I will be leaving the day after tomorrow to meet with my armies to escort them here," Prince Thorne continued. "It will take several days to make the journey, but while I'm here, I want her with me."

Claude refilled his brandy. His knuckles were bleached white as he gripped the glass and took a drink.

I started to sweat, anxiety building.

"I have no problem with your request," the Baron announced.

"What?" I gasped, twisting toward him.

"Perfect." The Prince nodded at Claude, then rose, turning to me. He smiled. "Our arrangement is agreed upon then."

Having not agreed to anything, I took a step back, bumping into the table.

His smile deepened. "You have an hour to ready yourself." He prowled past me, stopping as his arm brushed mine. He looked down, lashes lowered. "I so look forward to seeing you later."

Stunned speechless, I watched the Prince of Vytrus stalk out of the dining hall. I couldn't even move as I stood there, my skin flashing between hot and cold.

"How could you tell him that was okay?" I faced the Baron. Then it sank in, finally breaking through the anger. Hyhborn *could* take what they wanted, even from a *caelestia*. "You didn't have a choice," I admitted, but he could . . . he could've at least said that he wasn't okay with it.

"He gave a choice, Lis. Even if it didn't sound like he was, you know that he did." Claude stared from beyond the now-calm candlelight. "He could've simply compelled both of us into agreement."

Yes, the Prince *could've* done that. "Does that matter?"

"It should always matter," Claude stated softly, drinking.

It had mattered last night, but that had been different. "This is absurd!" I shouted, throwing up my hands. "I cannot—"

"Who?" Claude asked. "Who bruised you?"

I couldn't believe he was focused on that when he had basically handed me off to a Hyhborn prince. "That's not really important at the moment."

"I beg to differ. I want to know who."

"It isn't—"

"Answer me!" Claude yelled, smacking a hand onto the table and causing me to jump. He took a deep breath, looking away. "I'm sorry. I know I'm not perfect and there is so much that I could do better when it comes to you—with all of this." He gestured to the hall with a wide sweep of his arm as his gaze returned to me. Several moments passed. "But especially you. The gods know I want more for us—for you, but I know why you stay, Lis. I do."

I fell silent, a knot lodging in my throat.

"The fear you have of being back out there—you and Grady living off the streets? It's a horrible thing to live with, one that I've been lucky enough to never know." He laughed, but it was without humor. "But I've capitalized on that fear. I've benefited from it when I should've done the exact opposite."

I . . . I couldn't believe what I was hearing. I hadn't known that he . . . he realized. That he knew. The knot expanded.

"I wish I could say I'm a better person, but I know I'm not," he continued, jaw working. "However, I have never raised a hand against you—against any of my paramours. That is the one thing I could take comfort in providing you. Safety. Security. Because that is why you stay."

I clutched the back of a chair as my throat thickened and my eyes stung. "You . . . you have given me that."

"I clearly haven't." His stare met mine. "Was it Hymel?"

I hesitated, because the gods knew I didn't want to protect that bastard, but I feared what Hymel would do if Claude confronted him. To Grady. Even to the Baron. "No," I said. "I honestly don't know how I got it. I swear to you."

Claude said nothing for many moments; then he looked away, picking up his glass and swallowing the sweet liquor. "I'm actually relieved by the Prince's demand."

I blinked. "What?"

"Who else would you be safer with than the Prince of Vytrus?" he appealed.

My fingers pressed into the wood of the chair. "I don't need to be safe."

Claude raised his brows.

"Okay, that didn't come out right," I said. "What I meant is that I don't need to be protected."

"Obviously you do."

I stiffened. "I am safe here. I promise—"

"I'm not even talking about that," he interrupted. "Vayne Beylen and the Iron Knights are heading this way. You said so yourself. He's coming."

Well, I wasn't so sure that my premonition had been about Beylen, but that was beside the point. "We may get lucky, and the sheer force of the Royal regiment will sway the Westlands and the Iron Knights away from attempting to seize Archwood."

Claude snorted. "Beylen is many things, but easily swayed is not one of them. If he was given an order to take Archwood, he will follow through."

"How can you know that?"

The Baron said nothing.

Pressure clamped down on my chest, and my senses opened immediately. My intuition stretched out as that string formed in my mind. I came into that gray wall and *pushed*. "You *do* know him."

Claude turned a look of disapproval on me. "Don't read me, Lis."

"I would apologize for doing so, but my gods, if you know the Commander of the Iron Knights, don't you think that's something you should've let Prince Thorne know before either he or the King learns of this from anyone else?" I dropped into the seat. "If they find out . . ."

"I'll be hanging from the gallows?" Claude laughed roughly. "Trust me, I know." He let his head tip back against his chair. "We're actually related, Lis. Thankfully, a cousin distant enough that it would be hard to find exactly where our family tree meets."

If I hadn't been sitting, I would've fallen down. "If you're related . . ." I placed my hands on the table. "On which side of the family?"

"Father's."

"Then that . . . that would mean he's a *caelestia*," I whispered. "The leader of the lowborn rebellion isn't even a lowborn?"

Claude saluted his glass as answer, chuckling. "Sorry, I do love seeing you surprised. It is such a rarity."

I fell back in the chair. "Well, maybe that answers why he would join forces with a Hyhborn—something you pretended to have no clue about."

"I wasn't pretending. I too am . . . surprised by that, but Beylen isn't . . ." His eyes closed. "We spent a few years together when I was a boy."

"He's from the Midlands?" I asked. "How did he end up in the Westlands, a mortal commanding a Court army?"

"He's starborn," he said, and I frowned. Not only because that told me nothing at all, but because there was something vaguely familiar about that phrase. "None of that matters right now. What does is that Beylen won't be swayed and there's no place safer to be than with a Hyhborn prince."

I was still stuck on the fact that he was related to the Commander of the Iron Knights. That was more important than Prince Thorne's demand. "Then Beylen knows you're the Baron of Archwood. You're family."

"Family isn't always everything," he murmured, stare fixed on the candles. "Not when it comes to what he . . ." Claude shook his head. "There are things far stronger than blood."

A tiny shiver erupted, and my thoughts flashed to Maven and to what the Baron knew about my abilities—the gray shield protecting their thoughts. "How did you know it would be easier to crack the shield of a Hyhborn that wasn't as powerful as a prince?"

His brows knitted. "What?"

"This morning, you said that."

He took a drink. "I truly have no idea what you're speaking of."

Doubt rose. "How could—"

"You should be readying yourself, Lis," he interrupted. "The Prince will return for you and you have little time."

"I don't care about that right now."

A brief smile appeared. "You and I both know that's not true."

"All right, I do care about that, but we can get back to that mess in a minute."

"Mess?" He chuckled. "I'm not sure why you're even protesting so much. You appeared to *thoroughly* enjoy his attentions," he pointed out. "I don't think I've seen a person come as hard as you did."

My cheeks caught fire as I muttered, "I doubt that's true."

"Come now, pet. Nothing I've done with my cock or my tongue has ever come close to what he did with his fingers," he said. "Even I can admit I never brought that sort of ecstasy to your face."

"I can't believe I'm even having this conversation." I reached for a bottle of wine left on the table and drank straight from it. "None of that matters, Claude. I'm not an object to be given or taken."

"And you're not owned. You stated that clearly enough at supper, but you?" He lifted a finger from his glass, pointing it at me. "You're wrong. We all are owned by the King. We are his subjects, in flesh and spirit."

"Okay, well, besides that." I clutched the neck of the bottle. "He wants to use me so he can feed, Claude."

"I sincerely doubt that is the sole reason, Lis. There are innumerable ways he could feed that don't require him doing so from one person."

"Then why me?"

He raised a brow. "Good question, is it not?"

It wasn't. Not at all. "I don't want to go with him and be—be under his mercy, his command."

"I have a feeling that being under his command and at his mercy will only involve being *under* him," Claude replied.

A sharp twist of desire pulsed through me despite my anger, and that made me really want to smack myself. "I want to throw this bottle at you."

Claude laughed. "You should rest your throwing arm for when you're with the Prince. I have this distinct impression that such an act will arouse him."

"Oh my gods." I fell against the back of the chair, shaking my head. "What if he thinks I'm a conjurer?"

"But you're not."

"That hasn't stopped you from worrying about the Hyhborn accusing me of such in the past," I reminded him.

"Yes, but he won't think that," he argued.

"And how do you know that?"

"Because I do," he said. "He's a prince. If anyone would know, it would be him."

I wasn't sure if that made a difference or not. Nibbling on my lower lip, I struggled to beat back the rising tide of frustration. "I don't even know why he wants this."

"I can think of a couple of reasons," Claude remarked dryly.

I was sure he could. Staring at the arched ceiling and its gold veining, I shook my head again. Several moments passed. I looked over at Claude.

He was staring into his almost empty glass. "Do you really not want to go to him?"

I opened my mouth.

"Honestly?" he insisted. "I want an honest answer, Lis."

Snapping my jaw shut, I gave my head another shake. I didn't know how to answer that. There was nothing but confusing thoughts and feelings if I spared one thought for the Prince—for *my* Hyhborn prince. "If he simply asked me if I would like to keep him company while here, I could answer that question for you, but he didn't ask, so I can't."

"And if he had, you would've said . . . yes?"

I kept my mouth shut.

Claude raised his brows. "He's a prince, Lis. Their concept of asking is pretty much what you just witnessed."

"So?"

"Most lords wouldn't have even gone so far as to ask, let alone a prince. Hell, most Hyhborn wouldn't have even thought twice. They would've simply compelled you, then taken you."

Lowering my chin, I pinned him with a glare. "*So?*"

"You're losing time, pet." Grabbing the oval-shaped bottle of brandy, he rose. "Ready yourself."

I didn't move.

Claude sighed heavily as he crossed the chamber, stopping short of opening the door. "Grady will be fine while you're with the Prince. I promise you that."

I closed my eyes against the sudden, foolish rush of tears as it became so quiet in the hall that I would've thought Claude had left.

The Baron hadn't. "This is a good thing, Lis. I hope you come to understand that," he told me. "Because the Prince of Vytrus will be able to provide you with what I cannot."

"And what is that?"

"Everything."

Wiping my palms under my eyes, I twisted toward the door. "What . . . ?"

The space there was empty.

The Baron was gone.

CHAPTER 24

"I can't even imagine it," Naomi whispered from where she stood, staring out the window of my antechamber, her arms wrapped tightly around her waist. "The idea of there being a siege—a war."

Part of me thought that maybe I shouldn't have told Naomi what I'd learned about the Westlands army when I'd crossed paths with her upon leaving the dining hall. It wasn't because I feared that she would then go and tell others, possibly causing a panic. I knew she wouldn't. I just hated seeing her concerned—afraid.

"You know when I said that I'd hoped there'd be lords here in time for the Feasts?" Naomi looked over her shoulder at me, the pale lavender of her gown standing out starkly against the night sky beyond the window. "I didn't mean an army of them."

"I know," I said from where I sat on the settee, my legs tucked underneath me. Thoughts heavy, I fiddled with one of the laces on my gown.

"Have you told Grady yet?" she asked.

I shook my head. I wanted to, but seeing Grady right now meant that I would also have to tell him about this new *arrangement*—something I knew he wouldn't respond well to. I would somehow need to convince him that I had agreed to keeping the Prince company, but apparently, I wasn't all that convincing when it came to my emotions. I still couldn't believe that Claude had known why I stayed in Archwood—that he had always known. I didn't know how to feel about it. I didn't know why that made me . . . sad. I couldn't even begin to figure that out when I had *this* to deal with.

Pulling my gaze from where I'd placed the ruby headpiece on a small table, I glanced at the door. The hour was almost upon me. My stomach dipped. "When Claude summoned me last night, he sent me to one of the Hyhborn who'd arrived ahead of the regiment.

Claude hadn't known why the Hyhborn were here yet and he'd wanted me to find out why."

Naomi turned from the window, the delicate arches of her brows rising. "My gods, you're just now telling me about this?" she asked. "I would've expected you to have been at my chamber doors first thing in the morning. I'm so disappointed in you."

Unfurling my legs, I scooted to the edge of the settee. "Don't be disappointed. There wasn't much to tell."

"Don't bullshit me, Lis. There has to be a whole lot to tell." Her eyes widened as she stepped forward. "Unless you used the Long Night last night? On a Hyhborn lord?"

"I didn't try. I wasn't sure if it would work and I didn't risk it," I told her. "And it wasn't a lord. It was the Prince."

"The Prince?" she repeated, lips parting. "*The* Prince of Vytrus?"

I nodded.

"Holy shit. I need a moment to process this—Wait." Her eyes bravely met mine. "Did . . . did something happen when you were with the Prince?" Everything about Naomi changed in an instant. Gone was the teasing seductress, and in her place was an alert tigress. "What happened last night, Lis?"

"Nothing I didn't allow to happen—nothing that I didn't want," I assured her. "He was—I don't know." I shook my head. "Not as I expected."

"He's said to be—"

"A monster. I know, but he's . . ." Prince Thorne was a lot of things—infuriating and entitled, demanding and annoying—but he wasn't a monster. "I don't think a lot of what has been said about him is the truth."

"For real?"

"Yes. I promise."

"Good." She relaxed, unfolding her arms. "I would've hated having to get myself killed in the process of chopping off a Hyhborn prince's dick."

A loud laugh burst out of me.

Naomi crossed her arms. "You think I'm lying?"

"I don't. That's why I find it funny."

"This is the perfect distraction." She nudged my foot with hers. "I want every last juicy detail about how the dreaded Prince of Vytrus was not as you . . . *expected*." She winked. "And I may need a demonstration of exactly how."

"Well, there may not be time for that," I said with a nervous hitch to my voice. "There's more. The Prince requested—and I use the word 'requested' in the barest sense possible—that I keep him company during his time at Archwood."

She blinked once, then twice. "Seriously?"

"Unfortunately." I gripped the edge of the settee.

She stared at me for what felt like a full minute. "Okay, I don't believe nothing much happened last night. What are these things that you *willingly* did that must've impressed him enough to request such a thing?"

"Trust me, he wasn't impressed." Clearly he wasn't all that impressed, since he didn't believe I was as experienced as I'd tried and failed to present myself as. "I think he . . . You know, I honestly don't know why. It makes little sense to me."

Coming to the settee, she sat beside me. "It's obvious you're not thrilled about this. Did you not . . . enjoy your time with him?"

"It's not that." I brushed a strand of hair back from my face. "I did enjoy it."

"But?"

"He didn't really ask, Naomi. It was more like pretending to ask. He made it clear that he wouldn't be happy with a no for an answer."

"I'm surprised he even pretended, to be honest—and I know that's not the point," she added when I opened my mouth. "I've just never really heard of the Hyhborn actually asking for permission for anything."

Neither had I. "I don't like that he thinks he can just make such a demand, and I don't care if he's a prince or not. That shouldn't matter."

"No, it shouldn't," she agreed. "And it would piss me off too." She glanced over at me. "Did you agree to it?"

"Not really." I sighed.

"And what did Claude say about this?" Naomi asked, then

snorted. "Then again, what could he truly say? A Hyhborn is denied nothing."

"Exactly," I muttered. "But here's the strange thing. Claude has always behaved as if he feared that being around Hyhborn could lead to them accusing me of using bone magic. And I never really believed that to be the sole reason. I think he was also worried another would, I don't know, coax me away . . . but he was actually relieved by the Prince's request."

"I . . ." Naomi's nose scrunched. "That is strange."

"Yeah."

She was quiet for a couple of moments. "What are you going to do?"

"I don't know." I leaned back against the cushion, folding my arms. My thoughts raced. I knew it wouldn't be wise to deny a prince, so I had to proceed with caution. "But if he thinks that I'm just going to submit and make this easy for him? He has another think coming."

⤳

A knock came shortly after Naomi had left. I hadn't wanted her caught in the middle when Prince Thorne came for me. I had no idea what I was going to do, let alone how the Prince would respond.

Except it wasn't him at the door.

Lord Bastian stood in the hall, his mouth curved in a half grin. "Good evening," he said, bowing slightly. My eyes were drawn to the dagger strapped to his chest. "I'm to escort you to Prince Thorne."

My back stiffened as I clasped the side of the door, and I wasn't sure why, but Prince Thorne sending another to *escort* me hit every nerve in my body the wrong way. "He was unable to come himself?"

"Unfortunately no." He clasped his hands behind his back. "He is running a bit behind and asked that I go in his stead."

"I apologize for wasting your time." I spoke carefully, having no idea how this Hyhborn lord would respond. "But I have no intentions of joining Prince Thorne this evening."

Dark brows lifted. "You do not?"

"No. I'm not feeling all that well," I said. "He will need to find some other way to occupy his time."

The nearby buttery light of a wall sconce glanced off the smooth, dark skin above his neatly trimmed beard. "Is there something that I could get for you then?"

"Excuse me?"

"You're feeling unwell." The green of his eyes brightened to the point where I couldn't see the other colors. "Is there something I can retrieve for you?"

I blinked rapidly. "Th—" I stopped myself, and the other side of Lord Bastian's lips tipped up. "I appreciate your offer, but I have what I need."

"You sure?" he pressed. "It will be no trouble."

I nodded. "Again, I apologize for wasting your time, my lord. I do wish you a good evening." I moved to close the door.

Lord Bastian moved so fast I couldn't even hope to track his movement. One hand shot out, landing on the center of the door and stopping me from closing it. "May I ask what is ailing you?" Lord Bastian dipped his chin. "Thor will ask, after all."

"Thor?" I murmured.

"Short for Thorne. It annoys him when we call him that, so of course, that is all we call him." Lord Bastian winked.

"Oh." That was my most intelligent response. I was a little thrown by his teasing nature. "I . . . I, uh, have a headache."

"Ah, I see." Straight white teeth appeared as the Lord smiled more broadly. "I'm guessing that headache is a rather large one? Perhaps if you had to describe it, you'd say that it came in a six-foot-and-seven-inch frame?"

I snapped my mouth shut.

Lord Bastian chuckled. "I will let him know that you are . . . feeling under the weather." His hand slid off the door. "I do hope you don't find yourself plagued by an even larger headache." He stepped back, clasping his hands behind his back once more. "Good evening."

"Good evening." I closed the door, going rigid when I heard his muffled laugh from the hall.

Clearly, Lord Bastian didn't believe me. Or more accurately, he'd guessed the source of my fabricated headache.

But Prince Thorne would have to be a right ass if he sent another or came himself after hearing that I wasn't feeling well. I didn't think it would hold him off forever, but it should at least give me the night to figure out what I was going to do—what I could do—and possibly longer, since he said he had to leave to meet with his armies.

But do you really want to stop him from coming? that annoying voice whispered.

"Yes," I hissed, toeing off my shoes. I crossed the antechamber, my bare feet sinking into the soft area rug as I went to the small credenza and poured myself a half shot of whiskey. The liquor was the best Archwood had to offer, mellow and smooth with the barest taste of alcohol. Or so everyone said. I could still taste the bite of liquor, but I downed the whiskey, lips peeling back against the burn.

It did little to calm my nerves, and I poured myself another half shot and brought it with me as I walked to the window. I looked past the golden *sōls* dancing in the night sky.

By the time the Feasts were in full swing, the Prince's armies would be at Archwood. Then, how long before the Iron Knights made their way here? It took no leap of logic to assume that the act had more to do with the importance of the port and the Hyhborn Court seated just beyond than it did with the people who called Archwood home.

I rested my cheek against the window, thinking of what the people of Archwood would think once they saw the Hyhborn forces. Once they learned of the Westlands threat? The fear and dread would be palpable. I swallowed the whiskey, welcoming the bite this time. The aristo would likely abandon the city until the threat had passed. Many had families in other cities and the means with which to travel there. But the poorest among the Archwood—the miners and dockworkers, the laborers? Everyone who kept the city and the ports open and running? There'd be no easy escape for them. They'd have to ride it out—

I felt the sudden shifting in the chamber. Tiny hairs along the nape of my neck rose as a charge hit the air. A clicking noise sent a shiver over my skin—the distinctive sound of a lock.

Heart thudding, I slowly turned to the door. There was no way. I lowered the empty glass to my side.

The door swung open and he stood there, legs planted wide and shoulders squared, hair swept back from his striking features and knotted. The armor still shielding his chest. He looked like a warrior, and one thing became clear.

Prince Thorne had come to conquer.

CHAPTER 25

Prince Thorne crossed the threshold, the light of my chamber glinting off the golden hilt of the dagger strapped to his chest.

I didn't think. I should have, but I simply reacted.

I threw the glass at the Prince of Vytrus.

In the brief seconds following the glass leaving my hand, I realized I'd had no idea of how reckless, how idiotic I truly was until that very moment.

The glass stopped in midair, several feet from the Prince.

I sucked in a sharp breath, eyes widening.

"Na'laa," Prince Thorne rumbled softly, the blue of his eyes a brilliant shade. The glass shattered into nothing—absolutely *nothing*. Not even tiny shards remained. It was simply obliterated.

I took an unsteady step back.

He smiled, and I shivered like any prey would upon realizing they'd not only come face-to-face with a honed predator but had taunted them. "You have a very good arm on you," he said. "Though, I would've preferred to discover that in a way that didn't involve an object being thrown at my head."

My heart thumped so fast I feared I might be sick. "I . . . I didn't mean to do that."

"Really?" he drawled.

Swallowing, I nodded. "The glass slipped from my fingers."

An eyebrow rose. "Slipped all the way across the room?"

"You startled me," I argued, fully realizing how ridiculous my excuse was. "I wasn't expecting someone to unlock the door and barge in. Though, I should have. You do have a habit of such."

"You know very little of what habits I have." One side of his lips tipped. "But I do know *you* have a habit of lying, which I do enjoy immensely."

I stiffened. "I beg to differ. I know of at least two habits. Barging into places you're not invited and insisting upon insulting my honor each time you see me."

"How is it an insult to your honor when it's truth?" he countered. "Perhaps you dishonor yourself by lying."

My chest rose as anger lanced through me. "Why are you here, Your Grace?"

"We have an arrangement."

"We do not, but that's not the point. I have a headache."

"Yes, one that is six feet and seven inches in shape?"

I gaped. "It was not I who said that."

"I know. Those were Lord Bastian's words." He glanced around the room, gaze skipping over my shoes and the uncorked bottle of whiskey. "He always likes to shave an inch from my height so that I'm not taller than him."

My brow creased; then I gave a small shake of my head. "Be that as it may, I still have a headache and I'm not feeling up to company this evening."

Those swirling irises settled on me. "You and I both know that's not the case."

"How would you know?" I crossed my arms. "Are you telling me that you can be so tuned in to a person that you can sense if they have a headache?"

"No." His laugh was low and soft, sending a chill up my spine. "I simply don't believe you."

"Well, that's rude."

"The truth is never rude, only unwanted." His grin spread into a hint of a shadowy smile, causing the irritation to prick away at my skin. "You look like you wish to throw that whiskey bottle at me next."

"That would be a waste of fine liquor," I retorted.

"And much harder to claim it only slipped from your fingers." He'd come closer in that silent way of his. "We have an arrangement. Are you going to honor it?"

"No." I lifted my chin. "Because there is no arrangement for me to honor."

"Figured."

I stepped back an inch. That was as far as I made it. Prince Thorne was on me before I could take another breath. One of his arms went around my waist as he bent, and a second later I was hoisted up, onto his shoulder. For a moment, I was so shocked I could do nothing as I dangled there, my hair streaming over my face and the woodsy scent of his overwhelming me.

Then he turned.

"Oh, my gods," I shrieked, grabbing a fistful of his tunic. "Put me down!"

"I would, but I have a feeling you're going to want to argue." Prince Thorne strode into the bedchamber, passing the bed. "And I prefer to do that while I'm close to the bed I plan to sleep in."

"You can't do this!" Fury erupted, erasing all common sense. I pounded my fists against his back, kicking my legs—completely forgetting *what* I was hitting. "Put me—" I hissed as pain radiated across my balled fists and up my arms. "*Fuck.*"

"You should stop," he said, amusement clear in his tone. "I really don't want you to break your hands. We may have need of them later."

"Oh my gods." My eyes widened as the chamber door swung open. He was truly going to carry me to his quarters? He was out of his mind. "You can put me down."

"I don't trust you."

"You don't trust me?" I sputtered as my chamber doors closed behind us. "You're going to make a scene."

"It's not me who is making a scene." Prince Thorne's head turned, his chin grazing my hip. "It is your shrieking that will wake anyone who has gone to bed and alarm those who have not yet done so."

"I'm not shrieking!" I, well, shrieked. "I don't prefer any of this." I tried to lift myself off his shoulder, but his arm clamped down over my back. "This is ridiculous."

"I know."

Disbelief roared through me. "Then put me down or . . ."

"Or what?"

"I may vomit all over your back."

Prince Thorne chuckled. "Please try not to do that, but if you do, it would be a good enough excuse for you to aid me in my bath."

A growl of exasperation parted my lips as my gaze fell on the hilt of a short sword just above his right hip. I was lying across the sheathed blade. Once more, I was too angry to think about what I was doing. I lifted a hand, reaching for the hilt.

"I wouldn't do that," he warned.

I froze, fingers inches from the golden handle. Did he have eyes in the back of his head?

"Not unless you know how to wield it and plan to do so," he tacked on.

"And if I did?"

"I would be rather impressed," he remarked, and my brows shot up. "But I don't imagine you have such knowledge."

I could handle a dagger; Grady had taught me that much. But I knew a dagger and a sword were vastly different things, so I let out a frustrated, closed-mouth, and quiet scream as we passed through the darkened hallways.

"However, I also suspect that if you knew how to handle a sword, you wouldn't hesitate to use it," he surmised.

"You would be correct—" I yelped as he bounced me. "That was highly unnecessary, Your Grace."

"Thorne," he corrected with a laugh. "I apologize. My shoulder . . . *slipped*."

I saw red. "Oh, I'm sure it slipped, *Thor*."

The Prince came to a complete stop. "I see I'm going to have to kill Bas." He started walking again.

My lips parted as my already tumbling stomach dipped. "What?"

"He's only half kidding," another, whom I recognized as Lord Bastian himself, said. I lifted my head, catching only a glimpse of his chest and the opening doors of his quarters and the Lord who waited in the hall outside of them. "He'd miss me terribly if he killed me."

"I wouldn't count on that," Prince Thorne warned.

Lord Bastian snorted as he stepped aside. "May I ask why you're carrying your guest like a sack of potatoes?"

Warmth hit my cheeks, but before I could speak, Prince Thorne said, "She was proving to be rather difficult."

"Must be that six-foot-six-inch headache of hers," the Hyhborn lord remarked.

"Now I've lost two inches?" Prince Thorne muttered.

"I'm just stating facts."

Frustration boiled over. "He's kidnapping me, and you two are arguing over how much taller he is?"

"See." Prince Thorne squeezed me. "Even she knows I'm taller."

"Traitor," Lord Bastian said with a sigh.

"That's—" I gasped as Prince Thorne gripped my hips and I was suddenly lowered to the floor. A lamp flickered on along the wall as I pulled free, putting several feet of distance between us.

"Before I take my leave," Lord Bastian drawled. "Crystian has left for Augustine."

Augustine? That was the capital.

"Good."

"You know, the King will be displeased."

The Prince looked over at him. "We both know that."

"That we do," Lord Bastian murmured, then glanced at me, his smile returning. "By the way, Crystian also wants to meet her."

"I'm sure he does," Prince Thorne muttered.

"Who is Crystian?" I asked.

"A pain in my ass."

Lord Bastian laughed. "Well, don't have too much fun tonight. Morning will come soon enough, and it will be an early one."

The Prince nodded as the Lord angled his body toward me and bowed. My brow shot up. Grinning, the Lord straightened and then disappeared.

"He's . . . different," I murmured.

"That would be an understatement." The Prince closed the door. Without touching it.

I swallowed. "You're different."

"That's also an understatement, na'laa."

Alone with the Prince, I shifted from one foot to the next. "So, why will the morning be an early one? Have you changed your mind and will be leaving to meet your armies at dawn?"

Prince Thorne chuckled. "Don't fret. I will not be leaving you so soon. Tomorrow I will be meeting with those in Archwood to begin training those who are able and willing to defend their city."

"Oh," I whispered, clasping my hands together.

He glanced at me. "You seem unsettled by that."

"I am. It's not that I've forgotten what is to come. It's just hearing that makes it more real. And I wasn't fretting over your absence." I glanced beyond him, to the doors. I bit down on my lip, inching to the side. "I'm looking forward to it."

"Don't."

My gaze flew back to him.

"I would warn against attempting to run," he advised, walking past me.

"Because you will stop me?"

"Because I will give chase." He unhooked the straps holding the short sword to his back as he crossed into the bedchamber. "And I will capture you."

I tensed.

The Prince stopped in the bedchamber, angling his body toward me as he lowered the sword he'd withdrawn. "But perhaps that is what you'd want." He tossed the sheathed sword onto a chest. "To run. For me to chase."

An unwanted thrill hit my blood. It was yet further proof of something being very, drastically wrong with me. I swallowed, holding myself still. "I don't want that."

One side of his lips quirked up as he unhooked his baldric. "What do you want, na'laa?"

"Not this."

His laugh was like dark smoke. "What do you think *this* is?"

"I think I'm to be your own personal cattle."

A short laugh left him. "My what?"

"You want me so you can easily feed. You said so yourself—"

"That is not the sole reason," he cut in. "Your baron wanted *a* reason. I gave him one."

"Then why?" I stopped myself. His reasons didn't matter. "I didn't agree to anything."

He placed the weapons down, then kicked off his boots, apparently not having a small arsenal to unload this night. "That's not how I recall it happening."

"I'm sorry? That's not how you recall it?" I stared at him in disbelief. "I'm sure I was quite clear."

"Yes. You were quite clear." His head tilted. "Just as you were quite clear when you came on my fingers—not once but twice."

My mouth dropped open as heat flooded my cheeks and lower, deep inside me, where my body clearly knew no shame.

His nostrils flared, his eyes becoming luminous even in the distance, and I knew he sensed that curl of desire.

I gritted my teeth. "I'm not sure what that has to do with this arrangement you insist upon."

"It has everything to do with it." He disappeared for a moment, then reappeared, carrying a bottle of liquor and two glasses.

The breath I took went nowhere as I watched him stop by the table and pour two glasses. "Then if that is the case, there are many within this manor and city who would be willing to take my place."

He glanced over his shoulder at me. "But would any of them throw a glass at me?"

I drew a short breath through my nose. "Likely not, which should relieve you."

"But it doesn't."

I blinked, unsure of what to say to that, because he wanted blunt objects thrown at his head? Which meant Claude had been right about that.

"And I also know that none of them would remind me of cherries or taste as good on my fingers," he continued, offering the half-filled glass. "Nor are any of them a mystery to me."

"There's nothing about me that is a mystery." I stared at the glass, then snatched it from him.

Prince Thorne eyed me, his stare so intense it was hard to stand still. "Why are you so against this arrangement?" His brows knitted as I took a drink of what turned out to be some sort of dark wine. "Please do not tell me you have feelings for your baron."

That I hadn't been expecting. "And what if I did?"

His jaw hardened. "Then your feelings would be wasted on a man who is clearly not worthy of them."

Thrown by his statement, it took me a moment to respond. "You don't know the Baron well enough to decide that."

"I do know the only reason he lives is because you sat in his lap and I'd rather not see you covered in his blood."

My chest turned cold. "Because he spoke of cutting off your arm? He was only kidding—albeit stupidly, but he wasn't being serious."

"I'm not talking about that." He took a sip. "Though, I do agree that was stupid."

"Then what?"

"He was touching you," he answered. "I didn't like it."

"What? Are you saying you were jealous?"

"Yes."

My laugh shattered the silence that followed. "You cannot be serious."

Slowly churning eyes met mine. "Do I appear as if I am teasing?"

No, he did not. I gaped at him. "Why in the world would you be jealous?"

"I don't know." He brushed a strand of hair back behind his ear. "Not knowing has become quite commonplace when you're concerned. I'm not sure if it annoys me or excites me."

"Well, it confuses me."

"Your reluctance in this confuses me."

"Truly?" As he stared back at me, I could see that he spoke the truth. "You really don't get it? Like it doesn't even occur to you that demanding something like this from another would anger them?"

"If you and I had not known one another? If I didn't know how much you enjoyed my touch? Then yes, I could understand someone's anger, but that's not the case between us."

"Just because we know each other and I've enjoyed your touch doesn't mean I don't want to be asked, nor that I would continue to enjoy such things."

"But I know you want my touch," he countered. "Just a few minutes ago, your pulse rose in arousal—"

"Oh my gods." I lowered my glass to the table to prevent myself from throwing it. "I can't believe I'm even having to explain what should be taught at birth—"

"But I was not born," he interrupted, brows furrowed.

"That shouldn't mean . . ." I trailed off, staring at him. My lips parted as what he'd said earlier that day in my chambers struck me—the lack of humanity. A lot of things fell under that, going beyond just caring for another. Being understanding did. Thoughtful. Considerate. Without humanity, there was just . . . "Logic."

"Logic?" he repeated.

I shook my head. "Deminyens operate on logic and not emotion?"

He seemed to think that over. "That would be somewhat accurate."

But logic was cold, and he wasn't that. "Last night you asked me to join you in the tub. You didn't just assume that is what I wanted."

"I knew that was what you wanted," he said, and my eyes narrowed. "But I sensed your nervousness—the skip in your breath was part uncertainty and part arousal."

"Can we just stop saying 'arousal' for the rest of our lives?"

"Why?" The blue of his eyes lightened. "Because the truth of how you feel around me bothers you?"

"Maybe—oh, I don't know—I don't need you pointing it out every five seconds?"

His chin dipped. "So you do acknowledge that you are aroused by me."

I opened my mouth.

"I have this distinct feeling you're going to lie," he said, a hint of smile playing across his lips. "And claim that you will not enjoy your time with me."

"Whether or not I will doesn't matter. You should *always* ask."

"Why?"

"Why *what*?"

"Why when we both already know what is wanted?"

Blowing out an aggravated breath, I desperately clung to my waning patience. "Because you shouldn't assume that will never change. It can. It can change at any second for various reasons."

"Hmm." The sound hummed from him as his gaze flicked over me. "I suppose then I must endeavor to ensure that doesn't change."

My lips pursed. "That wasn't the point I was getting at."

"It's not?"

I sighed, twisting the laces on the gown. "I feel like we're speaking two different languages."

That half grin appeared as he finished off his wine. "So, *na'laa*, would you like to join me this evening and upon my return?"

I glared at him.

"What?" Somehow he was closer, less than a foot from me. "I'm doing as you requested. I'm asking."

"And why are you asking now?"

"Because it is important to you that I do so."

Surprised, I felt my eyes widen slightly. "Yeah, well, it's a little too late for that since you've kidnapped me."

Prince Thorne chuckled. "You are not kidnapped nor captive. If you wish to leave . . ." he said, lifting a hand. His fingers closed over mine. I looked down, momentarily consumed by the fact that our hands were touching, and I felt . . . I heard and felt nothing that wasn't my own. He stilled my fingers, drawing my gaze back to his. "I will not stop you, Calista. I am not . . ." A slight frown appeared.

"You're not what? Like other Hyhborn?"

That pinch of confusion that had etched into his features earlier that day, when he'd been in my chambers, reappeared. He inclined his head. "What are other Hyhborn like?"

"Is that . . . is that a serious question?"

"It is," he said. "What do you think of my kind?"

I opened my mouth, then wisely closed it.

He studied me. "It's clear you have thoughts on this. Share them."

For the thousandth time in my life, I wished my face didn't show what I was thinking. "I . . . I don't know any Hyhborn well. Actually, you are the only Hyhborn that I've spent any amount of time with, but from what I know? What I've seen? The Hyhborn don't seem to really care about us, despite claiming to be our protectors. I mean, the Feasts are a perfect example of this."

He drew his thumb along the top of my hand. "What about them?"

"The Feasts have always seemed more a celebration of the Hyhborn than of the lowborn."

"And why do you think that?" He grinned at my silence. "Do not be shy now, *na'laa*."

"Stop calling me that."

"But I'm intrigued to know what you think, and you *are* being stubborn, which is so—"

"Yes. I know. Fitting." I sighed heavily. "If King Euros and all the Deminyens wanted to prove their commitment to being our protectors, why only do it a few days out of a year? Why not do it every day? It's not like—" I stopped myself then, thinking that I probably should listen to the advice I'd given to Grady and shut my mouth. "It doesn't matter."

"Yes, it does." His thumb had stilled along my hand. "It's not like what?"

I shook my head. "It's not like . . . we're only starving a few days a year. Clearly, the Hyhborn Courts have enough food to share. Making sure as many mouths as possible don't go hungry throughout the year would be a better way of showing us that the Hyhborn are truly our protectors."

"And what do you know about starving?" he asked quietly.

His tone caught me off guard. It wasn't a challenge, but a genuine question, and it had me answering honestly. "I . . . I grew up without a home—"

"You were an orphan?" His voice had sharpened.

My heart turned over heavily as I held his stare, waiting for him to realize that we'd met before, waiting for me to even understand why my intuition was hesitant to tell him that we had.

"I was just one of many. Too many that never make it to adulthood," I said when no realization came from either of us. "I know what it's like to go to bed and wake up hungry, day after day, night after night, while some people have more food than they could ever hope to consume. Food they just throw away."

Prince Thorne was silent for several moments. "I'm sorry to hear that, Calista."

Uncomfortable with the sincerity in his voice and the sound of my name, I looked away as I nodded. "Anyway, I can think of better ways for the King to show his love of his people, be they Hyhborn or lowborn."

"You sound like Beylen."

My gaze snapped back to his, thoughts immediately going to what Claude had shared. "You know him?"

"I know he has said the same or very similar things," he said, not really answering my question. "You have never been to any of the Courts, correct?"

"Nope. Never had the honor."

His thumb began to move again, sliding slowly over the top of my hand. "Most would not find it to be an honor."

My brows rose. He'd given the impression that there was violence in his Court, but what he was saying now felt different. "What do you mean?"

"I know what the Courts look like from a distance. Decadent opulence from the rooftops to the streets, all glitter and gold," he said. "But as with most things that are beautiful on the outside, there is nothing but ruin and wrath on the inside."

A shiver curled its way down my spine.

"But you speak the truth. The King could do more. All of us could and should have. I imagine we would not face these issues with the Iron Knights if we'd gone about things differently."

"It's strange," I said after a moment. "And rather . . . nice."

"What is?"

"To be in agreement."

Prince Thorne laughed then. "I can think of other things we can be in agreement about that are far better than just nice."

"And then you ruined it."

Another laugh rumbled from him, and I felt my lips twitching. His laugh was almost as infectious as Naomi's, and that caused my heart to give an unsteady leap.

The sound faded, though, as did his smile. "I don't know how much I am like the others, but I know how I am not. I will not make you do what you truly do not want to do."

He released my hand then, but his touch lingered, warming my skin as I stepped back. Doubt filled me, even as he made no move, even as I made no move. I glanced at the door, pressing my lips together. I hesitated, searching for a reason to linger, and I found one. "Lord Bastian mentioned that the King will be displeased." I faced him. "What for?"

A smile appeared, but it was brief. "My decision regarding Archwood."

"I don't understand." I frowned. "You're planning to defend Archwood. . . ." I trailed off as his words from supper returned. *We've come to determine what course of action* . . . "Unless that was just an option. A choice to decide if we were worth saving or . . ." I couldn't bring myself to say it.

"Or not." The Prince had no trouble saying it. "Destroying Archwood was an option. Primvera would be abandoned and new ports along the Eastern Canal would be established. And that is what the King prefers."

CHAPTER 26

"Gods," I rasped, pressing a hand to my chest. "Why would you—? Wait." A new kind of horror rose. "Why would the King be displeased with you deciding not to destroy Archwood?"

The Prince eyed me for several moments. "Because destroying the city would be easier."

"Easier?" I whispered, bumping into the legs of a couch. "Killing and dislocating thousands of innocent people is easier?"

"It's less of a risk to the Hyhborn forces. Very few if any would be lost in . . . removing Archwood as possible leverage," he said, arms folded across his chest. "Our knights will die defending the city."

I couldn't believe what I was hearing, even if I shouldn't be surprised. It wasn't like I believed King Euros cared all that much for lowborn, but this was . . . it was brutal in his lack of caring. "So, the lives of lowborn mean that little to our king?"

The Prince said nothing.

A biting laugh burned my throat as anger flooded me. "Is this what happened to Astoria then? You were sent in, as judge and executioner?"

"Astoria was something else entirely," he said, features sharpening. "The city was already lost."

"Does the reason for destruction matter?" I questioned.

He was quiet again.

I inhaled deeply. "How many people have you killed?"

"Too many." The brown in his eyes darkened to a pitch black and spread over the rest of the colors, and I would've sworn the temperature of the chamber had dropped. "But just so you know, neither I nor my knights sack the cities that have fallen. We do not lift our weapons against those people. We do not kill indiscriminately. What deaths have occurred happened in spite of all we have done to prevent it."

"You mean those deaths occurred because the people who lived in these towns fought back? To protect their homes and livelihoods? Do you expect them not to?"

"I would expect nothing less from them," he said.

Suddenly cold, I wrapped my arms over my waist. "How many cities has our king decided weren't worth the precious lives of Hyhborn?" I asked, thinking of the small villages and towns that had disappeared over the years.

"Too many," he repeated flatly. "And far more than that would be lost if I sided with the King in every situation." His head tilted. "What? Do you think I can disobey the King's orders? I am a prince, and he is the King. Choice is limited, even for someone like me."

I stared at him, a part of me understanding that he was just another cog in the wheel—albeit a very powerful cog. I drew in a shaky breath. "What makes you decide which city is worth *your* protection and which one is to be sentenced to death? Better yet, why would you save Archwood after what was done to you?"

A muscle flexed along his jaw as he looked away. "You."

"What?"

"There's no one answer for why when it comes to other places, but for here? It was you. Your bravery. I figured that if you were that brave, then surely there were others like you."

"Others that would fight back?"

"That is another question you already know the answer to." The black faded from his eyes as the blue and green hues reappeared. "In a way, I'm glad that I was poisoned. If I hadn't been, I wouldn't have found you."

But you found me before. Those words whispered along my tongue but didn't make it past my lips. Swallowing what my intuition wouldn't allow me to speak, I looked to the window. In the distance, I saw the glowing *sōls*.

"Do you finally think of me as a monster?"

I closed my eyes.

"You should," he said softly. "The blood that is on my hands will never wash off. I wouldn't even attempt to do so."

A faint shudder worked its way through me, the heaviness of

his words speaking the guilt and maybe even the pain he carried. Should it be only his hands that bore that stain? Or the King's? Because he was right. Choice *was* limited. Everyone answered to someone, even the King. It was said he answered to the gods, but the Prince still had a choice. "What would happen if the King wasn't just displeased with your decision but demanded that you destroy the city anyway? And you refused?"

"War," he answered. "The kind that would make what is brewing in the Westlands seem like nothing more than a skirmish to be forgotten."

My breath caught. "You're talking about the Great War," I whispered.

He nodded, and a moment passed. "Do you know what the realm was like before the Great War?"

"Not really."

"Most don't." Prince Thorne returned to the credenza and poured himself another drink. "Would you like another?"

I shook my head.

He replaced the topper. "By the time the realm was stable enough after the Great War for anyone to begin chronicling the histories, all who could remember what it was like had long since passed, taking with them the memories of thousands and thousands of years of civilization. It was decided that it was best all of it was forgotten."

"Were you . . . alive during that time?"

"No. I was created shortly after, with the knowledge of what had come to pass." He went to the window, the angles of his face tense as he peered out. "In our language, the Great War was called the Revelations."

A chill slipped down my spine.

"Hyhborn have always been around, in the background, watching and teaching. Protecting not just man but the lands itself," he said. "We were known as many things throughout history, worshipped as gods at one point, called the fair folk of the forests—nymphs and magical beings from another realm—for a time." He laughed quietly. "Others believed us to be elementals—spirits that embodied nature. Some believed us to be angels, servants of one god, while others saw us as demons—both written in scriptures by mortals who barely understood the visions and premonitions that they had."

Air slowly leaked from my parted lips. Did he speak of visions similar to those I had?

"I suppose the first of the Deminyens were all of those things in different ways. Each name given fit in some way." He took a drink. "Either way, the Deminyens were *ancient*, Calista. As old as the realm itself. They were here when the first mortal was given life, and I imagine we will be here long after the last passes."

Another shiver curled its way down my spine as I moved to the couch and sat on the edge.

"Time is unrelenting, though, and even Deminyens are not immune to its effects." Prince Thorne eyed me as he drank. "And while in the beginning the Deminyens interacted with mortals, there came a time when that was not something that could continue. Deminyens moved more into the role of watcher, but they began to lose their connection to those they protected. The wisest of the Deminyens—his name was Mycheil—saw the dangers in that. He was already seeing it in others. How time was changing them, making them colder, less empathetic and humane. Accidents began to happen."

"What do you mean by accidents?"

"Deaths." His lips twisted in a wry grin. "The causes varied. Sometimes it was simply fright from seeing a Deminyen that took a life of a mortal. Other times it was due to the Deminyens attempting to stop a mortal from doing something that would either bring harm to the many or to the lands, and at that time, striking a mortal . . . it was unheard of."

"Well, that's definitely changed," I muttered.

"Yes, it has." He finished off his drink, placing it on the credenza. "Mycheil knew that it was time for his brethren to step back from mankind, to rest in hopes that when they reawakened, they'd be renewed. So, he ordered them to go to ground, to sleep, and they did. For centuries, becoming nothing more than forgotten myths and legends to most and unknown ancestors of others."

I picked up a soft, plush pillow and cradled it to my chest. "What . . . what happened?"

Prince Thorne didn't answer for a long moment. "Time continued. The world before this one? The world that fell? It was so much more advanced. Buildings that stretched as tall as mountains. Food was rarely hunted, but raised or engineered. Cities that were connected by roads and bridges that spanned miles. Streets that were clogged with powered vehicles instead of carriages, and steel cages that took to the air, transporting people across the seas. The world was not like this."

What he was saying sounded implausible and impossible to even fathom, but Hyhborn . . . they couldn't lie.

"Those great buildings replaced the trees and destroyed entire forests, the machinery choked the air, and ease of life pushed creatures all across the world into the brink of extinction or beyond. All of it came at a cost. The world was dying, and mortals were either incapable of changing their ways or didn't want to. The reasons really don't matter, because all that destruction awoke the Hyhborn. Those ancients tried to warn the people, but too few had listened, and too few of the reawakened Deminyens had returned with a renewed connection with man. Too many began to see them as a scourge upon this earth. A plague that needed to be culled, and that's what they did. Over half of the Deminyens turned on man, believing that they should be stripped of their freedom, convinced it was the only way to save them and the world, and as others attempted to defend the rights of man— that's when the war started. It was between Hyhborn. Their fighting shook the earth until the buildings fell, whipped the wind, sending fire through cities, and raised the oceans, swallowing . . . swallowing entire continents. Mortals were just caught in the cross fire."

"Continents?" I whispered.

"There used to be seven—large swaths of lands surrounded by vast bodies of water," he said. "There are no longer seven."

My gods. I squeezed the pillow tighter.

"Mortals weren't completely innocent of what occurred. After all, their actions, their selfishness and willful ignorance, are what woke the Hyhborn, but none of them deserved to face such wrath, such ruin." He looked at me. "The Great War didn't just end lives. It reshaped the world completely."

I tried to process all of that, but I didn't think it was something I ever could. "There are Deminyens now who were a part of that world, right?"

"A few. There were steep losses on both sides."

"The King?"

Prince Thorne faced me. "He was alive then."

"And what side was he on?" I asked, half afraid.

"Both? Many of the Deminyens who survived were those who existed somewhere in the middle. They believed that mortals needed to be protected but could not be trusted to rule the lands. That left alone or given any real power, they would repeat history."

Sometimes I thought that we lowborn couldn't be trusted to carry a pitcher of water without spilling it, but to say we would repeat history was unfair when that history was unknown to us. "What do you think?"

"I'm not sure." A wry grin appeared. "It truly varies from day to day." His eyes met mine. "But what I do know is that kind of war cannot come to pass again. Mortals would not survive it, and everything must be done to prevent that from happening."

"So, it's what then?" I rose, dropping the pillow where I sat. "Sacrifice the few to save the many? Is that what obeying the King's orders really means?"

"In the most simplified terms? Yes." He watched me. "There is a reason why most mortals do not know the history of their realm."

"Because if they did know, they would fear the Hyhborn?"

He nodded. "More than many already do."

Chilled, I ran my hands over my arms. I wasn't so sure that was the only reason the history was kept secret. Perhaps the King and those who ruled didn't want us to have the chance to do and be better than we had done and been before. "That's a lot to take in."

"I know."

"I suppose ignorance is bliss," I murmured.

"Knowledge rarely makes things easier." He inhaled deeply. "What I shared with you? It is forbidden to do so."

I looked over at him. "Then why would you?"

"Yet again, I don't know." He laughed. "I think I felt the need to explain why I've done the things that I have, because it feels . . ." He frowned. "It feels important that you understand that I'm not . . ."

That he wasn't a monster.

I drew in a ragged breath. I didn't know what to think. Was he a monster? Possibly. He claimed to feel no compassion and laid waste to cities at the King's orders, but he carried the weight of the King's orders. I could see that even now.

I did know that he was neither bad nor good. Nor was I, and I didn't need my intuition to confirm any of that or to know he saved those he could and mourned those he couldn't.

"If you wish to leave, Calista, I will not stop you. I wouldn't even blame you," Prince Thorne said, drawing my gaze to him. "That I promise."

Nodding, I backed up and turned from him, because that was . . . that was what I thought I needed to do. I crossed the space, the feel of his stare burning into my back. I reached the door, wrapping my fingers around the handle. It turned in my grasp. The door cracked open. My heart began to pound as I stared at the thin opening. I was frozen, at war with myself, because I . . .

I didn't want to leave.

Despite the fact that I should, and despite what I'd learned, I wanted to stay, and I knew what it meant if I did—what I was agreeing to. The kind of company he wanted didn't involve me teaching him the intricacies of consent or continuing to argue about only the gods knew what. He wanted me. My body. I wanted him. His body.

Why couldn't I have that?

There was no reason, except a . . . a keen sense of nervousness, because staying inexplicably felt like *more*.

Because it wasn't just pleasure I sought if I stayed with him. It was the companionship. His seeming unexplainable trust in me. The complexity of who and what he was. It was also the quiet I found with him.

Closing the door, I turned to see him standing where I'd left him.

Our gazes locked, and I thought I saw a hint of surprise in his features.

Slowly, he extended his hand. My chest felt too tight and too loose at the same time. I didn't feel the cool floor beneath my feet as I walked forward. His eyes never left mine as I lifted my trembling hand and placed it into his. The contact of my palm against his was a shock to the senses, and as his fingers threaded through mine, my intuition was silent, but somehow I knew that nothing would ever be the same after this moment, after tonight.

CHAPTER 27

There was a good chance that it was just my overactive imagination guiding my thoughts, filling in the gaps my intuition was silent on, but I couldn't shake the feeling that this one choice was the start of everything changing as Prince Thorne turned.

Without saying a word, he led me into the bedchamber. My heart was still pounding as I glanced from the doorway to the bathing chamber and then the bed. The nervous energy ramped up in me, a mixture of anticipation and the . . . the unknown. It had been so long since I'd been with anyone.

And I'd never been with anyone like him.

Prince Thorne stopped at the side of the bed and turned to me. He was still silent as he cupped my cheek, the colors of his irises swirling. Could he tell why my pulse hammered now? I dragged my lower lip between my teeth.

Holding my gaze, he drew the tips of his fingers down my throat, to my shoulder. He turned me so my back was to him. "What was it like for you? Growing up?"

"I . . . I don't know." The barely there touch had left a wake of shivers.

"Yes, you do." He brushed aside the heavy length of hair over my shoulder. "Tell me."

I stared ahead. "Why do you want to know?"

"I just do."

"It's not that interesting."

"I doubt that," he said. "Tell me what it was like, *na'laa*."

"It was . . ." My breath caught as his fingers found the row of tiny hooks along the back of my dress. A bedside lamp clicked on, startling me. His ability to do such things wasn't something I thought I could ever get used to. "It was hard."

He was quiet for a moment. "When did you become an orphan?"

"When I was born?" I laughed. "Or shortly thereafter, I suppose. I don't know what happened to my parents—if they had become sick or simply couldn't care for me—and I . . . I used to think about that a lot. Like why did they give me up? Did they have a choice?"

"You don't wonder that anymore?" he asked, the dress loosening as he slowly worked the clasps.

I shook my head. "There's no point in it. Doing so would drive one mad, so I decided that they just didn't have a choice."

"That's likely the truth no matter the scenario," he commented, and I nodded. "How did you survive?"

"By doing whatever was necessary," I said, and then quickly added, "I wasn't alone. I had a friend. We survived together."

"And this friend? It made surviving easier?"

I thought that over as the backs of his fingers brushed over the skin of my lower back. "It did make it easier, but . . ."

"But?"

"But it also made it harder," I whispered. "Because it wasn't just your own back you're looking out for, you know? It's someone else's too—someone you worry about every time you part ways, looking for food or money or shelter? So many things can happen on the streets. Everyone is . . ." I stopped myself, shifting uncomfortably from foot to foot.

"Everyone is what?"

I looked over my shoulder at him. The low light cast shadows in the hollows of his cheeks. "Do you really want to know this? Because you don't have to pretend to be interested for us to do whatever this is."

He stared down at me, eyes hidden beneath his lashes. "I'm not pretending," he said. "And I wasn't pretending at dinner either."

I raised a brow. "You were truly interested in the different types of sedum?" I laughed. "No one is interested in sedum."

"But you are."

"Yeah, well, I'm easily entertained."

Prince Thorne chuckled. "That is another thing I doubt," he said. "Everyone was what, *na'laa?*"

Nibbling on my lower lip, I gave a little shake of my head. "Everyone is a potential enemy. Other kids, even ones you shared space with and trusted. The person who gave you bread one day can call the magistrates on you the next and accuse you of stealing. The too-friendly gentleman down the street? Well, that friendliness comes with a cost." I shrugged as his fingers stilled along the last of the hooks. "So, you're not just looking out for yourself, but you're not alone. You do have someone else watching out for you too."

He was quiet for a moment. "You make it sound like it was nothing."

I did? "It just was what it was."

There was another short gap of silence. "You are braver than I even realized."

Face warming, I forced out a laugh. "That's not true. I spent my entire life scared. I still—" I dragged in a deep breath. "I don't think I was or am brave. I was likely just desperate to survive."

"Being afraid doesn't lessen one's bravery," he said, finishing the last of the buttons. "Nor does desperation. If anything, it strengthens the bravery."

"Maybe," I murmured, clearing my throat. "I would ask what it was like for you, but since you were never a child . . ." I trailed off, frowning. "That's a really weird thing to say out loud."

The Prince huffed out a laugh, his fingers pressing lightly against my skin, parting the sides of the gown as he drew them up my back. The sleeves of the gown slipped a little farther down my arm, stopping just above my elbows.

"What was it like?" I asked, my curiosity getting the best of me. "To be created?"

"It's hard to explain and likely impossible to understand." His hands grazed my upper back, sending another ripple of tight shivers through me. "But it's like . . . waking up, opening your eyes, and knowing everything."

I blinked. "Everything? Like in an instant?" I glanced back at him, but his head was turned in such a way that I couldn't see his expression. "You know everything?"

"Yes, but it takes a while to understand what you know and how it all applies to the world around you—the world you've yet to enter." His fingers traced the line of my shoulder blades. "It can take years to fully understand."

I tried to fathom what it would be like, to wake up with the knowledge I'd gained over the course of a lifetime in a matter of minutes. He was right. I couldn't understand. "That sounds . . . intense."

"Very much so."

I held still as he continued to explore the length of my back, enjoying his warm touch. "And when you were created, you looked like you do now?"

"Not exactly." His fingers trailed down my spine. "When I came into consciousness, I was deep underground."

I gasped. "You were buried alive?"

"No, *na'laa*." He drew his hands back up my spine. "I was created from the earth, like all Deminyens are, and when we come into our consciousness, we are not yet fully . . . formed."

"Not fully formed?" My gaze fell on his sheathed sword. "I'm going to need more details on that."

"It takes a while for our bodies to develop into what you recognize now, and things can go wrong in the process of creation," he explained. "We are but a consciousness at first, then over time, our bones are forged from the rock deep in the ground as our flesh is carved from stone." His fingers skimmed the sides of my ribs. "All the while, the roots of the Wychwoods keep us fed, creating our organs and filling our veins. The process can take years while we listen to the life around and above us."

My mouth was likely hanging open. I tried to wrap my head around all that and gave up because there was no way. "Years beneath the ground? I would go insane."

"Of course you would. You are mortal," he stated simply. "We are not."

"But I don't understand—I mean, you bleed blood. Not sap."

"As do the Wychwoods."

Recalling the rumors, my lip curled. "I'd heard that the Wych-woods bled, but I . . ."

"You didn't believe it?"

"I figured it was just red sap people saw, but I guess I now under-stand why the Wychwoods are so sacred." I gave a shaky laugh. "You know, the night in the gardens when you said you were a part of everything around us, I didn't think you meant literally."

"Most would not." His fingers glided along the curve of my waist.

I thought about what he'd shared with me about the past world. "Did those who lived before the Great War know about the Wych-woods?"

"If they did, it was forgotten, but there would've been signs upon entering the woods that they treaded on sacred ground. Warnings that had to have been ignored. It was the destruction of the Wych-woods that woke the firsts."

In a way, it was hard not to be angry with our ancestors when it seemed like they'd dug their own graves almost willingly. "There are Hyhborn that are born, right?" I asked. "I'm not talking about the *caelestias*."

"The children of Deminyens are born and they age just as a *cae-lestia* or mortal, but perhaps slower."

"That's what I thought." I paused. "Do you have children?"

"No."

I didn't know why I was relieved to hear that, but I was. "I'd heard that Deminyens can actually choose when to have a child. Like both parties have to want that for a child to be created. Is that true?"

"It is."

"Must be nice," I murmured.

"And you?" His hands slipped up my back again. "Have you had children?"

"Gods, no."

Prince Thorne laughed. "I take it you aren't fond of children?"

"It's not that. It's just what kind of . . ." I stopped myself. Grady's words resurfaced. Why would I want to bring a child into this world?

That was a damn good question for most, but for me? Even more so. How could I even touch my child?

"I understand," he said quietly.

I opened my mouth, but closed it, thinking that maybe he did understand that I wouldn't be able to give a child the life they deserved. That I feared that I would end up repeating history. I didn't want to do that to a child. I couldn't. But there was no way he could know how truly difficult it would be for me.

I cleared my throat. "Anyway, you said that things can go wrong during the creation?"

"If the process is disturbed, the creation is interrupted." He slid his hands down my arms, catching the sleeves of my gown. The breath I took snagged as the silky material slipped from my arms and from my hips, pooling at my feet. "What is unearthed is even less mortal than a Deminyen."

A chill hit my exposed flesh. "You're talking about the ones who don't look like us? Like the *nix*?"

"In a way," he said, his palms grazing my ribs once more, chasing away the coldness. "The *nix* are awakened early on purpose."

My mind went back to the last time I was in this chamber. "Is that what you meant when you talked about not trusting those who created the *nix*?"

His breath touched the nape of my neck, and then I felt his lips there. "Yes."

I wanted to ask him why one would attempt to disturb the process, but his hands made their way to my hips. His fingers slipped beneath the thin lace and he began to lower it.

My pulse sped up as I looked over my shoulder, seeing only the top of his bowed head as he drew the cloth down my legs, and then that too joined the gown on the floor. His mouth brushed against the curve of my ass, scattering my thoughts. Then his lips glanced off the dip of my lower back, the center of my spine, and then the nape of my neck as he rose once more.

"Tell me something, *na'laa*," he said, turning me in his arms. "Is that how you survive now?"

I looked up, my gaze immediately locking with his. The blue had deepened to a color like the sky at dusk, seeping into the other hues. "What do you mean?"

He gathered my hair, dragging it back over my shoulder. "Do you still survive by doing whatever is necessary?"

"Yes," I whispered.

Thick lashes lowered, shielding his eyes. "Is that why you decided to stay tonight?"

My stomach skipped. "No."

"Truly?"

A tremor skated down my arms as I lifted them, curling my fingers along the sides of his tunic. In my chest, my heart pounded as I tugged his tunic up. Silent, he took over, removing his shirt, so I reached for the flap on his pants. Unhooking the buttons felt nothing like the first time I'd done this with him. Nor did it when I drew the soft, worn material of his pants down.

"Yes," I answered as he stepped out of his pants. I placed the palms of my hands against his stomach, eyes closing as I soaked in the feel of his smooth skin beneath my hands. Another tremor went through me. "Truly."

The Prince said nothing as I ran my hands over his chest, thinking about how his flesh really was made of stone. For several moments, I allowed myself to get a little lost in just touching him. The friction of his hard skin against my much softer hands. The tight dips and rises of his stomach. The corded muscles. I had no idea what I must've looked like to him, but the novelty of touching another was far too strong to resist. He didn't stop me. He just stood there, allowing me to explore, much like I allowed him to do the same, and for that, I didn't think he could ever understand what he'd given me as I lowered myself onto my knees before him, the stone of the floor as hard as his skin but cold.

I opened my eyes, lifting my gaze to the rigid, thick length jutting out from his hips. "You're beautiful," I whispered.

His head tilted slightly, exposing one . . . deeper-hued cheek to the lamplight.

My lips parted. "Are you . . . blushing?"

"Am I?" He sounded genuinely uncertain.

There was something wholly charming in that faint stain to his cheeks—that someone as powerful and otherworldly as a Deminyen could blush. "Yes, Your Grace."

"Thorne," he corrected. "I don't think I've ever blushed before."

"Perhaps you have and no one has told you."

"Many wouldn't have the courage to do so," he remarked, head straightening. "But I think this is a . . . first."

It probably wasn't, but I liked the idea of being the first to make the feared Prince of Vytrus blush. I smiled as I ran my hands along his thighs, focusing on his length. On my knees, I had to stretch to reach him, he was so absurdly tall. I dragged my hands over his skin, feeling the hard curve of his ass and then the lean flesh of his hips once more, all the while my blood thrumming. His size was impressive . . . and intimidating, and even if this weren't something I hadn't done in a while, I still would've felt nervous—excited but nervous.

"I was thinking," I said, feeling bold and wanton. "That since you already had dessert, it would only be fair that I too have some."

His fingers grazed my cheek before slipping into my hair. "Then have it."

There was no hesitation, no uncertainty or pretense. I was on my knees before him, touching him, because I wanted to be, and there was nothing in my mind but my own thoughts. My hands didn't shake as I wrapped my fingers around him, but he did. It was a slight tremor as my grip tightened on him, and I felt it again as my breath teased the head of his cock. I drew my hand up his length, feeling those slight ridges as I glanced up at him.

Air snagged in my chest. There was a faint golden blur to his shoulders, his arms. His head was bowed, hair falling forward and against the sides of his face. I couldn't see his eyes, but his stare was intense and hot. It fanned the fire already simmering in my veins. The fingers in my hair curled.

I took him in my mouth and I shuddered at the deep, rumbling sound that came from him. I took him as far as I could, which wasn't all that far, but the Prince . . . His answering groan and the shallow flex of his hips told me he didn't mind at all. I ran my tongue along his length and over the ridges along the underside, reaching the indent under the tip of his cock. I drew him into my mouth again as he . . . he seemed to warm beneath my hand and inside my mouth, and that heat invaded my own senses. I sucked on the head of his cock, surprised by the taste of him. It wasn't salty like I'd experienced before, but . . . faintly sweet? Like a dusting of something akin to sugar? I'd never tasted anything like it before. His hand tightened in my hair, tugging on the strands as I sucked harder, my mouth filling with more of the taste of him—my mouth tingled and that sharp swirl of sensations moved throughout me, hardening the tips of my breasts and joining the muscles curling tight and low in my stomach. Feeling myself dampen, I moaned around him. The faint, fiery sting along my scalp as his entire body jerked only heightened my arousal.

I leaned into him, pressing my breasts to his thighs as I worked him with my mouth and my hand. The throb against my tongue echoed between my thighs, and I wanted to reach down and touch myself, but I hadn't ever done that—hadn't ever touched myself before another. Gods, I wanted to so badly the ache was almost painful as my fingers pressed into the back of his calf.

"Fuck," he growled, his body jerking again.

I'd never really enjoyed this act all that much before, but I was greedy now. I was insatiable as I drew him deeper, reveling in his taste, in the deep, guttural moans echoing from him. And when his hips started to rock, I wanted him to move faster, harder. I wanted all sorts of . . . of wicked things as I opened my eyes and looked up at him, my pulse thundering and my body aching. I squeezed my thighs together, shuddering at the flare of desire. His hold on the back of my head firmed, holding me in place as he moved. I wanted—

"Touch yourself."

My eyes flew open.

He drew his cock from my mouth, and then guided me up onto my feet. My legs shook as he turned me, sitting me so that I was on the edge of his bed. He stepped in, spreading my legs wide. Cool air kissed the heat between my thighs. He reached down between us, taking ahold of one of my hands. He drew it over the length and the head of his cock, his flesh wet with my mouth and . . . and *him*. The tips of my fingers immediately warmed and began to tingle.

"What . . . what is this?" I asked, barely recognizing my voice. It was throaty. Sensual. "My skin is tingling and you taste . . ." I swallowed, moaning softly. In the cloud of lust, I remembered something he'd said. "Your come . . ."

"Is an aphrodisiac," he finished.

"Good gods," I gasped, eyes widening. He hadn't even come yet, and it could have this kind of effect? "Now I—" I moaned as a dart of intense desire pulsed through me. "I understand why people would want it so badly."

His laugh was dark and sinful. "Touch yourself," he ordered, folding his hand along the back of my head once more. "Fuck your fingers while I fuck your mouth."

My body caught fire upon his demand—upon words that would've normally turned me off but now caused a whimper of pleasure to escape me. Eyes locked with his, I did as he demanded. I brought my hand to the space between my thighs as he watched, as he held completely still, his cock glistening between us. My fingers grazed my clit, and my hips nearly came off the bed. The tingling from my fingers transferred to the taut bud of nerves—

"Oh gods," I cried out at the shiver of pleasure that rippled through me, body shaking. "I don't think I can."

"You can." He drew my head closer to him. "I want those fingers inside you." His jaw flexed. "I want them in you."

Shuddering, I slipped them through the wetness and then inside me. He didn't blink, not once as I began to move my fingers. He towered over me, his hand balled tightly in my hair. The tingling warmth followed the plunge of my fingers.

"That's my girl," he murmured.

My pulse thrummed as I took him into my mouth once more, gripping him with my other hand. I sucked on him as I did what he'd demanded. My hum of approval was lost in his growl as he thrust harder, his movements roughening, but there was a line of control in each push of his hips. He didn't hurt me, and gods, I knew he could easily with how hard he was, how strong he was, but he took without *taking,* and I took more of that taste of him into my mouth, grinding against the bed as I touched myself. Muscles tightened and spun deep inside. He couldn't hear my moans, but I knew he felt them as he watched me work his cock with my mouth, work myself with my own fingers. The release hit me hard, stealing my breath—

The Prince pulled out of my mouth, pushing me onto the bed as he settled between my legs, trapping my hand and his cock between us as he braced his weight above me. The hand in my hair tugged my head back. My gaze met his as he shuddered, his release hot and tingling against my hand—against my core, his body just as heated as his flesh seemed to hum. My eyes went wide at the riot of sensations as the edges of his body glowed just like the *sōls.* The sound I made as I clutched his arm would surely embarrass me, but his laugh—his rich, sultry laugh as he rocked against me—tugged at my own lips as wave after wave of pleasure swept through me.

And it went on, seconds into minutes, long after he'd stilled against me. The tremors of pleasure kept coming even as he reached between us, easing my fingers from me. I shook as he . . . he held himself over me, brushing the strands of damp hair back from my face, touching my cheek, my parted lips, his eyes open and not missing a single moment. He watched me, petted me as I came and came until the final wave of pleasure faded and I was finally released from the thrall. I stared at him, eyes half open.

Good gods, Naomi hadn't been wrong about the orgasms. . . .

"Stay here," the Prince said.

I wasn't going anywhere as he lifted himself off me. I couldn't move, every muscle seeming to have lost the ability to work. I thought I heard the water turn on. My eyes drifted shut as I lay there, the warmth disappearing from between my thighs before the taste of him faded from my tongue. I might've actually dozed off, because when I blinked open my eyes to find him standing above me, I had a feeling that he'd been there for some time.

"Here." He bent, pressing one knee into the bed as he slid a hand under the nape of my neck and lifted my head. "Drink this."

I opened my mouth to the cup he held at my lips. It was water and I drank fiercely, not realizing until that moment how thirsty I was. He took the cup away when I finished, then picked up a cloth he must've brought with him. He took ahold of my arm, wiping the damp cloth over my limp fingers and then lowering my hand to the bed.

"Next time—and there will be a next time," he swore, dragging the cloth between my legs. The blue of his eyes turned luminous as I moaned, lifting my hips weakly against his touch. One side of his lips curled up. "You're going to come on my dick, and you're going to stay right there until the last bit of pleasure leaves you." He paused, head tilting. "Do you agree?"

My brows lifted at his attempt at asking, and I would've laughed if I weren't so tired. "Yes, Your Grace."

"Thorne," he said with another laugh. "And I'm glad we agree."

I snorted.

As he tossed the cloth aside, I knew I needed to get up and get dressed. The Prince wanted my company, but I knew there was a certain part of my company he desired that didn't include me passed out in his bed, despite his request the previous night. Ordering myself to get moving, I started to sit up.

I didn't make it very far.

Prince Thorne returned to my side, and before I knew what he was up to, he lifted me. He laid me down across the center of the bed, then settled in beside me. The click of the lamp turning off followed. I blinked open my eyes to the darkness of the room—to the chest I faced and *touched*. He planned on me staying the night with him? *Sleeping* beside him?

I'd only ever slept with Grady, and that was absolutely nothing like this. I didn't know what to think or feel as I lay there. My heart tumbled over itself, but beneath my palm, his chest was still except for the shallow rise and fall of his breath. What had he meant when he said his heart hadn't beat like a mortal's in a long time? Did it have to do with how he was . . . created?

"Are you asleep?" I whispered.

There was silence and then, "Yes."

My brows knitted. "Are you answering me in your sleep then?"

"Yes." The arm around my waist tightened.

I swallowed, my fingers pressing against his chest—against where his heart *should* be but I couldn't feel. "Can I ask you something?"

"You just did."

My nose wrinkled. "Can I ask you something else?"

"Yes, *na'laa*."

"Don't call me that," I muttered.

"You're being especially stubborn at the moment, though."

I rolled my eyes. "Whatever."

He sighed, but the sound wasn't an annoyed one. It was almost as if he were amused. "What's your question?"

Biting down on my lip, I stared at the shadowy outline of his chest beneath my palm. "Did your heart beat like a mortal's once before?"

"Yes." He yawned.

I curled a finger against his skin. "Why doesn't it beat like that now?"

"Because I . . ." His hand moved idly over my lower back. "I lost the *ny'chora*."

"And what is that?"

He didn't answer for so long that I thought he might have fallen asleep on me. "Everything."

Everything? I waited for him to elaborate, but there was only silence. "Are you still awake?"

"No," came the response with a soft laugh.

The corners of my lips rose, but the small grin quickly faded. I swallowed. "Would you prefer that I . . . that I return to my chambers?"

His arm tightened even more, pressing my stomach to his. "If I preferred that, you wouldn't be in the bed with me."

"Oh."

He shifted, somehow managing to tuck one of my legs between his. "*Na'laa?*"

"Yes?"

"Go to sleep."

"Good night, Your . . ." I closed my eyes, heart feeling . . . light. It had never felt that way before. "Good night, Thorne."

He didn't answer, but as I drifted off to sleep, I felt his lips brush against my forehead, and I thought I heard him whisper, "Good night, Calista."

CHAPTER 28

When I woke, the space beside me was empty, but the soft, woodsy scent clung to the sheets and to my skin. I placed my hand on the bed, feeling the warmth of his body heat that still lingered.

Thorne.

There was this vague memory of waking in the gray light of dawn to the touch of his fingertips along the curve of my cheek, the brush of his lips along my brow, and the sound of his voice. "Sleep well," he'd whispered. "I'll return to your side soon."

I opened my eyes, my chest . . . *swelling.* The feeling wasn't entirely unpleasant but was wholly unfamiliar, and it scared me, because it felt like a promise of something more.

Bringing my legs up, I tucked them against my chest. There couldn't be a promise of anything more, even if I wasn't sure exactly what the idea of *more* actually entailed. I knew enough. More went beyond pleasure shared in the darkest hours of night. More went beyond the physical. More was a future.

And none of those things were possible with a Hyhborn, let alone a prince. Especially the Prince of Vytrus.

But he claimed to have saved Archwood because he had found me.

Rolling onto my back, I shook my head. He couldn't have been serious about that, no matter what he thought of my supposed bravery.

But Hyhborn couldn't lie.

Smacking my hands over my face, I dragged them down, rubbing at the skin. Why was I even lying in his bed, thinking about this? There were far more important things I needed to be focused on. Claude's knowledge of how my abilities worked, because I doubted he had no recollection of speaking that. His relation to the Commander of the Iron Knights. The impending siege.

Thorne was the least of my worries.

But he was the prettiest of my worries.

"Gods," I groaned, throwing the sheet off. I sat up and scooted to the edge of the bed, looking for my gown. Not spotting it on the floor, I rose and turned, finding the gown folded on the chest, where his swords had lain the night before. A black robe lay across the foot of the bed. He must've left that there for me.

That strange and downright silly swelling motion returned to my chest as I donned the robe. It was . . . thoughtful of him.

I'll return to you soon.

I glanced around the quarters. He . . . Thorne had said he wanted me with him until he left to escort his armies. Did he expect me to wait around for him all day, in his chambers?

That was not going to happen.

Tugging my hair out from the robe, I picked up my gown. I cradled it to my chest and hurried toward the door, finding it locked. When I turned the latch and opened the door, I nearly plowed straight into Grady.

"Oh my gods." Gasping, I stumbled back.

Grady caught my arm, steadying me. "Sorry," he grunted. "I was trying to pick the lock—been at it for a half of an hour. He must've done something to it to prevent it from unlocking from the outside." His dark gaze swept over my face, and then he seemed to see what I was wearing and holding. "Are you all right?"

"Yes. Of course." I stepped around him, closing the door behind me. "Why were you trying to pick the lock?"

"Really?" His brows flew up.

"Really." I started down the hall.

He stared at me for a moment. "Do you even know what time it is? It's almost noon."

Surprise flickered through me. "Really? I never—"

"You never sleep this late," he finished for me. "I looked everywhere for you this morning, Lis. Your chambers, the gardens—I ran into Naomi, who was also looking for you," he said when he saw the look I gave him. "She told me about this arrangement."

Ugh.

I held the gown tighter. "She shouldn't have done that."

"Because you weren't planning to?"

"No, because she probably had to deal with you overreacting and freaking out," I said, quieting as we passed one of the staff carrying a load of towels. "And I was going to tell you."

"When?"

"This morning." I tucked a strand of hair back.

His jaw was working overtime. "It goes without saying—"

"You're not happy with this arrangement."

"And neither are you, according to Naomi," he shot back.

My lips pursed, but I stamped down on my annoyance. Naomi was likely just worried, and I'd clearly given her good reason to be. "I wasn't exactly thrilled with the arrangement," I began. "But Thorne and I talked it out, and I'm okay with it."

Grady had stopped walking. "Thorne?"

"Yes?" I glanced back at him. "That's his name."

"And since when are you on a first-name basis with him?" he demanded.

Since I'd decided to stay despite what he'd told me last night.

I didn't say that, because all of that was too hard to explain or understand. Hell, I wasn't sure if I even understood. I turned down the hall. "It's fine, Grady. Really—"

"I really wish you'd stop lying to me."

"I'm not." I stopped, facing him. "I wasn't thrilled with the arrangement, because he hadn't asked me how I felt—what I wanted—but we talked it out. We came to an . . . understanding." *I think.* "And I . . ." Pressing my lips together, I shook my head as I started walking. "I can touch him, Grady. I can touch him and not hear, feel, or think anything other than my own thoughts and feelings. I know you say you understand all of that, but there is no way you can truly fathom what that means."

"You're right," Grady admitted after a few moments. "I can't know what that means."

He fell quiet as he trailed behind me, but that didn't last long. "Is that the only reason, though?" he asked, voice low. "Because you can touch him?"

"Why?" I shot him a look over my shoulder. "What other reason could it be?"

"I don't know." He glanced up at the ceiling as he fell in step beside me. "Do you like him?"

"Do I like him?" I laughed as my stomach gave a weird wiggle. "What are we?" I nudged him with my elbow. "Sixteen?"

He snorted. "Do you?"

"I don't know. I mean, I like him well enough to want to touch him, if that is what you're asking," I said, skin prickling. "I don't know him well enough to like him more than that."

Grady stared ahead. "Yeah, but even if you did know him, you can't *like* him, Lis."

"Yeah, I know. You don't need to tell me that."

"Just making sure," he murmured.

Ignoring the sudden knot in my chest, I said, "Shouldn't you be working or something?"

"Yes, but the Baron is holed up in his study with Hymel."

They were likely trying to figure out where a thousand soldiers were going to camp. I pushed open the doors to my quarters. "Did Naomi tell you why the Hyhborn were here?"

"She did." He sat on the edge of the chair. "Got to admit, that surprised me."

"There's something else I learned last night."

"If it has anything to do with what went on in the chambers with the Prince, I'm not at all interested."

"It has nothing to do with Thor—" I caught myself when Grady's stare jerked toward me. "It has nothing to do with the Prince, but King Euros," I said, and then told him about how the King had preferred that Archwood go the way of Astoria. I didn't tell him about the past—about the world that had fallen. Thorne trusting me with that was important, and knowledge of the past felt . . . it felt dangerous.

"Can't say I'm surprised to hear the King would rather see the city leveled," Grady said when I went quiet.

"Really?" My brows rose.

"Yeah. Were you surprised to hear that?"

"A little," I said. "I mean, there's a huge difference between the King taking little interest in the welfare of us lowborn and deciding that our homes and livelihoods aren't worth the possibility of a Hyhborn being injured or dying."

"Yeah, I don't see a difference there." He shrugged. "All Hyhborn care about is themselves at the end of the day. Half of the time I'm surprised that they haven't just gotten rid of us and taken the realm for themselves."

"Gods." I stared at him. "That's dark. Even for you."

He snorted.

I shook my head. "There's more. It's about Vayne Beylen."

Curiosity filled his face. "I'm all ears."

"And it has to stay with your ears."

"Of course."

I glanced at the closed door. "Claude and Vayne are related."

His brow shot up. "What?"

"They're cousins, related on Claude's father's side of the family," I told him. "Beylen is a *caelestia*."

"Fuck . . ." He drew the word out. He leaned into the chair, draping an arm over the back. "How did you learn this?"

"Claude told me. The Hyhborn don't know." I crossed my arms, inhaling deeply and immediately regretting it, because the damn robe smelled of . . . of Thorne. "But him being a *caelestia* explains why the Iron Knights would back the Westlands."

"Yeah." He dragged a finger over his brow. "I suppose."

I studied him. "I'm sorry."

He looked up. "For what?"

"I know you kind of looked up to this Beylen, and hearing that he's a *caelestia* probably changes it."

"Why?" His brows knitted.

"Because *caelestias* aren't lowborn—"

"They basically are compared to the Hyhborn. I mean, look at Claude. He's about as dangerous as a half-asleep kitten."

I wrinkled my nose. "You really don't think that changes things? What he is? His support of the Westlands Hyhborn—a princess who wants to be queen?"

"Look, I know I said all Hyhborn are the same and shit, but I was . . . I don't know. I was talking out of my ass. Beylen and those who follow him are risking their lives. There must be a reason why Beylen would support her—why those already following Beylen are also supporting her. She could be different."

I huffed out a breath, shaking my head.

"You think your prince is different."

"He's not my prince," I snapped. "And I just . . ." I sat on the edge of the chair. "There's something I feel like I'm missing with Claude and everything, and that it's important. He said that Beylen was starborn or something like that. It sounded familiar, but I don't get it." There was a lot I didn't get, like how Claude had said the Prince of Vytrus could provide me with what he could not. Everything.

"Starborn?" Grady murmured, and I looked over at him. He rocked forward. "Wait. I've heard that before. Heard you say that."

"What do you mean?" I asked, fiddling with the collar of the robe.

"The Prioress of Mercy—the one you were given to," he said. "You told me when we were younger that she used to say that *you* were born of the stars."

"Holy shit." My hand fell to my lap. "You're right."

He gave me a cheeky grin. "I know. Probably just a weird coincidence."

"Yeah," I murmured, except I didn't believe in coincidences.

Neither did he.

⫸

Starborn.

I *knew* that meant something.

My intuition, usually silent on all things dealing with me, was telling me that it did.

That it was important.

Claude was still with Hymel, so speaking with him wasn't an option at the moment, and since this could be something only a *caelestia* knew, the only other person I could think of who might know what starborn meant was Maven.

That was if Naomi was right about her, and she was Claude's grandmother, on his father's side.

The thing was, I'd have to get her to talk or . . . I would have to get the information from her another way, without her permission.

That didn't sit well with me, but it also didn't stop me. I was a hypocrite and fully aware of it.

Bathed and dressed in the lightweight tunic and leggings often favored by the staff, my hair braided back from my face, I could *still* catch that woodsy, soft scent of Thorne on me. At this point, I was beginning to think it was my imagination, because how was that even possible?

I stepped into the alcove Maven's chamber door was set in, and knocked. There was no answer, but after a few moments the rounded, wooden door cracked open.

Hesitating, I took a deep breath and pushed the door open enough for me to get past, stepping into the chamber, which was lit by dozens of candles stacked on shelves along the stone walls and piled on nearly every flat surface. There had to be electricity in this chamber to heat the water, but Maven seemed to prefer the ambience of the candlelight.

Or the creepiness.

Closing the door behind me, I almost missed her. Shrouded in black, she was seated on one of the many stools, near the wardrobe, her head bowed as she stitched a piece of garment in her lap. The room smelled of laundry soap and faintly of mothballs.

Throat strangely dry, I inched forward. "Maven?" I winced at the hoarse sound of my voice. "I brought back the headpiece. I forgot to do it last night."

She jerked her head toward one of the shelves holding other elaborate pieces.

Nibbling on my lip, I walked the headpiece to the shelf and found an empty hook to hang it from. Anxiety settled in the center of my chest as I glanced over at her. Limp, dull gray strands of hair fell from the cowl, shielding her face.

"I . . . wanted to ask you something." I draped the chain over the hook and carefully placed the chains of rubies on the shelf below it.

There was no response as her gnarled fingers drew the needle and thread through the thin red garment.

"Are you Claude's grandmother?" I asked.

Still, she was silent.

I stared at her hunched shoulders. Like the other night, a shivery pressure settled in between my shoulder blades. The tingling spread throughout my arms and seeped into my muscles, guiding me toward her. Fingers twitching, I made no sound as I approached the woman, lifting my hand—

Faster than I would've thought her capable, Maven wheeled around on her stool.

I gasped, jerking back a step.

"You think to force an answer outta me, girl?" she demanded in a voice as thin as parchment and as brittle as her bones. "After all this time?"

"I . . ." I didn't know what to say as I drew my hand back.

She laughed, the sound more of a dry wheeze that shook her entire body. "You never spoke to me before. Never asked me about my kin before. Why now?"

"That's not true. I've spoken to you before, when I first started being brought to you," I told her, but that was neither here nor there. "Is Claude your grandson?"

The lines in her face were deep gouges. Watery, shadowed eyes met mine, but they were alert and full of curiosity. "What's it matter to you?"

"Can you just answer the question?"

Stringy silver hair slipped back as she lifted her chin. "Or?"

"Or . . ." My fingers tingled. "I will just get the answer the hard way." My stomach twisted; the hypocrisy still didn't sit well with me, especially after my lecture to Thorne about consent. Granted, gaining answers from Maven was nothing like demanding my time and my body, but it felt a lot like splitting hairs. It felt a lot like what I did every time I used my abilities for Claude. Maybe that was why I had such a problem with Thorne's demands. And maybe that was why I was able to accept them. Heart thudding, I took a step toward her. "You won't be able to stop me."

Maven's answering laugh was more of a cackle. "No, I suppose not." She rose slowly, shuffling forward, the hem of her black robes dragging unevenly along the floor. "Yeah, he's my grandson."

"On his father's side?"

"Yes."

I exhaled roughly as she laid the garment on a nearby table. It reminded me of a splash of blood in the darkness. "You understand what I can do."

"Clearly," she remarked, ambling back to the stool. She sat down heavily, cheeks puffing with exertion.

I ignored the surprisingly strong tone of sarcasm. "Do you know what 'starborn' means?"

"Why you asking me?" She picked up a tuft ball, stabbing the needle through it. "You could've asked the Baron."

"Because he's busy, and I figured if you're a *caelestia* then you may know what that is."

Maven shook her head, tossing the pincushion into a basket at her feet. "And why would you think that?"

Hell if I knew at this point. "Because I've heard it before, spoken by the Prioress of Mercy, and Claude mentioned it in . . . in passing."

"Funny gal, you are," she said, snickering. "Know so much and yet know so little."

My eyes narrowed. "Hymel said something like that."

"Yeah, well, that one knows too much."

"What do—?"

"Why don't you get me a drink out of that red bottle?" She lifted a frail arm. "There. On the table by the door."

I looked over my shoulder and saw it. I crossed the chamber, picked up the glass bottle, and pulled the stopper. The scent of whiskey was strong, nearly smacking me in the face. "You sure you want this?"

"Wouldn't ask for it if I wasn't."

"Okay," I murmured, pouring the deep brown liquor into an old clay cup. Bringing the drink to her, I hoped that the whiskey loosened her tongue and didn't kill her. "Here you go."

"Thanks." She wrapped thin, bony fingers around the cup, careful to avoid mine. She took a drink—a deep drink. My eyes widened as she swallowed, then smacked her lips. "Keeps my bones warm."

"Uh-huh."

Her chuckle wasn't very much more than a puff of air. "I was like you once. Not some orphan scraped off the streets, but nothing much better. A poor farmer's daughter, one of three with an empty belly but heart and head full of nonsense."

My brows inched up at what sounded distinctly like an insult, but I kept quiet.

"And just like you, I was more than willing to trade anything to not go to bed hungry every night," she said, staring at the candles along the wall as I sat on the edge of another stool. "Not to wake up every morning knowing I was going to end up just like my mama, dead before she entered the fourth decade of life, or like my pa, made miserable by the toll of working the fields. When I met Baron Huntington—Remus Huntington?" Her wizened features softened as she spoke of Claude's grandfather. "I was more than happy to give him what he wanted in exchange for being kept fed and sheltered. Comfortable. He was kind enough, especially when I gave him a son his wife passed off as her own. I raised Renald though. He was still my boy—Claude's father. I also gave him a daughter. Named her after my mama. Eloise. Raised her too. Somehow I outlived them all." She laughed again, shoulders sinking before she took another drink. "Old blood. That's my family. Our blood is old. That's what my pa used to say."

Slowly, she turned her head toward me. "You know what old blood is?"

I shook my head.

"It's another name they like to call the *caelestias*. Old blood. Meaning many of our ancestors can be traced all the way back to the Great War. Even before then. Can be traced all the way back to the first of them, those who were once the stars watching over us. Older than the king who rules now. As old as the one who came before."

"First of them?" My intuition went silent, and that told me enough. "The Hyhborn?"

Maven nodded. "To the Deminyens. The watchers. The helpers."

Thorne . . . he had called the ancient Deminyens that. *Watchers.* "What does that have to do with starborn?"

"If you stop making unnecessary comments, I'll get there."

I closed my mouth.

Maven laughed hoarsely. "Did you ever think about how strange *caelestias* are? For one to even come into creation? We come from a Deminyen—not their offspring. For a *caelestia* to be born, it has to be one of them and a lowborn, and ain't that strange?"

I guessed so, but I didn't want to speak.

"Think about it." She looked over at me. "Deminyens can fuck half this realm and never have a child."

A giggle crawled up my throat upon hearing her curse, but I wisely swallowed it.

"They got to choose to have one. Now why would they want to create a child with a lowborn?"

When I said nothing, she looked at me pointedly. "I don't know," I said. "Maybe because they're . . . in love?"

She cackled so deep and hard, liquor sloshed over the rim of her cup. I couldn't blame her. It sounded ridiculous to me. "Maybe. Maybe so, but every creation has to have the groundwork laid, and that's what the Deminyens were doing back then. Laying the groundwork for those born of the stars."

I really had no idea what she was rambling about, but I stayed quiet and listened.

"And I'm of the mind that some of them don't like that groundwork. At least that's what my pa always said. You probably think it's because they'd want to keep their blood pure, right?" she said, and yes, that was exactly what I thought. Her thin, bloodless lips curled, revealing yellowed, aged teeth. "I'm of the mind they don't want that because of what that old blood does. Allows the stars to fall."

The back of my neck tingled. "Starborn? You talking about *caelestias?*" I asked, confused.

"No. Not them. They ain't born from the stars." She raised a hand, pointing a finger at me. "The stars don't fall just for anyone, but they . . ." That spotted hand disappeared back into her sleeve as she lifted her cup with the other. "They used to say that when a star falls, a mortal is made divine."

My brows inched up my forehead. "Divine?"

"Divine like my other grandbaby, girl." She raised the cup in my direction as if she were saluting me. "Divine like you."

"Me?" I squeaked. "I'm not a *caelestia*—"

"You ain't no ordinary lowborn, now are you? With seeing the future. With peering into the minds of others. No, you ain't. Old blood," she repeated. "Once one is born, everyone that comes after has that chance. And there are more than you think." Her stare turned shrewd as she drank. "Ain't no one ever really questioning how conjurers got their knowledge, the know-how when it comes to Hyhborn parts. Old blood." She laughed hoarsely. "Ain't no one questioning anything."

Surprise rolled through me. Conjurers had descended from Hyhborn? "I didn't know . . ." I trailed off, a strangled sort of laugh leaving me. "Of course, I wouldn't know." Not if what she said was true. "My intuition has never been much help when it came to Hyhborn."

"Strange, ain't it?"

I nodded slowly. So many questions whirled about.

"Strange that we've all forgotten the truth."

"The truth?"

Maven stared down at her cup, face hidden once more. "Good and evil are real. They always have been. Yet the weight of the realm has always fallen on those in between, ones neither good nor bad. That's what my pa always said." She lifted her drink again. "But he was also a drunk, so . . ."

I blinked slowly.

"There are Deminyens moving about this town, these walls, right?"

"Yes. A prince and two lords."

"A prince." She humphed. "It was bound to happen."

"What was?"

"That he came." Her head turned to me. "For what is his."

CHAPTER 29

A sharp swirl of tingles erupted along the back of my neck. *That he came for what is his.* My heart thudded. That same feeling as before returned, settling in my chest. Rightness. Acceptance.

I leaned forward, clasping my knees. "Are you—" A burst of nervous energy pounded through me. My body moved without will, turning on the stool, toward the door a second before it swung open, slamming into the table with enough force to rattle the candles.

Hymel stood there, eyes narrowed. "What are you doing in here?"

"Nothing." I rose, wiping my palms on my thighs. "I was just returning the headpiece I wore last night."

Hymel's gaze shot to Maven. "And to do that you had to be sitting down?"

"Maven was a bit unsteady on her feet," I quickly said, not so much instinct guiding me to lie but just my general distrust of the man. "I got her something to drink and was just making sure she was okay."

Maven said nothing as she lifted her cup, finishing off the liquor I really hoped Hymel couldn't smell.

"She looks fine to me," Hymel growled.

"Yes. Thankfully." I turned, nodding at Maven. The old woman gave no indication of seeing me or anyone else. I hesitated, wanting confirmation of what I suspected, but she was staring at the candles, and Hymel waited. Stamping down on my frustration, I left the chamber.

Hymel stalked out behind me, closing the door. "What were you in there talking about?"

"Talking? With Maven?" I forced a laugh. "We weren't talking."

His upper lip curled. "I heard someone talking."

"You heard me speaking to myself," I replied, focusing on him. "And what would it matter if we were talking?"

Hymel's jaw clenched. "It doesn't," he said, glancing at the door and then back to me. "Don't think you're needed here."

Hands opening and closing at my sides, I turned stiffly and walked out from the alcove and through the narrow servants' corridor. When I reached the doors to the foyer, I looked back and saw that Hymel no longer stood there.

Since he most likely had gone back into Maven's chamber, there was not a single doubt in my mind that he knew all of what Maven had shared.

Three *sōls* danced together above the roses as I walked the gardens that evening. I hadn't ventured too far, able to still hear the music drifting from the lawns of Archwood Manor.

After speaking with Maven, I had searched for Claude, but hadn't seen him until this evening. There was no chance to talk to him. He was holding a party that likely rivaled what took place during the Feasts. The drive was full of jeweled carriages and the Great Chamber teeming with glittering aristo. I'd spent only a few minutes there, and knew that most had come to catch sight of the lords of Vytrus, and of course, *the* Prince.

I reached out, running my fingers over the silky petal of a rose. I'd been wrong in my assumption that most of the aristo would abandon the city upon hearing of the impending siege. None of them appeared at all concerned about why they were here, their thoughts consumed with catching a glimpse of the Hyhborn and more.

Which meant none of those in attendance had been with the Hyhborn that morning to prepare for the siege. That wasn't at all surprising. I still believed that many would be gone once the reality of what was to come settled in.

The Hyhborn weren't in attendance, and I didn't know if any of them would eventually show.

I didn't even know if Thorne had returned to the manor or had come to look for me yet.

One of the *sōls* dipped down, nearly brushing against my arm before it floated deeper into the roses as I heard Maven's words echo in my thoughts. *That he came for what is his.* The warm swirl of tingles rippled across the base of my neck, and that same feeling as before returned. Rightness. Acceptance. I didn't understand it.

I started walking, unsure if what I felt was from my intuition or not. Having felt only vague premonitions about them before, it was hard to know what fueled the feeling. It was also hard to believe what Maven had said—had suggested.

If she'd spoken the truth, then she was saying that I . . . that I was a *caelestia* and that was how I'd gained my abilities. Could that be impossible? No. I didn't know my parents, let alone my ancestry, but Claude had no gifts. I'd never heard of any having abnormal abilities, but both she and Claude spoke of Beylen as if he were different. Divine. As if I were different. *Divine.* Because we were . . . starborn?

I glanced up at the star-swept sky. Part of me wanted to laugh at the ridiculousness of it. Wouldn't Thorne have, I don't know, sensed that I was a *caelestia*? Wouldn't Claude have just told me this? Why keep it hidden from me? A horrible thought crossed my mind. Could he have kept it hidden from me because *caelestias* were automatically accepted into the aristo class? Certain opportunities presented themselves. I could seek education if that was what I wanted. I could own land. Buy a home. Start a business—

"No," I whispered. Claude wouldn't have kept that from me just to keep me by his side. If it was true, and I was a *caelestia*, there would be a damn good reason why Claude wouldn't have told me.

Unless I was incredibly naive, and I wasn't. At least, I didn't think I was.

I walked on for several minutes, stopping when I felt the sudden thickening of the air. The brief, unnatural stillness and then the sharp crescendo of humming insects and chattering night birds. Tiny bumps spread across my arms. Awareness pressed upon me.

Slowly, I turned. The breath I took was unsteady as the swelling motion returned to my chest.

Thorne stood on the walkway, a handful of feet from me, dressed in the black sleeveless tunic and pants. A warm breeze toyed with the loose strands of his hair, tossing them against the cut of his jaw.

There were no golden glints of weapons on him, at least that I could see, but their absence made him no less dangerous.

And that damn urge—the one to run, to provoke him into giving chase—rose in me again. My muscles tensed in preparation. It was a wild feeling.

"I've been looking for you," he said, drawing several *sóls* from the air above.

Clasping my hands together, I held myself still. "Were you?"

"I thought you'd be in my quarters or yours."

"You mean you thought I would be waiting for your return?"

"Yes," he answered without hesitation.

"You shouldn't have." I turned from him, heart pounding as I forced myself to move slowly. To not run. I didn't look back, because I . . . I knew he *followed*. A warm shiver curled down my spine.

"I thought we had come to an agreement on this arrangement," Thorne said, sounding as if he was only a foot, if that, behind me.

"Had we?"

"We have," he said. "I recall telling you that I would return as soon as I could."

"But I do not recall agreeing to sitting around and waiting on your return."

"I didn't expect you to sit and wait."

I halted, and faced him. He was close, having approached me in that unnerving silent way of his. "What did you expect then?"

The blue of his eyes was luminous as he stared down at me. "For you not to hide from me."

"I wasn't hiding, Your Grace." I lifted my chin. "I was simply enjoying an evening stroll."

One side of his lips curled up. "Or were you simply seeing if I would find you?"

I clamped my mouth shut. Had that been why I'd come out here? His smile deepened.

That he came for what is his.

Pivoting, I nibbled on my lower lip as I began to walk, the gown I'd changed into before supper whispering along the stone path. "You met with the people of Archwood today?"

"I did." He fell in step beside me.

I kept my gaze trained ahead. "Did many show?"

"Many but not all that could," he told me, his arm brushing mine as we walked. "Your baron did."

"What?" Surprise flickered through me as I looked at him. "He did?"

Thorne chuckled. "I was as surprised as you."

I blinked, focusing ahead. "Did he train?"

"No, but there wasn't much in the way of training to be had today, as Rhaz needed to differentiate those who had skill with sword or arrow from those who had none," he said, and I found it amusing, the shortening of their names. Rhaz. Bas. *Thor.* "You are likely not surprised to hear that most have no such skill."

"I'm not. Beyond the guards, I doubt many have lifted a sword," I said. "The only ones who likely have skill with a bow are the long hunters, and they are likely on a hunt. The rest work in the mines."

"For the most part, it was only they who showed and were eager to learn," he commented. "Yet they aren't the only ones capable of defending the city."

I knew he spoke of the aristo. "I imagine most of them had yet to awaken from their evening pursuits to join," I said, still stuck on the fact that Claude had gone. "What did the Baron do?"

"He mostly listened and watched, which is more than I expected from him."

I glanced at him, stomach dipping when our eyes locked. "He's not completely irresponsible, you know?"

"We shall see," he replied. "But I believe he is better suited for Court life than to govern a city."

What Maven had shared with me flickered through my thoughts. I twisted my fingers, having the sense that whatever I asked, I had to do so carefully. "Is that what most *caelestias* do?"

"Some. Depends on the Court and how they treat *caelestias*. Some Hyhborn treat them as if they are . . ."

"A lowborn?" I finished for him.

Thorne nodded.

"How so?"

He didn't answer immediately. "They are treated more like servants than equals."

I exhaled slowly. "And does that differ from your Court? I've always heard that lowborn were not welcomed."

"They aren't."

My head cut toward him. "And here I was beginning to think that what was said about you not liking lowborn was another false narrative."

Thorne stared ahead. "The Highlands are fierce lands, *na'laa*. Dangerous for even a Hyhborn to travel without knowledge."

I thought about that. I knew that the largest portion of the Wychwoods was in the Highlands. "Are there any *caelestias* that live there?"

"There are. Some are even knights of the Court."

"Oh." That made sense, since I knew that many *caelestias* were in the Royal regiment. I worried my lower lip, searching for a way to ask what I wanted to know and finding it. "I've always wondered something. Can you or other Hyhborn sense a *caelestia*?" I asked as I opened my senses, creating that cord. I came into contact with that white shield, and when I pressed upon it, it did nothing.

He nodded as I severed the connection. "Their essence is different than that of a mortal."

Well, that threw a wrench into what Maven claimed. The Prince had repeatedly referred to me as a mortal.

"That was an odd thing to wonder about," Thorne commented.

"I wonder about a lot of odd things," I said, which was true.

"Like?"

I laughed. "I'd rather not embarrass myself by sharing the things that cross my mind."

"Well, now I'm all the more interested."

Snorting, I sent him a look.

There was a pause as we neared the wisteria trees. Only then did I realize how far we'd walked. "Do you wonder about me?"

I had, many times over the years, and even more between the time he first appeared in Archwood and his return. Stopping, I trailed a finger over the lavender-hued blossoms. I'd wondered all sorts of random, irrelevant things. I had questions that were far less important than what I should be thinking about then.

"Do you have family?" I asked, which was something I'd wondered. "I mean, obviously not by blood but something similar?"

"Deminyens do have what would be similar to family—to a sibling," he answered, lifting a hand. His fingers folded around the thick braid of hair resting over my shoulder. "We are never created alone." He ran his thumb along the top of the braid as he drew his hand down. "Usually there are two or three created at the same time, sharing the same earth, the same Wychwood."

"So, in a way, you do have blood . . . siblings?"

His fingers reached the middle of the braid, where it crested over my breast. "In a way."

"And you? Do you have one? Or two?"

In the soft glow of the *sōls*, there was a tightening to his jaw. "Just one now." His brows knitted. "A brother."

"There was another?"

"A sister," he said. "Do you ever wonder if you had siblings?"

"I used to."

"But not anymore?" he surmised.

"No." Without his focus on the braid, I openly studied the striking lines and angles of his features. "What do you do when—" My breath caught as the back of his hand brushed against the tip of my breast. The buttery-yellow muslin gown was no barrier to the heat of his touch.

His lashes lifted. Eyes more blue than green or brown met mine. "You were saying?"

"What do you do while you're at home?"

"Read."

"What?" I said with a short laugh.

The half grin reappeared. "You seem surprised. Is it that hard to believe that I enjoy reading?"

I reached up to brush his hand away, but my fingers curled around his forearm and remained there. No thoughts intruded, but I did . . . I felt something. The warm whisper against the back of my neck. The sensation I'd felt earlier. Rightness. But was it from me?

Or him?

And what did it even mean?

"Na'laa?"

Clearing my throat, I refocused. "What do you like to read then?"

"Old texts. Journals of those who lived before my creation," he said. "Things most would find boring."

"It sounds interesting to me." Beneath my fingers I could feel the tendons of his arms moving under his hard flesh as he drew his fingers down to the tail end of my braid. "I've only ever seen a few history tomes in Claude's studies."

"Have you read them?"

I shook my head, realizing that he was being serious. After all, Hyhborn couldn't lie. Why I kept forgetting that was beyond me. "The pages appear ancient, and I'm too afraid of accidentally damaging them."

"What else?" His hand left my braid, grazing my stomach to stop along the curve of my waist, and my hand followed as if it were attached to his arm. It was the silent, simple contact I couldn't let go of. "What else have you wondered?"

If he ever thought of the young girl he'd met in Union City. I'd wondered that many times, but those words wouldn't come to my tongue. Instead, I asked only what I'd started to wonder today. "If you believed in old legends and rumors."

"Like?" His hand glided to my hip.

"Like the . . . the old stories of those starborn," I said, and his gaze shot to mine. "Mortals made divine or something of the sort?"

The blots of brown in his irises suddenly cast shadows against the vibrant blue. "What has made you think of that?"

I lifted a shoulder, willing my heart to remain slow. "It's just something I heard an older person talking about once. It all sounded fantastical," I added. "I'm not even sure if it's something real, so maybe you have no idea what I'm speaking of."

"No, it was real."

Was.

I stayed silent.

"And I did believe," he said.

"What does it even mean though?" I asked.

"It . . . it means *ny'seraph*," he said. "And that is everything."

Everything. He'd said that before, when he spoke of a *ny'chora*.

"What else?"

Distracted, I shook my head. "Have you ever called anyone else *na'laa*?"

"No." A shadow of a smile appeared. "I have not."

Our gazes locked again, and for some reason, that revelation felt just as important as learning that some of what Maven had said was true.

"I've wondered about you," he said in the silence. "I'm wondering right now."

"Oh?"

"I've told no mortal that I have a brother nor shared that I enjoy reading."

"Well, I've never told anyone I wanted to be a botanist, so . . .'"

"Not even your baron?"

I shook my head no.

"That pleases me."

"Why?"

"That is also what I wonder. Why. Why I would share anything with you, but you already know that," he said, and the way he said it was as vaguely insulting as it was before. "Even today, when I should be fully focused on those before me, I caught myself wondering what it is about you. It's still incredibly perplexing and annoying."

Oookay. I pulled my hand from his arm. "Well, then, perhaps I should leave so I don't continue to add to this perplexing annoyance."

The Prince chuckled. "It's more like I'm a perplexing annoyance to myself," he said. "And if you left, I would have to follow and I feel like that would lead to an argument when there are far more entertaining things we can do."

"Uh-huh." We'd started walking again.

The grin that crossed his lips held a boyish charm that made him seem . . . young and not so otherworldly, and it tugged at my heart. I quickly looked away.

"Dance with me."

My brows shot up as my head cut in his direction. That I hadn't expected. "I've never danced before."

He stopped. "Not once?"

I shook my head. "So, I don't know how to dance."

"No one knows how to dance the first time. They just dance." His gaze met mine. "I can show you that, Calista."

I sucked in a heady breath full of that soft, woodsy scent of his. My name was a weapon. A weakness. I nodded.

My gaze dropped to his hand as he offered it to me. This . . . this felt surreal. My heart was flipping all over the place. And was it my imagination or did the violin from the lawn seem louder, closer? As did the guitar? And was there suddenly a melody in the air, in the night birds' singing and the humming of summer insects?

"And if I prefer not to?" I asked, my hand opening and closing at my side.

A sliver of moonlight caressed the curve of his cheek as his head cocked. "Then we don't, *na'laa*."

A choice. Another that shouldn't matter all that much, but it did and I . . . I wanted to dance even if I were to make a fool of myself. I lifted my hand, hoping he didn't notice the faint tremor in it.

Our palms met. The contact—the feel of his skin against mine— was still startling. His long fingers closed around mine as he bowed his head slightly.

"Honored," he murmured.

A nervous giggle left me. "I thought Hyhborn can't lie."

"We can't. I spoke no lie." Thorne tugged gently on my arm, coaxing me closer as he stepped into me. Suddenly, his hips brushed against my stomach, my chest against his. The fleeting contact was sudden, unexpected, and only then did I realize this wasn't the kind of dancing I'd seen the aristo do at the less wild balls the Baron sometimes held, where there were at least several inches between their bodies and each step was a well-practiced, measured one. This was the kind of dancing the aristo took part in once the masks came out.

His hips swayed and the hand on mine urged me to follow. After a few moments, I realized that this kind of dancing was a lot like making love. Not that I knew what making *love* felt like. Fucking? Entirely different story, and this didn't feel like that.

"Silence your thoughts."

"W-What?" I glanced up, able to see only the lower half of his face.

"You're stiff. Usually that means your head is not where your body is," he said. "You're thinking too much. One doesn't need to think about their body to dance."

"Then what do they do?" I asked, because it was hard not to think about how close we were—how tall and broad he was, and how that made me feel dainty, and there was nothing about me that could be described as such. Not even my hands. When he turned, I stumbled over my own feet and maybe his.

"You just close your eyes," he told me. "Like you did last night, when your fingers were between your thighs and your mouth was on my cock. Just close your eyes and feel."

I wasn't sure how bringing up last night was going to help, because the sharp pulse of desire those words elicited was completely distracting, but I closed my eyes.

"Listen to the music. Follow it," he coaxed, his voice deeper. Thicker. "Follow me, *na'laa.*"

Breath shallow, I did what it took to use my abilities. I silenced my mind, letting myself listen to the music—to the ebb and flow of violin and the sounds of the night settling around us, charging the air. There was a rhythm, one that tugged at my legs and hips. I followed it and I followed him, my body loosening with each passing minute and my steps becoming lighter. When he turned his body this time, I didn't stumble. I followed. It was like floating, and I imagined that I was one of the *sōls* dancing above us—that we were.

And it was the strangest feeling, almost freeing as I danced with the Prince. I moved with the tempo, chasing the strings as they picked up. Sweat dampened my skin—dampened his. Strands of hair that had escaped the braid I'd twisted it into clung to my skin. The sweet-smelling wisteria vines tangled with us as we moved, as my breath came in quicker pants, each inhale causing the tips of my breasts to graze his chest. The gown was so thin that it always felt as if there were nothing between us. I wished it were the same for my hands, because I could feel his chest rise with shallow, longer breaths beneath mine.

His hand at my hip glided across my lower back, leaving a wake of shivers in its path as we spun beneath the wisteria. My pulse quickened, and I didn't think it had much to do with the dancing. I let my neck loosen, my head tip back as I opened my eyes. Above us, the *sōls* danced, mostly a blur of soft light as we spun and spun, and somehow his thigh had ended up snug between mine. Each movement I made, each one he gave, created this . . . this delicate, decadent friction.

I followed the music—followed him as the tempo gradually slowed. The realm stopped spinning and we moved in each other's embrace, the rhythm richer, thicker and throbbing, just like the blood was doing in my veins. Each breath I took felt like it was getting trapped in my throat as my hips moved with the churning music—moved against him. And I felt richer, thicker and throbbing, aching and swollen. The arm at my waist tightened, as did the hand that held mine. Low in my stomach, muscles twisted and tightened in desire, and I could feel him as I moved, a thick part of him harder than the rest against my stomach.

His chest rumbled against mine, and a throbbing dart of pleasure whipped through me. His breath teased the curve of my cheek and then the corner of my lips. He stopped there, but I didn't. Our bodies still moved, but I wasn't sure it could be considered dancing at this point. I was grinding against him, and the hand at my hip was encouraging it as a wild sense of abandonment swept over me. That primal urge to run. The feral want for him to chase. That savage need for him to capture.

He stilled completely against me, only his chest rising and falling rapidly. Slowly, I lifted my gaze to his. Bursts of starlight had appeared in the pupils. I didn't know if it was the dancing or the melody in the air, if it was knowing he called no one else *na'laa,* or if it was that strange feeling of rightness—it could've been all of those things that emboldened me.

I slipped away from him, taking a trembling step back. His head tilted. Tension poured into the space between us and into the air around us.

And I did it.

I caved to that urge.

I turned and ran.

CHAPTER 30

With my hand balled in the skirt of my gown, I ran through the wisteria vines, heart racing and blood . . . blood heating. I ran as fast as I could, darting to the left and then the right. Hair slipped free in the mad dash, tossing across my face, and I didn't slow.

Not until I felt him closing in on me.

Deep within the wisterias, I stopped. Panting, I scanned the *sōl*-lit canopy of vines as my grip on my skirt eased off. I didn't see him, but I felt him in the thickening of the air, in the electric charge that danced along my skin. I knew he was close as my fingers went to the dainty lace of my bodice. Watching and waiting, he the predator and I the prey. Anticipation swelled. A throbbing ache pulsed between my thighs so acutely I swayed. I didn't understand how I was so aroused or why, but it was like a different kind of instinct had taken over the moment I caved to the wild urge and it was in control now, guiding me farther back into the shadows of the wisteria. Every small sound—every snap of a twig or tousle of vines—heightened my senses, my desire. I almost felt as if I was losing my mind, because I ached as if I had been taunted and teased. I burned as if I had touched his come. Muscles low in my stomach curled. My eyes started to drift shut—

The Prince had made no sound. He came at me from behind, one arm folding around my waist, hauling me back against his chest. I could feel him breathing as hard as me. I could feel his arousal pressing against my back.

"Told you I would catch you," he said, his breath warm against my cheek. His other arm came around me, the fingers curling over where mine still clutched the bodice. "Didn't I?"

I let my head fall back against his chest. "Only because I let you."

His laugh was all smoke and sin, teasing my skin. "I hope you thought about this before you ran. What would happen when I caught you."

I shuddered.

"What I would do to you." His lips grazed my throat and then closed on the skin at the slope of my neck and shoulder. He sucked hard, wringing a sharp cry from me. "Are you ready?"

Yes. No? I found it hard to breathe as I trembled, expecting him to take me then. To drive me to the ground. But he waited.

Pulse pounding, I stared at the glowing orbs above us. He *was* waiting. That silly swelling motion returned, and I ignored it. The emotion had no place here. "Yes," I whispered. "I'm ready."

The sound he made was one I had never heard before. It came from deep within him, a triumphant growl of . . . of warning.

The fingers overlapping mine curled, catching the collar of the bodice. With one hard tug, my body jerked against his. Stitches loosened at my shoulders as he exposed my breasts to the warm night air. I looked down at the turgid peak of my breast as his hand closed over the flesh, as I wrapped my own fingers around his wrist. His mouth closed over the skin beneath my ear as he drew the skirt of my gown up. Humid air swirled around my bare legs, my thighs, the lacy undergarments. I held the gauzy skirts, and his hand slipped below, balling into the thin fabric there. Lust pounded through me as he tore the material free from my body with one quick, brutal jerk.

The Prince took me to the ground then, onto my knees, his large body caging mine in. The damp grass pressed into my palm as I held on to the wrist of the hand he braced in the soil. It was maddening—the way he held me there for several moments. Then he shifted behind me. His thigh parted mine. I shook.

"You're not going to be able to take all of me like this. Not yet." His voice was a heated whisper against my neck. "But *na'laa?*"

"What?" I gasped at the feel of the hard, unbelievably hot length of his cock sliding over my ass.

"You're going to want to." A guttural sound left him as the head of his cock pressed into the heat—

I cried out, hips jerking at the feel of him, just the crown of his arousal parting my flesh, as the sound of him kicked off a sharp, sudden explosion of sensation.

"Oh yeah. You're going to want to." His hand gripped my hip, steadying me. My legs shook as my hand slipped to rest atop his, and there was nothing in my mind but a haze of red-hot lust. His lips pressed a kiss to my wildly beating pulse. "Badly."

A rush of damp heat flooded me. He eased in another inch, his width, those ridges, stretching me.

"But I'm not going to let you," he swore.

"W-What?" I started to turn my head.

Thorne folded his arm over my hips, sealing my back to his, and then he thrust into me.

My cry was lost in his shout. Buried deep in me, he didn't move, and I couldn't think beyond the feel of him. The piercing, vibrating heat and hardness. My entire body shook.

Then he moved.

The Prince withdrew, and those ridges—oh gods, they dragged along the sensitive walls, catching that hidden spot just as he pushed back inside. And the sound I made, it was a whimper and a scream as he held me against him, moving in and out of me slowly, steadily. He was in complete control, the way he held me keeping me from moving my lower body—from pushing back on him or retreating. All I could do was kneel, my fingers curling between his, and take him.

And he took me.

His pace became faster, harder. He drove into me, his cheek pressed to mine, and I swore I could feel his stare on my bare breast, pushed up by the bodice. Tension curled and spun and tightened. He fucked, but I had never been fucked like this. My entire body pulsed, every nerve ending becoming raw. I could feel the release building, spinning each time he hit that spot. My eyes were wide, gaze fixed on my white-knuckled grip on his hand.

"Oh gods," I gasped as he plunged into me. My chest clenched. My core spasmed and everything unraveled as I moaned, *"Thorne."*

"Fuck," he snarled, slamming into me. He lifted my knees slightly, grinding into me as I came, as I felt him swelling, felt that knot at my opening as he pumped into me, and my body moved on its own, wiggling and trying to bring him even deeper into me, as pleasure rolled and rolled through me.

"Bad girl," he laughed, gasping as his arm tightened, stilling my movements.

He wouldn't allow me to take him where he was at his thickest, and I might've actually hissed . . . or growled. I wasn't sure, because the pleasure crested again, leaving me quivering and still hot, still . . . still throbbing.

Thorne pulled out suddenly, pressing his cock against the curve of my ass as he found his release, as the tension erupted inside me all over again.

Releases that could last for hours . . .

"Oh fuck," I moaned, the whirling sensation building in a crescendo once more. "I . . . I can't."

"You can." His lips grazed my flushed cheek as he moved us down. "You will."

The ground was cool against my chest, his body hot against my back even as he supported his weight on the hand beneath mine. The release took me again, and he wasn't even inside me any longer.

"Why . . . why did you pull out?" I gasped.

"I didn't want to," he said, holding me tight. "I think I would kill to be inside you right now, but if you think this is intense?"

It was. I had never felt anything like it.

"It would be a hundred times more if I stayed inside you." He eased us onto our sides. "It would drive you mad."

I might have already been a little mad as he stayed with me, petting the curve of my hip, my thigh, and the swell of my ass. He stayed with me as every small, delicate muscle inside me spasmed, and I held on, my grip on his hand never slipping. His hold on mine never waning. Not even when I finally went limp, exhausted and sated. Our hands remained sealed.

And my mind remained quiet.

~≫~

"No," I protested halfheartedly.

Thorne grinned from where he was nestled between my thighs. "*Yes*," he murmured, parting my swollen flesh with a swipe of his wicked tongue.

The low moan that rattled from my chest was only one of many I'd made since we left the gardens.

The Prince of Vytrus was insatiable when it came to giving pleasure.

I didn't remember much of our return to the manor, but from the moment we reached his quarters, time had become a sensual blur. We'd bathed—or more accurately, he'd bathed me, washing the dirt and blades of grass from my body as I'd washed away the blood from his skin once before. He made me come then, with his fingers, and when we made it to his bed, our bodies still damp, he'd started a slow exploration of my body, kissing a path along the curve of my jaw, down my throat, and over my breasts. His tongue had been wicked there too, swirling over my nipples just like his tongue now swirled inside me.

Thorne *feasted*.

My fingers balled into the sheets as his tongue dipped in and out. I hadn't thought I'd have the energy in me to move, but I'd been wrong. I lifted my hips to his thrusts, and his answering growl of approval inflamed me. A faint golden glow edged his bare shoulders as he shifted, working a finger inside me. I groaned.

Thick lashes lifted. Eyes a brilliant shade of blue dotted with silvery stars met and held mine. "Don't look away," he ordered. "I want to see your eyes when you come."

I shuddered, trembling all over.

"I want to see your eyes when you come, screaming my name." His finger curled deep inside me. "Understand?"

"Yes," I panted. "*Your Grace.*"

He nipped at my flesh, drawing a ragged moan from me. There was a flash of a grin along his damp lips and then his mouth closed over my clit. My back bowed and my hips lifted from the bed. I didn't look away. Our gazes remained locked, and I did scream when I came, his name spilling from my lips as I quivered.

I was boneless as he crawled up the length of my body, dropping a quick kiss on my navel, at my rib cage, the swell of my breast. As he settled beside me, his lips pressed against my temple.

"You okay?" he asked.

"Mmm-hmm," I murmured. He'd asked that when we'd been in the gardens, when the aftershocks had finally begun to ease. The question had caught me off guard then. It still did now. "Are you?"

Thorne chuckled. "I am."

I turned my head toward his. Our mouths were scant inches apart as I lifted my hand to his chest. I splayed my fingers across his chest. "But you didn't . . ."

"I don't have to find release to feel pleasure." The hand resting on my stomach glided up, folding over the swell of my breast. "The most exquisite kind of pleasure is derived from bestowing it upon another."

"You . . . you really aren't a mortal man then," I said.

He laughed, the sound light and causing my heart to skip. "If you're truly just now realizing that, I'm not sure what to tell you."

I huffed, eyes drifting shut. The silence that fell between us then was warm, companionable, and nothing like I'd experienced before with anyone I'd been with. There was always this need to speak, to fill the quiet either to stave off the inevitable awkwardness that often came or to keep my mind from slipping in another.

But the Prince was nothing like I'd ever experienced.

"I leave in the morning, by the way," Thorne said eventually.

"I remember." A pang of unease sliced my chest. Did I not want him to leave? Or was it something else? "When will you return?"

"I believe it will only take a few days."

I tried to decipher the feelings inside me. Shouldn't I feel relief that he'd be gone for a few days? I didn't. There was just unease, and maybe a little . . . sadness. Oh gods, I realized it was likely because I would miss him.

I needed help.

"Then you should be back in time for the Feasts," I said.

"I should be."

Some of the pleasant haze faded as the reality of what was to come resurfaced. "How long do you think it will be before the West-lands or the Iron Knights reach Archwood?"

"That I cannot answer for sure, but I suspect it will be before the month's end."

My stomach hollowed as I drew the pads of my fingers over the chiseled lines of his chest.

"Leave with me."

"What?" I blinked open my eyes.

The blue and green of his eyes swirled into the brown. "Come with me when I leave to meet with the armies."

My breath snagged on the word *yes*, but I stopped it from escaping. Anticipation swelled at the prospect of traveling with him, of being with him, *at his side*, but that . . . that felt like *more*. Dangerously so. I swallowed, closing my eyes. "I don't think that would be wise."

"Probably not," he said, then fell quiet for several moments. "Will you have dinner with me then, when I return?"

"You're actually asking if I will?" A tired smile tugged at my lips as I struggled to ignore the disappointment with myself—with him for not pushing that I go with him, which was entirely messed up.

"Is that not what you want from me?"

I shouldn't want anything from him. "Yes."

His thumb swept over the peak of my breast. "Then will you?"

"Yes."

Thorne was quiet for a moment, and then I felt his lips against my cheek. "Thank you."

A tripping motion went through my chest. Any Hyhborn, let alone a prince, expressing gratitude was, well, unheard of, and I didn't know what to do with that as I lay there, the Prince eventually slipping into sleep.

But I stayed awake, my fingers resting against his chest. I didn't know why in those quiet, dark moments I thought of the premonition I had in the Great Chamber when Ramsey Ellis had come to the Baron with news of the Westlands.

He's coming.

I knew that premonition had been about Thorne.

That he came for what is his.

That was what Maven had said, and I knew that when Thorne had been here before, he had been searching for something.

Or someone.

⇒⇒⇒

A light touch to my cheek woke me. I opened my eyes to the faint rays of dawn glancing off the cut of Thorne's jaw and the golden hilt of the dagger strapped to his chest. It was morning, and that meant . . .

"You're leaving?" I whispered, voice heavy with sleep.

Thorne nodded. "I didn't mean to wake you," he said, thick lashes lowered as he drew his fingers along my chin.

"It's okay." I started to sit up.

"No, stay. I like the idea of you being here, in the bed I've slept in," he told me, his brows furrowing. A moment passed, and those lashes lifted. His gaze slipped over my face, lingering on my . . . my lips.

Though I was only half awake, my pulse started to pound. I thought he looked at me like he . . . like he wanted to kiss me.

I wanted him to kiss me.

I wanted to kiss him.

Neither of us moved, though. Not for several moments. Then he lowered his head. My eyes drifted shut. His lips didn't touch mine. They brushed over my brow, and for some reason, that sweet, chaste kiss . . . it undid me.

"I'll return to you as soon as I can," Prince Thorne said. "I promise."

Eyes remaining closed, because I was afraid that if they opened they would start watering, I nodded.

"Go back to sleep, *na'laa*." He tugged the sheet up over my arm. His touch lingered at my shoulder. "Till later."

"Till later," I whispered hoarsely.

Prince Thorne stood, and though he moved so quietly, I knew the exact moment he'd left the chamber. I opened damp eyes.

Do you like him?

That was what Grady had asked.

Gods.

I thought I did.

—————— ⤜⤜⤜

I found Claude in his study that afternoon, alone as he sat behind his desk. He looked up as I entered, his smile a little off.

"Do you have a moment?" I asked.

"Always for you." He folded a piece of parchment and set it aside. I glanced at the ever-increasing stack of letters. "I'm glad you've come by. I've been wondering if the arrangement between you and the Prince has fared well or if you're glad for the momentary reprieve."

My cheeks warmed as I thought of last night. "Surprisingly well."

"I can see," he chuckled, leaning back as he crossed one leg over the other. "So, you're not so against this arrangement now?"

I lifted a shoulder, having not come to talk about the Prince. I sat in one of the chairs before his desk. "He told me that you were with the people of Archwood yesterday."

"I was." He brushed a lock of dark hair back from his face, his pale cheeks turning pink. "I thought it would be wise that I see what is being done. That I be seen." He cleared his throat. "I was there this morning for a little bit."

"I think it's a good idea." I smiled at him. "Hopefully it will inspire others to take part."

"Hopefully," he murmured, lowering a hand to the arm of his chair. "We shall see, I suppose."

I nodded, taking a deep breath. "I actually had something I wanted to talk to you about." I twisted my fingers together, unsure of why I was so nervous. Actually, that wasn't true. I was worried I was going to prove myself a naive fool today. "It's about your other cousin."

"Is it?" He glanced at the closed door.

I opened my senses, letting that connection forge between us. I saw the gray wall. "Does he . . . does he have abilities like me?"

His brows knitted as his head tilted. "Are you trying to read me, Lis?"

I stiffened. "Can you tell?"

He laughed roughly. "Only because I've known you long enough to recognize when you're reading someone. Your stare becomes rather intense and you don't blink."

"Oh." I squirmed a little in my chair.

"He does," he answered.

I stopped fidgeting. Everything stopped.

"That's how I knew what you said when we first met could be true. He had the same knack for knowing. He had other . . . knacks." His shoulders rose with a deep breath. "And if you're wondering why I didn't tell you, it was because by the time I met you, Vayne was already committing acts of treason. I thought that if I told you that there was another like you, you would want to meet them, and meeting him would endanger you."

I was still connected to him, and his thoughts reflected what he said, but he knew I was in his mind. Hearing thoughts didn't mean I couldn't be fooled. "Then you know what I . . . I am?" I whispered.

He stared at me, brow furrowing. "Did the Prince tell you something?"

"No."

"Then I don't understand—"

"Am I a *caelestia*?" I interrupted.

He blinked rapidly. A moment passed. "I don't know."

"Claude." I leaned forward, fingers pressing into the knees of my tights. "Have you known this whole time that I wasn't really mortal?"

"*Caelestias* are mortal too, Lis. We just have stronger blood. That is all," he said.

Except *caelestias* weren't treated like lowborn. "Have you known?"

He held my stare, then looked away. "At first, I . . . I suspected that you were."

An ache pierced my chest as I sucked in a breath that went nowhere. "And you never told me? Why wouldn't you—"

"Because I'm not sure *what* you are," he cut in. "And I speak the truth. You don't bear the mark."

I frowned. "What mark?"

"Your eyes. They're brown. A beautiful shade of brown," he added quickly. "But all *caelestias* have eyes like mine. Some are different in other ways." He looked away. "But you don't bear the telltale trait of a *caelestia*."

"My eyes . . ." I thought of how they'd looked different the other day, an inner ring of . . . of blue appearing around the pupils. My throat tightened. The night in Union City? Thorne and Lord Samriel . . . they had been looking at the eyes of the children there. My palms dampened.

"Has the Prince sensed that you were a *caelestia*?" Claude asked.

"No," I said, wiping my palms on my knees. "The Prince has always referred to me as a mortal, but . . ."

"But what?"

"But he says there's something about me that he can't figure out," I said, breathing through the stinging in my throat. "He feels as if he met me before."

"Because he has, hasn't he?"

Losing my connection with him, I went rigid. Even my heart stuttered.

"He's the Hyhborn you met in Union City, isn't he?" Claude drew his fingers over his brow. "The one you thought was a lord?"

"Yes," I whispered. "How did you know it was him?"

"I didn't till the other night, at dinner. It was the way he behaved toward you. The way he . . ." His eyes squinted. "The way he claimed you."

That he came for what is his.

"I don't understand," I whispered.

"Neither do I, and I mean that. I truly do." He dropped his hand to the arm of the chair. "You have abilities similar to my cousin, but if a prince cannot sense that you're a *caelestia* and you don't bear the mark, then there was no way for me to know for sure."

I looked away, swallowing. "You still could've told me."

"Then what? Do you know how a *caelestia* is proven if there are no parents to make the claim? They are taken to the Hyhborn Courts, where a prince or another Deminyen confirms their lineage," he explained. "And if a Deminyen couldn't sense it now, what would've been the likelihood of one being able to do so then? I know I said I wasn't worried about Prince Thorne believing you to be a conjurer, but others? It would be too risky."

I tried to accept what he said. He had a point, but . . . "You don't have abilities."

Claude laughed roughly. "No, I don't. Neither does Hymel. Neither do most *caelestias*."

"Then why would your cousin have them?"

"Or you? If that is what you are?" He said what I hadn't. "Because my cousin is starborn. A mortal made divine."

"And what does that mean exactly?" I demanded.

"That is not something I can answer," he said, dragging a hand over his head.

I stood, flashing from confusion to anger and then disappointment. "You can't or you won't?"

"I *can't*," he insisted, and several moments passed. "Maybe I should've told you anyway. I'd be lying if I said that fear for your safety was the only reason I remained quiet, but you already know that."

"I do."

Claude flinched, and damn it, seeing that hurt. I didn't want it to, but it did. "I know I'm not a good man and that's also something you already know," he said, and it was I who winced then. "So my advice likely means nothing, but you need to ignore your intuition this time. When the Prince returns, you need to tell him that you've met before. You need to tell him."

CHAPTER 31

I got little rest that night, and I wasn't sure if it was the knowledge that I'd been wrong about Claude or if it was because of Thorne's absence. I was also uncertain which one of those things was worse—which one was leading to my general sense of unease.

And that unease followed me through the morning and afternoon, as I walked the busy halls of the manor. Staff rushed to and fro, some cradling vases full of banana-hued daisies and streaming, white-petaled petunias while others carried trays of meats provided by Primvera and yet to be prepared. All were far too busy to pay much attention to me.

The Feasts began tomorrow.

Thorne would likely return the day after or the following one.

I stopped by the breezeway, thoughts heavy as they drifted to Claude. What I felt was a mixture of disappointment and anger, confusion and a little bit of heartache. I tried to understand his position, and I did. Mostly. Because he still should have told me what he suspected. I had a right to know, even if there was nothing to be done with that knowledge.

But wasn't I doing the same thing with Thorne? I didn't understand why my intuition stopped me, but that didn't change the fact that our meeting in Union City was likely why Thorne felt like we'd met. What it didn't explain was how it all tied into what both Maven and Claude had shared. Why it even mattered. My intuition was quiet except for that unease.

I turned, spotting Grady entering the hall. I started toward him. I started to speak.

"Whatever you have to tell me is going to have to wait for a few," he said, placing his hand on my lower back. "There's something you need to see."

Curiosity rose, but so did that anxious energy. It made me jumpy, chest too tight.

"Hymel just came out of the Great Chamber." Grady led me through the narrow hall, to one of the many interior doors. He kept his voice low as we entered the main hall, one now filled with vases overflowing with those flowers I'd seen earlier, placed upon numerous marble pedestals. "He wasn't alone."

I glanced down the wide hall of the foyer that opened on both sides to the outside, my gaze landing on the pillared, stone doors. "Who was he with?"

"You'll see." Grady nodded toward one of the windows that looked over a part of the circular drive leading to the manor.

I saw Hymel standing with his back to us, but it was those he stood below that caught and held my attention. There were three of them astride sable-black horses that towered over the shires. One had long, fair hair that reminded me of the lord we'd seen in Union City, knotted at the nape of his neck, but the blond wasn't the icy white of Lord Samriel's. Another's skin was a warm clay in the sun, and the third was raven-haired, and that was who spoke to Hymel.

It was clear they were Hyhborn, but none that I knew who had arrived with Thorne. Besides, Commander Rhaziel and Lord Bastian had left with Thorne.

"Are they from Primvera? Bringing more food?" I asked.

"That's what I thought until I saw the one who's speaking to Hymel now," Grady said, placing his hand on the window. "That's Prince Rainer."

My eyes widened as I stepped closer to the window, unable to make out much of any of their features.

"What the hell is he doing here?" Grady questioned.

"Maybe it's about the Westlands threat," I said, though I never knew the Prince to have visited Archwood before. "Or about the shadow market."

"Yeah." Grady angled his body toward me. "But what the hell is he doing talking with Hymel about those things and not the actual baron?"

That was a damn good question.

Hymel handled quite a bit of the day-to-day functionality of Archwood, but there was no way that the Baron would not be available to speak to the Hyhborn.

Especially not a prince.

The anxiety was now a dread I couldn't name, but it was pumping through my veins as I hurried through the maze of halls, the hem of the pale gray tunic snapping at my knees. My thoughts bounced between the possibility that Claude and his family had descended from Deminyens—that I had—and what that really meant. If it meant anything. But I set aside what I'd learned from Maven as I reached the gold-adorned doors of the Baron's personal apartments.

Something wasn't right.

When I knocked and there was no answer, I tried the handle, finding the door locked. Cursing, I pulled a pin holding the shorter strands back from my hair and knelt.

A wry grin tugged at my lips as I gripped the handle and worked the thin edge of the pin into the keyhole. One thing I could appreciate from my life before Archwood was the certain . . . skills I'd acquired.

Taking a deep breath, I willed my hand to be steady and gentle as I wiggled the pin left and then right. Picking locks was truly an exercise in patience, a virtue that neither living on the streets nor in a nice home had helped me develop. Must be nice to be a Hyhborn and able to just will the door to unlock.

Or able to simply kick it in.

If I tried that, I'd likely break my foot.

Finally, I heard the soft snick of finding the tumbler. Biting down on my lip, I continued to wiggle the pin until I felt the mechanism give a little. I kept my hand steady as I turned counterclockwise. The handle turned in my palm.

A brief smile of satisfaction tugged at my lips as I shoved the pin back into the braid and rose, pushing open the door.

The private quarters of the Baron were all wealth and luxury. I remembered the first time I'd been in these chambers. I hadn't been able to stop touching everything.

It had been at least two years since I'd entered Claude's chambers. Maybe even longer, and it was strange being in here now. I ran a hand over the plush back of a couch. Fruits and meats were left out, half eaten, on a polished table. Ceiling fans stirred silk curtains finer than any clothing most lowborn would ever own.

"Claude?" I called out.

There was no answer.

I snatched what appeared to be an untouched slice of orange and popped it into my mouth. The sweet and tart taste coursed down my throat as I walked past a chair outfitted with thick velvet cushions. I stopped, letting the memories of sitting in that chair and being held by Claude as he read mail from a neighboring baron engulf me. That had been a habit of ours for a little while. We'd wake and have breakfast in bed, something I'd only heard of people doing before. (The first time we'd done it, I'd been so afraid of getting crumbs on the sheets, but Claude made a far larger mess than I could ever hope to and he laughed while doing so.) Then he'd lead me out to this chair, where we'd spend hours doing nothing much. I remembered feeling . . . safe. Warm. Wanted.

But I never felt like I belonged. Like I was supposed to be there.

Not much had changed since then, but everything felt different.

A knot lodged in my chest as my hand slipped off the chair. Claude had always known that—known how I felt, even if I hadn't realized it. He knew as he laughed and smiled, as he kissed my lips and my skin. He knew.

And he tried to change that.

It just wasn't in his heart, and it hadn't been in mine. But if it had? If Claude had loved me and I'd felt the same? Would I have ended up like Maven, a mistress raising the children that another woman, one deemed suitable by the aristo, claimed as hers? Or would Claude have continued to buck tradition and married me?

I didn't even know why I was thinking about any of that as I walked past a brightly colored tunic left on the floor. In a way, it felt like I was . . . I was mourning what could never be.

Walking through the rounded archway, I glanced around the bedchamber. A breeze carried the floral and woodsy scent of the gardenias filling the tall vases positioned along the walls of the circular chamber.

Gardenias were a favorite of Claude's.

Allyson had been smelling a lot like gardenias.

I focused on the bed seated on a slightly raised platform beneath open windows, a tremor hitting my hands. I sucked my lower lip between my teeth. My steps were light as I stepped onto the platform. Through the rippling fabric, I could make out only lumps.

My heart began to pound as I reached forward, parting the curtains.

The bed was empty.

Letting the curtains fall into place, I stepped off the platform and went to the bathing chamber. That too was empty, and didn't appear to have been used that morning. If so, there would've been towels scattered about and puddles of water. Claude was messier than me.

I turned back to the bed, that dread increasing. A cool finger pressed against the nape of my neck. A tingling pressure settled between my shoulder blades.

Something isn't right.

I took a step and it happened. Without warning, my skin prickled all over. Pressure settled between my shoulder blades as the skin behind my left ear tingled. Claude's chamber fell away and I saw *blood.*

Pools of blood. Rivers of it streaming between still limbs, seeping into gold veining. Bare arms with deep gouges. So many of them, their mouths gaping open in frozen, silent horror. Brocade and jewel-encrusted masks torn, strewn across the floor. Silver and sapphire drenched in blood.

Sucking in a sharp breath, I stumbled back, bumping into the wall. I'd . . . I'd seen death.

CHAPTER 32

The vision warned of death, and the masks? The glittery jewels and gowns? The Feasts. Something terrible—something horrible was going to happen during the Feasts. I jerked forward, then halted.

Silver and sapphire.

I'd seen a sapphire necklace dripping with blood.

Naomi.

I spun, racing from Claude's chambers. Adrenaline coursed through my veins as I hurried along the opposite wing of the manor. The hall was quiet and the air stagnant. A fine sheen of sweat dotted my upper lip as I reached Naomi's quarters. I rapped my knuckles on the door, hoping she was there. I waited, shifting my weight from one foot to the other. She had to be. It was still early.

"Naomi?" I called out, knocking louder. "It's me."

After a few moments, I heard the sound of footsteps. Relief swept through me as the door cracked and a sleepy Naomi appeared.

"Good morning." Smothering a yawn, she stepped aside, the deep blue of her silky slip somehow unwrinkled. Only Naomi could look so stunning upon waking. "Or is it good afternoon?"

"Afternoon. Sorry to wake you." I stepped inside, closing the door behind me. "But I needed to speak with you."

"It's okay. I was already half awake." Naomi tucked her hair back from her face as she stepped over a pair of heeled slippers and thick, vibrant-colored plush cushions as she went over to a chaise and sat. "But you didn't bring coffee with you, which is rude."

"I didn't even think about that." Stomach twisting itself into knots, I glanced at the fuchsia curtains hung in the doorway to her bedchambers. "Are you alone?"

"I hope so." She curled her legs, leaving room for me.

"Good." I sat beside her, needing a moment to collect my thoughts.

I'd come to her without really even thinking it through. I swallowed. "There's . . . there's something I need to talk to you about."

"Without coffee? Or even tea?" Leaning into the arm of the chaise, she yawned again. "I'm not sure how much you're expecting me to retain . . ." She trailed off, eyes narrowing on me. "Wait. Did the Prince come for you that night? I haven't seen you since, so I'm guessing that is a yes."

"Yes. But—"

Naomi straightened, all the sleep vanishing from her gaze in an instant. "And what happened? I want all the details."

"Nothing really happened—okay, things happened," I added when her eyes narrowed. "I threw a glass at him. We sort of argued. Then he actually carried me to his chambers—"

"I'm sorry. Back up. You threw a glass at him?"

"Yes."

She rubbed at her eyes. "Are you a ghost?"

"What?" I shook my head. "No. He wasn't angry if that's what you're getting at. He actually laughed, then carried me to his chambers, where we continued to argue . . . then talked it out."

Naomi stared at me as if I'd admitted to being a god. "And then what?"

"And then we . . ." Squeezing my eyes shut, I pressed my fingers to my temple. I thought about the night before he left. "What you said about the kind of pleasure Hyhborn can give? It's true."

"I know it's true." A slow grin appeared on her lips. "Lis, tell me all about—"

"I had a vision," I interrupted her, and the smile faded from her lips. I sat on the edge of a chair. "I just had this vision of blood—lots of blood and bodies."

Naomi had gone still. Her eyes were full of shadows as she stared at me. "Is it the *ni'meres* again? Do you . . . do you know whose bodies you saw?" There was a slight tremble in her lips as she sat up, placing her feet on the floor. "Do you?"

A slice of panic and fear lanced my chest. "I couldn't see who they were or if *ni'meres* are involved. I don't know all who will be . . . will be caught up in what I'm seeing, but I . . . I think it's going to happen during the Feasts. I saw masks, and . . ." My gaze followed her fingers, to the collar of her robe, where the silver chain she normally wore would be. Anyone could've been wearing that sapphire necklace, but . . . "You should leave Archwood. I don't want you here."

"Lis—"

"You know I care about you, right?" I twisted toward her. "And you care about me."

"Yes. Of course I do."

"And if you thought something bad might happen and I could be caught up in it, you wouldn't just warn me. You'd do something about it," I said. "The difference is that I *know* something bad is coming, and it's going to hit a lot of people. Maybe you'll be fine. I don't know, but I don't want you here. At least for the Feasts."

"You want me to leave, but what about you?" Her voice dropped. "Grady? Claude?"

"I'm going to ask Grady to do the same, and Claude." If I could find him.

"And what about you?"

"I . . . I can't."

"Why?" she demanded.

Because Thorne claimed that it was I who would save Archwood, and even if I couldn't believe that, Hyhborn didn't lie. And I wasn't even sure if that was the reason I couldn't leave. I *needed* to be here when Thorne returned. I knew that.

Naomi's lips pressed together as she looked away, head shaking. "If you don't leave, neither will Grady."

Another cut of fear sliced through me. I also knew that. My fingers dug into my knees. "If you don't want to leave Archwood, at least go spend some time with your sister." I took a deep breath. "And you *really* should do that before it's too late."

Her gaze swung back to mine, her skin paling. "You told me she would recover from the fever. She *is* recovering."

"I know, but . . ."

Naomi's chest rose with a heavy breath. "But what, Lis?"

I briefly closed my eyes, hating myself a little for using her sister like this. "But you only asked if she would recover from the fever, and she will; however, you should spend time with her."

"Because?" Her chin lifted as her lips trembled.

The back of my throat stung. "You know why."

Her eyes turned glassy. "I want to hear you say it."

"She won't live to see the end of the Feasts," I whispered. "I'm sorry."

Her eyes squeezed shut and several moments passed. "So, you're telling me this now to get me to leave the manor?" Her lashes lifted, eyes glimmering. "You should've told me this before."

"I know," I agreed. "I really am sorry."

Naomi huffed as she looked away. She pressed her lips together, shaking her head. "I know."

My heart cracked a little. "Will you do as I ask?"

"Yes." When she faced me, her eyes were damp. "And you need to leave my quarters." She rose, turning from me.

I stood. "Naomi—"

"Don't." She whirled toward me, the robe fluttering around her feet. "You knew what I asked when I came to you about Laurelin. I wasn't just speaking of the fever, and you lied. I could've been with her more—" She sucked in a sharp breath, fisting the skirt of her robe. "Please. Leave. I need to pack."

I stepped toward her, but she turned again and walked through the curtains. I stopped myself, breathing through the sting. Blinking back tears, I left her chambers, hoping that she would heed me. That she would leave the manor and that whatever damage I'd done to our friendship wouldn't be in vain.

       ~≫≫~

"Not going to happen." Grady leaned against the ledge of the breezeway I sat on. I'd drawn him away from the wall, and was in the process of attempting, and failing, to convince him to leave Archwood. "I can't believe you would ask that of me. Better yet, I can't believe you would even waste your time asking me this when you already know what the answer is going to be."

"I had to try."

"More like you had to piss me off," he retorted. "If you want to leave, then we can hit the road right now, but you won't since you've got it in your head you need to be here when the Prince returns."

I really should've kept my reason for staying to myself. It hadn't helped matters. "I'm not trying to upset you." A warm breeze caught a shorter strand of hair that had slipped the pins, tossing it across my face. "I've already upset Naomi today."

He crossed his arms. "Is she leaving?"

I nodded. "Hopefully, but she's angry. She has every right to be. I didn't tell her everything about her sister." I leaned my head back against the pillar of the breezeway. "And I can't find Claude anywhere. Have you seen him?"

"No."

Throughout the day, I'd tried to get my intuition to tell me where Claude might be, to tell me anything, but there was nothing but those three words repeating.

Something isn't right.

Worry gnawed at me as I stared at the manor walls, my thoughts going to Prince Rainer's visit. "Don't you think it's strange that the Prince of Primvera showed only after the others left?"

"I think everything is fucking strange right now." He squinted, watching one of the stable hands brush down a mare. "Especially this stuff with you possibly being a *caelestia*."

That was another thing I should've kept to myself, because Grady had looked at me like I'd grown a third eye. He was having a hard time wrapping his head around it, and I couldn't fault him for that, but I thought of what I'd seen in that mirror. I wasn't so sure that the brief change in color had been my imagination.

If it hadn't, what was it?

But that wasn't really important at the moment. The vision was.

I swung my legs off the ledge and stood. "I'm going to try to look for Claude in his study once more," I told him, brushing off the bottom of my tunic. "And if I find him, I'm going to try to convince him to cancel the Feasts."

"Good luck with that," Grady replied.

"I'll let you know if I find him," I told him, hesitating. "I wish you—"

"Don't say it, Lis." He backed up. "I'm not going anywhere without you."

I sighed, nodding. We parted ways, him heading back to the wall and me going inside. I made my way to Claude's study, hope sparking when I saw that the door was ajar. I hurried forward, pushing it open. I came to a complete stop.

Claude wasn't in his study.

His cousin was.

Hymel's head jerked up from where he sat behind the Baron's desk, slips of paper in his hand.

Something isn't right.

"What are you doing in here?" I blurted out.

The splash of surprise quickly faded from his features. "Not that it's any of your business, but I'm going through the stack of letters." He lifted the parchments he held. "Which happen to be notices from debtors, namely the Royal Bank."

My stomach sank as I glanced at the ever-growing stack. "What do they want?"

He looked at me as if I had asked the silliest question, and I had.

"How late is he?" I asked. "And does he have the coin to settle his debts?"

"Not too late," Hymel answered, tossing the parchments onto the desk. "And there's enough coin. Or will be." He looked up at me. "What are you doing here?"

"I was looking for Claude," I said, deciding that the prevalent financial issues were something I was going to have to stress over later. "I can't find him."

Hymel's dark brows rose. "He's not here."

My lips pursed. "I can see that. Do you know where he is?"

"Last I knew, he was in his quarters, but I'm not his keeper."

"Clearly," I muttered. "He's not there. I've checked twice."

"Then he's probably with the Bowers." Hymel leaned back in the chair, looking mighty comfortable where he didn't belong. "And he's likely on a bender with it being the start of the Feasts tonight—well, at midnight."

"And because of that, shouldn't he be here and not off someplace else?"

"One would think that," Hymel stated dryly. "But this is Claude we're talking about. Last Feasts, he spent half of them hallucinating winged creatures in some abandoned mine with the Bower brothers."

That sounded so bizarre it had to be true. "So, there's a chance he won't show for the start?"

Hymel shrugged. "Possibly. He hasn't before."

And I wouldn't know that since I never saw him during the Feasts.

"Considering the mood he was in when I last saw him, I'm thinking he'll probably be seeing winged beasts once more."

My chest tightened. "What do you mean about his mood?"

"He's been morose since the meeting with the Prince of Vytrus." Hymel picked up a paperweight carved from obsidian. "After he apparently agreed to give you to the Prince."

My mouth dropped open. "He did not give me to the Prince," I said, and I doubted that was what caused Claude to be depressed. He'd been relieved by it. "And I saw him after that. He didn't appear bothered." At least not until we'd started to talk.

"That's not how I heard it," Hymel countered. "The Prince wanted you, a lowborn, and Claude agreed. I think his fragile feelings were hurt."

I frowned, concentrating on him. The string connected us, but I saw the grayish shield obscuring his intentions—his future.

Hymel tossed the obsidian ball and caught it. "Is there something you needed from Claude?"

Pulling my senses back, I crossed my arms and made no attempt to approach Hymel. He'd know what I was up to the moment I attempted to touch him. "I had a vision."

One side of his lips kicked up. "Do tell."

"Of blood and death. I think—no, I know something bad is going to happen at the Feasts," I told him. "I think Claude should cancel them—"

"Cancel the Feasts?" Hymel laughed. "The Westlands armies could descend on us tomorrow, and the Feasts will not be canceled."

My brows knitted. "Hymel, I know you like to act like my visions aren't real, but you know better. The celebrations could at least be canceled here."

"Not going to happen." He tossed the obsidian ball once more.

Frustration burned as I stared at him, and suddenly that shiver at the nape of my neck and between my shoulder blades came. I saw nothing, but I heard three words whispered. I stiffened. "The Prince of Primvera," I said, and Hymel's gaze flashed to mine. He caught the ball. "What was he doing here today?"

"Sharing good news." Hymel placed the obsidian on the stack of parchment. "Prince Rainer will be joining us for the Feasts."

CHAPTER 33

I stood at the edge of the Great Chamber the following night, staring at the dais. The elaborate ruby-encrusted chair sat vacant.

Claude was still missing.

Thorne had yet to return.

Fingers pressing into the skirt of my plain white gown, I felt the hilt of the *lunea* dagger sheathed to my thigh. I didn't know why I'd grabbed it when I left my chambers. It had been an unconscious act, but it made me feel a little better.

I scanned the crush of vividly dressed and masked aristo. Luckily I hadn't seen Naomi here or in the solarium, where Grady was stationed. Nor did I see Hymel.

Something isn't right.

My gaze settled on a fair-haired man, drawn to him simply because he was one of the fully unmasked in attendance, but even if he had been masked, I would've known immediately what he was. He was taller than most in the chamber, the silk of his shirt and the cut of his dark breeches more finely tailored than the clothes of the wealthiest of aristo in attendance. His features were perfectly symmetrical, giving him an unreal beauty. He was a lord.

And it was one of the two I'd seen with Prince Rainer yesterday. The one who reminded me of Lord Samriel. This Hyhborn in the crowd looked so much like him. There were other Hyhborn, more in the solarium than in here, but I hadn't seen Prince Rainer.

The Lord angled his head, his stare colliding with mine. I sucked in a startled breath.

He smiled.

Swallowing, I took a step back as he was surrounded by fawning aristo. Unmasked as I was, I stood out. My heart fluttered like a trapped bird as I hastily turned and left the Great Chamber, entering the wide hall and slipping out one of the doors leading to the outside.

I was jumpy, partly due to the lack of sleep and the creeping dread that had haunted me throughout the day. I tried several times throughout the day to get my intuition to work—to tell me anything about where Claude could be. I'd even drawn myself a bath and held myself underwater so that no sound or distraction could find me, but there was silence. Nothing.

And that could mean one of only two things—Hyhborn were somehow involved in whatever Claude was doing or his seeming disappearance involved me somehow.

Claude could very well be off with the Bowers, but . . .

Something isn't right.

Aristo had spilled out into the lawn, where laughter joined the music. I strode past the masked revelers, stomach knotting. I was tired, each step dogged, but the anxious energy invading my veins made it impossible for me to attempt any rest.

Using the narrow stone bridge, I crossed the small stream and stopped to look back at the manor. Torchlight lit those dancing and lounging on the lawn.

They were completely unaware of the looming violence of even the Westlands armies but gods, I wished I were one of them, blissfully ignorant and losing myself in the potent drink and rich food, in the sensual presence of the Hyhborn.

I fought the urge to race back and warn them, but how could I explain? Most wouldn't believe me. Others might think I was a conjurer, and with Hyhborn lords in attendance, the act would be foolish.

So I walked on, the *sōls* drifting in the air above me as I followed the path I'd walked a thousand times. They'd be gone at the end of the Feasts, not returning until the days leading up to the next.

I kept my gaze on them, because the low hum of conversation wasn't the only sound echoing out from the many different pathways and hidden-away nooks of the grand gardens. There were softer, sultrier gasps and thicker, deeper moans, a kind of song one didn't normally hear while traveling the hedged walkways.

The Feasts were in full, decadent swing.

Dragging my teeth over my lower lip, I watched the *sōls* dip and rise as if they were joined in a dance until a soft peal of laughter drew my attention from them. A trio drifted out from one of the shadowy lanes. Two women and one man, and there was no telling if they were aristo or not, but there was a whole lot of skin on display. Bare arms and legs that played peekaboo with the pastel panels of skirts. The man's shirt was left undone and open. Crimson ribbons fell from the women's masks, and the man's was a plain, shiny black.

I stepped aside, allowing the two women walking arm in arm with a man to pass by. One woman nodded in my direction. The other smiled.

"Good evening," the man said, his head tilting as he eyed me. All I saw was the curve of his mouth tip up in approval as he eyed the lacy straps crisscrossing over my breasts and the gauzy material clinging to my hips.

"Would you care to join us?" he asked.

I bit on my lip, fighting a grin. "Thank you for the invitation, but it looks like you already have your hands full."

One of the women giggled. "He does, but our hands?" She shared a glance with the dark-haired one. "Are not quite as full."

Interest sparked as the man chuckled, leaning in to kiss the shorter woman on her cheek, the one who spoke. I opened my senses just a little. They . . . they were a couple. The three of them.

What a lucky man.

"I'm on the way to meet someone," I lied. "But I wish you good Feasts."

"What a shame," the man murmured, bowing elaborately. "Happy Feasts."

I murmured the same, hanging back as the trio moved farther down the path. Then I kept walking, this time following two *sōls* circling one another as my mind alternated between the vision, what Maven had shared, and Claude's disappearance. My thoughts strayed, though, to *him*. It was kind of hard for them not to when I was in the gardens, and the breeze stirred up the scent of catmint.

Would Thorne return tomorrow? Then what? I would be his? But wasn't I already—

"Stop," I whispered, refusing to let that thought even finish. My stomach tumbled nonetheless as I shook my head.

The only thing that I needed to think about that concerned Thorne was telling him about having met before.

As I neared the wisteria trees, I stopped and looked up. Stars blanketed the sky. It was such a . . . a strange coincidence that all of this was happening at the same time.

Thorne's sudden appearance, fulfilling a twelve-year-old premonition. My near-visceral reaction to him. His interest in me that he couldn't explain and that I felt went beyond him not realizing we'd met before. My intuition stopping me from telling him. The Princess of Visalia and the Westlands' Iron Knights making a move on Archwood. Learning that lowborn could descend from Hyhborn. Claude's absence. The vision. Hymel. That smiling lord who resembled Lord Samriel. All of it happening at the same time, and I . . .

I didn't believe in coincidences.

Or fate.

I lowered my gaze to the still lilac blossoms. A faint tingle danced at the nape of my neck and then between my shoulder blades. Like a slumbering giant, my intuition sparked.

Everything is related.

All of it.

A warning.

A reckoning.

A promise of what was to come—

Pools of blood. Rivers of it streaming between still limbs, seeping into gold veining. Bare arms with deep gouges. So many of them, their mouths gaping open in frozen, silent horror. Brocade and jewel-encrusted masks torn, strewn across the floor. Silver and sapphire drenched in blood. And this time there were screams. *Screams of pain. Screams of death—*

I jerked out of the vision just as the wisteria limbs began to shudder, swaying in the absence of any sort of breeze.

Breath catching, I took a step back. A shiver coursed down my spine as tiny bumps prickled my skin. Hair along the nape of my neck rose as an icy, unnatural energy built in the air. I looked up to see what looked like dark clouds gathering in the sky, blotting out the stars.

My muscles seized for a moment and then instinct kicked in, fueled by the heightened sense of intuition. I spun and took off, running faster than I ever had through the maze of pathways as the streams of moonlight faded and disappeared.

Something is coming.

I could feel it building in the air—in the sudden silence and growing darkness—and I didn't think what was filling the sky was clouds. Every part of my being was focused on finding Grady, and I didn't dare waste time by going for the bridge. Knowing the levels were low this time of year, I half slipped, half ran down the muddy bank. Water splashed as I stomped through the shallow stream, losing a shoe in the process. I kept going, reaching the other side, the hem of my gown soaked and clinging to my legs. I climbed the short hill, swallowing a cry as sharp rock cut through the thin sole of my remaining shoe, slicing into my skin.

I didn't let that slow me down. I flew across the lawn, startling many of those who were on the ground, their bodies pressed tightly together.

"Get inside," I screamed, dodging others who were rising to look at the sky. "Get inside now!"

I had no idea if anyone was listening as I stumbled, nearly falling. Had Naomi listened to me? I hadn't seen her all day, and gods, I hoped so, but my heart lurched, because I still saw that bloodied sapphire necklace.

Panting, I raced up the wide steps of the Baron's manor, and I was mere inches from the doors when the clouds fell from the sky in a chorus of wings beating at the air.

Then the screams of pain—the screams of death—began.

CHAPTER 34

It was happening. The vision. I knew it.

Grabbing the handle of the door, I looked over my shoulder and my legs almost gave out on me.

What had snuffed out the light of the moon and stars was something straight from a nightmare—creatures with a wingspan of over seven feet and talons longer and sharper than the claws of a bear. They looked as if a lowborn had been fused with a giant eagle.

Ni'meres.

They dived from the sky, faster than a charging horse. Those still on the lawn had no chance of escaping them. The *ni'meres'* talons ripped into flesh and bone, tearing open backs and shoulders and piercing even the skulls of those fleeing.

Horror seized me as a *ni'mere* lifted a man high into the air. He screamed, beating at the talons tearing into his bare shoulders. The *ni'mere* let out a terrifying sound, somewhere between a shriek and laugh, before releasing the man. He fell, plummeting back to the ground—

Another *ni'mere* caught him, its talons sinking deep into the man's stomach, splitting him open.

Gagging, I spun away and flew into the receiving hall. I didn't understand why the *ni'meres* were doing this—had a Hyhborn been attacked? There was no time to figure it out.

My other shoe, slippery with blood, fell off as I dodged pedestals holding tall vases of summer flowers. I raced down the wide hall, heading for the solarium, where I'd last seen Grady. When I was halfway through the hallway, doors all along both sides burst open. Lowborn flooded the chamber in a panicked tide, toppling pedestals and spilling petunias and daisies across the marble floors. In a heartbeat, I was swallowed in the crush.

Someone slammed into me, spinning me around. My feet slipped.

I fell into another, knocking them aside as wings beat upon the walls of the manor.

"Sorry," I gasped, reaching for the woman. "I'm so—" I choked as she turned her head to me. Deep gouges scoured her cheeks.

She had no eyes.

"Help me," she rasped as I jerked away from her reach. "Please. Help me."

"I . . . I don't know how." I backed up, bumping into another. I twisted to a man—a man who was undressed but covered in so much blood he appeared to be wearing a sheath of glistening red. I pressed my hands to my chest. "I'm sorry."

Chest squeezing, I turned away and pushed forward, desperately trying not to look too closely at those around me, trying not to hear the screams as I yelled for Grady, but it was impossible. I saw flesh shredded and hanging in tatters as if they were strips of nothing more than silky garments. Cheeks split open. Limbs hanging and attached by strands of sinew. There was so much gore that my stomach cramped.

"Grady!" I yelled, straining to see above those crowding the hall. "Grady!"

The doors leading to the Great Chamber and the rest of the manor appeared miles away as bodies pressed in; bodies slick with sweat and blood crowded mine, and it was too much. Something was happening in my mind as I stumbled forward. Dozens of strings formed in my mind, stretching out and connecting all around me and all at once. Their thoughts pressed against the inside of my mind as strongly as their bloodied bodies did.

Why is this happening? a voice screamed in my head, jerking me around before quickly being taken over by another shrieking *Where is Julius—did he make it inside?*

My wide eyes darted from a pale face to a crimson-streaked one in confusion. *I should've helped her. I just left her there—I left her out there.*

Get up. Gods damn you, get up. If we stay here, we're going to die.

"Leave me," the wounded man pleaded out loud. "Just leave me."

"Like hell I am," another man grunted.

Their thoughts—oh gods, I couldn't block them. I couldn't sever the connection as I pushed through the frenzied bodies, my heart thumping as the moans of the dying became final words in my mind.

It's too soon.

This isn't happening.

Why me?

I can't feel my legs. Why can't I feel—

They merged together, making it impossible for me to tell exactly how many I was hearing, if it was one or many.

I'm dying.

Oh blessed gods, save me.

I'm dead. I'm dead. I'm dead.

Gasping for air, I tripped over something—someone. I caught myself on a still-standing pedestal, my stare fixed on the man's face. His mask hung from one ear, his lips parted as if they had frozen mid-inhale. His throat . . . it was torn wide open. Through the mess of snapped bone and jellied flesh, I could see the floor—see the blood streaming through the gold veining of the marble.

My body locked up as I clutched the cool marble. Their thoughts. The sights and sounds. My own rising terror. My legs shook, knees weakening. I couldn't move as my throat seized. I couldn't shut them out. I slid to the floor, pressing back against the base of the pedestal. It was too much. They were inside me—their fear, their panic, their last thoughts—and I couldn't pull myself out of it. Couldn't stop them from being a part of me. I tucked my knees to my chest, squeezing my eyes closed as I pressed my balled fists to my ears.

Help me!

I'm dying!

It hurts—oh gods, it hurts.

He's gone. He's dead.

I'm bleeding—

Lis. Lis. Lis.

I don't want it to end like this.

I can't.

It's not fair—

"Lis!" Hands clamped my arms, shaking me. *"Calista,"* the voice demanded. "Look at me."

Dragging in air, I was terrified to do so—terrified by what I'd see—but it was brown eyes staring back at mine, eyes a shade darker than mine. *Grady.* He'd found me—like always, he'd found me.

"I can hear them," I rasped, shaking. "Their thoughts. Their screams. I can't stop it—"

"Just focus on me. Just me, and take a breath—a deep, long breath. Okay? Focus on me and breathe," he ordered, the warm brown skin around his mouth taut as another's voice started to intrude on my thoughts. "You focused?"

"I—" I began to look away from him. Blood pooled along the floor. Rivers of crimson, slick and shiny. Blood splattered along the base and up the sweeping golden pillars. Still arms and legs. Skin torn apart by deep gouges. . . .

"I saw this," I whispered. "This is what I saw, Grady. This is—"

"I know. That doesn't matter right now." He clasped my cheeks then, forcing my gaze back to him. "Tell me how I'm supposed to make catmint continue to bloom?"

His question caught me off guard. "W-What?"

"Tell me how I can get your favorite flower to keep blooming?"

"I like catmint, but it's . . . it's n-not my favorite. Tickseed is." My mind suddenly filled with images of tiny, daisy-like yellow blossoms. "The moonbeam kind."

"Okay. Whatever. How do you get moonbeam to keep blooming?"

My brows knitted. "You have to deadhead them—cut off the little black buds, the spent blossoms."

"Good to know." His hands smoothed the hair back from my cheeks. "You picturing those flowers?"

I nodded as my mind finally began to calm. Grady . . . he'd done this before, when we were younger and I hadn't learned how to sever the connection with others. Pushing off the floor, I threw my arms around him. "I don't know what I would . . . I would do without you."

"It's okay. I got you. It's okay." His arms tightened around me. "You hurt?"

I shook my head. "N-No. It was just their thoughts. I couldn't—"

"I know. I know." He rose, bringing me with him. "We've got to get out of here. Get farther into the house and hide before they get in."

"The *ni'meres?*"

"Not just them." He pulled back, quickly scanning my face and body for any injury I might have lied about. "I saw the Rae coming over the hill."

"W-What? Why?"

"I don't know." He grabbed my arm, squeezing as he looked around. "But something bad is going down, Lis. Primvera is burning."

My chest went cold. "What?"

He began to lead us through the crowd. "I saw the Rae from the solarium. Saw it before the *ni'meres* came. That's when I started to look for you. Careful," he warned, guiding us around a motionless pair of legs.

I didn't look to see what had caused those legs to become so still.

"Knew right off something bad was going down." Grady shoved his other hand through his mop of curly hair.

"Do you think it's the Westlands?"

"Who else could it be?" he said. "They must've made it farther into the Midlands than anyone knew. That's the only answer." He grunted as someone knocked into us. "We've got to hide," he repeated. "And then the first chance we get, we've got to get out—"

Glass shattered behind us. Grady looked over his shoulder as I did the same.

Ni'meres came through the broken window, their feathered bodies slick with blood and gore. Their wings beat at the air as they swooped down, aiming for those still standing with talons that dripped red.

Chaos erupted. Those who could scattered in every direction, as we ran toward the main hall. We weren't the only ones who reached the narrow hall that led to the Great Chamber and the remaining halls and spaces within the manor.

"Not the Great Chamber," I gasped. "We can't go there."

"Shit." Grady's gaze briefly met mine. "Hold on. Don't let go, Lis. Whatever you do, don't let go."

I clutched the back of his tunic as people crowded in all around us, quickly choking the hall.

But they didn't know the house like we did.

Narrow tables fell, clogging the path even more as we were pressed farther down the hall. I tugged on Grady's arm. "The blue door!" I yelled. "The back halls."

Grady nodded, keeping his footing and mine as we were nearly shoved right past the door. We dug in, him grunting and me gasping as several people slammed into us. The door was stuck, forcing Grady to throw his weight behind it.

The door groaned, swinging open, and we all but fell through. I spun around, spotting Allyson's pale curls in the madness. "Allyson," I screamed. Her head whipped toward us. She started fighting toward the door.

"Come on," Grady yelled, pulling us aside as a young fair-haired man and then Allyson dashed into the chamber.

I went to her. "Are you okay?" Her light blue gown was splattered with blood. "Are you hurt?"

"No," she rasped, her curls falling haphazardly into her face. "Are you?"

"I'm okay." My heart thundered. "I'm so glad I saw you. Have you . . ." I froze. A silver chain circled her neck, and from it, a sapphire jewel hung. "Is that Naomi's necklace?"

Confusion marked her brow as she stared at me like she couldn't believe I was asking such a question. "Yeah, I wanted to wear it with my gown. She gave it to me a few days ago."

Oh gods.

I'd been wrong. It hadn't been Naomi I'd seen. . . .

Allyson glanced up at the ceiling. "I . . . I got separated from the others," she said, and I looked away, heart cracking at the realization. "The *ni'meres*—they came in through the windows there. I don't know if . . ."

"This way!" Grady shouted, and I whipped around. "Come on. Damn it," he cursed as people scrambled past the door. "This way, you fuckers!"

No one listened.

I shook my head, heart sinking as a *ni'mere*'s shriek entered the hall.

"They're coming," Allyson whispered, backing away from me. She bumped into a settee. "We can't stay here with the door open."

She was right.

"Damn it," Grady snarled, slamming the door shut. "Damn it!"

"Th-This way," I said, glancing at the other man. He was pale. "There's another hall. It leads to the servant quarters and—"

"The wine cellar," Grady finished. "That door is heavy. No one, not even *ni'meres*, can get through it."

"Perfect. If I'm going to die tonight, I'd rather be drunk off my ass," the man said, dragging a hand down the front of his torn shirt. "Name's Milton, by the way."

"Grady." He nodded in my direction. "This is Lis and that's—"

"Allyson," she said, nervously rubbing her hands over her bare arms.

A scream pierced the air, causing both Allyson and me to jump.

Milton swallowed. "Let's get to this cellar so we can get drunk enough that we don't think about what's happening on the other side of that wall."

"Sounds like a plan. You good?" Grady asked of Allyson, who nodded. Then he turned to me. "You?"

Foot stinging, I limped slightly as I started for the door at the other end of the chamber. I couldn't look too long or too closely at Milton and . . . especially not Allyson. Not because I worried that what had happened in the receiving hall would overwhelm me again. I feared I'd discover how the night would end for them, and I already . . . I already knew how it would end for Allyson.

As I proceeded forward, an all-too-familiar sense of fragile calmness descended upon me, one that had sprung from dark, scary nights that had come before we'd fled Union City and after, when we'd slept on streets and in ditches, when we were chased off by lawmen or were running from adults whose thoughts were full of terrible things. We'd been in a lot of bad spots, many I didn't think we'd make it out of.

It wasn't that I wasn't scared. I was terrified. My heart hadn't stopped pounding. I felt sick with fear, but this was . . . it was just another bad spot to get past. To survive, and I would. We would.

I opened the door that fed into another hall, which was the length of the manor and wrapped around the whole back. It was empty. Grady motioned the other two forward. We hurried down the dimly lit hall, the muted sounds of screams coming from the other side of the wall following us, haunting us.

Remembering the dagger, I halted and hitched up the skirt of my gown. I unsheathed the dagger. I looked up.

Beside me, Milton raised his brows as he spotted the *lunea* blade. "I'm not going to even ask."

"Probably best that you don't." I let the skirt fall back into place.

"Why are they doing this?" Allyson asked, nibbling on her fingernails.

"Don't know," Grady said, then repeated what he'd told me about the Hyhborn Court. "But a bunch of the *ni'meres* flew over the manor, heading straight for Primvera."

"You can't be serious," Allyson gasped. "They're attacking their own?"

"He is. Saw it myself," Milton confirmed, and I had a feeling we'd see it soon enough when we reached the back hall. "Looked like the whole city was burning, but I think it was just the wall outside Primvera."

"But why attack us?" Allyson stuck close to Grady. "We weren't doing anything."

No one answered, not even my intuition, but I didn't think this was the Westlands or the Iron Knights. This was something else entirely.

"You lied to me," Grady muttered under his breath.

"What?" I glanced at him.

"You said you weren't hurt." He raised his brows. "Your foot is bleeding."

"You're bleeding?" Concern filled Allyson's voice.

"It's not a big deal. Just a minor cut on my foot."

"Minor cuts get infected all the time, Lis. Then you end up with your foot getting cut off."

My brows shot up.

"That escalated quickly," Milton commented under his breath from behind us.

Grady ignored him. "As soon as we get a chance, we're washing it out."

I sighed heavily. "I was planning to, but currently, I'm more worried about the *ni'meres*."

"Agreed," Milton commented.

We neared the corner where the hall turned to continue along the back of the manor. I peered around. The hall was dark. "The windows are intact."

Grady strode forward, his hand around the hilt of his sword. His steps slowed. "Sweet mercy."

I crept forward as Allyson cried out, smacking her hand over her mouth. She stumbled back, pressing against the wall. I told myself not to, but I joined Grady at the chest-high window and regretted it at once.

The moon was no longer blocked. Silvery light flooded the manor grounds. Bodies were strewn about the lawn, being . . . being picked at by a few lone *ni'meres*.

My stomach churned with nausea, but I couldn't look away from the horrifying and grotesque display. I'd only ever seen a *ni'mere* once before and at a distance. I'd been a child then, but they were no less terrifying now than they were then, with their feathered bodies that were vaguely mortal-like, and their faces a palish-gray shade. Their yellow eyes were nearly iridescent, a shade of gold that matched the streaks cutting through their onyx-hued wings and their long, straggly hair. Their teeth . . .

They were pointed, as razor-sharp as any beak or talon would be, and yet their features were delicate. Pretty even, if not for the ghastly shade of skin and the blood smearing their lips and chins.

I dragged my stare from them. Beyond the *ni'meres* was a wholly different sight. Archwood Manor sat atop a hill, and on sunny days, the sun glinted off the tops of the walls surrounding Primvera. Tonight, the entire horizon was lit in a golden glow. Primvera *was* burning.

"Shit," Grady cursed, jerking back. "The Rae. Get down."

I crouched beside Grady, stomach knotting. "If there's Rae . . ."

"Then there are princes near," he finished, his eyes briefly meeting mine.

"'Prince Rainer will be joining us for the Feasts,'" I whispered. "That's what Hymel said."

Grady's jaw clenched. "Your prince decided to leave at one hell of a time, didn't he?"

"He's not my prince," I retorted.

"We should try to keep going," Milton said from where he was crouched farther down the hall. "How far do we have to go?"

Grady rose halfway, keeping himself below the window. "At the end of the hall. Just keep low to the floor."

"End of the hall" felt like it was in a wholly different realm. "It's the second-to-the-last door . . ." I trailed off as a tingle of awareness erupted between my shoulder blades and traveled up the nape of my neck. Tiny goose bumps spread across my bare arms, and there was a strange warmth in my . . . in my chest even though the temperature had dropped, just as it had in the gardens. The hair along the nape of my neck rose. I lifted my gaze to the window above me as I rubbed my chest.

"Lis?" Grady called out quietly. "What is it?"

"I . . ." Intuition was guiding me as I reached up, gripping the bottom of the windowsill.

"Shouldn't we be hurrying?" Milton hissed.

We should be.

But there was something I needed to see. I rose just high enough to peer over the ledge of the window.

Rae rode past on horses shrouded in black cloth; the wispy mist seeping from openings in their cloaks trailed down the sides of their horses, spilling upon the ground like fog. There had to be well over two dozen of them. Warning bells started to ring throughout me when the Hyhborn rode forward on large reddish-brown steeds draped in indigo banners that bore a crimson insignia of what resembled several interlocking knots. I'd seen the sigil before. It was the Royal Crest and represented all the territories joined to form one.

If this was the Westlands or the Iron Knights, would they ride into battle bearing the sigil of the king they sought to overthrow? I didn't think so. But if it was the King, why would he have Primvera destroyed? Unless he believed Primvera would be a loss too?

A flash of silvery white in the moonlight drew my gaze. Hair. Long blond hair so pale it was nearly white. Paler than the hair of the lord I'd seen in the Great Chamber.

I recognized him.

Even though I'd been too scared as a child to look him the face, I knew it was him.

"Grady," I whispered. "*Look.*"

He turned from me, rising slightly.

"You see him?"

"Yeah," he spat between gritted teeth. "Lord Samriel."

CHAPTER 35

What in the world was *he* doing here? I didn't know, but I didn't believe in coincidences. Or fate. My fingers pressed into the windowsill.

"We really need to get out of here," Grady urged.

I started to move when the Hyhborn who rode beside Samriel turned their cloaked head to the window. Their horse drew to a sudden halt.

"Shit," I gasped, ducking. My wide gaze met Grady's as my grip tightened on the dagger. "He couldn't have seen us. There's no way—"

A *ni'mere* shrieked, sending a bolt of raw fear straight through me.

"Go!" Grady yelled to the others as we half scrambled, half ran along the wall.

Quickly catching up with Milton and Allyson, we raced for the door to the underground chambers, but while my intuition had been quiet seconds earlier, it no longer was. Wings beat against the window. *I knew* . . .

"We're not going to make it," I gasped.

"We will," Grady argued. "We—"

"No." I grabbed ahold of the back of his tunic. "We won't."

Understanding flashed across his features. He cursed, yelling for the others while I racked my brain for where we could go. I looked around—

"The library!" I shouted.

Allyson nodded, and darted across the hall, heading for the door I knew led to another part of the manor. There'd be chambers there; they weren't as safe as those underground, but they were places to hide, and that was the best we could do.

She pushed open the door, holding it open as the feeling of pressure continued to settle between my shoulders. There was no way

Lord Samriel had seen us, but something had alerted him to our presence.

Glass exploded as we hit the other hall. Allyson's sharp scream spun me around. A *ni'mere* came at us, its wings skimming the walls on both sides. I froze, just for a heartbeat as I stared at the creature's fragile, doll-like features smeared with blood—the smooth flesh that gave way to small, layered feathers and breasts. Actual breasts. The *ni'mere* was a female.

And I was never going to unsee this.

"Get down!" Grady shouted.

Allyson grabbed my arm, tugging me to my knees. The *ni'mere* twisted in the air, about to turn as Milton grabbed the creature by the legs. With a yell, he threw it against the wall.

Plaster cracked from the impact. Milton jumped back, breathing heavy as the *ni'mere* fell forward. It rose onto its hind legs inches from me, shrieking.

I moved without thought, lurching to my feet. I didn't think about what I was doing. I didn't hesitate. It was almost like I was someone else as the *ni'mere* swung at me with sharp, bloodied talons. I dipped under its arm and spun. Snapping upright, I thrust the dagger deep into the *ni'mere*'s chest. The creature's stunned gaze met mine as I jerked the blade free. The *ni'mere* stumbled back, its legs folding. The creature went down, dead before it hit the floor. I looked up.

Grady stared at me, eyes wide. "What the fuck?"

I glanced at my blade. "Holy shit."

A shriek cut through the air as another *ni'mere* entered the hall.

"Shit," Grady cursed.

I scrambled past Allyson, catching the door and slamming it shut. I threw the lock, knowing it would only slow the others down, as Grady shot forward. He didn't thrust the sword into the *ni'mere*. The steel would do very little. He twisted at the waist, sweeping up with the sword. The blade sliced through the *ni'mere*'s neck. Blood sprayed as Grady severed its head. He stepped back, blood splattered across the side of his face. I really hoped the *ni'meres* were one of the Hyhborn that couldn't regenerate.

"You okay?" I whispered, coming to Grady's side.

"Yeah." He glanced down at himself, swallowing. "Yeah." He turned to me, eyeing the dagger. "You?"

I nodded.

"How the hell did you do that?" He took ahold of my arm.

"I don't know." I swallowed, heart thumping.

Allyson jumped as something hit the door. "There's more." She began backing up. "Library. Now."

Stomach twisting, I shoved my sudden, inexplicable, and rather impossible prowess with the dagger away to deal with later. I turned as Allyson shoved open the doors. We raced into the chamber just as the sound of wood splintering reached us. Allyson cried out, fingers curling against the chest of her gown as Milton and Grady closed the doors behind them.

"Get the chairs—the settee," Milton ordered. "We'll block the door."

Quickly sheathing the dagger, I rushed forward and slammed my hands into the side of the settee. It barely budged. I whipped toward Allyson. "Help me."

Her wide, frightened eyes met mine as she hurried to my side, and I locked on to her. It happened so quick. I connected with her, and my second sense came alive so fast there was no stopping it as she moved forward to help. My entire body jerked.

Then I saw her falling—*fresh red running down the front of her blue gown*. Then I felt it—*sharp agony along my throat, burning and final as the silver chain snapped and the necklace fell, the sapphire splattered with blood*—

Breaking eye contact with her, I pushed harder on the settee, its legs tearing the carpet. "Hide," I rasped. "Go and hide."

"You need help. You can't push this—"

"No." I shoved her away, toward the stacks.

She stumbled back. "Lis—"

"You need to hide. Now. Don't make a sound. Don't come out. You hide. Do you understand me? You stay hidden, no matter what."

"Y-Yes." She wrapped her arms around herself.

"Go. *Now*."

Allyson slowly backed away and then turned, disappearing between the rows of books.

Grady joined me, grabbing the side of the settee. We carried it over to the door. Milton shoved a heavy chair against it—

A thump hit the doors, causing the three of us to jump again. Another bang hit it. A *ni'mere* shrieked, turning my blood cold.

"Really wish I had that wine now," Milton muttered.

"We'll get you a dozen bottles after this," Grady assured him. The *ni'mere* hit the door again, shrieking. "We need to hide."

My mind raced for a good hiding place. I thought of the heavily curtained recesses that many of the staff liked to sneak to, either for a brief rendezvous or a quick nap. Some of them even had doors in them that led to other chambers or to stairs that went to the mezzanine above. Which ones, I couldn't remember. "The alcoves. To our left. Some of them have doors."

Milton nodded, swallowing hard as he glanced around. "Best of luck."

Then he darted off, heading toward the wall. Grady and I did the same. We rushed through the maze of bookcases. The wall of alcoves came into view as the library doors crashed open.

Somewhere in the library, Allyson cried out in fear, and my heart sank. *Please be quiet. Please. Please.* Grady shoved one of the heavy drapes aside, and then we were quickly enveloped in the dark, stale air of the cramped space as the drape settled back in place.

Grady held me tight to him as I stared through the gap between the curtains, my entire body shaking. It was no more than an inch, but it felt like we stood completely exposed as the *ni'meres* flew through the library. Books fell, one by one, hitting the floor, and I jumped. Each time, I jumped.

A louder crash came seconds later, sounding like an entire row of heavy bookcases toppling over. Silence followed, and then . . .

Slow, steady footsteps.

Then quiet.

Seconds ticked by as I strained to hear any sound. Minutes. There was nothing. Did the *ni'meres* leave? Wouldn't we—

"There's no reason to hide," a Hyhborn said, and my body flashed hot then cold. I hadn't forgotten that voice. It was Lord Samriel. "I will not harm you."

Grady made no move to come up. Neither did I.

"Come out," Lord Samriel called, his tone gentle and coaxing. "You will be safe if you do."

I reached up, curling my fingers around Grady's sleeve, wishing I hadn't sheathed the *lunea* blade. I wasn't sure what I'd do with it. Then again, I hadn't expected being able to use it before, but I didn't dare breathe too deeply or make any other movement. Not even as the air turned frigid around us.

"Please don't hide from me." Lord Samriel's voice was drawing closer. "We want to help you."

We?

Through the gap in the curtain I saw a *ni'mere* land on one of the bookcases, its back to us as it stretched out its massive wings. Its head twisted from side to side in the quiet.

Then I heard a soft, trembling voice call out, "You . . . you promise?"

The *ni'mere*'s head swiveled to the right as I jerked forward. Grady's arms tightened around me.

"Don't," he whispered in my ear.

Heart sinking, I shuddered. I told her to hide—not to come out. Why hadn't she listened? I wanted to scream at her, but I couldn't. I knew that, but my entire body strained against Grady's hold.

"Of course. I promise," Lord Samriel assured, his voice so syrupy it dripped poisonous sugar. "Come on—ah, there you are."

No. No. No.

The *ni'mere* shook out its wings, a cruel, bloody smile twisting its lips.

"That's not her," another voice answered, one both Grady and I recognized. Hymel. What was he doing here, with them? Hymel was a bastard, but he couldn't be involved in this.

There was a heavy sigh and then Lord Samriel said, "Kill it."

It.

Kill *it*.

Allyson. Her. Not it. *Her.*

"Stop," another voice intruded, one that was colder, flatter.

The *ni'mere* listened, tucking its wing back as it strained from where it was perched on the bookcase.

"You said it was here." The unknown male spoke again. "Are you sure?"

"I'm positive," Hymel answered, and my stomach hollowed. I had never heard him sound so scared. "I saw her run with Allyson. She has to be in here, Your Highness."

I suddenly understood why Hymel sounded so afraid, because that man he spoke to was a prince. Was it Prince Rainer? But why would he be here when his Court burned?

Grady stiffened behind me. They were . . . they were talking about me. My thoughts raced, a mess of confusion and fear.

"Then we shall see," the Prince said.

Suddenly, Allyson's scream ripped through the air, high-pitched and terrifying. I jerked forward, knees nearly collapsing. Grady held on, keeping me standing.

"Shush now," the Prince ordered, that voice of his almost gentle if not for the iciness, and Allyson's screams ended in a soft sob.

Then there was . . . there was just the sound of my heart pounding.

"I'm going to give this lovely creature a chance," the Prince said, and through the curtains, I could see the *ni'mere* twist its head back and forth. "And I'm going to give *you* a choice." There was a pause. "Lis."

I went rigid against Grady, heart pounding. I could barely get enough air into my lungs.

"Come to me, and she will not be harmed," the Prince said. "Don't?"

There was a crack. A deafening, sickening snap.

Allyson's sharp, pain-filled scream pierced the air. My entire body jerked.

"That was just one small bone," the Prince continued. "There are many more to break. I don't want to do it. I also don't want to spend precious minutes searching every inch of this manor for you. Come to me."

Grady's other arm came around me as he pressed his cheek against mine, his body shaking just as violently.

Another snap shattered the silence, cracking my heart and something deeper, more important. My soul. I didn't know why this was happening. Why this prince, whoever he was, was looking for me. What Hymel had to do with any of it. But us standing by and doing nothing, letting this happen? I knew Grady didn't want to. I didn't, but the moment we reached the alcove, it was like the years in Archwood had never happened. It was just Grady and me against the world, watching out for each other and only each other. It was how we survived this long, but Allyson's screams . . . I wanted to pierce my eardrums. I wanted to claw out my own eyes. She didn't deserve this. My gods, none of those who had suffered tonight deserved any of this. And us? Me? What did we deserve for letting this happen? What did it make us? The monster Thorne had asked if I thought he was. That's what it made us. I slammed my eyes shut against the tears, my fingers digging into Grady's sleeve.

"Don't," he whispered just above a breath.

I shook my head frantically as Allyson's screams turned to moans. I couldn't do this. Just like I couldn't ignore my intuition when it guided me to intervene. I couldn't let myself become this. I wouldn't let Grady become a monster just to protect me from whatever it was that they wanted.

"Please," I whispered to Grady. "Please stay hidden."

"Lis—"

I didn't give myself time to think too much about what I was doing or time for Grady to prepare. Fear and desperation were a heady mix, giving one strength one normally wouldn't have. Or maybe it was adrenaline. Maybe it was something else—something that came from that hidden, deep part of me that had erupted when I'd grabbed Hymel's arm. I didn't know, but when I lurched forward, I broke Grady's hold.

"Stop! Don't hurt her!" I screamed as I rushed through the drapes, and I was fast—faster than I had ever been. I flew into the library.

And into a new nightmare.

Because Grady was right behind me. I should've known he wouldn't listen. He caught me with the arm around my waist, hauling me back as the *ni'mere* turned toward me, feather wings whipping out as it screeched a warning. I skidded to a stop as I saw the Hyhborn who had to be the Prince. It wasn't Prince Rainer. This male was blond like Lord Samriel. Blood splattered the exquisitely formed jaw and cheek. He held Allyson to his chest by her throat, forcing her onto the tips of her toes. Her left arm hung at an awkward, deformed angle. Her wide, terrified gaze met mine as Grady tried to edge me back, but I saw past them, to where Lord Samriel stood to the Prince's right, a towering icy beauty. He smiled as he took a step forward.

Grady shoved me behind him, brandishing his sword. I cried out, grabbing his arm, but he shook me off. "Don't come up any closer," he warned, and the Lord halted.

The Prince tilted his head to the side, his grasp on Allyson easing up.

"Yeah, that's right. You all are going to stay right there and you're going to let my friend here leave," Grady continued. "You're not going to stop her." He spared a quick glance over his shoulder. "Get out. I'll catch up with you."

Shock blasted through me as I stared at that brave, loyal fool in disbelief. Did he really think I would leave him? That I would run and leave him behind even if the Hyhborn allowed it? "No."

His nostrils flared. "Damn it, go! Get the hell out—"

"*No,*" I repeated, trembling as I grasped his sides, holding on to him with everything I had.

His head kicked toward mine. Panic filled his eyes, and I hadn't seen that since . . . since the night in Union City. "Please."

Tears burned my eyes. "I told you to stay hidden," I whispered.

"So very charming," Lord Samriel said, and I jolted. There was no impatience or annoyance tainting his words. He . . . he sounded like he meant it. He lifted a pale hand.

Grady cursed as his sword was ripped free of his hand. Lord Samriel snatched it from the air.

"Iron and steel? Cute." Lord Samriel tsked softly. He slammed the sword down into the floor, piercing the wood. The sword reverberated from the impact. "Seize him."

It happened fast—too fast.

Figures drifted out from the stacks, wispy gray tendrils seeping out from the openings of their cloaks and spilling along the floor. They moved so quietly and quickly they could've been wraiths, but the Rae weren't spirits. They were bone and . . . some flesh.

They were on us in a heartbeat.

Grady broke free from my grasp, swinging his fists as he crashed into the Rae. The heavy thuds of the blows he landed knocked hooded heads back, scattering the gray mist, but he was outnumbered. A Rae captured his arms, forcing them to his back as he was driven to his knees and another held a . . . a sword to Grady's throat. A blade that shone a milky white. I shot toward the Rae, reaching for the arm that held the sword at Grady's neck.

Lord Samriel stepped in front of me.

I jerked back so quickly, I lost my balance and slipped, landing on my ass hard.

Chuckling, Lord Samriel glided—actually *glided* toward me. "That was unbelievably graceful."

Shit. Shit. Shit. I crawled backward, my legs getting tangled in the skirt of my gown.

"You son of a bitch! Get away from her!" Grady shouted, struggling against the one holding him. "Let me go, or I swear I'll—"

"Silence him," the Prince ordered.

The Rae's cloaks whispered along the floor as it spun, bringing down the hilt of a sword onto Grady's head. He went down, sending a burst of panic through me as I scrambled to my feet. I rushed to his side, dropping to my knees. "Grady?" I whispered as the Rae moved quietly back, forming a loose circle around Grady and me. "Grady?"

"Calm yourself." Hymel walked out from between two standing stacks as I jerked to a halt, my gaze immediately drawn to his empty hands and then to his hips, where his . . . his sword was still sheathed. He hadn't been disarmed.

And I was a naive fool to believe that Hymel's presence had been forced. That he wasn't capable of taking part in what was happening.

"You bastard," I seethed, fingers curling around empty air as I glared up at him.

"That's her, Prince Rohan," he said, the relief evident in his features. "That's the one that belongs to the Prince of Vytrus."

My entire body locked up. "What?"

"Perfect." Prince Rohan let go of Allyson.

She stumbled, cradling her arm to her stomach as she sobbed. Prince Rohan looked at the *ni'mere* perched on the shelf, and that was all it took. The *ni'mere* took flight, aiming straight for her.

"Allyson!" I screamed.

Her head jerked up. She spun, taking off between the stacks. The *ni'mere* shrieked, diving down between the rows. "No!" I shouted. I knew what was coming. I had seen what would happen, and still I shook as her screams hit the air, high-pitched and terrifying before ending in a wet gurgle.

Then silence.

"Why do they always run?" Lord Samriel asked. "Where do they think they're running off to?"

"Death," Prince Rohan answered, eyeing me.

Lord Samriel chuckled, sickening me. "So very morbid."

"You . . . you said you wouldn't hurt her." I could barely breathe; my chest was too tight and I was shaking so fiercely. "You said—"

"I said I would give her a choice," Prince Rohan interrupted. "I did not say I wouldn't hurt her."

My lips parted. "What choice did you give her?"

"To die quickly or slowly, screaming in pain the entire time," he said. "And that was a quick death."

"My gods," I whispered, a part of my mind unable to process the cold brutality of his words.

"I hope you're not praying to them." Prince Rohan looked down at me coolly. "Because they stopped listening long ago."

"I wasn't," I rasped, not having the brain space to even consider if what he said about the gods was true or not. I glanced at Grady, seeing his chest rise and fall. I placed my palms there, letting each breath he took calm me. "Why . . . why are you all doing this?"

"You can say we're changing the rules," Prince Rohan answered.

"What?" I looked between him and Lord Samriel. "What rules?"

Prince Rohan's lip curled in disdain; then he turned his back without answering. The Lord stepped in closer, peering down at me. He squinted. "She doesn't bear the mark."

The mark.

The mark Claude had spoken of.

"I'm not sure what you're looking for," Hymel said from where he hung back. "But she has abilities. The gift of foresight and intuition. She can read intentions and the future."

"Her eyes," Lord Samriel explained, head cocked. "The mark would be in her eyes."

I sucked in a sharp breath, my mind flashing from the brief sight of them changing in the mirror. It hadn't been my imagination, but didn't I already know that? Deep down?

"She could've been glamoured," Prince Rohan mused, and I didn't have a single clue what he meant by that. "We will know once Lord Arion returns. In the meantime, get rid of that one—"

"No. No. Please," I pleaded, stretching over Grady. "Please do not hurt him. Please. I'll do whatever it is that you ask." I trembled, not above begging—bargaining. "Please."

Prince Rohan turned slowly toward me. His eyes . . . they were like Thorne's, a kaleidoscope of shifting colors, except the brown was closer to a shade of crimson. "Anything?"

My heart plummeted, but I nodded. *"Anything."*

Lord Samriel glanced at Hymel.

"She speaks the truth." Hymel crossed his arms. "Those two are thick as thieves. He's leverage."

Anger flooded my veins but I choked it back, focusing on the Prince. "Promise me you won't hurt him, and I will do whatever you want. I swear it."

A faint smile appeared, and as I stared up at him, I could see that his features were even more finely crafted than Thorne's, but there was no . . . no *life* to them. He was a perfectly molded shell. "Okay."

I didn't let myself feel an ounce of relief. "Promise me you won't hurt him."

That smile grew, and still, it did nothing to soften his jaw or warm his stare. "You are a quick learner."

I glanced at Hymel and then toward the stacks, where Allyson had . . . where she'd taken her last breath. "No, I'm not." I swallowed. "Promise."

"I, Prince Rohan of Augustine, promise that no harm will come to him," he said, and I shuddered with relief despite the knowledge he hailed from the Lowlands—the *capital*. Hyhborn couldn't lie. They also couldn't break an oath. That I remembered. "As long as you give no reason for that to occur."

Trepidation tiptoed through me, but I held on to Prince Rohan's oath.

"Take her to her quarters," Prince Rohan directed.

"I'm not leaving Grady," I warned, latching on to his tunic. "He stays with me."

Lord Samriel's brows inched up as Prince Rohan refocused on me, his stare more unnerving than Thorne's because it was so cold, so lifeless despite the churning. The Prince moved so fast I didn't even have time to scream.

His hand came around my neck, and he lifted me, forcing me to stand on the tips of my toes. "I promised no harm would come to him," he said as I grasped his arm. My mind opened wide to him, and I saw nothing . . . nothing but darkness. "Whether or not I honor that oath will be up to you. Making demands is one way to guarantee that oath is broken." His fingers bit into my throat, sending a flare of pain along my neck. "Do you understand me."

"Yes," I forced out.

"Good." He didn't so much let go of me as shove me away. I stumbled back, caught by the arms by Lord Samriel. His grip was firm but not nearly as painful as I knew it could be. "Take her to her quarters and make sure she stays there while the horses are readied. We will leave as soon as Lord Arion confirms what is claimed."

Lord Samriel began to move, and I wasn't given much of a choice. My stare desperately clung to Grady's unmoving form. What were they going to do to him? I didn't dare ask out of fear of giving Prince Rohan reason to break his oath.

"Your Highness." Hymel spoke up, unfolding his arms. "What about the Prince of Vytrus? He left to escort his knights to Archwood. They will be returning by tomorrow night, at the latest."

My heart skipped. In the panic and terror, I'd forgotten the return of Thorne and his knights.

"They will run into some unexpected trouble en route, which should give us time," Prince Rohan said with a smile, and that quick burst of hope deflated. He looked to me. "Don't worry, my dear. We will keep you safe from the Prince of Vytrus."

My mouth dropped open. Of all the things I might have expected the Prince to say, that was not it. "Keep me safe from *him?*"

"It may not seem that way now, but we are saving your life," Prince Rohan said. "After all, it's Prince Thorne you should fear. You are his to kill."

CHAPTER 36

Thrown by what Prince Rohan had said, I was barely aware of Hymel leading Lord Samriel to my quarters. There was no way what the Prince had said was true. I wasn't Thorne's to kill. He wasn't a threat to me. I wasn't scared of him. I felt safe with him.

But Hyhborn couldn't lie.

They could kill, though.

My chest hollowed as I walked, the slice along the bottom of my foot a dull burn. Everywhere I looked, no matter how quickly I averted my gaze and despite the fact that Hymel took us through the staff halls, I saw bodies. I saw blood streaking the floor and pooling in the crevices. When we reached the hall to my chambers, it was devoid of gore and bloodshed. If not for the faint smell of burning wood, one could almost pretend that such violence hadn't touched us, but I could still hear the moans and whimpers, and distant screams.

My vision had come to fruition, but it hadn't encapsulated the true horror of what had come to pass.

Lord Samriel ushered me into the chambers after Hymel opened the doors. Hymel started to follow, but the Lord held up his hand. "Leave us."

My heart stuttered as my gaze flicked to Hymel's. He hesitated, his gaze bouncing between the Lord and me, and good gods, I'd never thought I'd prefer his company, but here I was, wishing it weren't him closing the doors and remaining in the hall.

Alone with the Lord in a chamber that no longer felt familiar and was strangely cold, I was too aware of the Lord's stare. It was much like Thorne's. Intense. Unflinching. I folded my arms over my chest and backed up against the settee. Several moments of silence passed as the Lord watched me. I peeked at him. The silvery-blond hair was longer than it had been when I last saw him, reaching the middle of his back and a shock against the leather-adorned black armor protecting his chest and shoulders. He looked . . . curious and perplexed. Did he recognize me? Like with Thorne, I doubted it, but the same instinct that warned me to stay quiet resurfaced.

"Sit," Lord Samriel instructed.

Not wanting to tempt the Lord's ire and endanger Grady, I sat on the edge of the settee, curling my feet beneath the hem of my gown.

Slowly, he sat on the settee, his long and lean body angled toward mine. "Your name? It's Lis?"

I nodded.

"Is it short for anything?"

Pressing my arms close to my waist and chest, I didn't want to answer him, but the risk of lying was too great. "Calista."

"Calista," he repeated, and hearing him speak my name drew a shiver down my spine, but not the kind elicited from Thorne. "A beautiful name for a beautiful lady."

Fingers pressing into my sides, I forced myself to respond. "That is kind of you to say."

His answering smile was tight and knowing. "You worry for your friend?"

My stomach dipped and twisted. "Yes."

"The Prince will not break his oath unless given reason to," he told me. "You just don't want to give him reason."

"I won't," I swore.

"Relieved to hear that," he replied. "Tell me about your abilities, Calista."

"I . . . I can do as Hymel said," I told him. "But I'm not a conjurer."

"I know." Lord Samriel leaned back, resting one ankle on his knee. The shafts of his boots were polished, but something dark smeared the foot. I glanced at the tile near the door. A footprint in red stained the floor. Blood. I quickly looked away, stomach churning. "I want to hear how you would describe them."

Not at all experienced in speaking of my abilities, I squirmed. "I have . . . heightened intuition and I can sometimes see the future—in visions or when asked a question."

"Interesting," he murmured, the curve of his lips doing nothing to soften the harsh angles of his features. "This heightened intuition you speak of? How does it work?"

"It . . . it guides me toward certain choices. Sometimes I'm unaware of it until I'm doing something."

"Like?"

My thoughts were so scattered it took a moment for me to think of an example. "Sometimes I'll see someone and know what is about to occur. It can happen in a premonition—something I see happening in my mind before it occurs—and other times it's a voice I hear."

"Voice?" he questioned.

"My own voice. It'll . . . whisper what is about to occur or it will tell me to stop and listen, take another path or enter a different—" A scream from outside caused me to jump. My pulse sped up, and my head swung toward the window, but I could see nothing beyond the curtains. Who was that? Someone I knew? A stranger?

"Pay that no mind," Lord Samriel said, tone gentle and almost kind. His tone had been that way this entire time. Casual, even. "There is nothing you can do for them. Focus on what you can do for yourself and for your friend. What is his name?"

A knot lodged in my chest as I dragged my gaze from the window. "Grady," I whispered, clearing my throat. "My intuition is just very heightened."

"And seeing the future?" Lord Samriel asked.

I nodded. "Usually it takes someone asking me a question. I . . . I will need to concentrate on them and sometimes I need to touch them."

"But you also have premonitions without being asked. Did you not see this coming?"

"I did, but . . ." I swallowed, unnerved as I focused on the hand resting on the arm of the settee. The ring finger on his left hand was missing. Could he not regenerate it? There was no doubt in my mind that Lord Samriel was powerful enough, which meant that keeping from him the fact that I could hear thoughts was not wise, but Hymel hadn't mentioned it. The others might not know. "But it was vague. I knew there'd be . . . bloodshed but I didn't know what would cause it."

"Is it because the events involved you?"

My gaze shot to his as my heart skipped.

His smile deepened as his chin dipped. "I'll take that as a yes."

"How . . . how did you know that?"

"I knew of someone like you once, with similar gifts. Their future was often hidden to them." His gaze, like shards of obsidian except for the green ring around the pupil, flickered across my face. "For a time." His head straightened. "You were an orphan?"

Surprise ripped through me, then understanding. "Hymel?"

Lord Samriel nodded.

Anger built, tasting of ash on my tongue. It was clear that Hymel had been working with these Hyhborn, who likely hailed from the Lowlands. For how long was anyone's guess. "Hymel . . . he said Prince Rainer would be joining us for the Feasts."

"He did," Lord Samriel said. "Or I suppose it would be more accurate to say that he *was* going to. However, the Prince of Primvera wasn't in agreement with the King's wishes." He paused. "May the gods rest his soul."

The breath I took went nowhere. "Prince Rainer . . . he's dead?"

"Unfortunately."

Oh my gods. I rocked back, toes pressing into the thick rug. "The King . . ." I couldn't bring myself to say what I suspected.

"What has Prince Thorne told you?" Lord Samriel asked.

I tensed. "About . . . about what?"

"About the King."

"Nothing much," I said, and that wasn't a lie. Not exactly. "All I know is that he was sent here to determine if Archwood was worth defending against the Iron Knights."

Lord Samriel made a noncommittal sound.

"Was that not true?" I asked, not daring to open my senses to him. Not then.

"Hyhborn cannot lie." The green circles churned slowly around his pupils. "Prince Thorne is unaware of your abilities, isn't he? He's unaware of what you are to him?"

"No, he doesn't know about my abilities." My throat tightened. "And I'm nothing to him."

"That's not true at all, Calista," he said, and my skin chilled at the sound of my name. "He may not yet be aware of what you mean to him on a conscious level, but on a primal one? I'm confident he does. He's drawn to you, whether he understands why or not."

I jolted, recalling Thorne's own confusion as he admitted as much. "I . . . I don't understand."

"Well, it's quite simple," Lord Samriel said. "You are everything to him."

A shivery wave of awareness swept through me. "*Ny . . . ny'chora.*"

Lord Samriel's pale brows lifted. "So, he has spoken to you about something."

"It was . . . I was asking why his heart didn't beat."

Everything about the Lord changed in an instant. The friendly if cold smile slipped from his face. His entire body tensed, and when he spoke, gone was the gentleness. "And what did he say to that?"

My jaw clamped shut with the sudden feeling that I . . . I needed to be careful. It was the faint stirrings of my intuition. "He just said that his heart doesn't beat because of his *ny'chora.*"

His lips thinned as they curled slightly on one side. "Did he tell you what the *ny'chora* was?"

"Only that it was everything. That was all he said," I quickly added. "It was at night, and he was tired. He went to sleep."

Those unblinking eyes didn't leave mine. "He slept with you?"

I wet my dry lips. "Do you mean literally or figuratively?"

Lord Samriel chuckled. "Literally."

"Yes."

"And figuratively."

"No," I lied, and I wasn't even sure why I did. It slipped from my mouth so quickly that it sounded genuine.

"Interesting." His gaze flickered over me. "But you two have been intimate in other ways, I imagine?"

"Yes." Swallowing, I looked away, my gaze settling on the door. "What does that have to do with anything?"

"Nothing. I'm just being impolite and nosy."

I huffed out a dry laugh.

"What do you feel when you are with him?" he asked. "And this is not an impolite question, Calista. It's one I need you to answer."

Unfolding my arms, I clasped my tightly pressed-together knees. "I don't know how to answer that."

Lord Samriel raised his brows. "Are you drawn to him? Attracted to him? Or does he frighten you like I do?"

My heart skipped, and that faint smile returned. The Lord was . . . how did Thorne put it? Tuned in?

"I'm enjoying the openness of our conversation," he shared in my silence. "I hope it continues to be pleasurable and easy."

"Or?" I whispered.

"Or I will simply make it an easy conversation, though it may not be enjoyable for you."

I looked up, understanding what he meant. He'd use a compulsion—seize my will and take control—like he'd done with Grady in Union City. A whole new kind of terror seized me. That I didn't want. Ever. "I am drawn to him and find him attractive. After all, he is a Hyhborn prince."

Lord Samriel smirked. "Are you afraid of him?"

"No."

That smile returned. "He's the only one you won't fear."

"And yet I'm his to kill?" I forced out the words that felt so very wrong to say.

"If he wants to survive, yes."

I sucked in a shaky breath, chest tightened until I felt like I would suffocate. "I don't understand."

The Lord was quiet for a few moments. "Do you know anything about your birth? Your bloodline?"

"No," I said, thinking of what Maven had shared—gods, was Maven still alive? I shuddered. "I just know I was given to the Priory of Mercy as a babe."

His stare sharpened as he stared at me; then a slow smile spread across his face. "Did you ever tell Prince Thorne that you were given to the Priory?"

My heart was pounding once more. I shook my head.

"Calista?" He drew his booted foot from his knee, lowering it to the floor. "I have a very important question for you. Was Prince Thorne unknown to you when you met him here? Am I unknown to you?"

A tremor started in my hands and traveled up my arms. "No," I admitted in a hushed voice.

"Oh, the irony is so sweet." He scooted to the edge of the settee. "You were right there, in front of us, and yet neither of us knew," he said, letting out a thick laugh. "You were glamoured even then."

That word again. "Glamoured?"

"Your divinity was hidden, likely by the Prioress. You wouldn't be the first that they've attempted to hide. Their actions are . . . righteous in nature, if infuriating. They see themselves as protectors of those born of the stars."

I stared at him. "So . . . you believe me to be a *caelestia?*"

"I believe that you're more than just that. You see, quite a number of mortals carry the blood of Hyhborn in them," he said, and I thought of what Maven had said about the conjurers. "There could even be more *caelestias* than there are mortals. It's hard to tell, but when the stars fall, a mortal is made divine."

That phrase again. "And what does that mean exactly?"

"It means the gods blessed those born in the hour that the stars fell with certain gifts—with abilities that would make them useful in times of . . . strife."

I thought of Vayne Beylen. "There are others like me."

"There used to be many *ny'seraphs,*" he said, and my breath caught. "One for every Deminyen. You see, the *ny'seraph* is bonded to a Deminyen at birth, becoming their *ny'chora.*"

Why doesn't it beat like that now?

Because I lost the ny'chora.

"Bonded?" I whispered.

He nodded. "If you weren't glamoured, Prince Thorne would've recognized you the moment he laid eyes on you, but even so, he was still drawn to you and vice versa. That is how powerful the link is."

"You're saying that the gods bond a mortal to a Deminyen at birth?" I swallowed. "Why?"

"Because once the bond is completed, the Deminyen gains their *ny'chora*—their connection to humanity. The *ny'chora* keeps them—"

"Humane. Compassionate," I whispered.

Lord Samriel nodded. "The gods found that necessary after, well, that is a conversation for a different day."

I thought I already knew what conversation he spoke of. The Great War. Based on what Thorne had told me, the Deminyens had gone to rest because they'd been losing their ability to connect to mankind and when many awoke they did so without compassion.

My gods, I didn't . . . I didn't know what to think about that—any of that. It was almost too much to consider. "How is that bond completed?" I asked.

"A few ways, but that's not what you need to worry about," he said, and I started to open my senses to him. The white wall shielding his thoughts throbbed as he leaned forward suddenly, his movements severing the connection. "The completion of the bond will not happen."

I looked away. Just for a few seconds. "Why . . . why would he need to kill me to survive?"

"Because the *ny'seraph* can be a strength to a Deminyen, but also their greatest weakness," Lord Samriel explained, his tone gentle once more. "Through you, he can be killed."

My lips parted as my breath caught.

"But we won't allow that." He rose. "Prince Rohan will want all of this confirmed, just to be sure. You should rest till then."

Rest? Was he serious? I stayed seated as he crossed to the door, treading over the smear of blood there. "And then what?"

"Then you will be taken to Augustine," Lord Samriel said. "And you will be given to King Euros."

CHAPTER 37

Unsure of how much time I had, I didn't want to risk anyone return-ing for me while I was undressed, so I grabbed the robe from the bedchamber, cinching it tightly around my waist. I kept the *lunea* blade on me, but moved it to my ankle. Having this on me was a risk. I doubted the Hyhborn would take kindly to seeing it, and the last thing I wanted to do was jeopardize Grady.

But I needed something to defend myself.

I hastily washed the cut on my foot. It had stopped bleeding, but I wrapped it with a piece of gauze. I returned to the antechamber, limping slightly. My scattered thoughts immediately went to Lord Samriel's parting words.

I was to be given to the King? In what manner? Without my in-tuition, my imagination went to all sorts of places. I dragged a trem-bling hand through my tangled hair and stopped by the window. I pulled the curtain back. My bedchamber faced a part of the gardens and the front of the manor. Only a faint gleam of moonlight cast light over the dark grounds. There weren't even any *sōls* in the dis-tance, but I could make out just the hint of . . . of lumps scattered about the grounds. Bodies. I swallowed thickly. I couldn't see the stables. Was Iris okay? I knew it seemed wrong to worry for a horse with the loss of so much life, but animals were often the most vul-nerable.

Letting the curtain slip back in place, I closed my eyes, but the horror and the confusion still found me. I wasn't so shocked that I hadn't been able to read between what I already knew and what Lord Samriel had said. It made sense and yet didn't.

What I didn't understand was how Thorne was a risk to me de-spite what Lord Samriel had shared. How I could feel safe with him yet he would kill me to survive. I couldn't believe it.

But Hyhborn couldn't lie.

They spoke the truth. A shaky breath left me as I pressed my balled hand against my chest, where my heart . . . it ached from the loss, from the fear, and from the knowledge that . . . that Thorne would harm me, and I didn't even understand why that would affect me so. I barely knew him. He wasn't anything to me. . . .

Except that thought had never felt right.

Maybe it was because of this . . . this bond. Maybe it was something more. I didn't know, but I had started to feel—

The chamber door suddenly opened, spinning me around as my heart lurched into my throat. It wasn't a Hyhborn who entered and closed the door.

It was Hymel.

I couldn't even feel relief then. I didn't feel anything but rage as I crossed the floor and swung. I didn't slap him. I punched him right in the jaw.

Hymel's head snapped back as pain lanced my knuckles, and I welcomed that pain with a savage satisfaction.

"Fuck," Hymel grunted, clasping his jaw as he straightened. He turned his head to me. "That was unnecessary."

I swung again, but Hymel was prepared this time. He caught my arm. With a cry of fury, I went at him with my other hand, fingers curled into claws. He jerked his head back, but my nails scraped his cheek. He hissed as two bright red streaks appeared above his beard.

"Bitch," he snarled, snatching my arm.

"Let me go!" I shrieked, pulling on my arms as he shoved me hard. The back of my calves hit the settee, taking my legs out from underneath me. I landed on the settee, and immediately started to stand, but Hymel still had ahold of my arms. He forced me down on my back, trapping my legs with his. "Get off me!"

"Stop shouting," he spat, inches from my face. "You'll draw one of those Hyhborn here—"

"Get the fuck off me!" I screamed in his face. "You traitorous motherfucker!"

"Gods damn it." He jerked my arms up, pressing them into the cushion behind my head. He pinned my wrists together under one hand. His other smacked down on my mouth, silencing my curses.

"I swear to the gods," he growled, pushing my head down into the cushion. "I would love nothing more than to choke the ever-loving shit out of you, but since they want you alive and I want to survive, I need you to keep it the fuck down. Fuck," he snapped. "The only reason why I came in here was to make sure you were still breathing. I don't know or trust that white-haired Hyhborn. Knowing my fucking luck, he'll end up killing you and all of this will be for nothing." The hand around my wrists tightened brutally. "So are you going to act right? Are you?"

Breathing heavily through my nose, I glared up at him as I nodded as best as I could.

He slowly lifted his hand from my mouth, his entire body tense as if he was ready for me to start screaming again. "Did you pick up anything from Lord Samriel?"

"Fuck you."

"As I've told you before, not interested in where my cousin has been."

"And where is Claude?" I demanded, shaking with anger. "I want the honest truth. Is he—" My voice cracked. "Is he alive?"

"What? You can't answer that yourself?"

My intuition wouldn't tell me where he was, and gods, it hadn't occurred to me until then that it could very well be because he was no longer a part of this realm.

His eyes squinted. "You too afraid to see if you can find out?" He laughed. "You care that much about him? Fuck. I told you before. I don't know where the hell he is, but I can wager a guess." He met my glower with his own. "He hit the road the first chance he could."

Disbelief coursed through me. "You're suggesting that Claude ran away? That he abandoned his home? His people—"

"You? Gods damn, that is exactly what I'm suggesting. The fucker is a coward who has always been more concerned with getting off and getting drunk or high than he ever has running Archwood. He never should've been baron. You'd be lying if you didn't agree with that."

The thing was, I couldn't disagree. Claude was terribly irresponsible, but reckless enough to run? Gods, I knew the answer to that. It wasn't impossible.

"If he was here, though? If I could find him, he would be dead," Hymel said. "I would've slit his fucking throat myself."

And I knew he spoke the truth then. I could see it in those pale eyes that were full of so much hate and bitterness.

"Gods," I whispered, wanting to be angry with Claude, but damn it, I couldn't help but be relieved. At least he wasn't here. He was alive.

And if I ever saw him again, I'd punch him too.

"So, what? Is that what this is about?" I asked, staring into his eyes as I opened my senses. Intuition shuddered through me. "You think you should be baron, and you helped orchestrate this so you can take the title?"

"Get the fuck out of my head."

Disgust flooded me. "You did this because of your own envy? Do you know how many people died tonight?"

"Would've been more if it weren't for me," he said. "If the King learned of you, and came for you, while the Prince of Vytrus was here? The whole fucking city would be gone. Instead, I've saved people tonight. Not only that, I saved the title and the manor from going bankrupt. Those debtors? They need to be paid, and you? You're going to bring in enough coin that every debt Claude has racked up will be paid and then some. So, yeah, I should've been the fucking baron."

I stared at him. He didn't know the King wanted Archwood wiped off the map anyway. I shook my head. "You're a fool."

"You really think that? You don't know anything." He pushed off me and rose. Lifting a hand to his cheek, he wiped away the faint trickle of blood from where I scratched him. "Fucking bitch," he muttered.

I sat up, clutching the edge of the cushion. "You didn't tell them I could read thoughts, did you?"

"No." He glanced at the door.

"Why?" When he didn't say anything, it occurred to me. "It's because you don't trust the Hyhborn, do you? You were hoping I would listen in on their thoughts and warn you if they were planning to betray you?"

Hymel didn't answer, so I rose. He hadn't gone far, and when he faced me, he likely thought I was about to hit him again. He lifted a hand, but I wasn't about to strike him. Instead, I grasped his hand with my senses wide open and I pushed, *shattering* that shield.

I didn't see or hear the answer to my question.

I saw something else entirely.

I *felt* it.

A laugh parted my lips, spilling out from me.

Hymel jerked his hand free, backing up as he stared at me. "What did you see?" The skin above his beard paled. "What did you see?" He took a step toward me—

The door behind him opened then, stopping him. My gaze lifted, and my laugh died on my lips. The sight of the cloaked Rae waiting in the hall sent my heart racing, but what came into the chamber behind Hymel caused me to take a step back.

The too-shallow breath I took felt heavier, thicker, and tasted of . . . of something I hadn't thought about in years—mints the Prioress used to keep in the pockets of her robes. Power suddenly drenched the air, seeping along the walls and across the floor, soaking every nook and cranny of the space. My skin danced with static.

Cloaked shoulders almost too wide to fit filled the entrance; the male was so tall he had to dip his head to step through the doorframe. He straightened, revealing sculpted, sharp features, and hair a light, silvery blond.

I recognized him.

It was the Hyhborn I'd seen in the Great Chamber, earlier this evening. He'd looked at me and had *smiled*. The one I thought looked so much like Lord Samriel, and he did. His hair was shorter, though, reaching his shoulders, and his face even thinner, crescentshaped.

"Lord Arion." Hymel bowed quickly.

I would swear the *lunea* blade heated in its sheath as I took another step back.

"So this is her?" Lord Arion asked, his appraisal cooler than Lord Samriel's.

"Yes, my lord."

His head tilted in a distinctively serpentlike manner. "For your sake," he said to me, "I hope he is correct. My brother seems to think so, but we shall see."

Lord Arion was so quick, and there was no place for me to go. He was standing before me in a heartbeat, one hand at my throat, his eyes identical to Lord Samriel's. "Well, let's not delay this, shall we?"

"What—?" I gasped.

His other hand flattened against my temple. His lips moved. He spoke low and quick in a language that sounded like Enochian—

A sudden sharp pain darted across the back of my skull, then over the front of my face. Pressure built inside me. I cried out, squeezing my eyes shut as the pain traveled there. Bright white lights exploded behind my closed lids. The agony, it felt like a fire. My legs shook, and I thought I would fall. That I'd fall and be burned from the inside—

Then the pain eased off as quickly as it had started, leaving only a dull ache behind, in my temples and below my brow.

"Open your eyes," Lord Arion demanded.

I blinked them open, half afraid to discover that I was now blind, but I wasn't. My eyes locked with the Lord's.

"My brother tells me you were given to the Priory as a babe." Lord Arion stared down at me, his lips parted. "He was right. They tried to hide you, but you're no longer hidden. I see you for what you are." The grip on my throat vanished. "Our liege will be very pleased that we've found him an unbound *ny'seraph*."

I stumbled back, hitting the settee but keeping my balance.

Lord Arion smiled, turning away. He spoke to the Rae in Enochian. Half of them departed quietly, leaving two remaining.

"Where are they going?" Hymel asked.

The Lord turned his head to him. "They are going to share the good news."

"All right." Hymel nodded, a tentative smile appearing. "Then I should go to them, to close out our deal."

Slowly, my gaze shifted to Hymel, and I knew when I read him moments earlier that whatever deal Hymel had struck with the Hyhborn, it hadn't been a wise one. He hadn't laid out whatever terms he'd agreed to clearly. He *was* a fool.

"You did well." Lord Arion faced Hymel, his cloak fluttering over the floor as he approached him. "Our king will be forever appreciative of your service." He cupped the man's cheeks, pressing his lips to Hymel's forehead. He lifted his head. "It will not be forgotten."

Hymel's tentative smile faded.

There was a quiet moment.

Just a heartbeat.

The crack of Hymel's neck snapping shattered the silence.

I watched as Hymel . . . as he crumpled, just as I'd seen, dead before he hit the floor.

CHAPTER 38

"I think we're being followed," Grady whispered in the darkness of the unfamiliar chamber of the Bell's Inn, somewhere in the Midlands.

We lay facing one another on a narrow, stiff-as-a-board bed, but at least it was an actual bed indoors. We'd spent a few hours the night before camped alongside the Bone Road while coyotes howled and whined as if they could sense the Hyhborn's presence and were unsettled.

The only reason we were together was because the Bell's Inn didn't have a lot of rooms, and the Hyhborn, well, they might have curled their lips at the accommodations, but they weren't all displeased when they discovered that the owner offered more than food and drink to his patrons. The owner, a thin man who went by the name Buck and didn't seem all that concerned when he spotted me barefoot and Grady bloodied, also had flesh on the menu.

Just then, a cry of pleasure came from the floor above, momentarily overshadowing the steady thump of a headboard hitting the wall.

The Hyhborn were clearly enjoying themselves.

My gaze flicked up, where thin slivers of moonlight crawled across the ceiling. We were supposed to be sleeping. That was Prince Rohan's order, but the thin walls did nothing to block sound. We could hear every grunt and moan.

"Gods," Grady muttered wearily. "Do they ever stop fucking? They've been at it for hours."

"I hope not." I pulled my gaze from the ceiling. "They may separate us."

"Yeah." Grady sighed, and he shifted slightly, trying to get comfortable, but he couldn't move very much with his arms bound above his head with chain secured to the headboard.

I wasn't bound.

Because according to the Prince, I wasn't being held captive. I was being *rescued*, and I thought they really believed that. But I also knew they had no reason to fear me attempting to make an escape. They were partly correct there. The first thing I did the moment they left was try to free Grady. I even used the *lunea* blade they'd yet to discover on me, but the chain . . . it was constructed of the same material, and I learned then that *lunea* could not pierce, crack, or shatter itself. But again, they were partly correct. Thanks to Hymel, they knew I wouldn't leave Grady behind. I glanced at him, hating that he was in this situation because of me.

"Your eyes," he said, voice thick. "I can't get used to them."

My eyes . . .

I'd finally seen them when we were placed in here and I was able to use the bathing chamber. There was a dirty mirror above the vanity and the light in there had been dim, but I'd seen them. The incandescent blue rings circled my pupils, just like they briefly had before. Whatever glamour the Prioress supposedly used had hidden them all these years, and I didn't know if the glimpse of them before had been the glamour weakening or something.

"Are they . . . weird?" I asked.

"Kind of," he admitted. "They're also kind of pretty."

I shook my head. "You were saying you think we're being followed?"

"I heard Lord Arion talking to one of their knights this evening, before we stopped here. I didn't hear why he thought this, but that's why they wanted off the Bone Road for the night," he said.

I swallowed, throat dry. There hadn't been much in the way of food and water. Just a glass for each of us and something that was supposed to be a beef stew that we'd been given on our arrival. But if we were being followed? A tiny bit of hope sprang alive. Was it . . . was it Thorne? And if it was, what would happen then? "Do you think it could be . . . Thorne and his knights?"

Grady didn't answer immediately. "I don't know."

"Neither do I." I squeezed my eyes shut, opening my senses to find an answer to no avail. "I don't see anything. I don't know if it's because a Hyhborn is following us or if it's just that I'm . . . I'm tired and . . ." I sucked in a shallow breath that did nothing to alleviate the pressure gathering in my chest and stomach. "We're what? About two days' ride from Archwood?"

"Based on our pace, probably a little farther out than that," he replied. "Prince Thorne went north, right? To meet with his knights. Even if he managed to still return to Archwood when he expected to, he would still be at least a day or so behind us."

Whatever little hope had sparked was quickly extinguished as the thumping continued overhead. Not only would Thorne have to have ridden like hell to catch up with us, there was this trouble Prince Rohan had ensured Thorne and his knights would encounter.

There was also the fact that Thorne had no reason to come for me. He had no knowledge of me being this *ny'seraph*. I didn't even know what it was. The journey had been a tense, silent one. That was how Prince Rohan preferred it.

Another guttural moan echoed from above.

At least, that was how the Prince preferred it up until now.

"But if it is him? Prince Thorne?" Grady said after a few moments. "I'm not sure that's going to be a rescue."

I closed my eyes as that pressure increased, feeling as if it would drag me through the bed. I'd told Grady everything while I tried to free him. I still couldn't wrap my head around the idea of Thorne killing me, especially when I felt safe with him. I wasn't afraid of him.

But he also didn't know what I was, I reminded myself. That could change the moment he discovered that I was this . . . this thing that basically stripped him of his immortality. Why was that even the case? There was so much I didn't understand or know, and it made this all the more frustrating.

"Lis?"

I opened my eyes. "Yeah?"

"You like him, don't you?"

"Gods," I muttered as a piercing pain hit my chest. He'd asked this before, but it felt different now. More real. Harsher.

"Lis," he said, and the sorrow in the way he said my name, the sympathy and . . . "Do you remember when I was getting with Joshua?"

I stiffened. "Yeah, of course I do."

"And do you remember what you told me?"

"To stop messing around with someone who was married?"

He huffed out a dry laugh. "Besides that. You told me to cut it off before I got deeper and got hurt."

"Yeah," I said, thinking of the handsome banker. "And you didn't listen, if I recall."

"I know." There was a pause. "I'm telling you the same thing."

"What? It's not like that. It's nowhere near like you and Joshua—"

"You and this prince may not have known each other long. You might not have been pretending make-believe like Joshua and I were, but I know you, Lis. You don't get interested in anyone. It might be because you could touch him. It might be whatever the fuck you are to him and he's to you, but—"

"Okay. I understand what you're saying. I do. But what I feel or don't feel for him doesn't matter." I rolled onto my back. "We have way bigger problems to deal with."

"You're right. It doesn't." His exhale was heavy. "What does is that you need to get out of here."

All tiredness vanished in an instant. "What?"

"You're not bound. You can escape. There's a window right above us that looks like it can be easily opened," he said. "You should've already made a run for it."

I turned my head toward him. "Are you out of your mind?"

"Lis—"

"I'm not leaving you. Gods, I can't believe you would even suggest that again. That you would think I'd be okay with doing that . . ." I trailed off, suddenly understanding Naomi's anger. *Naomi.* My breath snagged. I stopped myself before I could learn of her future, like I'd done the last two days. I didn't want to know, because I needed to believe that she was alive. That she'd gone to her sister's house and that it remained untouched despite the fact that I knew Laurelin wouldn't live to see the end of the Feasts. That this attack could have been what ended her life.

I just needed that little piece of hope, because I knew when I closed my eyes again, I would see what I had when we'd been taken from the manor. The bodies of staff and guards I'd seen every day in *pieces*. Bodies strewn about the lawn, lit by moonlight. And the city? Homes had been burning and the path to the city gates had been cluttered with stone, broken wood, and . . . and shattered bodies. So many bodies, lowborn and Hyhborn. The old. The young, some that were—

"What happened in Archwood wasn't your fault." Grady interrupted the spiral of my thoughts.

Clamping my mouth shut, I scrubbed my hands down my face, wiping away the dampness that had found its way to my lashes.

"I know that's what you've been thinking. It's not," he said, voice low and hard. "The King didn't want Archwood defended. He wanted the city destroyed. Prince Thorne told you that."

I flinched at the sound of his name.

"Archwood was fucked whether or not you ever set foot in that city."

Dropping my hands to my stomach, I shook my head. "Well, it was mighty convenient that Prince Rohan came for me the same night they laid waste to a city."

"It wasn't convenient. It was fucking Hymel. What was going to happen to Archwood was going to go down. They just took two birds with one stone."

Maybe Grady was right. That Archwood would've fallen no matter what, and if Hymel had never gone to the Hyhborn, then we might have died that night in Archwood. Maybe we would've escaped. I didn't know.

But what I was sure about? What I needed no intuition to know? Grady wouldn't be in this situation, his life hanging on whether or not I displeased the Hyhborn. He wouldn't be here, for better or worse, if it weren't for me.

The only thing I could do now was make sure that Grady got

out of this in one piece, and I would, even if it was the last thing I ever did.

⇒⇒⇒

I didn't remember dozing off, but I must have, because I was suddenly wide awake and my heart was pounding.

The chamber was quiet—the entire inn was *silent,* but something woke me.

"Lis?" Grady nudged my leg with his knee. "There was screaming."

Swallowing, I turned my head toward him, able to make out the line of his profile. His head was tipped back. I followed his gaze to the ceiling, where there was nothing but silence. A chill skated down my spine as the streams of moonlight retreated from the ceiling, slipping across the beams and out the window—

The gas lantern in the bathing chamber suddenly turned on. Every muscle in my body tensed. The glow pulsed. Ice drenched my insides as the lamp on the table flickered to life, pulsing wildly. Air lodged in my throat as the air all around us charged with static—with power.

"The Hyhborn," I whispered. "Something is going—"

A cry pierced the silence, sudden and abrupt.

Sitting up, I grasped the front of Grady's tunic. The air was torn apart by a shrill shout, then another scream . . . and another.

"What's happening?" Grady gasped, straining against the chains.

"I don't know." Heart thumping, I scrambled to my knees and peered out the window, but I saw nothing but darkness. I jerked back from the window at the sound of a skin-chilling wail that ended sharply. That had come from outside, in the distance of whatever village we'd entered.

Twisting, I slipped off the bed and stood, wincing as sore muscles protested. Breathing raggedly, I reached for the dagger—

"Don't," Grady warned. "Keep it on you and run, Lis. Please. Fucking make a run for it."

My fingers curled around empty air as a shriek sent a shudder of dread through me. I backed up, each breath feeling too shallow, too quick. Turning, I crawled back into bed.

"Lis, please," Grady begged, his voice thickening.

Shaking my head, I stretched out beside him, pressing my face to his chest as I gripped his tunic once more.

Then the screaming began in earnest.

CHAPTER 39

Don't look.

That's what I kept telling myself as I was led through the inn, keeping my gaze trained on the backs of the Rae and the Hyhborn knights. My legs and arms were shaking so badly I was surprised I could actually put one foot in front of the other.

Grady had been taken from the chamber a few minutes after those . . . those screams had stopped. I didn't see Prince Rohan or Lord Samriel as I walked, Lord Arion beside me.

Don't look.

But the taproom floor was sticky and slick beneath my bare feet and there was a smell here that hadn't been when we entered earlier that night. A biting, metallic scent mixed with a too-sweet one. Pungent. Overwhelming.

I looked.

My eyes skated to my right, and I stumbled as I saw the owner. *Buck.* I saw others I didn't know the names of. Some were half dressed. Others didn't have a stitch of clothing on them, but all of them were nothing more than bodies now.

Bodies were splayed across tables, missing limbs, and others hung from the second floor, draped over the railing of the staircase. There was so much blood. It looked like a wild animal had gotten ahold of them, clawing open their chests and stomachs, leaving their insides on the outside. Hanging from them. In clumps and pools on the floor behind them. Someone . . . someone was burning in the fireplace. I'd seen so much violence, but this was—

Bile rose so quickly there was no stopping it. I turned, bending as I vomited water and what remained of the stew I'd eaten hours ago. I heaved until my legs gave out and I hit the bloodied floor on my knees, until my stomach cramped and tears streamed down my face.

Lord Arion waited silently through it all, speaking only once I quieted. "Is that all?" he asked as I shook. "Or will there be more yet to come up?"

I shook my head. There was nothing left inside me.

"Then stand. We must be on our way."

I rocked back. I didn't know any of these . . . these people, but there was nothing they could've done to deserve this.

"Why did this happen?" I rasped, throat sore. I had to know what could drive a living creature to be this cruel to another, because I couldn't fathom such destructive evil. It didn't matter what I'd seen in Archwood. This brutality was something else entirely. "Why did you all do this to them?"

There was a heavy sigh, one of boredom or impatience, maybe both. "Why not?"

I stared at him in disbelief.

"I was kidding," he said as if that somehow was better. "One of our knights got a bit out of hand. The screaming started, and well, Prince Rohan is not a fan of such annoyances. If they had only stayed silent, they might have lived to see the sun rise."

"They . . . they were slaughtered because someone screamed?" My voice pitched high.

"I can see that answer displeases you," Lord Arion noted. "Will it help you regain your footing to know that most of the town has been left untouched? Because I do hope so."

Most of the town? I thought of the wails Grady and I had heard coming from outside the inn. Were the ones not so lucky left like this? Split open and left to rot when the sun did rise like they had been in Archwood?

"Do you not care for lowborn at all?" I asked, even though I knew the answer. Or I thought I did. I knew that the King had taken little interest in us, but this was . . . it went beyond anything I believed the Hyhborn capable of. "Does the King think this is okay?"

"The King abhors violence," Lord Arion replied. "He also abhors dens of vice and sin. He would see this for what it is. A cleansing. There was no life of value lost tonight. Now, we need to continue."

A bone-deep rage unfurled, chasing away the coldness of terror and disbelief. My throat burned with my fury. "Fuck you."

Fair brows rose above the black-and-green eyes. That was all I had a chance to see. He moved so fast.

The blow he landed stung my cheek and lip, knocking me to the side. I threw out my hands, catching myself before I hit the floor. Burning, throbbing pain radiated across my jaw, up the side of my head. Blood soaked my palms as I breathed through the ringing in my ears.

Good gods. . . .

This wasn't the first time in my life I'd been struck, but I'd never been hit so hard that I could hear ringing in my ears.

Blood coated the inside of my mouth. I spat, wincing at the sharp spike of pain from a tear in my lip. I tentatively ran my tongue along my lips, half surprised that no teeth had been knocked free.

"Look at me." His whisper touched my skin like a breath of winter.

I drew back, sucking in a short breath as I lifted my head to the Lord once more. The lamplight was bright here—brighter than a few seconds before. Tiny hairs along the nape of my neck rose as power charged the air.

His smile grew. "Listen to me."

Before I could take another breath, his voice reached inside me and seized control. An unseen weight settled on my ankles first and then traveled up my legs, circling my waist and wrists, slipping over my shoulders. A quick, sharp pain lanced my skull, and then the pressure was there, filling my mind, and every breath I took tasted of . . . of *mint*.

The center of his eyes—where the blots of green ringed his pupils—brightened and expanded until only a thin strip of black was visible. "Stand," Lord Arion commanded.

I didn't want to. Every part of my being rebelled against it, but my body moved without conscious effort. He'd seized control of my body—my will. I rose.

The Lord brushed his cloak aside, grasping the black hilt of a sword. Lamplight glinted off the *lunea* blade as he withdrew it, leveling the pointed end at my chest. "Walk forward."

A foot lifted, then another.

He smirked. "Farther."

My heart thundered as I stared at the wickedly sharp edge of the sword. He was . . . he was going to have me impale myself? *No.* I wouldn't do this. I *couldn't* do this. *No,* I whispered, then screamed the single word, over and over, but none of those sounds made it to my tongue. My hands opened at my sides, fingers splaying wide.

"Interesting," the Lord murmured. "Look at me *now.*"

Pressure expanded in my head, sending spikes of agony through my temples until my gaze returned to his. Only then did the pain retreat.

The green in his eyes pulsed. *"Walk forward."*

My feet dragged across the bloodied floor. One foot. Then the other—and a sudden, sharp pain radiated across the right side of my chest, stealing my breath even as I took another step.

"Stop," he demanded.

I stopped.

The Lord pulled the sword back, holding it up between us. The very tip was glossy with blood—*my* blood. "I could order you to slit your own throat on this blade and you'd do it." He lowered it, resting the sharp blade against the base of my throat. "I *could* have you on your knees and your mouth around my dick. I *could* have you take this sword and go from house to house, disemboweling those who sleep. Do you understand me?"

Disgust joined the mint taste in my mouth as my lips moved. "Yes."

"Good." The Lord inched the sword down. "Now, did you get a good enough look at those around you?"

"Yes," I breathed.

"You can either do what you're told or live to regret not doing so. You've seen all the many, many ways to find regret. Starting with your brave friend. Do you understand? Say, 'Yes, my lord.'"

"Yes." My throat ached as the words left me. "My lord."

He drew the sword over the small puncture wound, dragging a ragged gasp from me. "The only control you have now is in what happens from this moment until you're handed over to our liege. My orders are to bring you to him alive and in somewhat good condition. Nothing was said about your friend. He is living only on the generosity of Prince Rohan and your actions."

My hands twitched as the tip of the sword grazed the swell of my breast and then the curve of my stomach before pointing to the floor.

The Lord's close-lipped smile returned as he sheathed his sword. "It can either be pleasant or I can have you begging for death every moment between now and then. Do you, my dear, understand?"

My lips moved once more. "Yes."

The green rings shrank until they were once more just blotches in the darkness of his eyes. The weight entrenched into my body lifted without warning, slipping from my ankles and wrists and then my mind. The fuzziness cleared from my thoughts as his—his power retracted its hold on me. Now having felt what a compulsion was like, I understood the terror I'd seen on Grady's face when we were children and he'd been under one. I staggered back, breathing heavily.

"Now, it's time for us to go."

Slowly, I turned around, my movements stiff and jerky. A tremor had started in my hands and had made its way throughout the entirety of my body as I took note of the small circle of blood that stained the chest of my robe. It was nothing compared to what I'd seen—compared to what I knew this lord was capable of. I walked out into the clouded, cooler night sky.

The courtyard was empty.

I barely felt the cold ground beneath my feet as I searched for any sign of Grady and the others. I didn't see them. Panic took root as all I saw beyond the stone fencing was the outline of a massive black steed, one as large as the horses I'd seen at the Archwood stables. "Where is he? Where are the others?"

"You will see him again." The Lord strode past, grasping my arm in the process. His grip was bruising, but I didn't protest. The manhandling was far better than him using another charm and making good on one of his many threats. "He was taken ahead with the Prince and my brother."

Confusion rose, and then I remembered what Grady had said. "We're being followed, aren't we?"

"We're being cautious," the Lord said with a chuckle, and I

flinched, reminded of Lord Samriel's apathy. "If we are, they'll follow the Prince. Not us."

My heart thudded as I entered the empty, dark street. I had to remind myself that Hyhborn couldn't lie. If he said the Rae were taking him ahead of us, then that was what was happening. Grady was strong and clever. If he had a chance to escape, he would. I latched on to that as the Lord gripped me by the waist and hoisted me up onto the horse.

The Lord swung up onto the saddle behind me. "Ask another question of me?" he said, picking up the horse's reins. "And you will find yourself occupying your mouth in a way that will be less grating to me."

I clamped my jaw shut, and that hurt, causing half of my face to throb. Why did men, no matter what they were, always resort to such threats? As if threatening our lives wouldn't be enough to ensure cooperation? My fingers dug into the pommel of the saddle.

"Do not fall," he instructed. "It will annoy me if you do, and you don't want that to occur."

With that, he dug his heels into the steed's sides, and the horse launched into movement. Refusing to use any part of the monster behind me as support, I held on to the pommel. The pace quickly picked up and we were rushing through the dark streets, forcing me to clamp my thighs against the saddle to stay upright. My heart sank as soon as we reached the end of the street.

An orange glow rose above the hill, and the scent of burnt wood grew. Smoke poured into the night, blanketing the roads. I tried to see what kind of damage had been done, but the horse charged on, turning the streets of the unnamed village into a blur.

As we approached the open, unguarded gates of the village, the clouds began to break apart. Silvery moonlight flowed over the road, washing over lumps scattered at the edges. Shapes that were—

My stomach cramped. Dead city guards lay scattered about. Dozens of them as we left the village, the horse's pace never slowing.

Good gods, how many had died tonight? I shuddered. And all these deaths . . . Was their blood on my hands? Like the blood the Prince of Vytrus carried on his?

No. That one word burned through me, forging my spine into steel. I'd done nothing to cause this. Nor had any of those who'd suffered tonight. This was on the Hyhborn. Grady was right. I wasn't responsible for Archwood either. The only thing I'd done was be born, but I wasn't completely free from guilt.

I cared about others, but I obviously hadn't cared *enough*. Because I never paid attention to Court politics whenever other barons visited with news and gossip. Whatever I gleaned from them for Claude I quickly forgot about. I didn't pay all that much attention when news of the Westlands unrest first broke. I used my abilities when asked, when it served me, or simply by accident. I could've worked harder at cracking that shield that surrounded Claude and Hymel, and I would've been able to, since I'd done it with Commander Rhaziel without touching him. I could've learned what Hymel was up to, but I'd been too afraid—not just for Grady but for myself. I hadn't wanted to jeopardize my life and all the privileges I'd obtained, whether warranted or not. I'd been looking out for him *and* myself. I was too wrapped up in my own life and my own fears. I could've done more. There were so many choices I could've made that would've changed and maybe even prevented what had become of Archwood.

What had happened here.

So how was I any better than the King at the end of the day? Just because I cared didn't make me different, because I hadn't cared enough. And the gods knew I wasn't the only lowborn who stuck her head in the sand, but I had been in a position of privilege, of protection, where I could've done more, and I hadn't. I thought of how I'd warned Grady to not get involved with the Iron Knights. I had done the exact opposite of *more*. Because I didn't want to risk ending up on the streets again. How did that make me any better?

It really didn't.

The fact that it had taken this for me to realize that sickened me, because now I had to live with those choices.

And who knew how many others would have to because of them.

⇛

We stayed on the road for a short period of time before Lord Arion guided the steed into moonlight-drenched meadows with a brutal urging of his knees.

Tall thistle weeds lashed at my legs, stinging my skin, but it was nothing compared to the throbbing in my chest and across my jaw, nor could it compare to the mounting dread of what was to come. The meadow seemed endless, my thoughts staggering over one another as I tried to piece together what I knew to figure out what was coming. How I could somehow make better . . . better choices but still protect Grady—still get him out of this situation.

Icy water jerked me from my thoughts, soaking my feet and the edges of my clothing as we crossed a narrow stream. The shivering ratcheted up as the steed climbed the steep bank and carried us into the . . . the Wychwoods.

Dear gods, there were things in these woods possibly even more frightening than the Hyhborn lord behind me.

When I glanced down at the packed earth, a silly yet slightly terrifying thought occurred to me. Were there still Deminyens in these woods, being created deep underground? Gods, thinking about that didn't help anything.

I didn't know how much time had passed. All I could focus on was staying atop the horse and not falling beneath his hooves as he raced at neck-breaking speeds through the maze of trees. I held on, even as every part of my body protested—as my hands and thighs ached. Only when the trees became too crowded together did Lord Arion slow the horse enough that I didn't feel as if I would fall at any given second.

But my grip didn't relent, not even as the pieces of sky visible through the heavy limbs lightened, shifting through all shades of blue. I held on.

The horse slowed even more, eventually coming to a near stop. Wearily, I turned my head toward the Lord. He was staring up at the thick clusters of trees taller than any building I'd ever seen. I followed his gaze to where the faint light of dawn struggled to penetrate the heavily leafed branches. The steed blew out ragged breaths as Lord Arion shifted in the saddle—

Something hissed through the air. Reins snapped free from the Lord's grip as he pitched forward without warning. He crashed into me, and my numb fingers slipped from the pommel. His sudden weight took both of us off the saddle.

I hit the ground with a jarring thud I could feel in my bones. I lay there, stunned for a heartbeat, staring at the patches of . . . of deep *violet* grass. I'd never seen such grass before.

But that really wasn't important at the moment.

Lord Arion . . . he was sprawled half on top of me, unmoving. Gathering every bit of strength I had, I rolled him off. He flopped onto his side, one arm still lying across my stomach. I looked at his face—

"Holy shit," I whispered at the sight of the arrow embedded deep between Lord Arion's eyes.

Tossing his arm off my stomach, I scuttled back across the ground as I stared at the rapidly expanding pool of red beneath his head. He looked dead, but I didn't know how powerful this lord was. I didn't know if he was only unconscious or whether that arrowhead through his brain was enough to kill him. That *milky-white* arrowhead—

A call came from the trees. Lord Arion's steed took off, its hooves pounding into the ground inches from me. I pushed onto my knees, twisting toward the sound of the sharp whistle. Through my tangled strands of hair, I saw a dark shape fall from the trees—no, the dark *shapes* had *flown* from above.

Ravens.

Dozens of them.

Their black wings cut silently through the air as they flew in rapid circles, coming closer and closer to each other with every pass until they . . . they came together feet above the ground, merging into . . . into one.

Into the figure of a man crouched several feet ahead, his dark cloak pooling over the violet grass like smoke.

A shiver tiptoed its way down my spine, then spread out over my skin. That feeling came over me, the one I first felt as a child.

A *warning*.

A *reckoning*.

The *promise* of what was to come.

But this time, something unlocked in my mind, and out of its darkness, a vision I'd never had before swamped me, and in a flash, I saw what Lord Samriel claimed.

I saw *his* arms, his hand wrapped around the hilt of the blade plunged deep into my chest—

A cry tore from my throat. Death. I'd seen mine. I'd seen it come at *his* hands.

"Move. Move, move," I whispered, trying to get my frozen muscles to unlock. "*Move.*"

He rose to that impossible, intimidating height as I shoved to my feet. Spinning around, I took off as fast as I could, running back toward the creek. I ran, arms and legs pumping as rocks dug into the soles of my feet. Branches slapped at my hair and cheeks, snagging my robe and nightgown. Every step *hurt*, but I didn't stop. There was no time to think about where I was going or the fruitlessness of—

A body collided with mine, knocking my legs out from underneath me. For a moment, I was weightless and falling; then arms snapped around mine. The body twisted, and I was suddenly no longer staring at the hard ground racing up toward me, but at the trees.

We landed hard, the body beneath mine taking the brunt of the fall, but the impact still knocked the wind out of me, and for a moment, neither of us moved. Then he rolled me onto my stomach. Weight pressed onto my back, trapping the entire length of body. My fingers curled into the damp grass.

"*Na'laa,*" he whispered. "You should've known better than to run. I will always catch you."

I dragged in a shallow breath. A . . . a woodsy, soft smell surrounded me. The scent of . . . *sandalwood.*

Of him.

My Hyhborn prince.

My salvation.

And my doom.

ACKNOWLEDGMENTS

I want to thank my agent, Kevan Lyon; the wonderful team at Bramble: Ali Fisher, Dianna Vega, Devi Pillai, Anthony Parisi, Giselle Gonzalez, Saraciea Fennell, Monique Patterson, Jessica Katz, Steven Bucsok, Heather Saunders, and Rafal Gibek; and Melissa Frain for helping bring Calista and Thorne to life.

A huge thank-you to Malissa for making sure things were still getting done while I was writing. Another big thank-you to Jen F. and Steph for letting me bounce ideas off of you guys. Vonetta and Mona—you guys are the best.

And the members of JLAnders? You guys rock, as always.

None of this would've been possible without you, the reader. THANK YOU.